CLASSIC ENGLISH
SHORT STORIES

1930–1955

CLASSIC
ENGLISH
SHORT STORIES

1930–1955

Selected and Introduced by
DEREK HUDSON

Oxford New York
OXFORD UNIVERSITY PRESS

Oxford University Press, Walton Street, Oxford OX2 6DP

Oxford New York Toronto
Delhi Bombay Calcutta Madras Karachi
Kuala Lumpur Singapore Hong Kong Tokyo
Nairobi Dar es Salaam Cape Town
Melbourne Auckland Madrid

and associated companies in
Berlin Ibadan

Oxford is a trade mark of Oxford University Press

First published 1956 in The World's Classics as
Modern English Short Stories: Second Series
First issued as an Oxford University Press paperback 1972

British Library Cataloguing in Publication Data

Data available

Library of Congress Cataloging in Publication Data
Modern English short stories second series.
Classic English short stories, 1930–1955/selected and introduced by Derek Hudson.
p. cm.
Originally published as: Modern English short stories. Second
series. 1956.
1. Short stories, English. 2. English fiction—20th century.
I. Title.
823'.0108'009041—dc20 PR1307.M64 1989 89-16119
ISBN 0-19-281121-5

15 17 19 20 18 16 14

Printed in Great Britain by
Biddles Ltd
Guildford and King's Lynn

Contents

Editor's Note

THIS volume is a sequel to the collection of *Modern English Short Stories* selected by Phyllis M. Jones and published in The World's Classics in 1939. That first volume drew on the work of several outstanding short-story writers of contrasting aims and talents who had died before 1932, writers as varied and distinguished as Thomas Hardy, Arnold Bennett, Saki, D. H. Lawrence, and Stacy Aumonier. It also contained stories by many writers still living in 1939.

In compiling this second volume of *Modern English Short Stories*, the year 1930 has been taken as an approximate starting-point, so that the collection is virtually an anthology of the stories of the twenty-five years up to 1955. All the stories have been drawn from books published since 1930, though they may in a very few cases have originally appeared shortly before that date. Three writers from the earlier selection are again represented: Somerset Maugham, Elizabeth Bowen, and H. E. Bates.

Some explanation of the use of the term 'English' in the present connection may be desirable. It excludes the Commonwealth (collections of Australian and New Zealand short stories have appeared in The World's Classics); it excludes American writers; and it also excludes the many admirable indigenous short stories of Ireland, Scotland, and Wales, which are properly the subject of collections in their own right. On the other hand, it has not been allowed to exclude Miss Bowen of County Cork, Mr. Eric Linklater of Ross-shire, or a Manxman like Mr. Nigel Kneale, all of whom have made reputations in England.

D. H.

Acknowledgements

Thanks are due to the following for permission to reprint copyright material:

The author's literary executor and William Heinemann Ltd. for 'The Kite', from *Creatures of Circumstance* by W. Somerset Maugham (William Heinemann, 1947)

The author's literary estate and The Hogarth Press Ltd. for 'The Duchess and the Jeweller', from *A Haunted House and Other Stories* by Virginia Woolf (Hogarth Press, 1943)

The author's estate and Winant, Towers Ltd. for 'The Little Willow', from *Tea with Mr. Rochester* by Frances Towers (Michael Joseph, 1949)

The author's estate and A. D. Peters & Co. for 'The Hostage', from *The Nightmare* by C. S. Forester (Michael Joseph, 1954)

The author's estate and A. D. Peters & Co. for 'Sealskin Trousers', from *Sealskin Trousers* by Eric Linklater (Rupert Hart-Davis, 1947)

The author and A. D. Peters & Co. for 'The Voice', from *It May Never Happen* by V. S. Pritchett (Chatto & Windus, 1945)

The author's estate and Jonathan Cape Ltd. for 'Ever Such a Nice Boy', from *Four Countries* by William Plomer (Jonathan Cape, 1949)

The author's estate and A. D. Peters & Co. for 'On Guard', from *Mr. Loveday's Little Outing* by Evelyn Waugh (Chapman and Hall, 1936)

The author and Laurence Pollinger Ltd. for 'The Basement Room', from *Twenty-one Stories* by Graham Greene (William Heinemann, 1954)

The author's estate and Laurence Pollinger Ltd. for 'The Woman Who Had Imagination', from *The Woman Who Had Imagination* by H. E. Bates (Jonathan Cape, 1934)

The author's estate and A. D. Peters & Co. for 'Local Boy Makes Good', from *Tiger, Tiger* by John Moore (William Collins, 1953)

The author for 'The Sacred and the Profane', a revised version of a story first published in *Character and Situation* by Christopher Sykes (William Collins, 1949)

The author and Elaine Greene Ltd. for 'The Vertical Ladder', from *The Stories of William Sansom* (Hogarth Press, 1963), © William Sansom 1963

The author and Laurence Pollinger Ltd. for 'Man About the House' by Fred Urquhart, from *Horizon Stories* (Faber and Faber, 1943)

The author and The Hogarth Press Ltd. for 'Mr. Minnenick', from *Innocents* by A. L. Barker (Hogarth Press, 1947)

The author and A. M. Heath & Co. Ltd. for 'The Putting Away of Uncle Quaggin', from *Tomato Cain and Other Stories* by Nigel Kneale (William Collins, 1949)

The author's estate and Jonathan Cape Ltd. for 'Maria', from *The Cat Jumps* by Elizabeth Bowen (Victor Gollancz, 1934)

The author's estate and Laurence Pollinger Ltd. for 'The Dearly Beloved of Benjamin Cobb', from *Fate Cries Out* by Clemence Dane (William Heinemann, 1935)

The author and The Society of Authors for 'A Dream of Winter', from *The Gipsy's Baby* by Rosamond Lehmann (William Collins, 1946)

Introduction

MOST of the stories in the first two volumes of *Selected English Short Stories** were written in the nineteenth century, and many of their authors were American. In his book *The Modern Short Story* (1941) Mr. H. E. Bates used this fact to emphasize 'the poverty of the short story' in nineteenth-century England. Mr. Bates did not mean that the Victorians were not eager readers and writers of the short story; their interest was sustained by an army of magazines which published innumerable stories, often with a domestic flavour, which were illustrated by woodcuts of a sentimental, improving nature and were especially looked for at Christmas time. But it is true that, for the greater part of the nineteenth century, the short stories of England were more conspicuous in quantity than in quality. Even such eminent novelists as Scott, Dickens, Thackeray, and Meredith failed, when writing on a smaller scale, to show that they had any clear view of the short story as an art-form in its own right. Mrs. Gaskell is respectfully remembered; but about her lesser competitors—as about the cobwebby bundles of Victorian magazines in our attics which contain so many of their earnest attempts—there lingers an unmistakable suspicion of dry rot.

Meanwhile, across the Atlantic, Irving, Hawthorne, Poe, Melville, Bret Harte, Crane, and Bierce were pouring out stories that were destined to be fruitful in their influence on English writers. These Americans brought to their developing art a mastery of construction, a terseness and clarity of expression, that gave them authority. They taught the lesson that the success of a story depends on atmosphere, on the instilling into a reader of a mood of almost hypnotic attention. There was to be no room for verbiage or pomposity, none of the

* Published in three volumes in The World's Classics in 1914, 1921, and 1927.

novel-reader's indulgence for creaking machinery; each stroke had to be directed to the total effect.

Towards the end of the century the American example began to show appreciable results on this side of the ocean in the stories of R. L. Stevenson, George Moore, Oscar Wilde and the contributors to the *Yellow Book* and the *Savoy*. American short-story writers had demonstrated the possibilities of the art; they had aroused a spirit of emulation. Theirs were not, of course, by any means the sole influences that affected the English writers of the nineties or their immediate successors such as Wells, Conrad, Bennett, Kipling, and Maugham. Many imaginations were stirred by Poe and Bierce; but in England our homespun tradition was transformed by the massive contrasting powers of Tolstoy and Chekhov, by the attacking force of Maupassant, and, most notably, by the precision and poetic delicacy of Turgenev and Flaubert. In 1914 a book of short stories by James Joyce, *Dubliners*, began to exercise a similar spell. These were giants whose presence is still perceptible in the background of this volume of *Modern English Short Stories*.

And yet it is largely owing to the original American impetus—the 'lend-lease' of a century ago—that we have been able in this volume and its predecessor to dispense, though not ungratefully, with American aid. For the past fifty years an English school of short-story writers has flourished. The aims and achievements of its members have been most various. The honour-boards commemorate the bitter poetry of D. H. Lawrence alongside the mordant humour of Saki and the irony of Maugham; Stacy Aumonier (perhaps our English O. Henry) is remembered beside H. E. Bates and Elizabeth Bowen whose tender re-creation of landscape and atmosphere owe as much to Turgenev as to Chekhov. The present volume adds such names as Virginia Woolf (a potent influence on several of her fellow contributors), V. S. Pritchett, Graham Greene, Eric Linklater, Rosamond Lehmann, C. S. Forester, William Sansom, Fred Urquhart, A. L. Barker, and Nigel Kneale, all of whom have produced work that is noticeably individual. It is one of the pleasures of the short story that it gives opportunities to writers of refinement who will never be among the 'big guns' of literature. Frances Towers, for example, was not a prolific writer and spent years working in the Bank of England. Her special qualities of grace and intuition were first widely appreciated in her posthumous *Tea with Mr. Rochester*. Yet her death in 1948 meant a distinct loss to English letters.

The modern short-story writer has had to steer between the Scylla of popular journalism and the Charybdis of preciosity. It has seemed, at times during the past twenty-five years, that some of our most distinguished writers were bent on establishing an era of plotlessness which might drive the intellectual short story out of the reach even of a 'general reader' sympathetically disposed to experiment. Fortunately a reaction among our younger writers has lessened this danger. An Irish-American, Mary Lavin, argued the point in a story in her book *A Single Lady* (1951). 'Life itself has very little plot,' she said; 'Life itself has a habit of breaking off in the middle.' This is true, as far as it goes. Readers of the short story do not look for any elaborate formal mechanism of composition in an art which is essentially fluid and elastic. But life is not the whole of fiction; a prime requirement of the short story is that it should sustain the illusion of suspense. The most beautifully written presentation of a state of mind will not do this unless the author can seize the reader's attention from the start and hold it as the story develops. Miss Elizabeth Bowen, in a foreword to Mr. Nigel Kneale's *Tomato Cain* (1949), recognized that the short story could all too easily have fallen under a blight 'and become an example of too much prose draped around an insufficiently vital feeling or a trumped-up, insufficiently strong idea . . . . A story must *be* a story.'

The present volume does not ignore experiment; in some cases the quality of the writing and a consummate skill in evoking mood and atmosphere have triumphed over a certain lack of form. And the collection demonstrates on page after page the new awareness of the lights and shadows within the human mind which has been generated by modern psychology and by the nervous intensity of contemporary life. In his compelling story 'The Kite' Somerset Maugham shows that he had moved in step with the times. But the selection has not been made to display any particular point of view; it would have been incomplete without examples of C. S. Forester's and

Graham Greene's narrative power, without Eric Linklater's and Evelyn Waugh's contrasting fantasies, without William Plomer's or John Moore's shrewd appreciations of native character, or Clemence Dane's classic account of a village tragedy that would have moved Thomas Hardy.

The war of 1939–45 has left its mark on many of these tales. We hear of 'Munich' and the Eighth Army, of bomb damage, of an English soldier who did not return, and of a German general who fought to keep his honour. The past quarter of a century has been sombre enough; inevitably these pages reflect its tension. Yet the dominating impression in these English stories is of humour—not necessarily in the comic sense (though some of the stories are extremely funny)—but in the sense in which Bret Harte used it of his own country's stories, the sense of a humorous perspective of life. They are English, again, in their strong vein of poetry and in the undiminished respect that their authors have shown, throughout a period of change, for the saving graces of personality. Some loving passages of landscape insist, too, that we are still a nation of water-colourists.

A selection remains a personal thing. This selection aims only at presenting some of the best modern stories that have been written in their various kinds. Other readers will have different preferences. This much is certain—that these stories do not derive from a dying art. Among them perhaps one or two will live to speak, fifty years hence, for English literature.

D. H.

W. SOMERSET MAUGHAM

The Kite

I KNOW this is an odd story. I don't understand it
myself and if I set it down in black and white it is
only with a faint hope that when I have written it I
may get a clearer view of it, or rather with the hope
that some reader, better acquainted with the com-
plications of human nature than I am, may offer me
an explanation that will make it comprehensible to
me. Of course the first thing that occurs to me is that
there is something Freudian about it. Now, I have
read a good deal of Freud, and some books by his
followers, and intending to write this story I have
recently flipped through again the volume published
by the Modern Library which contains his basic
writings. It was something of a task, for he is a dull
and verbose writer, and the acrimony with which he
claims to have originated such and such a theory
shows a vanity and a jealousy of others working in
the same field which somewhat ill become the man
of science. I believe, however, that he was a kindly
and benign old party. As we know, there is often a
great difference between the man and the writer.
The writer may be bitter, harsh and brutal, while
the man may be so meek and mild that he wouldn't
say boo to a goose. But that is neither here nor there.
I found nothing in my re-reading of Freud's works
that cast any light on the subject I had in mind. I can
only relate the facts and leave it at that.

First of all I must make it plain that it is not my

story and that I knew none of the persons with whom it is concerned. It was told me one evening by my friend Ned Preston, and he told it me because he didn't know how to deal with the circumstances and he thought, quite wrongly as it happened, that I might be able to give him some advice that would help him. In a previous story I have related what I thought the reader should know about Ned Preston, and so now I need only remind him that my friend was a prison visitor at Wormwood Scrubs. He took his duties very seriously and made the prisoners' troubles his own. We had been dining together at the Café Royal in that long, low room with its absurd and charming decoration which is all that remains of the old Café Royal that painters have loved to paint; and we were sitting over our coffee and liqueurs and, so far as Ned was concerned against his doctor's orders, smoking very long and very good Havanas.

'I've got a funny chap to deal with at the Scrubs just now,' he said, after a pause, 'and I'm blowed if I know how to deal with him.'

'What's he in for?' I asked.

'He left his wife and the court ordered him to pay so much a week in alimony and he's absolutely refused to pay it. I've argued with him till I was blue in the face. I've told him he's only cutting off his nose to spite his face. He says he'll stay in jail all his life rather than pay her a penny. I tell him he can't let her starve, and all he says is: "Why not?" He's perfectly well behaved, he's no trouble, he works well, he seems quite happy, he's just getting a lot of fun out of thinking what a devil of a time his wife is having.'

'What's he got against her?'

'She smashed his kite.'

'She did what?' I cried.

'Exactly that. She smashed his kite. He says he'll never forgive her for that till his dying day.'

'He must be crazy.'

'No, he isn't, he's a perfectly reasonable, quite intelligent, decent fellow.'

Herbert Sunbury was his name, and his mother, who was very refined, never allowed him to be called Herb or Bertie, but always Herbert, just as she never called her husband Sam but only Samuel. Mrs. Sunbury's first name was Beatrice, and when she got engaged to Mr. Sunbury and he ventured to call her Bea she put her foot down firmly.

'Beatrice I was christened,' she cried, 'and Beatrice I always have been and always shall be, to you and to my nearest and dearest.'

She was a little woman, but strong, active and wiry, with a sallow skin, sharp, regular features and small, beady eyes. Her hair, suspiciously black for her age, was always very neat, and she wore it in the style of Queen Victoria's daughters, which she had adopted as soon as she was old enough to put it up and had never thought fit to change. The possibility that she did something to keep her hair its original colour was, if such was the case, her only concession to frivolity, for, far from using rouge or lipstick, she had never in her life so much as passed a powder-puff over her nose. She never wore anything but black dresses of good material, but made (by a little woman round the corner) regardless of fashion after a pattern that was both serviceable and decorous. Her only ornament was a thin gold chain from which hung a small gold cross.

Samuel Sunbury was a little man too. He was as

thin and spare as his wife, but he had sandy hair,
gone very thin now so that he had to wear it very
long on one side and brush it carefully over the
large bald patch. He had pale blue eyes and his
complexion was pasty. He was a clerk in a lawyer's
office and had worked his way up from office boy
to a respectable position. His employer called him
Mr. Sunbury and sometimes asked him to see an
unimportant client. Every morning for twenty-four
years Samuel Sunbury had taken the same train to
the City, except of course on Sundays and during
his fortnight's holiday at the seaside, and every
evening he had taken the same train back to the
suburb in which he lived. He was neat in his dress;
he went to work in quiet grey trousers, a black coat
and a bowler hat, and when he came home he put
on his slippers and a black coat which was too old
and shiny to wear at the office; but on Sundays
when he went to the chapel he and Mrs. Sunbury
attended he wore a morning coat with his bowler.
Thus he showed his respect for the day of rest and
at the same time registered a protest against the
ungodly who went bicycling or lounged about the
streets until the pubs opened. On principle the Sunburys were total abstainers, but on Sundays, when
to make up for the frugal lunch, consisting of a
scone and butter with a glass of milk, which Samuel
had during the week, Beatrice gave him a good
dinner of roast beef and Yorkshire pudding, for his
health's sake she liked him to have a glass of beer.
Since she wouldn't for the world have kept liquor
in the house, he sneaked out with a jug after morning service and got a quart from the pub round the
corner; but nothing would induce him to drink
alone, so, just to be sociable like, she had a glass too.

Herbert was the only child the Lord had vouchsafed to them, and this certainly through no precaution on their part. It just happened that way.
They doted on him. He was a pretty baby and then
a good-looking child. Mrs. Sunbury brought him up
carefully. She taught him to sit up at table and not
put his elbows on it, and she taught him how to use
his knife and fork like a little gentleman. She taught
him to stretch out his little finger when he took his
tea-cup to drink out of it and when he asked why,
she said:

'Never you mind. That's how it's done. It shows
you know what's what.'

In due course Herbert grew old enough to go
to school. Mrs. Sunbury was anxious because she
had never let him play with the children in the
street.

'Evil communications corrupt good manners,' she
said. 'I always have kept myself to myself and I
always shall keep myself to myself.'

Although they had lived in the same house ever
since they were married she had taken care to keep
her neighbours at a distance.

'You never know who people are in London,' she
said. 'One thing leads to another, and before you
know where you are you're mixed up with a lot of
riff-raff and you can't get rid of them.'

She didn't like the idea of Herbert being thrown
into contact with a lot of rough boys at the County
Council school and she said to him:

'Now, Herbert, do what I do; keep yourself to
yourself and don't have anything more to do with
them than you can help.'

But Herbert got on very well at school. He was a
good worker and far from stupid. His reports were

excellent. It turned out that he had a good head for figures.

'If that's a fact,' said Samuel Sunbury, 'he'd better be an accountant. There's always a good job waiting for a good accountant.'

So it was settled there and then that this was what Herbert was to be. He grew tall.

'Why, Herbert,' said his mother, 'soon you'll be as tall as your dad.'

By the time he left school he was two inches taller, and by the time he stopped growing he was five feet ten.

'Just the right height,' said his mother. 'Not too tall and not too short.'

He was a nice-looking boy, with his mother's regular features and dark hair, but he had inherited his father's blue eyes, and though he was rather pale his skin was smooth and clear. Samuel Sunbury had got him into the office of the accountants who came twice a year to do the accounts of his own firm and by the time he was twenty-one he was able to bring back to his mother every week quite a nice little sum. She gave him back three half-crowns for his lunches and ten shillings for pocket money, and the rest she put in the Savings Bank for him against a rainy day.

When Mr. and Mrs. Sunbury went to bed on the night of Herbert's twenty-first birthday, and in passing I may say that Mrs. Sunbury never went to bed, she retired, but Mr. Sunbury who was not quite so refined as his wife always said: 'Me for Bedford,'—when then Mr. and Mrs. Sunbury went to bed, Mrs. Sunbury said:

'Some people don't know how lucky they are; thank the Lord, I do. No one's ever had a better son than our Herbert. Hardly a day's illness in his life and he's never given me a moment's worry. It just shows if you bring up somebody right they'll be a credit to you. Fancy him being twenty-one, I can hardly believe it.'

'Yes, I suppose before we know where we are he'll be marrying and leaving us.'

'What should he want to do that for?' asked Mrs. Sunbury with asperity. 'He's got a good home here, hasn't he? Don't you go putting silly ideas into his head, Samuel, or you and me'll have words and you know that's the last thing I want. Marry indeed! He's got more sense than that. He knows when he's well off. He's got sense, Herbert has.'

Mr. Sunbury was silent. He had long ago learnt that it didn't get him anywhere with Beatrice to answer back.

'I don't hold with a man marrying till he knows his own mind,' she went on. 'And a man doesn't know his own mind till he's thirty or thirty-five.'

'He was pleased with his presents,' said Mr. Sunbury to change the conversation.

'And so he ought to be,' said Mrs. Sunbury, still upset.

They had in fact been handsome. Mr. Sunbury had given him a silver wrist-watch, with hands that you could see in the dark, and Mrs. Sunbury had given him a kite. It wasn't by any means the first one she had given him. That was when he was seven years old, and it happened this way. There was a large common near where they lived and on Saturday afternoons when it was fine Mrs. Sunbury took her husband and son for a walk there. She said it was good for Samuel to get a breath of fresh air after being cooped up in a stuffy office all the week. There were always a lot of people on the common, but Mrs. Sunbury who liked to keep herself to herself kept out of their way as much as possible.

'Look at them kites, Mum,' said Herbert suddenly one day.

There was a fresh breeze blowing and a number of kites, small and large, were sailing through the air.

'*Those*, Herbert, not them,' said Mrs. Sunbury.

'Would you like to go and see where they start, Herbert?' asked his father.

'Oh, yes, Dad.'

There was a slight elevation in the middle of the common and as they approached it they saw boys and girls and some men racing down it to give their kites a start and catch the wind. Sometimes they didn't and fell to the ground, but when they did they would rise, and as the owner unravelled his string go higher and higher. Herbert looked with ravishment.

'Mum, can I have a kite?' he cried.

He had already learnt that when he wanted anything it was better to ask his mother first.

'Whatever for?' she said.

'To fly it, Mum.'

'If you're so sharp you'll cut yourself,' she said.

Mr. and Mrs. Sunbury exchanged a smile over the little boy's head. Fancy him wanting a kite. Growing quite a little man he was.

'If you're a good boy and wash your teeth regular every morning without me telling you I shouldn't be surprised if Santa Claus didn't bring you a kite on Christmas Day.'

Christmas wasn't far off and Santa Claus brought Herbert his first kite. At the beginning he wasn't very clever at managing it, and Mr. Sunbury had to run down the hill himself and start it for him. It was a very small kite, but when Herbert saw it swim through the air and felt the little tug it gave his hand he was thrilled; and then every Saturday afternoon, when his father got back from the City, he would pester his parents to hurry over to the common. He quickly learnt how to fly it, and Mr. and Mrs. Sunbury, their hearts swelling with pride, would watch him from the top of the knoll while he ran down and as the kite caught the breeze lengthened the cord in his hand.

It became a passion with Herbert, and as he grew older and bigger his mother bought him larger and larger kites. He grew very clever at gauging the winds and could do things with his kite you wouldn't have thought possible. There were other kite-flyers on the common, not only children, but men, and since nothing brings people together so naturally as a hobby they share it was not long before Mrs. Sunbury, notwithstanding her exclusiveness, found that she, her Samuel, and her son were on speaking terms with all and sundry. They would compare their respective kites and boast of their accomplishments. Sometimes Herbert, a big boy of sixteen now, would challenge another kite-flyer. Then he would man- œuvre his kite to windward of the other fellow's, allow his cord to drift against his, and by a sudden jerk bring the enemy kite down. But long before this Mr. Sunbury had succumbed to his son's enthusiasm and he would often ask to have a go himself. It must have been a funny sight to see him running down the hill in his striped trousers, black coat, and bowler hat. Mrs. Sunbury would trot sedately be- hind him and when the kite was sailing free would take the cord from him and watch it as it soared.

Saturday afternoon became the great day of the week for them, and when Mr. Sunbury and Herbert left the house in the morning to catch their train to the City the first thing they did was to look up at the sky to see if it was flying weather. They liked best of all a gusty day, with uncertain winds, for that gave them the best chance to exercise their skill. All through the week, in the evenings, they talked about it. They were contemptuous of smaller kites than theirs and envious of bigger ones. They discussed the performances of other flyers as hotly, and as scornfully, as boxers or football players discuss their rivals. Their ambition was to have a bigger kite than anyone else and a kite that would go higher. They had long given up a cord, for the kite they gave Herbert on his twenty-first birthday was seven feet high, and they used piano wire wound round a drum. But that did not satisfy Herbert. Somehow or other he had heard of a box-kite which had been invented by somebody, and the idea appealed to him at once. He thought he could devise something of the sort himself and since he could draw a little he set about making designs of it. He got a small model made and tried it out one afternoon, but it wasn't a success. He was a stubborn boy and he wasn't going to be beaten. Something was wrong, and it was up to him to put it right.

Then an unfortunate thing happened. Herbert began to go out after supper. Mrs. Sunbury didn't like it much, but Mr. Sunbury reasoned with her. After all, the boy was twenty-two, and it must be dull for him to stay at home all the time. If he wanted to go for a walk or see a movie there was no great harm. Herbert had fallen in love. One Saturday evening, after they'd had a wonderful time on the common, while they were at supper, out of a clear sky he said suddenly:

'Mum, I've asked a young lady to come in to tea tomorrow. Is that all right?'

'You done what?' asked Mrs. Sunbury, for a moment forgetting her grammar.

'You heard, Mum.'

'And may I ask who she is and how you got to know her?'

'Her name's Bevan, Betty Bevan, and I met her first at the pictures one Saturday afternoon when it was raining. It was an accident like. She was sitting next me and she dropped her bag and I picked it up and she said thank you and so naturally we got talking.'

'And d'you mean to tell me you fell for an old trick like that? Dropped her bag indeed!'

'You're making a mistake, Mum, she's a nice girl, she is really, and well educated too.'

'And when did all this happen?'

'About three months ago.'

'Oh, you met her three months ago and you've asked her to come to tea tomorrow?'

'Well, I've seen her since of course. That first day, after the show, I asked her if she'd come to the pictures with me on the Tuesday evening, and she said she didn't know, perhaps she would and perhaps she wouldn't. But she came all right.'

'She would. I could have told you that.'

'And we've been going to the pictures about twice a week ever since.'

'So that's why you've taken to going out so often?'

'That's right. But, look, I don't want to force her on you, if you don't want her to come to tea I'll say you've got a headache and take her out.'

'Your mum will have her to tea all right,' said Mr. Sunbury. 'Won't you, dear? It's only that your mum can't abide strangers. She never has liked them.'

'I keep myself to myself,' said Mrs. Sunbury gloomily. 'What does she do?'

'She works in a typewriting office in the City and she lives at home, if you call it home; you see, her mum died and her dad married again, and they've got three kids and she doesn't get on with her stepma. Nag, nag, nag all the time, she says.'

Mrs. Sunbury arranged the tea very stylishly. She took the nicknacks off a little table in the sitting-room, which they never used, and put a tea-cloth on it. She got out the tea service and the plated tea-kettle which they never used either, and she made scones, baked a cake, and cut thin bread-and-butter.

'I want her to see that we're not just nobody,' she told her Samuel.

Herbert went to fetch Miss Bevan, and Mr. Sunbury intercepted them at the door in case Herbert should take her into the dining-room where normally they ate and sat. Herbert gave the tea-table a glance of surprise as he ushered the young woman into the sitting-room.

'This is Betty, Mum,' he said.

'Miss Bevan, I presume,' said Mrs. Sunbury.

'That's right, but call me Betty, won't you?'

'Perhaps the acquaintance is a bit short for that,' said Mrs. Sunbury with a gracious smile. 'Won't you sit down, Miss Bevan?'

Strangely enough, or perhaps not strangely at all, Betty Bevan looked very much as Mrs. Sunbury must have looked at her age. She had the same sharp features and the same rather small beady eyes, but her lips were scarlet with paint, her cheeks lightly rouged and her short black hair permanently waved. Mrs. Sunbury took in all this at a glance, and she reckoned to a penny how much her smart rayon dress had cost, her extravagantly high-heeled shoes and the saucy hat on her head. Her frock was very short and she showed a good deal of flesh-coloured stocking. Mrs. Sunbury, disapproving of her make-up and of her apparel, took an instant dislike to her, but she had made up her mind to behave like a lady, and if she didn't know how to behave like a lady nobody did, so that at first things went well. She poured out tea and asked Herbert to give a cup to his lady friend.

'Ask Miss Bevan if she'll have some bread-and-butter or a scone, Samuel, my dear.'

'Have both,' said Samuel, handing round the two plates, in his coarse way. 'I like to see people eat hearty.'

Betty insecurely perched a piece of bread-and-butter and a scone on her saucer and Mrs. Sunbury talked affably about the weather. She had the satisfaction of seeing that Betty was getting more and more ill at ease. Then she cut the cake and pressed a large piece on her guest. Betty took a bite at it and when she put it in her saucer it fell to the ground.

'Oh, I am sorry,' said the girl, as she picked it up.

'It doesn't matter at all, I'll cut you another piece,' said Mrs. Sunbury.

'Oh, don't bother, I'm not particular. The floor's clean.'

'I hope so,' said Mrs. Sunbury with an acid smile, 'but I wouldn't dream of letting you eat a piece of cake that's been on the floor. Bring it here, Herbert, and I'll give Miss Bevan some more.'

'I don't want any more, Mrs. Sunbury, I don't really.'

'I'm sorry you don't like my cake. I made it specially for you.' She took a bit. 'It tastes all right to me.'

'It's not that, Mrs. Sunbury, it's a beautiful cake, it's only that I'm not hungry.'

She refused to have more tea and Mrs. Sunbury saw she was glad to get rid of the cup. 'I expect they have their meals in the kitchen,' she said to herself. Then Herbert lit a cigarette.

'Give us a fag, Herb,' said Betty. 'I'm simply dying for a smoke.'

Mrs. Sunbury didn't approve of women smoking, but she only raised her eyebrows slightly.

'We prefer to call him Herbert, Miss Bevan,' she said.

Betty wasn't such a fool as not to see that Mrs. Sunbury had been doing all she could to make her uncomfortable, and now she saw a chance to get back on her.

'I know,' she said. 'When he told me his name was Herbert I nearly burst out laughing. Fancy calling anyone Herbert. A scream, I call it.'

'I'm sorry you don't like the name my son was given at his baptism. I think it's a very nice name. But I suppose it all depends on what sort of class of people one is.'

Herbert stepped in to the rescue.

'At the office they call me Bertie, Mum.'

'Then all I can say is, they're a lot of very common men.'

Mrs. Sunbury lapsed into a dignified silence and the conversation, such as it was, was maintained by Mr. Sunbury and Herbert. It was not without satis-

faction that Mrs. Sunbury perceived that Betty was
offended. She also perceived that the girl wanted to
go, but didn't quite know how to manage it. She was
determined not to help her. Finally Herbert took
the matter into his own hands.

'Well, Betty, I think it's about time we were getting along,' he said. 'I'll walk back with you.'

'Must you go already?' said Mrs. Sunbury, rising
to her feet. 'It's been a pleasure, I'm sure.'

'Pretty little thing,' said Mr. Sunbury tentatively
after the young things had left.

'Pretty my foot. All that paint and powder. You
take my word for it, she'd look very different with
her face washed and without a perm. Common,
that's what she is, common as dirt.'

An hour later Herbert came back. He was angry.

'Look here, Mum, what d'you mean by treating
the poor girl like that? I was simply ashamed of
you.'

'Don't talk to your mother like that, Herbert,' she
flared up. 'You didn't ought to have brought a
woman like that into my house. Common, she is,
common as dirt.'

When Mrs. Sunbury got angry not only did her
grammar grow shaky, but she wasn't quite safe
on her aitches. Herbert took no notice of what she
said.

'She said she'd never been so insulted in her life.
I had a rare job pacifying her.'

'Well, she's never coming here again, I tell you
that straight.'

'That's what you think. I'm engaged to her, so
put that in your pipe and smoke it.'

Mrs. Sunbury gasped.

'You're not?'

'Yes, I am. I've been thinking about it for a long time, and then she was so upset tonight I felt sorry for her, so I popped the question and I had a rare job persuading her, I can tell you.'

'You fool,' screamed Mrs. Sunbury. 'You fool.'

There was quite a scene then. Mrs. Sunbury and her son went at it hammer and tongs, and when poor Samuel tried to intervene they both told him roughly to shut up. At last Herbert flung out of the room and out of the house and Mrs. Sunbury burst into angry tears.

No reference was made next day to what had passed. Mrs. Sunbury was frigidly polite to Herbert and he was sullen and silent. After supper he went out. On Saturday he told his father and mother that he was engaged that afternoon and wouldn't be able to come to the common with them.

'I daresay we shall be able to do without you,' said Mrs. Sunbury grimly.

It was getting on to the time for their usual fortnight at the seaside. They always went to Herne Bay, because Mrs. Sunbury said you had a nice class of people there, and for years they had taken the same lodgings. One evening, in as casual a way as he could, Herbert said:

'By the way, Mum, you'd better write and tell them I shan't be wanting my room this year. Betty and me are getting married and we're going to Southend for the honeymoon.'

For a moment there was dead silence in the room.

'Bit sudden like, isn't it, Herbert?' said Mr. Sunbury uneasily.

'Well, they're cutting down at Betty's office and she's out of a job, so we thought we'd better get married at once. We've taken two rooms in Dabney Street and we're furnishing out of my Savings Bank money.'

Mrs. Sunbury didn't say a word. She went deathly pale and tears rolled down her thin cheeks.

'Oh, come on, Mum, don't take it so hard,' said Herbert. 'A fellow has to marry sometime. If Dad hadn't married you, I shouldn't be here now, should I?'

Mrs. Sunbury brushed her tears away with an impatient hand.

'Your dad didn't marry me; I married 'im. I knew he was steady and respectable. I knew he'd make a good 'usband and father. I've never 'ad cause to regret it and no more 'as your dad. That's right, Samuel, isn't it?'

'Right as rain, Beatrice,' he said quickly.

'You know, you'll like Betty when you get to know her. She's a nice girl, she is really. I believe you'd find you had a lot in common. You must give her a chance, Mum.'

'She's never going to set foot in this house only over my dead body.'

'That's absurd, Mum. Why, everything'll be just the same if you'll only be reasonable. I mean, we can go flying on Saturday afternoons same as we always did. Just this time I've been engaged it's been difficult. You see, she can't see what there is in kite-flying, but she'll come round to it, and after I'm married it'll be different, I mean I can come and fly with you and Dad; that stands to reason.'

'That's what you think. Well, let me tell you that if you marry that woman you're not going to fly my kite. I never gave it you, I bought it out of the house-keeping money, and it's mine, see.'

'All right then, have it your own way. Betty says it's a kid's game anyway and I ought to be ashamed of myself, flying a kite at my age.'

He got up and once more stalked angrily out of the house. A fortnight later he was married. Mrs. Sunbury refused to go to the wedding and wouldn't let Samuel go either. They went for their holiday and came back. They resumed their usual round. On Saturday afternoons they went to the common by themselves and flew their enormous kite. Mrs. Sunbury never mentioned her son. She was determined not to forgive him. But Mr. Sunbury used to meet him on the morning train they both took and they chatted a little when they managed to get into the same carriage. One morning Mr. Sunbury looked up at the sky.

'Good flying weather today,' he said.

'D'you and Mum still fly?'

'What do you think? She's getting as clever as I am. You should see her with her skirts pinned up running down the hill. I give you my word, I never knew she had it in her. Run? Why, she can run better than what I can.'

'Don't make me laugh, Dad!'

'I wonder you don't buy a kite of your own, Herbert. You've been always so keen on it.'

'I know I was. I did suggest it once, but you know what women are, Betty said: "Be your age," and oh, I don't know what all. I don't want a kid's kite, of course, and them big kites cost money. When 've started to furnish Betty said it was cheaper in the long run to buy the best and so we went to one of them hire-purchase places and what with paying them every month and the rent, well, I haven't got any more money than just what we can manage on.

They say it doesn't cost any more to keep two than one, well, that's not my experience so far.'

'Isn't she working?'

'Well, no, she says after working for donkeys' years as you might say, now she's married she's going to take it easy, and of course someone's got to keep the place clean and do the cooking.'

So it went on for six months, and then one Saturday afternoon when the Sunburys were as usual on the common Mrs. Sunbury said to her husband:

'Did you see what I saw, Samuel?'

'I saw Herbert, if that's what you mean. I didn't mention it because I thought it would only upset you.'

'Don't speak to him. Pretend you haven't seen him.'

Herbert was standing among the idle lookers-on. He made no attempt to speak to his parents, but it did not escape Mrs. Sunbury that he followed with all his eyes the flight of the big kite he had flown so often. It began to grow chilly and the Sunburys went home. Mrs. Sunbury's face was brisk with malice.

'I wonder if he'll come next Saturday,' said Samuel.

'If I didn't think betting wrong I'd bet sixpence he will, Samuel. I've been waiting for this all along.'

'You have?'

'I knew from the beginning he wouldn't be able to keep away from it.'

She was right. On the following Saturday and on every Saturday after that when the weather was fine Herbert turned up on the common. No intercourse passed. He just stood there for a while looking on and then strolled away. But after things had been going on like this for several weeks, the Sunburys had a surprise for him. They weren't flying the big kite which he was used to, but a new one, a box-kite, a small one, on the model for which he had made the designs himself. He saw it was creating a lot of interest among the other kite-flyers; they were standing round it and Mrs. Sunbury was talking volubly. The first time Samuel ran down the hill with it the thing didn't rise, but flopped miserably on the ground, and Herbert clenched his hands and ground his teeth. He couldn't bear to see it fail. Mr. Sunbury climbed up the little hill again, and the second time the box-kite took the air. There was a cheer among the bystanders. After a while Mr. Sunbury pulled it down and walked back with it to the hill. Mrs. Sunbury went up to her son.

'Like to have a try, Herbert?'

He caught his breath.

'Yes, Mum, I should.'

'It's just a small one because they say you have to get the knack of it. It's not like the old-fashioned sort. But we've got specifications for a big one, and they say when you get to know about it and the wind's right you can go up to two miles with it.'

Mr. Sunbury joined them.

'Samuel, Herbert wants to try the kite.'

Mr. Sunbury handed it to him, a pleased smile on his face, and Herbert gave his mother his hat to hold. Then he raced down the hill, the kite took the air beautifully, and as he watched it rise his heart was filled with exultation. It was grand to see that little black thing soaring so sweetly, but even as he watched it he thought of the great big one they were having made. They'd never be able to manage that. Two miles in the air, mum had said. Whew!

'Why don't you come back and have a cup of tea, Herbert,' said Mrs. Sunbury, 'and we'll show you the designs for the new one they want to build for us. Perhaps you could make some suggestions.'

He hesitated. He'd told Betty he was just going for a walk to stretch his legs, she didn't know he'd been coming to the common every week, and she'd be waiting for him. But the temptation was irresistible.

'I don't mind if I do,' he said.

After tea they looked at the specifications. The kite was huge, with gadgets he had never seen before, and it would cost a lot of money.

'You'll never be able to fly it by yourselves,' he said.

'We can try.'

'I suppose you wouldn't like me to help you just at first?' he asked uncertainly.

'Mightn't be a bad idea,' said Mrs. Sunbury.

It was late when he got home, much later than he thought, and Betty was vexed.

'Wherever have you been, Herb? I thought you were dead. Supper's waiting and everything.'

'I met some fellows and got talking.'

She gave him a sharp look, but didn't answer. She sulked.

After supper he suggested they should go to a movie, but she refused.

'You go if you want to,' she said. 'I don't care to.'

On the following Saturday he went again to the common and again his mother let him fly the kite. They had ordered the new one and expected to get it in three weeks. Presently his mother said to him:

'Elizabeth is here.'

'Betty?'

'Spying on you.'

It gave him a nasty turn, but he put on a bold front.

'Let her spy. I don't care.'

But he was nervous and wouldn't go back to tea with his parents. He went straight home. Betty was waiting for him.

'So, that's the fellows you got talking to. I've been suspicious for some time, you going for a walk on Saturday afternoons, and all of a sudden I tumbled to it. Flying a kite, you, a grown man. Contemptible I call it.'

'I don't care what you call it. I like it, and if you don't like it you can lump it.'

'I won't have it and I tell you that straight. I'm not going to have you make a fool of yourself.'

'I've flown a kite every Saturday afternoon ever since I was a kid, and I'm going to fly a kite as long as ever I want to.'

'It's that old bitch, she's just trying to get you away from me. I know her. If you were a man you'd never speak to her again, not after the way she's treated me.'

'I won't have you call her that. She's my mother and I've got the right to see her as often as ever I want to.'

The quarrel went on hour after hour. Betty screamed at him and Herbert shouted at her. They had had trifling disagreements before, because they were both obstinate, but this was the first serious row they had had. They didn't speak to one another on the Sunday, and during the rest of the week, though outwardly there was peace between them, their ill feeling rankled. It happened that the next two Saturdays it poured with rain. Betty smiled to

herself when she saw the downpour, but if Herbert
was disappointed he gave no sign of it. The recollection of their quarrel grew dim. Living in two rooms
as they did, sleeping in the same bed, it was inevitable that they should agree to forget their differences. Betty went out of her way to be nice to her
Herb, and she thought that now she had given him
a taste of her tongue and he knew she wasn't going
to be put upon by anyone, he'd be reasonable. He
was a good husband in his way, generous with his
money and steady. Give her time and she'd manage
him all right.

But after a fortnight of bad weather it cleared.

'Looks as if we're going to have good flying
weather tomorrow,' said Mr. Sunbury as they met
on the platform to await their morning train. 'The
new kite's come.'

'It has?'

'Your mum says of course we'd like you to come
and help us with it, but no one's got the right to
come between a man and his wife, and if you're
afraid of Betty, her kicking up a rumpus, I mean,
you'd better not come. There's a young fellow we've
got to know on the common who's just mad about
it, and he says he'll get it to fly if anybody can.'

Herbert was seized with a pang of jealousy.

'Don't you let any strangers touch our kite. I'll be
there all right.'

'Well, you think it over, Herbert, and if you don't
come we shall quite understand.'

'I'll come,' said Herbert.

So next day when he got back from the City he
changed from his business clothes into slacks and
an old coat. Betty came into the bedroom.

'What are you doing?'

'Changing,' he answered gaily. He was so excited, he couldn't keep the secret to himself. 'Their new kite's come and I'm going to fly it.'

'Oh, no, you're not,' she said. 'I won't have it.'

'Don't be a fool, Betty. I'm going, I tell you, and if you don't like it you can do the other thing.'

'I'm not going to let you, so that's that.'

She shut the door and stood in front of it. Her eyes flashed and her jaw was set. She was a little thing and he was a tall strong man. He took hold of her two arms to push her out of the way, but she kicked him violently on the shin.

'D'you want me to give you a sock on the jaw?'

'If you go you don't come back,' she shouted.

He caught her up, though she struggled and kicked, threw her on to the bed and went out.

If the small box-kite had caused an excitement on the common it was nothing to what the new one caused. But it was difficult to manage, and though they ran and panted and other enthusiastic flyers helped them Herbert couldn't get it up.

'Never mind,' he said, 'we'll get the knack of it presently. The wind's not right today, that's all.'

He went back to tea with his father and mother and they talked it over just as they had talked in the old days. He delayed going because he didn't fancy the scene Betty would make him, but when Mrs. Sunbury went into the kitchen to get supper ready he had to go home. Betty was reading the paper. She looked up.

'Your bag's packed,' she said.

'My what?'

'You heard what I said. I said if you went you needn't come back. I forgot about your things. Everything's packed. It's in the bedroom.'

He looked at her for a moment with surprise. She pretended to be reading again. He would have liked to give her a good hiding.

'All right, have it your own way,' he said.

He went into the bedroom. His clothes were packed in a suitcase, and there was a brown-paper parcel in which Betty had put whatever was left over. He took the bag in one hand, the parcel in the other, walked through the sitting-room without a word and out of the house. He walked to his mother's and rang the bell. She opened the door.

'I've come home, Mum,' he said.

'Have you, Herbert? Your room's ready for you. Put your things down and come in. We were just sitting down to supper.' They went into the dining-room. 'Samuel, Herbert's come home. Run out and get a quart of beer.'

Over supper and during the rest of the evening he told them the trouble he had had with Betty.

'Well, you're well out of it, Herbert,' said Mrs. Sunbury when he had finished. 'I told you she was no wife for you. Common she is, common as dirt, and you who's always been brought up so nice.'

He found it good to sleep in his own bed, the bed he'd been used to all his life, and to come down to breakfast on the Sunday morning, unshaved and unwashed, and read the *News of the World*.

'We won't go to chapel this morning,' said Mrs. Sunbury. 'It's been an upset to you, Herbert; we'll all take it easy today.'

During the week they talked a lot about the kite, but they also talked a lot about Betty. They discussed what she would do next.

'She'll try and get you back,' said Mrs. Sunbury.

'A fat chance she's got of doing that,' said Herbert.

'You'll have to provide for her,' said his father.

'Why should he do that?' cried Mrs. Sunbury. 'She trapped him into marrying her and now she's turned him out of the home he made for her.'

'I'll give her what's right as long as she leaves me alone.'

He was feeling more comfortable every day, in fact he was beginning to feel as if he'd never been away, he settled in like a dog in its own particular basket; it was nice having his mother to brush his clothes and mend his socks; she gave him the sort of things he'd always eaten and liked best; Betty was a scrappy sort of cook, it had been fun just at first, like picnicking, but it wasn't the sort of eating a man could get his teeth into, and he could never get over his mother's idea that fresh food was better than the stuff you bought in tins. He got sick of the sight of tinned salmon. Then it was nice to have space to move about in rather than be cooped up in two small rooms, one of which had to serve as a kitchen as well.

'I never made a bigger mistake in my life than when I left home, Mum,' he said to her once.

'I know that, Herbert, but you're back now and you've got no cause ever to leave it again.'

His salary was paid on Friday and in the evening when they had just finished supper the bell rang.

'That's her,' they said with one voice.

Herbert went pale. His mother gave him a glance.

'You leave it to me,' she said. 'I'll see her.'

She opened the door. Betty was standing on the threshold. She tried to push her way in, but Mrs. Sunbury prevented her.

'I want to see Herb.'

'You can't. He's out.'

'No, he isn't. I watched him go in with his dad and he hasn't come out again.'

'Well, he doesn't want to see you, and if you start making a disturbance I'll call the police.'

'I want my week's money.'

'That's all you've ever wanted of him.' She took out her purse. 'There's thirty-five shillings for you.'

'Thirty-five shillings? The rent's twelve shillings a week.'

'That's all you're going to get. He's got to pay his board here, hasn't he?'

'And then there's the instalments on the furniture.'

'We'll see about that when the time comes. D'you want the money or don't you?'

Confused, unhappy, browbeaten, Betty stood irresolutely. Mrs. Sunbury thrust the money in her hand and slammed the door in her face. She went back to the dining-room.

'I've settled her hash all right,' she said.

The bell rang again, it rang repeatedly, but they did not answer it, and presently it stopped. They guessed that Betty had gone away.

It was fine next day, with just the right velocity in the wind, and Herbert, after failing two or three times, found he had got the knack of flying the big box-kite. It soared into the air and up and up as he unreeled the wire.

'Why, it's a mile up if it's a yard,' he told his mother excitedly.

He had never had such a thrill in his life.

Several weeks passed by. They concocted a letter for Herbert to write in which he told Betty that so long as she didn't molest him or members of his family she would receive a postal order for thirty-five shillings every Saturday morning and he would pay the instalments on the furniture as they came due. Mrs. Sunbury had been much against this, but Mr. Sunbury, for once at variance with her, and Herbert agreed that it was the right thing to do. Herbert by then had learnt the ways of the new kite and was able to do great things with it. He no longer bothered to have contests with the other kite-flyers. He was out of their class. Saturday afternoons were his moments of glory. He revelled in the admiration he aroused in the bystanders and enjoyed the envy he knew he excited in the less fortunate flyers. Then one evening when he was walking back from the station with his father Betty waylaid him.

'Hulloa, Herb,' she said.

'Hulloa.'

'I want to talk to my husband alone, Mr. Sunbury.'

'There's nothing you've got to say to me that my dad can't hear,' said Herbert sullenly.

She hesitated. Mr. Sunbury fidgeted. He didn't know whether to stay or go.

'All right, then,' she said. 'I want you to come back home, Herb. I didn't mean it that night when I packed your bag. I only did it to frighten you. I was in a temper. I'm sorry for what I did. It's all so silly, quarrelling about a kite.'

'Well, I'm not coming back, see. When you turned me out you did me the best turn you ever did me.'

Tears began to trickle down Betty's cheeks.

'But I love you, Herb. If you want to fly your silly old kite, you fly it, I don't care so long as you come back.'

'Thank you very much, but it's not good enough. I know when I'm well off and I've had enough of married life to last me a lifetime. Come on, Dad.'

They walked on quickly and Betty made no attempt to follow them. On the following Sunday they went to chapel and after dinner Herbert went to the coal-shed where they kept the kite to have a look at it. He just couldn't keep away from it. He doted on it. In a minute he rushed back, his face white, with a hatchet in his hand.

'She's smashed it up. She did it with this.'

The Sunburys gave a cry of consternation and hurried to the coal-shed. What Herbert had said was true. The kite, the new, expensive kite, was in fragments. It had been savagely attacked with the hatchet, the woodwork was all in pieces, the reel was hacked to bits.

'She must have done it while we were at chapel. Watched us go out, that's what she did.'

'But how did she get in?' asked Mr. Sunbury.

'I had two keys. When I came home I noticed one was missing, but I didn't think anything about it.'

'You can't be sure she did it, some of them fellows on the common have been very snooty, I wouldn't put it past them to have done this.'

'Well, we'll soon find out,' said Herbert. 'I'll go and ask her, and if she did it I'll kill her.'

His rage was so terrible that Mrs. Sunbury was frightened.

'And get yourself hung for murder? No, Herbert, I won't let you go. Let your dad go, and when he comes back we'll decide what to do.'

'That's right, Herbert, let me go.'

They had a job to persuade him, but in the end Mr. Sunbury went. In half an hour he came back.

'She did it all right. She told me straight out. She's

proud of it. I won't repeat her language, it fair
startled me, but the long and short of it was she was
jealous of the kite. She said Herbert loved the kite
more than he loved her and so she smashed it up
and if she had to do it again she'd do it again.'

'Lucky she didn't tell me that. I'd have wrung her
neck even if I'd had to swing for it. Well, she never
gets another penny out of me, that's all.'

'She'll sue you,' said his father.

'Let her.'

'The instalment on the furniture is due next week,
Herbert,' said Mrs. Sunbury quietly. 'In your place
I wouldn't pay it.'

'Then they'll just take it away,' said Samuel, 'and
all the money he's paid on it so far will be wasted.'

'Well, what of it?' she answered. 'He can afford
it. He's rid of her for good and all and we've got
him back and that's the chief thing.'

'I don't care twopence about the money,' said
Herbert. 'I can see her face when they come and
take the furniture away. It meant a lot to her, it did,
and the piano, she set a rare store on that piano.'

So on the following Friday he did not send Betty
her weekly money, and when she sent him on a letter
from the furniture people to say that if he didn't pay
the instalment due by such and such a date they
would remove it, he wrote back and said he wasn't
in a position to continue the payments and they
could remove the furniture at their convenience.
Betty took to waiting for him at the station, and
when he wouldn't speak to her followed him down
the street screaming curses at him. In the evenings
she would come to the house and ring the bell till
they thought they would go mad, and Mr. and Mrs.
Sunbury had the greatest difficulty in preventing

Herbert from going out and giving her a sound thrashing. Once she threw a stone and broke the sitting-room window. She wrote obscene and abusive postcards to him at his office. At last she went to the magistrate's court and complained that her husband had left her and wasn't providing for her support. Herbert received a summons. They both told their story and if the magistrate thought it a strange one he didn't say so. He tried to effect a reconciliation between them, but Herbert resolutely refused to go back to his wife. The magistrate ordered him to pay Betty twenty-five shillings a week. He said he wouldn't pay it.

'Then you'll go to prison,' said the magistrate. 'Next case.'

But Herbert meant what he said. On Betty's complaint he was brought once more before the magistrate, who asked him what reason he had for not obeying the order.

'I said I wouldn't pay her and I won't, not after she smashed my kite. And if you send me to prison I'll go to prison.'

The magistrate was stern with him this time.

'You're a very foolish young man,' he said. 'I'll give you a week to pay the arrears, and if I have any more nonsense from you you'll go to prison till you come to your senses.'

Herbert didn't pay, and that is how my friend Ned Preston came to know him and I heard the story.

'What d'you make of it?' asked Ned as he finished. 'You know, Betty isn't a bad girl. I've seen her several times, there's nothing wrong with her except her insane jealousy of Herbert's kite; and he isn't a fool by any means. In fact he's smarter than the average. What d'you suppose there is in kite-flying that makes the damned fool so mad about it?'

'I don't know,' I answered. I took my time to think. 'You see, I don't know a thing about flying a kite. Perhaps it gives him a sense of power as he watches it soaring towards the clouds and of mastery over the elements as he seems to bend the winds of heaven to his will. It may be that in some queer way he identifies himself with the kite flying so free and so high above him, and it's as it were an escape from the monotony of life. It may be that in some dim, confused way it represents an ideal of freedom and adventure. And you know, when a man once gets bitten with the virus of the ideal not all the King's doctors and not all the King's surgeons can rid him of it. But all this is very fanciful and I dare say it's just stuff and nonsense. I think you'd better put your problem before someone who knows a lot more about the psychology of the human animal than I do.'

VIRGINIA WOOLF

The Duchess and the Jeweller

OLIVER BACON lived at the top of a house overlooking the Green Park. He had a flat; chairs jutted
out at the right angles—chairs covered in hide. Sofas
filled the bays of the windows—sofas covered in
tapestry. The windows, the three long windows, had
the proper allowance of discreet net and figured
satin. The mahogany sideboard bulged discreetly
with the right brandies, whiskies and liqueurs. And
from the middle window he looked down upon
the glossy roofs of fashionable cars packed in the
narrow straits of Piccadilly. A more central position could not be imagined. And at eight in the
morning he would have his breakfast brought in on
a tray by a man-servant: the man-servant would
unfold his crimson dressing-gown; he would rip his
letters open with his long pointed nails and would
extract thick white cards of invitation upon which
the engraving stood up roughly from duchesses,
countesses, viscountesses and Honourable Ladies.
Then he would wash; then he would eat his toast;
then he would read his paper by the bright burning
fire of electric coals.

'Behold Oliver,' he would say, addressing himself. 'You who began life in a filthy little alley, you
who . . .', and he would look down at his legs, so
shapely in their perfect trousers; at his boots; at his
spats. They were all shapely, shining; cut from the

best cloth by the best scissors in Savile Row. But he dismantled himself often and became again a little boy in a dark alley. He had once thought that the height of his ambition—selling stolen dogs to fashionable women in Whitechapel. And once he had been done. 'Oh, Oliver,' his mother had wailed. 'Oh, Oliver! When will you have sense, my son?' . . . Then he had gone behind a counter; had sold cheap watches; then he had taken a wallet to Amsterdam . . . At that memory he would chuckle—the old Oliver remembering the young. Yes, he had done well with the three diamonds; also there was the commission on the emerald. After that he went into the private room behind the shop in Hatton Garden; the room with the scales, the safe, the thick magnifying glasses. And then . . . and then . . . He chuckled. When he passed through the knots of jewellers in the hot evening who were discussing prices, gold mines, diamonds, reports from South Africa, one of them would lay a finger to the side of his nose and murmur, 'Hum-m-m,' as he passed. It was no more than a murmur; no more than a nudge on the shoulder, a finger on the nose, a buzz that ran through the cluster of jewellers in Hatton Garden on a hot afternoon—oh, many years ago now! But still Oliver felt it purring down his spine, the nudge, the murmur that meant, 'Look at him—young Oliver, the young jeweller—there he goes.' Young he was then. And he dressed better and better; and had, first a hansom cab; then a car; and first he went up to the dress circle, then down into the stalls. And he had a villa at Richmond, overlooking the river, with trellises of red roses; and Mademoiselle used to pick one every morning and stick it in his buttonhole.

'So,' said Oliver Bacon, rising and stretching his legs. 'So . . .'

And he stood beneath the picture of an old lady on the mantelpiece and raised his hands. 'I have kept my word,' he said, laying his hands together, palm to palm, as if he were doing homage to her. 'I have won my bet.' That was so; he was the richest jeweller in England; but his nose, which was long and flexible, like an elephant's trunk, seemed to say by its curious quiver at the nostrils (but it seemed as if the whole nose quivered, not only the nostrils) that he was not satisfied yet; still smelt something under the ground a little farther off. Imagine a giant hog in a pasture rich with truffles; after unearthing this truffle and that, still it smells a bigger, a blacker truffle under the ground farther off. So Oliver snuffed always in the rich earth of Mayfair another truffle, a blacker, a bigger farther off.

Now then he straightened the pearl in his tie, cased himself in his smart blue overcoat; took his yellow gloves and his cane; and swayed as he descended the stairs and half snuffed, half sighed through his long sharp nose as he passed out into Piccadilly. For was he not still a sad man, a dissatisfied man, a man who seeks something that is hidden, though he had won his bet?

He swayed slightly as he walked, as the camel at the zoo sways from side to side when it walks along the asphalt paths laden with grocers and their wives eating from paper bags and throwing little bits of silver paper crumpled up on to the path. The camel despises the grocers; the camel is dissatisfied with its lot; the camel sees the blue lake, and the fringe of palm trees in front of it. So the great jeweller, the greatest jeweller in the whole world, swung down

Piccadilly, perfectly dressed, with his gloves, with his cane; but dissatisfied still, till he reached the dark little shop, that was famous in France, in Germany, in Austria, in Italy, and all over America—the dark little shop in the street off Bond Street.

As usual, he strode through the shop without speaking, through the four men, the two old men, Marshall and Spencer, and the two young men, Hammond and Wicks, stood straight and looked at him, envying him. It was only with one finger of the amber-coloured glove, waggling, that he acknowledged their presence. And he went in and shut the door of his private room behind him.

Then he unlocked the grating that barred the window. The cries of Bond Street came in; the purr of the distant traffic. The light from reflectors at the back of the shop struck upwards. One tree waved six green leaves, for it was June. But Mademoiselle had married Mr. Pedder of the local brewery—no one stuck roses in his buttonhole now.

'So,' he half sighed, half snorted, 'so——'

Then he touched a spring in the wall and slowly the panelling slid open, and behind it were the steel safes, five, no, six of them, all of burnished steel. He twisted a key; unlocked one; then another. Each was lined with a pad of deep crimson velvet; in each lay jewels—bracelets, necklaces, rings, tiaras, ducal coronets; loose stones in glass shells; rubies; emeralds, pearls, diamonds. All safe, shining, cool, yet burning, eternally, with their own compressed light.

'Tears!' said Oliver, looking at the pearls.

'Heart's blood!' he said, looking at the rubies.

'Gunpowder!' he continued, rattling the diamonds so that they flashed and blazed.

'Gunpowder enough to blow Mayfair—sky high,

high, high!' He threw his head back and made a sound like a horse neighing as he said it.

The telephone buzzed obsequiously in a low muted voice on his table. He shut the safe.

'In ten minutes,' he said. 'Not before.' And he sat down at his desk and looked at the heads of the Roman emperors that were graved on his sleeve links. And again he dismantled himself and became once more the little boy playing marbles in the alley where they sell stolen dogs on Sunday. He became that wily astute little boy, with lips like wet cherries. He dabbled his fingers in ropes of tripe; he dipped them in pans of frying fish; he dodged in and out among the crowds. He was slim, lissome, with eyes like licked stones. And now—now—the hands of the clock ticked on, one, two, three, four . . . The Duchess of Lambourne waited his pleasure; the Duchess of Lambourne, daughter of a hundred Earls. She would wait for ten minutes on a chair at the counter. She would wait his pleasure. She would wait till he was ready to see her. He watched the clock in its shagreen case. The hand moved on. With each tick the clock handed him—so it seemed—paté de foie gras, a glass of champagne, another of fine brandy, a cigar costing one guinea. The clock laid them on the table beside him as the ten minutes passed. Then he heard soft slow footsteps approaching; a rustle in the corridor. The door opened. Mr. Hammond flattened himself against the wall.

'Her Grace!' he announced.

And he waited there, flattened against the wall.

And Oliver, rising, could hear the rustle of the dress of the Duchess as she came down the passage. Then she loomed up, filling the door, filling the room with the aroma, the prestige, the arrogance, the

pomp, the pride of all the Dukes and Duchesses
swollen in one wave. And as a wave breaks, she
broke, as she sat down, spreading and splashing and
falling over Oliver Bacon, the great jeweller, covering him with sparkling bright colours, green, rose,
violet; and odours; and iridescences; and rays shooting from fingers, nodding from plumes, flashing
from silk; for she was very large, very fat, tightly
girt in pink taffeta, and past her prime. As a parasol
with many flounces, as a peacock with many feathers,
shuts its flounces, folds its feathers, so she subsided
and shut herself as she sank down in the leather
armchair.

'Good morning, Mr. Bacon,' said the Duchess.
And she held out her hand which came through the
slit of her white glove. And Oliver bent low as he
shook it. And as their hands touched the link was
forged between them once more. They were friends,
yet enemies; he was master, she was mistress; each
cheated the other, each needed the other, each feared
the other, each felt this and knew this every time
they touched hands thus in the little back room with
the white light outside, and the tree with its six
leaves, and the sound of the street in the distance
and behind them the safes.

'And today, Duchess—what can I do for you
today?' said Oliver, very softly.

The Duchess opened her heart, her private heart,
gaped wide. And with a sigh but no words she took
from her bag a long washleather pouch—it looked
like a lean yellow ferret. And from a slit in the
ferret's belly she dropped pearls—ten pearls. They
rolled from the slit in the ferret's belly—one, two,
three, four—like the eggs of some heavenly bird.

'All's that's left me, dear Mr. Bacon,' she moaned.

Five, six, seven—down they rolled, down the slopes
of the vast mountain sides that fell between her
knees into one narrow valley—the eighth, the ninth,
and the tenth. There they lay in the glow of the
peach-blossom taffeta. Ten pearls.

'From the Appleby cincture,' she mourned. 'The
last . . . the last of them all.'

Oliver stretched out and took one of the pearls
between finger and thumb. It was round, it was
lustrous. But real was it, or false? Was she lying
again? Did she dare?

She laid her plump padded finger across her lips.
'If the Duke knew . . .' she whispered. 'Dear Mr.
Bacon, a bit of bad luck . . .'

Been gambling again, had she?

'That villain! That sharper!' she hissed.

The man with the chipped cheek bone? A bad
'un. And the Duke was straight as a poker; with side
whiskers; would cut her off, shut her up down there
if he knew—what I know, thought Oliver, and
glanced at the safe.

'Araminta, Daphne, Diana,' she moaned. 'It's for
them.'

The ladies Araminta, Daphne, Diana—her daughters. He knew them; adored them. But it was Diana
he loved.

'You have all my secrets,' she leered. Tears slid;
tears fell; tears, like diamonds, collecting powder
in the ruts of her cherry blossom cheeks.

'Old friend,' she murmured, 'old friend.'

'Old friend,' he repeated, 'old friend,' as if he
licked the words.

'How much?' he queried.

She covered the pearls with her hand.

'Twenty thousand,' she whispered.

But was it real or false, the one he held in his hand? The Appleby cincture—hadn't she sold it already? He would ring for Spencer or Hammond. 'Take it and test it,' he would say. He stretched to the bell.

'You will come down tomorrow?' she urged, she interrupted. 'The Prime Minister—His Royal Highness . . .' She stopped. 'And Diana . . .' she added.

Oliver took his hand off the bell.

He looked past her, at the backs of the houses in Bond Street. But he saw, not the houses in Bond Street, but a dimpling river; and trout rising and salmon; and the Prime Minister; and himself too, in white waistcoat; and then, Diana. He looked down at the pearl in his hand. But how could he test it, in the light of the river, in the light of the eyes of Diana? But the eyes of the Duchess were on him.

'Twenty thousand,' she moaned. 'My honour!'

The honour of the mother of Diana! He drew his cheque book towards him; he took out his pen.

'Twenty——' he wrote. Then he stopped writing. The eyes of the old woman in the picture were on him—of the old woman his mother.

'Oliver!' she warned him. 'Have sense! Don't be a fool!'

'Oliver!' the Duchess entreated—it was 'Oliver' now, not 'Mr. Bacon.' 'You'll come for a long week-end?'

Alone in the woods with Diana! Riding alone in the woods with Diana!

'Thousand,' he wrote, and signed it.

'Here you are,' he said.

And there opened all the flounces of the parasol, all the plumes of the peacock, the radiance of the wave, the swords and spears of Agincourt, as she rose from her chair. And the two old men and the two young men, Spencer and Marshall, Wicks and Hammond, flattened themselves behind the counter envying him as he led her through the shop to the door. And he waggled his yellow glove in their faces, and she held her honour—a cheque for twenty thousand pounds with his signature—quite firmly in her hands.

'Are they false or are they real?' asked Oliver, shutting his private door. There they were, ten pearls on the blotting-paper on the table. He took them to the window. He held them under his lens to the light . . . This, then, was the truffle he had routed out of the earth! Rotten at the centre—rotten at the core!

'Forgive me, oh, my mother!' he sighed, raising his hands as if he asked pardon of the old woman in the picture. And again he was a little boy in the alley where they sold dogs on Sunday.

'For,' he murmured, laying the palms of his hands together, 'it is to be a long week-end.'

FRANCES TOWERS

The Little Willow

THE first evening, Simon Byrne was brought to the
house by a friend of Charlotte's, one of those with
whom she would have to settle an account after the
war—unless, of course, he didn't come back. The
stranger stood on the threshold and took in the
room, and a look of such extraordinary delight came
over his face that the youngest Miss Avery's heart
gave a little leap, almost as if, independently of her
mind and will, it greeted of its own accord another
of its kind.

It was, of course, a peculiarly gracious room, with
its high ceiling and Adam chimney-piece. The shiny
white walls were painted with light and dim reflections of colours, and a thick black hearthrug
smudged with curly pink roses—an incongruous
Balkan peasant rug in that chaste room—somehow
struck a note of innocence and gaiety, like the
scherzo in a symphony. That rug, and the photographs on the lid of the grand piano; the untidy
stack of books on a table; and a smoky pseudo old
master over the fireplace, with the lily of the Annun-
ciation as a highlight, a pale question mark in the
gloom, gave the room an oddly dramatic quality.
Lisby had often thought—'It is like a room on the
stage, in which the story of three sisters is about to
unfold.'

The passing reflections of Charlotte in red, Brenda

in green made a faint shimmer on the walls as they drifted about, as if a herbaceous border were reflected momentarily in water.

'Charlotte dear, I've brought a friend. He was at Tobruk. Comes from South Africa, and doesn't know a soul over here,' said Stephen Elyot. 'He's just out of hospital.'

'I am so glad!' said Charlotte glowingly, giving him both her hands. 'You must come as often as you like.'

His eyes dwelt on her dark, lovely face, and he said, 'You don't know what it feels like to be in a drawing-room again.'

'I can very well imagine. It must feel like the peace of God,' said Brenda, in that soft, plangent voice of hers, which was so perfect an instrument for the inspired remarks that seemed to fall effortlessly from her lips.

She could say the most divinely right things without a throb of real sympathy, and would spend pounds on roses rather than write a letter of condolence. As for her 'cello playing, it was strange how deeply she could move one, while she herself remained quite aloof. It was because she knew what the music was meant to say and was thinking about the music all the time, and not of how she played or how she felt. It was a great charm in her.

Lisby said nothing. She had no poetic conception of herself to impose on the minds of others. However, she had her uses. She cut the sandwiches and made the coffee and threw herself into the breach when some unassuming guest seemed in danger of being neglected. And unassuming guests often were. Charlotte and Brenda had such brilliant friends— musicians and artists and writers. The truest thing about those girls was that they were charmers. Every other fact sank into insignificance beside that one supreme quality. Though each had her own strongly marked individuality, they had this in common: that by lamplight they acquired, in their trailing dresses, a timeless look, as if they might have stood for types of the seductive woman in any age. Not a modern girl; but the delicate creature who through the ages has been man's rose of beauty, or his cup of hemlock.

Always, destroying friendship, there was this allure —the glow, the fragrance, the what-you-will, which, sooner or later, ensnared every young man and made him the captive of one or the other of the two elder Misses Avery.

'Charlotte dear,' said Stephen Elyot, wandering about the room with his coffee cup in his hand, 'I wonder, with your exquisite taste, you let that picture hang there! It's all *wrong*, my dear, as I've told you before. A Watteau, now, or a Fragonard, for this eighteenth-century room. And yet your *décors* for the stage are so perfect! You are *quite* my favourite designer.'

'Lisby would die if we banished the picture. It's been in the family for generations,' said Charlotte.

'It has been loved by people who are dead, for its . . . holiness, not for aesthetic reasons; and that makes it spiritually precious,' said Simon Byrne in a low voice to Lisby, by whom he chanced to be sitting.

She gave a little start. The thick white paint of the lily, and its golden tongue, had fascinated her as a child, making all lilies seem not quite earthly flowers. How did he know so quickly that the dark picture in the white room brought spiritual values into it, brought her mother saying, 'Yes, darling; perhaps the angel has a queer face—perhaps he *is* a little bit like Miss Nettleton. How interesting that some-one we know should have a face that an old master chose for the Angel Gabriel! I shall always think of Miss Nettleton as a very special kind of person.'

'It almost seems as if he might be my kind of per-son,' she thought. Perhaps one would have thought his face unremarkable if one had not caught that look on it. 'He has known horror and violence, and is terribly vulnerable to beauty,' she had said to herself, with one of her flashes of insight.

Brenda played that evening, and Simon Byrne never took his eyes off her. In her long green dress, with her gold hair like an inverted sheaf of corn, she held him spellbound. Or perhaps it was the music.

When she went to bed that night, Lisby caught herself hoping quite desperately that it was, after all, the music; and for such a foolish reason. Because as he was leaving he took her little willow tree in his long thin hands.

'So cool,' he said, 'and watery. Willows and wâter —I used to dream of them.'

'In the desert?' she asked.

'When I was lost,' he said, 'and parched with thirst, and terribly frightened.'

'It's the loveliest thing I have,' she said.

It was made of jade and crystal and it stood on the lacquer cabinet in the hall. She had fallen in love with it in an antique shop and had expended on it, with wild extravagance, her first term's salary as a teacher. Charlotte and Brenda had thought her too utterly feckless—almost wicked. The sun by day and the moon by night made it throw a lovely shadow on the wall. She couldn't explain that what

she loved was the *idea* of a willow that had been in
the mind of the Chinese artist—the glitter and coolness and bewitchment. But he would know.

He came several times. 'Naturally,' thought Lisby,
'one would like the house, wouldn't one? Its oldness
and peace.' And Charlotte arranged the flowers so
beautifully and there were music and conversation:
Brenda and her friends practising their quartets for
concerts and Charlotte's friends talking of art. Anyone could come to the Court House as a place in
which to forget the war. There was the strangeness
of its being so near London and yet completely hidden in a wood, an oasis in the desert of ribbon
development that had spread around it in the past
few years. Many young men on leave found it a
place of refuge.

He was a person one could talk to. The things that
made Lisby laugh made him laugh too. Sometimes
he would catch her eye and they would go off into
a silent fit of laughter at some absurd thing that no
one else had remarked. She knew, once or twice, the
strange feeling of strings being plucked in her mind
by a chance word or gesture of his, and he had a
way of humming some tune that had been haunting
her, even something she had not heard for a long
time: a phrase from a symphony, perhaps, that had
suddenly come back to her quite distinctly between
sleeping and waking, as if a record had been put on
in her mind.

And then, one day, Brenda, in her delicate way,
appropriated his friendship. A person versed in
Brenda-ish modes of behaviour could guess what
she thought. When she said charming things a little
frostily, as if offering an ice-chilled gardenia, when
she smiled with dazzling sweetness one moment and

raised her eyebrows rather coldly the next, one knew
what was in her mind. She was dealing with a situation that required delicacy and tact. Love was sacred,
even unwanted love. The little flame must not be
allowed to go out. So one blew on it prettily one
moment, and damped it down the next. For a con-
flagration meant the end of everything, it meant
stamping on the heart in which it burned. And how,
in wartime, could one bear to do that?

She said, 'You know, Simon is rather an in-
triguing person. He can say rather divine things—
when one is alone with him. Still waters, my dear,
run deep.'

Yes. He wouldn't wear his heart on his sleeve. But
to be the person to whom he said 'rather divine
things' must be to feel oneself unimaginably exquisite.

There was that night they all went out into the
garden when the all clear sounded. The scent of the
tobacco plants was so sweet it was like a presence,
like a naked nymph following one about, and the
moon was so bright that the red roses kept their
colour, and the white were luminous like the moths.
Standing apart, Lisby was fascinated by his shadow
lying clearcut on the lawn. She stared at it, and then,
looking up, saw it printed, gigantic, across the sky.
It gave her a queer cold feeling, seeming to confirm
an idea she had had of him lately: that everything
he was concerned in here and now was the beginning of something that would go on happening outside this sphere. It would always be there, behind
her eyelids.

After that, she couldn't go on trying to make up
to him for the times that Brenda was too much

occupied with someone else to bother about him. It would be a kind of mockery. The only thing was to keep out of his way.

But the last evening of his embarkation leave, when he came to say good-bye, it was she who had to see him to the front door. Brenda was fey that night, with a kind of febrile gaiety, because the favoured lover of the moment was home on forty-eight hours' leave, and she had no eyes for anyone but him; and Charlotte was deeply involved with Richard Harkness. When they said good-bye, they would doubtless be driven into each other's arms. One could see it in their eyes when they looked at each other.

Lisby's eyes fell on the little willow. She seized it and put it into his outstretched hand. 'Please take it —for luck,' she said.

'But you can't give this away, Miss Avery. It's— it's . . . much too lovely,' he stammered.

'Please, please—it's more yours than mine.'

'It's terribly kind of you. Your sisters—you've been so kind letting me come. I shall dream of this house.'

'But you'll come again,' said Lisby, speaking as lightly as she could.

'I'd try to . . . in the spirit, if not in the flesh,' he said, with his crooked smile. Why must he say a thing so devastating?

'Look at Orion—like some secret heavenly diagram,' said Lisby, at the open door, because she had no word of comfort for him (Oh, dear! He'll think I'm trying to be appealing, trying to be a poetical little puss, trying to get at him, she thought despairingly.) If only Brenda would come out for a moment and be very sweet in that way she had of being responsive to another's mood! She could have given him something to take away with him, some cryptic remark, that he could dwell upon and cherish, as if it were a tiny key she had put into his hand to unlock a door in the future. But she was caught away into a private heaven, and so he had to go without any hope.

He looked up at the heartbreaking glitter of Orion, so serene, so triumphant above the tortured world. 'A lover might use it as a code,' he said, almost under his breath. 'Abelard signing his letters to Héloise.'

He looked down at her, hesitating a moment, as if there were something he wanted to say. And then, with a sigh, he turned away. As he looked back at the gate to salute her, the little tree in his hand caught the starlight and shone with a faint blue fire.

He never wrote. Lisby, sorting out the post, sometimes looked wonderingly at a letter addressed to Brenda in a hand-writing she didn't know, but the name on the flap of the envelope was never his.

When the war was over at last, Richard Harkness, liberated from a prison camp in Germany, came back to claim Charlotte. Their wedding was fixed for the autumn.

'By the way, Brenda,' Charlotte said casually one day, looking up from a letter she was writing, 'I forgot to tell you. Richard says that Simon Byrne was a prisoner in the same Offlag. He died last year.'

'Oh, poor darling!' said Brenda, in the sweet, hollow voice she used when the conventions demanded an assumption of sorrow. One's heart had been wrung so often that there had come a time when it recorded merely a mechanical spasm. She went on arranging the flowers with a set expression.

Lisby said nothing. She sat very still in the recesses of the armchair and clasped her knees to still their trembling. 'So much death, one cannot bear it,' she said at last, and got herself out of the room somehow. She always took things to heart—as if she suffered in her own body the agony of unknown millions.

'It's all very well for Lisby,' said Brenda with a shrug. 'But, after all, she hasn't had any *personal* loss in this war. Not like you and me. I mean, when someone's killed who's been in love with one, it makes it all so terribly poignant. I sometimes think I've felt so much, I can't feel any more. Those poor lambs!' She sighed and dipped her face into the roses, as if she would leave with them the expression of grief she could now decently abandon. It was almost as though she were leaving them on his grave to symbolize her thoughts of him, that would fade more quickly than they. 'He was sweet, but rather dumb,' she said.

'Did he ever——' asked Charlotte, looking over her tortoise-shell glasses.

'Not in so many words. You all took it for granted it was me. But perhaps, after all, *you* were the attraction, Charlotte.' But the hint of doubt found no expression in the tones of her voice.

'Or Lisby. It really is rather awful the way we leave her out of account.'

Charlotte sealed her letter and took off her glasses. She had a face like La Belle Ferronière, on which the glasses had the air of an amusing affectation. But Brenda had the flowerlike delicacy of a Piero della Francesca. Lisby had seen the resemblances and had made her sisters a present of them. But no one had noticed that she herself was like a watching girl who holds a basket on her head in the background of El Greco's *Christ in the Temple*.

'Of course,' said Charlotte, affixing a stamp, 'it wasn't I. That's a thing I never make a mistake about. A woman always knows.'

'Well, I am not so cocksure about love as you seem to be. I mean, I'm inclined to say to myself, "*If* he does so and so, *if* he remembers what hat I wore the day before yesterday, *if* he bothers to look up the address I'm staying at in the telephone book, *then* I shall know for certain." But I don't remember applying any such tests to Simon. Somehow we never got that far. Though I had my suspicions, of course.'

Brenda carried the roses across the room and put them on the piano, in the midst of the numerous photographs, of young men in uniform. Surreptitiously she changed the place of one. He had been shot down over Hamburg, and his place was among the dead. Perhaps no one but herself, who was responsible for it, was aware of this arrangement of the photographs. She had a feeling about the matter of which she would not have spoken for the world. It did not exactly amount to a superstition. Perhaps it meant no more than did the meticulous dividing up of her books into their respective categories. It irritated her to find a novel thrust in between two volumes of poetry. Death, perhaps, was poetry, and life, prose. Or was it the other way round?

In the midst of preparations for the wedding, no one, it seemed, gave another thought to Simon Byrne.

'Lisby seems rather odd these days—sort of

strung-up,' said Charlotte one day. 'Do you think, Brenda, that subconsciously she minds my getting married and your being engaged? I mean, it can't be much fun, poor child, seeing happiness through other people's eyes, as Shakespeare has already remarked.' She snapped off a thread and took the pins out of a seam.

Brenda looked down with a preoccupied expression at the ring on her long pale hand, where it lay on a fold of crêpe de Chine she had been sewing. 'How incredibly lucky we are that our two have come through alive!' she said. 'Gerald doesn't know *how* lucky he is; because it *might* have been John. I don't know, but I *think* it might have been. I was devastated when he was killed. I dare say you are right about Lisby. But what can we do . . .?'

'That cyclamen colour you've chosen for the bridesmaids—of course, you'll look divine in it, but it's trying for Lisby. Heaven knows, she's sallow enough.'

'But, my dear, what was I to do? We had the stuff and we've got no coupons. If only Gerald were back, we could have had a double wedding and both got out of Lisby's way. I feel we rather swamp her, you know—like two arc lamps putting out the moonlight. Now, isn't that a tribute to our Lis?'

Charlotte was married on a golden day. While they waited for her in the porch, Lisby thought that Brenda looked more like an Italian primitive than ever, pale and bright as an angel. (But we are all wrong for the blue horizon and the golden leaves—too shrill, too springlike, she thought.) Their reflections stained with pink the dewdrops in a spider's web slung between two tombstones.

A cab drove up to the lich-gate, and Charlotte came down the path on the arm of an uncle, her dark eyes shining through her veil. She was so majestic, so withdrawn that they did not venture to speak to her, but spread out her train, whispering nervously together.

Richard Harkness stood at the altar steps. To Lisby he had rather a vulpine look. It argued a certain spirituality in Charlotte, not to be deceived by outward appearances, but to swoop unerringly on the qualities she wanted. But he hadn't been Simon's sort. He had never mentioned Simon's name in Lisby's presence. She was grateful to him for that, but she couldn't forgive him.

She stole a glance apprehensively at the best man. He had been in the camp too—a doctor, they said. He had a dark, ascetic face, sensitive and melancholy. One must keep out of his way.

The wedding reception was like any other: the strained hilarity, the desperate frivolity, lit with a perilous brightness as of unshed tears. Corks popped, the cake was cut, the toasts proposed. Charlotte came out of her trance, and Richard made a speech so charming that all her friends began to think they knew, after all, what she saw in him.

There was Brenda by the window, trying desperately to make conversation with Captain Oliver. When her voice was high and strained like that, one knew she was wilting; and there were those faint mauve shadows under her eyes. The man was difficult. He appeared to have no capacity for small talk.

'By the way, did you come across someone who was a friend of mine—Simon Byrne? He was in the tanks,' she said.

Brenda ... don't ... Don't! Lisby cried out soundlessly, with a pain like cramp about her heart. His name seemed to sound through the room like a clash of cymbals. She felt that it must pierce every breastbone. It made a stranger of Brenda. It was incomprehensible that she could use it to make conversation, that to her it could be a name like any other.

Lisby saw the start that Captain Oliver gave. He turned quickly and looked at Brenda—a long, searching look.

'Yes, I knew Byrne,' he said.

'He was such a dear. We liked him so much. Look, Charlotte has gone up to change. I must fly after her.'

They were gone at last. Charlotte leaned out and waved. Someone threw a slipper after the taxicab.

In the throng at the gate, Lisby was aware of Captain Oliver edging his way toward her.

'Miss Avery,' he said in her ear, 'may I speak to you a moment alone?'

'In the morning room,' said Lisby, very pale. For some unfathomable reason she picked up her bouquet from the hall table before preceding him into the little yellow room.

A picture glowing with evening appeared in the frame of the window. In the foreground, the black trunk of the mulberry tree, about which still dangled a few heart-shaped leaves of sour green, and to the right the long silver plumes of the pampas grass, had a strange significance, as if the words 'black, gold, silver' were being reiterated in a poem. The blue October mist lay beyond, veiling the lawn, and a little sumac tree burned like a torch at the edge of the mist. A bird that had abandoned music for the winter made a grasshopper sound.

The pampas grass. Charlotte had tried to dig it up—a vulgar interloper, she had said. Lisby clung desperately to her thoughts. She did not want to hear what this man had to say. She sank down on the sofa and began mechanically to take her bouquet to pieces. The colour was drained out of her face, and she looked ghastly in the cyclamen shade that was so becoming to Brenda.

'So you knew Simon Byrne,' said Captain Oliver, looking down at her. 'I wonder . . . perhaps you could help me, Miss Avery? I was with him when he died.'

'Have you, perhaps, a message . . . for my sister?' asked Lisby faintly, arranging little sprigs of heather on her knee.

'That's what I don't know,' he said with a sigh. 'There is something I'd like to tell someone—but not the wrong person. You see, Simon meant a great deal to me. Could you tell me, did she ever give him a little tree, a willow? I suppose it was one of those Chinese things.'

'No,' said Lisby, very low, 'she never gave him anything.'

'I am going to tell *you*,' said Captain Oliver, as if making a sudden decision. 'A secret would be safe with you, wouldn't it? He was badly hurt, you know. His wound never healed. He was terribly ill all the time; but the odd thing was that through it all, he was never less than himself. They couldn't do anything to Simon. They couldn't strip him of a single one of his qualities. It was as if he had some inward source of happiness, a core of peace in his heart. The camp was short of doctors and they were only too pleased to make use of me, so I was able to make things a little easier for him.'

'I am glad,' she said, bent over her flowers, 'that he had you to look after him.'

'The night before he died,' went on Captain Oliver, in a low deliberate voice, 'he dictated a letter to his mother in South Africa. He was a bit of a poet, you know. It was a very touching letter. I suppose she has it now, poor soul. I said, "Is there no one else, Simon?" He shook his head. "There was a girl," he said, "but she never knew she was my girl." I asked him to tell me about her, thinking it might comfort him. He said, "She is a little, quiet creature —like mignonette—and her eyes go light and dark with her thoughts. I knew in my bones she was meant for me. Once, when the pain was very bad, I thought she came and kissed me. I felt her cheek against mine. It was soft and cool—like young buds, as I always imagined it would be. And the pain went away and I went to sleep. You know, Robert, she wouldn't mind my dreaming that. She has such exquisite compassion. When I said good-bye, she gave me the loveliest thing she had—a little willow tree. It was smashed to bits in my kit when the shell got us." I thought to myself, "Perhaps she did care, that girl." He died toward morning, very peacefully, without speaking again.'

Lisby sat very still. 'So cold . . . so cold,' she said, chafing her hands as if the hands of the dying lay between them.

'So *you* were his girl,' said Robert Oliver.

'He was my dear, dear love,' whispered Lisby. She bowed her head on her knees and wept soundlessly.

He thought, 'It is sad for a girl when her first avowal of love has to be made to a third person.' And, going softly to the door, he turned the key in the lock and let himself out by the window.

'Lisby cried her eyes out after you left,' wrote Brenda to Charlotte. 'But at night she looked so radiant, one might have thought it was *her* wedding day. There were dozens of letters for you by the evening post (I've sent them on) and some for me. I sorted them out, and said, as one usually does, "None for you, I'm afraid, Lisby darling." She looked at me so strangely, and said, "I have had mine—one that was never written." What could she have meant? I said, "What on earth do you mean?" But I knew from the look on her face that it is one of those things she will never tell.'

C. S. FORESTER

The Hostage

IT was in the autumn of 1944, when the allied
armies had come bursting out of the Cotentin penin-
sula, flooding across France and advancing towards
the frontiers of the Fatherland, that General of
Infantry Friedrich von Dexter received his new
orders. They were brought by motor-cycle despatch
rider to the little house in the Welfenstrasse, having
presumably been teletyped to Army District Headquarters from the higher command of the armed
forces. Air raids on the town had been infrequent
lately; and the ruins had ceased to smoke, but traffic
was scanty, so that the roar of the motor-cycle engine was heard by everyone, and neighbours peeped
out of their windows to find out what was happening. They saw the general himself at his front door
receive the envelope and sign the receipt for it, and
then the motor-cycle roared away again and the
general went back inside his house.

Indoors the general found it hard to read the
typewritten sheet with its printed heading, for the
general was not wearing his spectacles and he had
to hold the message at arm's length, which was in-
convenient as the shattered windows had been
boarded up, making the stuffy old-fashioned sitting-
room almost dark. Aloise his wife stood motionless
by him while he read the message, motionless because as a soldier's wife she was trying to conceal
the anxiety she felt. Dexter handed it to her without

a word when he had finished reading it, and she read it with less difficulty.

'Does this mean—?' she began, and then she cut the question short. There were factory workers billeted in the house, and although they were presumably asleep, having been on the night shift, she could not risk being overheard discussing orders which had come from the Fuehrer himself. The two old people substituted glances for words; even in that twilit room they understood each other, after forty years of married life. The general looked over at the marble clock on the mantelpiece—the gift of the 91st Infantry on the occasion of their colonel's promotion—and reached a decision.

'We have ten minutes,' he said. 'Let us go for a walk.'

They went out into the shattered streets; there, among the hurrying pedestrians, and the cyclists bumping their way over the uneven surfaces, they could talk safely as long as they did not display any deep emotion. The general was in civilian clothes, because when he had been dismissed from his command by a frantic Fuehrer order he had been deprived of the right to wear uniform. So he wore his battered twenty-year-old tweeds, and Aloise walked beside him in her old-fashioned coat and skirt; and they appeared, as indeed they were, survivors of a past generation—even though, thanks to his spare figure and straight back, and with his hat concealing his white hair, the general's age was not apparent.

'What does it mean, dear?' asked Aloise before they reached the first corner.

'A direct order from the Fuehrer,' said the general. 'I have been appointed to the command of Fortress Montavril.'

'Yes, dear. That is in France?'

'The Belgian frontier. Near the Channel coast.'

'What sort of a fortress is it?'

The general looked casually round him, back over his shoulder, before he answered.

'I doubt if it is any fortress at all,' he said. 'I am quite sure there is none, in fact.'

'But dear——?'

The general looked over his shoulder again.

'The Fuehrer has a new system,' he said. 'It began in Russia last year—no, two years ago. He designates a particular area as a "fortress" and he appoints a garrison and a commandant for it.'

'And then, dear? And then?'

'Because it has been designated a fortress the place is expected to hold out to the last man.'

'I understand,' said Aloise.

It was hard, dreadfully hard, to have to carry on this conversation in public, while trying to appear as if merely taking a casual stroll.

'There is much for you to understand, dear,' said the general. 'He is obsessed with this idea. And he still believes, in spite of everything, that what he wishes must come true. A place is a fortress and so it must hold out, no matter what the conditions. A barbed-wire perimeter—that is all that is necessary. Disorganized troops—worn-out guns—shortage of ammunition—to speak of them is treason.'

They could not exchange a significant glance here in the street; they must stroll along looking idly about them as if talking of nothing except trivialities.

'It is hopeless, then?'

'My duty——' began the general, and then he paused while making the effort to marshal all the multitudinous ideas called up by that word, the most significant in the vocabulary of a soldier. 'It is my duty to obey my orders, and to fight for my country, no matter what the future.'

'Of course, dear.'

'But——' The general paused again, as a soldier well might pause after saying 'but' when speaking of his duty.

'But what, dear?'

'That is not all. In a siege——'

The general had been married forty years. During that time he had come gradually to discuss professional matters with his wife in a way that often violated the convention that a wife should confine her interests to Church, children and kitchen; but it was hard to convey to her in a few words the same picture of a siege that he carried in his mind's eye, called up with the ease of long professional experience.

'In a siege, dear?'

'There comes a time when further defence is useless. When the perimeter is broken. When the enemy has captured the commanding heights. When his artillery is overwhelming. Until then the garrison has been doing what it was intended to do. It has detained a larger force in its front. It has caused more casualties than it has suffered. Probably it has blocked some important line of communication. But after that moment is reached——'

The general talked with the fluency he could display when discussing professional subjects—he had talked in this way to several generations of young men at the War Academy many years ago. He broke off now, for they were passing a long line of people waiting outside a shop. When they had passed it Aloise recalled him to his explanation.

'You were talking about a siege, dear.'

'Yes. So I was. After a certain point defence usually becomes futile. The besiegers have an overwhelming artillery, good points of observation, have breached the defences. Then the losses become heavy among the defenders with no corresponding loss to the besiegers. To hold out longer than that means a massacre; men are killed with no chance of hitting back. Sometimes it is necessary, even so.'

'It is hard to see why, dear.' Aloise tried to speak with a professional tone. Woman-like, her first reaction when 'casualties' were mentioned was not to think of figures in a return, or of a commanding officer deciding that a unit was 'fought out', but of dead men and tortured men, of childless mothers and widowed wives—of herself when the news came about their sons. She knew that was not the way a general's wife should think at a time when professional subjects were under discussion, and she steadied her voice in consequence.

'It may happen,' explained Dexter, 'that the garrison may still be blocking some important line of communication. Then it may be worth while to incur those losses, to fight to the last man to keep that line blocked for the last few hours. It might be worth any sacrifice.'

'I suppose so,' agreed Aloise doubtfully.

'But that is an unusual situation,' went on Dexter, 'rarer than you would think.'

Aloise in her heart of hearts believed that there could never be any situation worth the sacrifice of thousands of lives, but she did not say so. She waited dutifully for her husband to continue.

'Generally speaking,' he said, 'a neutralized garrison under final attack has no useful part to play.'

Aloise could make no contribution to the conversation, and her husband, interpreting her silence as lack of full understanding, went on to produce a specific instance, even though when lecturing to budding staff officers he had been careful to warn them not to think exclusively along arithmetical lines.

'Supposing,' he said, 'I have twenty thousand men in my garrison. That's a likely number. For two or three weeks I detain forty thousand of the enemy in front of me. Well and good. They attack at the decisive points. If their armour is not overwhelmingly strong I inflict heavy casualties on them. By the time they have mastered those decisive points I have lost—say five thousand men.'

Aloise tried to picture in her mind's eye five thousand dead men, and failed.

'But the enemy has lost ten thousand—twelve thousand, perhaps,' went on her husband. 'That is well and good, as I said. Now my guns are wearing out, my ammunition failing, and I am under constant searching bombardment. The assault is going to succeed whenever the enemy cares to make it. If I fight on my fifteen thousand men are killed. And what does the enemy lose? One thousand? I doubt if it would be as many as that.'

'I see,' said Aloise, nodding her head as she walked. The general looked at his watch.

'My dear,' he said. 'I—I am afraid we must turn back.'

Aloise glanced sharply at him, sidelong, at that break in his voice. It would have told her, even if she had not already guessed, how deep were his feelings, and how great was the strain he was enduring. After they had turned back he added a supplement to his little lecture.

'You might think,' he said, 'that it did not really matter. One garrison more or less—But that is not true. There is the rest of the army to think about. And there is the Germany of the future.'

The general turned almost self-conscious as he entered into a discussion of the psychology of warfare. It was a very theoretical subject for a practical soldier.

'Soldiers will always fight under good officers. You can ask for extraordinary sacrifices from them.' The general paused, and his faded blue eyes looked out over dreadful distant vistas of memory. 'But they will not endure the thought of their lives being thrown away uselessly. They sulk, they desert. They shirk their duty. Once let it be known that they are going to certain death to no purpose and—no garrison would ever hold out. Do you understand that, dear?'

'I understand,' said Aloise.

'Already the army is not what it was.'

The general looked quickly over his shoulder after he had said that. It had slipped out, and if he had been overheard he might be a dead man that very night—and die a shameful death at that. They walked on their homeward way for some hundred yards in silence; the general was silent not merely because he was shaken by the risk he had just run but because he found it hard to continue with what he had to say, to advance the conversation to the next stage. It may have been accidental, or it may not, that Aloise made it easy by her next question.

'And you, dear,' she asked. 'Have you thought about what you will do?'

'I have my orders,' said Dexter. There was a grim, hard tone in his voice, and the glance that Aloise directed at him showed her that his face bore a bleak hopeless expression.

Most people would have thought there was very little about General Friedrich von Dexter for any woman to love, a professional soldier, hard, tough, limited both in his education and outlook, and more than sixty years old. Some men might laugh at him, some even despise him, although there had been many young men who had admired him, and there had been young captains who had loved him, back in the days of that other nightmare, when his fighting spirit alone had held his regiment together in face of utter disaster at the Butte de Warlencourt. And long after that, too; only last year at Kharkov, after he had fought his way with the remnants of his army corps out of the ring of encirclement, his staff had been moved to the deepest pity and sympathy when the savage message arrived from headquarters depriving him of his command. 'The weak-kneed gentleman with a von to his name' was how that message had described him. Sorrow at losing him had been the first and principal emotion of those young staff officers. The feeling that something must be desperately amiss at Fuehrer Headquarters for such a message to be sent came only secondarily—and of course could not be expressed in any spoken words.

And the hard professional soldier had read that message without allowing his expression to change in the least. He had left with only the briefest good-byes, to return home in disgrace, humiliated; only Aloise when she welcomed him home knew the depths of that humiliation. And she loved him; perhaps she loved him the more. An old woman of sixty; an old man of sixty-two, walking together along the shattered street in the bleak autumn sunshine, and discussing horrors, discussing the death of twenty thousand men—how could there be love there? Yet there was, just as flowers grow among the rocks.

'I have to obey,' said Dexter.

'I know you must, dear,' said Aloise.

Even if there were no question of duty one obeyed orders from the Fuehrer, or died.

'My dear,' said Dexter, looking straight before him, not daring even for a moment to meet his wife's eyes; it was as if, although speaking low, he was addressing the horizon.

'Yes, dear?'

'You know there is a law of hostages?'

'Yes.'

'Do you understand about it?'

'Yes.'

No one in Germany could fail to understand it. The law had been promulgated that summer, although it had been in operation, to everyone's knowledge, long before. Now it had been announced in cold print. Men's families were to be held responsible for their actions. If a man were to desert, his father or his mother, his wife or his sister or his children would be killed. Not only the man who deserted, but the man who faltered in his duty, the man whose spirit failed him, the man who could not overcome his physical weaknesses, condemned in that moment those who were dearest to him to a death which might or might not be speedy. There was to be no human weakness displayed in the defence of the Third Reich and in the prolongation of the lives of the inhuman creatures who ruled it.

'You are the only one now, dear,' said Dexter, still addressing the horizon.

'I know,' said Aloise.

The younger Friedrich von Dexter had died at El Alamein; Lothar von Dexter at Stalingrad. Ernst was 'missing, believed killed' at Rostov. There were only the two old people left. One would command at Montavril, and one would be a hostage at home.

'Did you notice in my orders who was to be my chief-of-staff?' asked Dexter.

'A gruppenfuehrer—I can't remember his name at the moment, but I did not know it. An SS officer, of course?'

'Gruppenfuehrer Frey,' said Dexter. 'I don't know him either. But I know why he has been appointed.'

'To spy on you?'

'To keep me up to my duty,' said Dexter.

They were nearly home again now. Everything had been said except the good-bye which would have to be said immediately.

There were several good-byes of the same sort being made at that time in Germany. Hitler was recalling to service many of the generals he had previously dismissed in disgrace, and appointing them to the command of 'fortresses'. He needed officers of high rank and authority, officers of experience, for those posts, to make sure the troops would obey. And he could rely on the Law of Hostages to make the generals themselves obey, however harshly he had treated them previously, and whatever their feelings towards him—about which he could have no doubt. As Dexter kissed his wife good-bye before going out to the waiting car he had the Law of Hostages in his mind.

On the seventeenth day of the siege of Montavril the Allies launched their third attack, and succeeded in breaking through the outer perimeter of the defences and in overrunning the whole of the area beyond the canal which the German forces had so far contrived to maintain. It was a desperate fight, in driving rain. The general himself had taken part in it. It was he personally who had saved the day. He had rallied the broken infantry, had brought up his last reserve, and had plugged the gap which yawned in the defences between the canal and the crossroads. He himself had posted the guns, and by his own example had kept them firing. The counter-attack which he had launched might even have succeeded in regaining the vital higher ground beyond the crossroads if it had not been for the shell which momentarily disabled him. It had wounded his aide-de-camp, and had torn to pieces the brigadier a few yards from him, but by some freak of ballistics the fragment which struck the general on the shin did not even break a bone. But he had been dazed and shaken by the explosion and by the time he could stand steady on his feet again the counter-attack had failed, and the battle had died away into desultory firing. The heavy rain limited visibility on all sides, turning the low fields into swamps, soaking —and perhaps in some instances even drowning— the helpless wounded who lay in the ill-defined No Man's Land round the crossroads. Perhaps the Allies would send in a flag of truce to arrange a brief armistice to attend to them.

The general left instructions on the matter with the colonel now in command of the sector before he went limping off—alone, because he left his runner to look after his aide-de-camp—to inspect the defences along the canal bank. Here the Allies were already in touch, in a manner of speaking. With extraordinary celerity they had brought up a loud-speaker which was braying ceaselessly across the nearly dry canal bed. It spoke almost perfect German—the sort of German one might expect from a German-American who had used the language at home in his childhood—and it was appealing to the troops to give up a hopeless struggle. The general listened to it with the division commander at his side. Normally the penalty for listening to Allied broadcasts was death, the same as for possessing an Allied leaflet, but in these circumstances the penalty could hardly be exacted—too many of the garrison were within hearing. It was good sense that the loud-speaker talked, too, pointing out that now the Allies had direct observation over the whole of the de-fences, and that there was no part of the perimeter now which was not subject to enfilade. The sensible thing to do would be to surrender, said the loud-speaker, and if the mad folly of the officers prevented that, then it would be equally sensible to desert, to slip over to the Allied lines where honourable treat-ment awaited anyone who accepted the invitation. The general listened, with the rain beating down on his helmet and waterproof coat.

'I am going back to headquarters now,' he said to the division commander. 'If they telephone for me, say that I am on my way.'

'Very well, sir,' said the division commander.

He was a man in his forties, white with fatigue and with red rims to his eyes. He watched with something like envy the stiff figure of the man in his sixties, limping solitary down the muddy path; but there was pity mingled with the envy.

The briefness of Dexter's journey from his outer defences by the canal to his headquarters in the church of Montavril demonstrated vividly the difficulties of the defence. It took Dexter not very long, even though he had to pick his way. Here was a score of dead horses, already beginning to bulge with corruption—there was no fuel with which to burn them nor labour available to bury them. The general thought bitterly of how the Allies, fully mechanized, had not a horse in their organization. They were four times stronger numerically, ten times better equipped, a hundred times stronger in the air. He exchanged a few words with the artillery commander here, a man as worn out as the division commander he had just left. Whatever compulsion was called for, those horses must be buried. The whole entrenched camp stank—the stench of modern war, foulness and corruption and high explosives. Here, where the dead had been buried, the shells of the Allies had horribly caused the earth to give up its dead. He must remember to give orders about that.

He stumbled through a filthy puddle. By his action today he had prolonged the defence by a few hours. The Allies would have to regroup and replenish with ammunition before they renewed their assault. If the counter-attack had regained the crossroads he might have gained a day—two days, even. But it had failed, and there was not a single battalion—not even a battalion as battalions were measured nowadays, with less than company strength—in reserve. Infantry, engineers and cooks were all in the front line. No; in a cellar in the village were two men under arrest. At headquarters they were waiting for him to confirm the court-martial sentences; he had postponed his decision until his return. Yet the sentences would have to be carried out. He had been remiss in even allowing that short delay. Prompt and inevitable punishment was necessary to keep the garrison fighting. Yet did it matter about two miserable men who had attempted to desert, when ten thousand men were going to die? Dexter shook his head, not in dissent but rather to shake off evil thoughts, as he plunged on.

Headquarters were in the church, in the crypt below the church, for of the building itself only a fragment of one wall still stood. The rest was piled about in jagged heaps of masonry. Dexter went in through the sandbagged and camouflaged entrance, down the stone steps, past the signallers in the outer dug-out, and into the crypt, where four candles struggled to burn in the foul air, and the chairs and tables of the staff were ranged round the tomb of the saint. Gruppenfuehrer Frey, left in charge when the general went to Canal Corner, rose to greet him.

'Congratulations, General,' he said, in his shrill voice, and the general stared at him in astonishment. There was nothing in the events of the past few hours—or days—or weeks—which called for congratulation. Frey turned back to take a little box from his improvised desk, opened it, and handed something to the general with an extravagant gesture; it was something metallic, which glittered, and lay cold in the general's hand.

'The Knight's Cross of the Iron Cross!' said Frey. 'The Ritterkreuz! What a pleasure it is to hand it to you, General. It was never better deserved.'

'How did this get here?' demanded Dexter.

'The plane—you didn't see it pass over? This morning—it dropped a message packet.'

'I did not see it,' said Dexter. Perhaps it had flown

over while he had been rallying the Landeschuetzen battalion at Oak Tree Corner. He had been too busy to notice the only German plane the garrison had seen since the siege began.

'Was there anything else in the message packet?' asked Dexter, sharply still.

Frey's fingers fluttered back to the desk.

'The letter from the Chief of the Military Cabinet enclosing the Ritterkreuz,' he said. 'A most flattering letter, General.'

Dexter glanced through it. A flattering letter, certainly—nothing beyond flattery either. The higher command, now that Germany was falling in ruins, avoided realities and confined its attention to trivialities like Knight's Crosses.

'Anything else?'

'Personal orders for me from SS head office.'

In the fantastic disorder into which Germany had fallen it was possible—it was a certainty—that an SS officer should receive orders independently of his commanding officer. Dexter could not even ask what those orders said.

'Anything else?'

'Yes. A small amount of mail for some of the units of the garrison. I have not yet decided to distribute it. As political officer I have to consider——'

'Anything for me?'

'One letter, General.'

Dexter knew what it was the instant he saw it. He snatched it from Frey's hand; Frey's fingers were twitching to open it, the born spy that he was; and as political officer with Himmler's authority behind him he could have demanded that it be shown him, but he knew that—at least in an isolated garrison like this—there was a practical limit to the power delegated to him. Dexter would not have allowed him to see Aloise's letter, not for anything on earth. Dexter stood holding it, yearning inexpressibly to open it and read it, but he would not do so in Frey's presence. When he could get a moment's privacy he would read it. It would afford him a brief glimpse of another world; it would be torment as well as unmeasured happiness, he knew. He would be reminded of Aloise's steadfast love for him, the comfort of it, the security of it, even while he was here, plunged deep into hell. Hell was all round him, and he would never escape from it; the letter he held in his hand would open a chink through which for one small moment he would be able to peer through into heaven.

Hell was all round him, demanding his attention.

'Have any reports come in?' he asked. He must attend to his duty before reading Aloise's letter.

Busse, the assistant chief-of-staff, had them ready.

'Verbal reports, sir,' he said, holding his notes of the telephone conversations in his hand. 'Barmers says—perhaps I had better give you his exact words, sir.'

'Very well,' said Dexter. Barmers was the senior medical officer in the garrison.

'He says "It is my duty to report to the General that I can do nothing for the wounded that are coming in. Anaesthetics and dressings are completely at an end, and plasma nearly so. The regimental aid stations are asking for morphine, and I have none to give them. The newly wounded must lie in the open outside the hospital to wait their turn for operative treatment without anaesthesia, and that will not be until tomorrow morning. I should

not really have spared the time to make this report."
That is the end of the report, sir.'

'Thank you,' said Dexter.

'The adjutant of the Five Hundred and Seventh
Artillery Regiment reports——'

'I saw him on my way back. I know what his
report says.'

Ten rounds left per gun, and very few guns
serviceable.

'General Fussel asks for the return of his Ost battalion.'

Fussel commanded the 816th Division on the far
side of the perimeter. His division had been stripped
of every available man to make the counter-attack.

'I left that decision to you, sir,' interposed Frey.

'The Ost battalion must stay where it is,' decided
Dexter.

'Fussel has no reserves at all, sir,' said Busse, in
gentle warning.

'I know that. Anything else?'

'The assistant quartermaster-general——'

'I can guess what he has to say,' said Dexter, looking round at the gloomy face of Becker, the officer
mentioned. 'Anything else?'

'The court-martial findings, sir.'

'Yes,' said Dexter.

Two men waiting to be shot, two men who had
been detected in the act of desertion. There could
be no mercy for them if the garrison were to be held
together. The sooner they were shot the stronger the
effect on the others. It was his duty not to delay.
And yet—he had fought a good fight. His iron will
had implemented his immense tactical experience.
Under his leadership his garrison had beaten off two
assaults and had at least temporarily checked the

third. In the hands of a bungler the defence might well have collapsed on the third day, and now it was the seventeenth. Surely he was entitled to some reward for that, something more satisfying although less tangible than the Ritterkreuz? He could spare two lives. Or could he even spare ten thousand? He was suddenly aware that Frey's eyes were fixed on his face, and he hoped that his expression had revealed none of his feelings.

The squawk of the telephone came as a fortunate diversion. Any call through to the central command post must be important, as only half a dozen officers had the right of direct access; routine calls were dealt with by the staff officer in the outer room. Frey picked up the telephone, as was his natural duty as chief of staff, but Dexter bitterly attributed to him a greedy inquisitiveness even in this hour of disaster.

'Chief-of-staff,' said Frey. 'Yes, I hear. Yes. Yes.'

He looked over at Dexter, the telephone still in his hand.

'Fussel,' he said. 'He thinks he can hear armour moving up behind the embankment at La Haye. Co-ordinates——'

'I know the place,' said Dexter. 'Tell him it makes no difference to his orders.'

Fussel apparently expostulated at the far end of the wire; there was a brief argument before Frey put down the telephone again. Well might Fussel expostulate, too. If the Allies were bringing up tanks they could burst through Fussel's sector as if it were a paper hoop. So far the garrison had seen none.

'It may be only a ruse,' said Busse.

That was possible. There were plenty of ways in which the Allies might simulate the sound of tanks advancing in the shelter of the embankment. Dexter could not believe that it was only a ruse, all the same. Nor could Frey, obviously. There was a pinched look about his thin face as he stood still fingering the telephone. But when he raised his head and met Dexter's eyes again the pinched look was transmuted into something more vicious. Rat-like, perhaps. Frey was a cornered rat facing finality with bared teeth. He drew attention with a gesture to the letter still unopened in Dexter's hand.

'I *hope* the Baroness is well,' he said, his shrill voice shriller even than usual with the heightened tension. 'I *hope* she is well.'

There was an hysterical edge to the remark; in other circumstances the words might have been utterly casual, but now there could be no doubt about their implication. Frey was using a threat to ensure the death of ten thousand men. He was infected with the same madness that was being displayed by the whole Party from the Fuehrer downward, with the same insane lust for destruction. If the Party were doomed to perish then nothing German was to survive. The men could die, the women and children starve, the whole area of the Reich was to be left a depopulated desert in the final Götterdämmerung, without one stone left upon another in its silent villages and cities; that was the only way left for the Party to assert itself, and those stony deserts the only memorial the Fuehrer could now hope for. Frey for his own part was ensuring for himself, like some petty Attila, the company of ten thousand spirits of men when he himself should pass on to whatever he thought lay beyond the grave. That was why he was reminding Dexter about the letter, about Aloise.

Dexter's pistol was at his belt, and he was actually

tempted at that moment to draw it and to kill this madman. But that would be no help to Aloise. It would not remove her from the power of the SS; rather would it—if the news reached Germany, as it might with so many informers about—rather would it ensure the worst, the torture chamber, the pincers—the—the—Dexter felt his own sanity to be on the point of breaking down, and he mastered himself by a frightful effort. He wanted to shout and storm; the steadiness of his own voice when he spoke surprised him—it was as if someone else were speaking.

'I had forgotten my letter,' he said.

Of a sudden he felt intensely weary. And he was cold, too; shuddering a little. That had to be controlled in case they thought he was trembling. Another determination was forming in his mind.

'I shall go and rest,' he said. 'For fifteen minutes.'

Frey and Busse nodded, their eyes fixed on his face, and their gaze followed him as he walked slowly and heavily over the flagstones to the corner where a suspended blanket screened his bed. He remembered to take a candle with him, and once inside the screen he set it on the bracket at the head of the bed. He would need that much light to read his letter, even though he would need no light for what he was going to do after that. He turned back from the bracket to draw the screen close, and in that moment he saw Busse's face, tortured with pity. That was the last thing he saw before he drew the blanket.

Inside the screen there was only room for the bed. He had to lie down on it to read his letter. He ought to take off his boots. Otherwise he would smear the bed with mud, and the thought disturbed his orderly mind; he remembered the general orders he had issued to the garrison on his taking command, to the effect that every man who allowed himself to be unclean would be severely punished. That had been necessary to keep the garrison up to the mark, to maintain them as disciplined soldiers to the very end. But this was the very end, for him at least. And if the bed were soon to be fouled with blood and brains a little mud hardly mattered. He lay down and swung his muddy boots up on to the bed.

His hand holding the letter lay on his breast, and there was a moment's incredible temptation not to read it. He was so weary. The deed he had in mind to do was an easy way out for him. It would be the end of his troubles. It might well save Aloise's life, too. A bloody sacrifice might appease the madmen of the SS. And even if it did not, he would know nothing about it. He would be at peace, even if Aloise—no; he must not think along those lines.

Nor would it solve the problems of the garrison. With his death Frey would take command, and the ten thousand men were still doomed. He must not think about that, either. As he could do nothing to save them he must congratulate himself on ending his own misery and he must give no further thought to theirs. That was cowardly. The horrible system that had mastered the Reich was forcing even Friedrich von Dexter into cowardice; could there be better proof of its inherent evil?

To draw his pistol he had to lay down the letter. As his hand touched the cold butt he withdrew it again. He must read Aloise's letter, of course. He would read it twice, and when for the second time he had read the last dear word he would draw the pistol, quickly. His mouth actually softened into something barely like a smile as he thought of Aloise's tenderness and love. He opened the letter.

My dearest,—This letter brings you from your loving wife every good wish, wherever you may be, whatever may be happening, and with my good wishes my deepest love, which you know you have had during all the years of our marriage.

But, dearest, I am afraid that this letter is going to add to your unhappiness. I have bad news for you. I did not tell you about it when we were last together, because at that time you had too many troubles already and I could not add to them. I kept it a secret from you then, but now I have to tell you.

Dearest, I shall not be alive when you receive this letter. I have a cancer. Doctor Mohrenwitz has told me so, but I knew it before he told me. I made him tell me. And he told me that it is in the same place as Frau Engel had hers, and you remember what happened to her, dearest. It has not been too bad until now, but now I cannot go on. Doctor Mohrenwitz has been giving me pills to make me sleep and to ease the pain, and I have been saving them up. Tonight after I have posted this letter I am going to take them all at once. I have made all the arrangements and I know I shall die.

So, I have to say good-bye to you, dearest. I have to thank you for every bit of happiness I have enjoyed during the last thirty years. You have always been the best, the kindest, the tenderest of husbands to me, and I have loved you with all my heart. And I have admired you as well—I have been such a fortunate woman to have a husband I could admire as well as love—your honesty and your sincerity and your thoughtfulness and your care.

I only wish I could have done more for you, dearest. I used to wish I could bear all your sorrow as well as my own when we lost our dear boys. But now you know that I have no more sorrow or unhappiness or pain and that while you read this letter I shall be at peace. Tonight I shall only be thinking of you, dearest, as I always have done. My last thoughts will be of you, always and ever my very dearest.

Good-bye, darling, Good-bye.
Eternally your A.

That was the letter. Dexter read it twice, as he had planned, but not twice through from beginning to end as he had thought he would. He read it jerkily, going back to re-read each line. It was hard to focus his eyes on the words; perhaps because the light of the single candle was so dim. But he finished the reading and lay still, the letter on his breast. He was conscious only of his dreadful sense of loss. A world that did not have Aloise in it was not the same world as he had lived in for all these years. It was not a world in which he wanted to live. He remembered why he had come in here. He put his hand down again on the butt of the pistol, and perhaps it was the cold contact that recalled him to other realities. Aloise was dead—was dead—was dead. She had said she would have no more sorrow or unhappiness or pain. She had not said that now she would be beyond the power of the SS, but that was equally true. Dexter stiffened, as he realized that he still had a duty to do, a duty which he could now carry out.

The realization held him rigid for some seconds as he thought about the situation, and then he relaxed as his numbness vanished and his thoughts began to flow freely again. He was a man of action, bred and trained to make rapid decisions, and born with the firmness of will to execute them. There was no time to waste. He must act, and he burst instantly into harsh action. He drew his pistol as he swung his legs off the bed; he released the safety catch as he stood up. With his left hand he held aside the screening blanket, and he emerged into the crypt with his pistol pointed and ready.

They were all three of them still there, Frey and Busse and Becker; they were waiting to hear the pistol shot behind the screen, and they looked round in surprise as he came bursting out. Dexter pointed the pistol at Frey, who was the dangerous man—he could trust the other two.

'Move and you're dead!' said Dexter, his lips hardly parting sufficiently to allow the words to escape him.

'But—but—' began Frey, backing away in astonishment from the weapon.

'Stand still! Put your hands on your head!'

Perhaps some unconscious memory of the American western films that he had seen long ago, in the days of the Weimar Republic, prompted Dexter to give that order, but he had seen long lines of Russian prisoners emerging from strong points after surrender, with their hands on their heads too. Frey obeyed; no sound came from his lips although they moved.

'Busse!' snapped Dexter.

'Sir!'

'Telephone to Fussel. Get through to him at once.'

'Yes, sir,' said Busse, advancing to the telephone.

'You're going to surrender!' said Frey, finding his

shrill voice again, his body jerking with emotion while he could not gesticulate, hands on head.

'Yes,' said Dexter.

He was going to save ten thousand lives for the Germany of the future.

'But your wife!' said Frey. 'Remember——'

'My wife is dead.'

'But *my* wife—my children——'

Frey's voice went higher still, into a scream. It all happened in a second. Frey's excitement completely overcame him, and he put his hand down to his pistol. But to draw the weapon took far too long. Western films had not taught Frey to be quick on the draw. Before he even had the holster unfastened Dexter shot him twice, the reports resounding like cannon shots in the restricted space of the crypt, and Frey fell dying on the tomb of the saint.

'That's better,' said Dexter. 'Now I can speak to Fussel myself.'

That night the B.B.C. broadcast the news of the surrender of Montavril. In five languages the news was broadcast over Europe. Ten thousand men came out from the shadow of imminent death into the prisoner of war camps of the Allies. All through the night Allied doctors toiled over the German wounded. Far away in East Prussia, in a gloomy headquarters dug-out deep below the gloomy pine woods, a frantic tyrant raved like a maniac—like the maniac that by now he was—because ten thousand men were alive whom he wished dead.

That night four men knocked at the door of a house in the Welfenstrasse. A dignified old lady opened the door to them, and at a glance recognized their uniform.

'I was expecting you gentlemen,' she said. 'You want me to come with you?'

'Come,' said one of the four.

The old lady's hat and coat hung in the hall ready to hand, and she put them on quickly, and walked out with them to the waiting car. She was still alive, and she showed no signs of the cancer she had said she had. But as she had promised, her last thoughts were of the husband to whom she had written.

ERIC LINKLATER

Sealskin Trousers

I AM not mad. It is necessary to realize that, to accept it as a fact about which there can be no dispute. I have been seriously ill for some weeks, but that was the result of shock. A double or conjoint shock: for as well as the obvious concussion of a brutal event, there was the more dreadful necessity of recognizing the material evidence of a happening so monstrously implausible that even my friends here, who in general are quite extraordinarily kind and understanding, will not believe in the occurrence, though they cannot deny it or otherwise explain—I mean explain away—the clear and simple testimony of what was left.

I, of course, realized very quickly what had happened, and since then I have more than once remembered that poor Coleridge teased his unquiet mind, quite unnecessarily in his case, with just such a possibility; or impossibility, as the world would call it. 'If a man could pass through Paradise in a dream,' he wrote, 'and have a flower presented to him as a pledge that his soul had really been there, and if he found that flower in his hand when he woke—Ay, and what then?'

But what if he had dreamt of Hell and wakened with his hand burnt by the fire. Or of Chaos, and seen another face stare at him from the looking-glass? Coleridge does not push the question far. He was too timid. But I accepted the evidence, and while

I was ill I thought seriously about the whole proceeding, in detail and in sequence of detail. I thought, indeed, about little else. To begin with, I admit, I was badly shaken, but gradually my mind cleared and my vision improved, and because I was patient and persevering—that needed discipline—I can now say that I know what happened. I have indeed, by a conscious intellectual effort, *seen and heard* what happened. This is how it began. . . .

How very unpleasant! she thought.

She had come down the great natural steps on the sea-cliff to the ledge that narrowly gave access, round the angle of it, to the western face which to-day was sheltered from the breeze and warmed by the afternoon sun. At the beginning of the week she and her fiancé, Charles Sellin, had found their way to an almost hidden shelf, a deep veranda sixty feet above the white-veined water. It was rather bigger than a billiard-table and nearly as private as an abandoned lighthouse. Twice they had spent some blissful hours there. She had a good head for heights, and Sellin was indifferent to scenery. There had been nothing vulgar, no physical contact, in their bliss together on this oceanic gazebo, for on each occasion she had been reading Héaloin's *Studies in Biology* and he Lenin's *What is to be Done?*

Their relations were already marital, not because their mutual passion could brook no pause, but rather out of fear lest their friends might despise them for chastity and so conjecture some oddity or impotence in their nature. Their behaviour, however, was very decently circumspect, and they already conducted themselves, in public and out of doors, as if they had been married for several years.

They did not regard the seclusion of the cliffs as an opportunity for secret embracing, but were content that the sun should warm and colour their skin; and let their anxious minds be soothed by the surge and cavernous colloquies of the sea. Now, while Charles was writing letters in the little fishing-hotel a mile away, she had come back to their sandstone ledge, and Charles would join her in an hour or two. She was still reading *Studies in Biology*.

But their gazebo, she perceived, was already occupied, and occupied by a person of the most embarrassing appearance. He was quite unlike Charles. He was not only naked, but obviously robust, brown-hued, and extremely hairy. He sat on the very edge of the rock, dangling his legs over the sea, and down his spine ran a ridge of hair like the dark stripe on a donkey's back, and on his shoulderblades grew patches of hair like the wings of a bird. Unable in her disappointment to be sensible and leave at once, she lingered for a moment and saw to her relief that he was not quite naked. He wore trousers of a dark brown colour, very low at the waist, but sufficient to cover his haunches. Even so, even with that protection for her modesty, she could not stay and read biology in his company.

To show her annoyance, and let him become aware of it, she made a little impatient sound; and turning to go, looked back to see if he had heard.

He swung himself round and glared at her, more angry on the instant than she had been. He had thick eyebrows, large dark eyes, a broad snub nose, a big mouth. 'You're Roger Fairfield!' she exclaimed in surprise.

He stood up and looked at her intently. 'How do you know?' he asked.

'Because I remember you,' she answered, but then felt a little confused, for what she principally remembered was the brief notoriety he had acquired, in his final year at Edinburgh University, by swimming on a rough autumn day from North Berwick to the Bass Rock to win a bet of five pounds.

The story had gone briskly round the town for a week, and everybody knew that he and some friends had been lunching, too well for caution, before the bet was made. His friends, however, grew quickly sober when he took to the water, and in a great fright informed the police, who called out the lifeboat. But they searched in vain, for the sea was running high, until in calm water under the shelter of the Bass they saw his head, dark on the water, and pulled him aboard. He seemed none the worse for his adventure, but the police charged him with disorderly behaviour and he was fined two pounds for swimming without a regulation costume.

'We met twice,' she said, 'once at a dance and once in Mackie's when we had coffee together. About a year ago. There were several of us there, and we knew the man you came in with. I remember you perfectly.'

He stared the harder, his eyes narrowing, a vertical wrinkle dividing his forehead. 'I'm a little shortsighted too,' she said with a nervous laugh.

'My sight's very good,' he answered, 'but I find it difficult to recognize people. Human beings are so much alike.'

'That's one of the rudest remarks I've ever heard!'

'Surely not?'

'Well, one does like to be remembered. It isn't pleasant to be told that one's a nonentity.'

He made an impatient gesture. 'That isn't what I

meant, and I do recognize you now. I remember your voice. You have a distinctive voice and a pleasant one. F sharp in the octave below middle C is your note.'

'Is that the only way in which you can distinguish people?'

'It's as good as any other.'

'But you don't remember my name?'

'No,' he said.

'I'm Elizabeth Barford.'

He bowed and said, 'Well, it was a dull party, wasn't it? The occasion, I mean, when we drank coffee together.'

'I don't agree with you. I thought it was very amusing, and we all enjoyed ourselves. Do you remember Charles Sellin?'

'No.'

'Oh, you're hopeless,' she exclaimed. 'What is the good of meeting people if you're going to forget all about them?'

'I don't know,' he said. 'Let us sit down, and you can tell me.'

He sat again on the edge of the rock, his legs dangling, and looking over his shoulder at her, said, 'Tell me: what is the good of meeting people?'

She hesitated, and answered, 'I like to make friends. That's quite natural, isn't it?—But I came here to read.'

'Do you read standing?'

'Of course not,' she said, and smoothing her skirt tidily over her knees, sat down beside him. 'What a wonderful place this is for a holiday. Have you been here before?'

'Yes, I know it well.'

'Charles and I came a week ago. Charles Sellin,

I mean, whom you don't remember. We're going to be married, you know. In about a year, we
hope.'

'Why did you come here?'

'We wanted to be quiet, and in these islands one is
fairly secure against interruption. We're both working quite hard.'

'Working!' he mocked. 'Don't waste time, waste
your life instead.'

'Most of us have to work, whether we like it or
not.'

He took the book from her lap, and opening it
read idly a few lines, turned a dozen pages and read
with a yawn another paragraph.

'Your friends in Edinburgh,' she said, 'were
better-off than ours. Charles and I, and all the
people we know, have got to make our living.'

'Why?' he asked.

'Because if we don't we shall starve,' she snapped.

'And if you avoid starvation—what then?'

'It's possible to hope,' she said stiffly, 'that we
shall be of some use in the world.'

'Do you agree with this?' he asked, smothering a
second yawn, and read from the book: '*The physical factor in a germ-cell is beyond our analysis or
assessment, but can we deny subjectivity to the primordial initiatives? It is easier, perhaps, to assume
that mind comes late in development, but the assumption must not be established on the grounds
that we can certainly deny self-expression to the
cell. It is common knowledge that the mind may
influence the body both greatly and in little unseen
ways; but how it is done, we do not know. Psychobiology is still in its infancy.*'

'It's fascinating, isn't it?' she said.

'How do you propose,' he asked, 'to be of use to the world?'

'Well, the world needs people who have been educated—educated to think—and one does hope to have a little influence in some way.'

'Is a little influence going to make any difference? Don't you think that what the world needs is to develop a new sort of mind? It needs a new primordial directive, or quite a lot of them, perhaps. But psychobiology is still in its infancy, and you don't know how such changes come about, do you? And you can't forsee when you *will* know, can you?'

'No, of course not. But science is advancing so quickly——'

'In fifty thousand years?' he interrupted. 'Do you think you will know by then?'

'It's difficult to say,' she answered seriously, and was gathering her thoughts for a careful reply when again he interrupted, rudely, she thought, and quite irrelevantly. His attention had strayed from her and her book to the sea beneath, and he was looking down as though searching for something. 'Do you swim?' he asked.

'Rather well,' she said.

'I went in just before high water, when the weed down there was all brushed in the opposite direction. You never get bored by the sea, do you?'

'I've never seen enough of it,' she said. 'I want to live on an island, a little island, and hear it all round me.'

'That's very sensible of you,' he answered with more warmth in his voice. 'That's uncommonly sensible for a girl like you.'

'What sort of a girl do you think I am?' she demanded, vexation in her accent, but he ignored her and pointed his brown arm to the horizon: 'The colour has thickened within the last few minutes. The sea was quite pale on the skyline, and now it's a belt of indigo. And the writing has changed. The lines of foam on the water, I mean. Look at that. There's a submerged rock out there, and always, about half an hour after the ebb has started to run, but more clearly when there's an off-shore wind, you can see those two little whirlpools and the circle of white round them. You see the figure they make? It's like this, isn't it?'

With a splinter of stone he drew a diagram on the rock.

'Do you know what it is?' he asked. 'It's the figure the Chinese call the T'ai Chi. They say it represents the origin of all created things. And it's the sign manual of the sea.'

'But those lines of foam must run into every conceivable shape,' she protested.

'Oh, they do. They do indeed. But it isn't often you can read them—There he is!' he exclaimed, leaning forward and staring into the water sixty feet below. 'That's him, the old villain!'

From his sitting position, pressing hard down with his hands and thrusting against the face of the rock with his heels, he hurled himself into space, and straightening in mid-air broke the smooth green surface of the water with no more splash than a harpoon would have made. A solitary razorbill, sunning himself on a shelf below, fled hurriedly out to sea, and half a dozen white birds, startled by the sudden movement, rose in the air crying 'Kittiwake! Kittiwake!'

Elizabeth screamed loudly, scrambled to her feet with clumsy speed, then knelt again on the edge of the rock and peered down. In the slowly heaving clear water she could see a pale shape moving, now striped by the dark weed that grew in tangles under the flat foot of the rock, now lost in the shadowy deepness where the tangles were rooted. In a minute or two his head rose from the sea, he shook bright drops from his hair, and looked up at her, laughing. Firmly grasped in his right hand, while he trod water, he held up an enormous blue-black lobster for her admiration. Then he threw it on to the flat rock beside him, and swiftly climbing out of the sea, caught it again and held it, cautious of its bite, till he found a piece of string in his trouser-pocket. He shouted to her, 'I'll tie its claws, and you can take it home for your supper!'

She had not thought it possible to climb the sheer face of the cliff, but from its forefoot he mounted by steps and handholds invisible from above, and pitching the tied lobster on to the floor of the gazebo, came nimbly over the edge.

'That's a bigger one than you've ever seen in your life before,' he boasted. 'He weighs fourteen pounds, I'm certain of it. Fourteen pounds at least. Look at the size of his right claw! He could crack a coconut with that. He tried to crack my ankle when I was swimming an hour ago, and got into his hole before I could catch him. But I've caught him now, the brute. He's had more than twenty years of crime, that black boy. He's twenty-four or twenty-five by the look of him. He's older than you, do you realize that? Unless you're a lot older than you look. How old are you?'

But Elizabeth took no interest in the lobster. She had retreated until she stood with her back to the rock, pressed hard against it, the palms of her hands fumbling on the stone as if feeling for a secret lock or bolt that might give her entrance into it. Her face was white, her lips pale and tremulous.

He looked round at her, when she made no answer, and asked what the matter was.

Her voice was faint and frightened. 'Who are you?' she whispered, and the whisper broke into a stammer. 'What are you?'

His expression changed and his face, with the water-drops on it, grew hard as a rock shining undersea. 'It's only a few minutes,' he said, 'since you appeared to know me quite well. You addressed me as Roger Fairfield, didn't you?'

'But a name's not everything. It doesn't tell you enough.'

'What more do you want to know?'

Her voice was so strained and thin that her words were like the shadow of words, or words shivering in the cold: 'To jump like that, into the sea—it wasn't human!'

The coldness of his face wrinkled to a frown. 'That's a curious remark to make.'

'You would have killed yourself if—if——'

He took a seaward step again, looked down at the calm green depths below, and said, 'You're exaggerating, aren't you? It's not much more than fifty feet, sixty perhaps, and the water's deep.—Here, come back! Why are you running away?'

'Let me go!' she cried. 'I don't want to stay here. I—I'm frightened.'

'That's unfortunate. I hadn't expected this to happen.'

'Please let me go!'

'I don't think I shall. Not until you've told me what you're frightened of.'

'Why,' she stammered, 'why do you wear fur trousers?'

He laughed, and still laughing caught her round the waist and pulled her towards the edge of the rock. 'Don't be alarmed,' he said. 'I'm not going to throw you over. But if you insist on a conversation about trousers, I think we should sit down again. Look at the smoothness of the water, and its colour, and the light in the depths of it: have you ever seen anything lovelier? Look at the sky: that's calm enough, isn't it? Look at that fulmar sailing past: he's not worrying, so why should you?'

She leaned away from him, all her weight against the hand that held her waist, but his arm was strong and he seemed unaware of any strain on it. Nor did he pay attention to the distress she was in—she was sobbing dryly, like a child who has cried too long —but continued talking in a light and pleasant conversational tone until the muscles of her body tired and relaxed, and she sat within his enclosing arm, making no more effort to escape, but timorously conscious of his hand upon her side so close beneath her breast.

'I needn't tell you,' he said, 'the conventional reasons for wearing trousers. There are people, I know, who sneer at all conventions, and some conventions deserve their sneering. But not the trouser-convention. No, indeed! So we can admit the necessity of the garment, and pass to consideration of the material. Well, I like sitting on rocks, for one thing, and for such a hobby this is the best stuff in the world. It's very durable, yet soft and comfortable. I can slip into the sea for half an hour without doing it any harm, and when I come out to sun myself on the rock again, it doesn't feel cold and clammy. Nor does it fade in the sun or shrink with the wet. Oh, there are plenty of reasons for having one's trousers made of stuff like this.'

'And there's a reason,' she said, 'that you haven't told me.'

'Are you quite sure of that?'

She was calmer now, and her breathing was controlled. But her face was still white, and her lips were softly nervous when she asked him, 'Are you going to kill me?'

'Kill you? Good heavens, no! Why should I do that?'

'For fear of my telling other people.'

'And what precisely would you tell them?'

'You know.'

'You jump to conclusions far too quickly: that's your trouble. Well, it's a pity for your sake, and a nuisance for me. I don't think I can let you take that lobster home for your supper after all. I don't, in fact, think you will go home for your supper.'

Her eyes grew dark again with fear, her mouth opened, but before she could speak he pulled her to him and closed it, not asking leave, with a roughly occludent kiss.

'That was to prevent you from screaming. I hate to hear people scream,' he told her, smiling as he spoke. 'But this'—he kissed her again, now gently and in a more protracted embrace—'that was because I wanted to.'

'You mustn't!' she cried.

'But I have,' he said.

'I don't understand myself! I can't understand what has happened——'

'Very little yet,' he murmured.

'Something terrible has happened!'

'A kiss? Am I so repulsive?'

'I don't mean that. I mean something inside me. I'm not—at least I think I'm not—I'm not frightened now!'

'You have no reason to be.'

'I have every reason in the world. But I'm not! I'm not frightened—but I want to cry.'

'Then cry,' he said soothingly, and made her pillow her cheek against his breast. 'But you can't cry comfortably with that ridiculous contraption on your nose.'

He took from her the horn-rimmed spectacles she wore, and threw them into the sea.

'Oh!' she exclaimed. 'My glasses!—Oh, why did you do that? Now I can't see. I can't see at all without my glasses!'

'It's all right,' he assured her. 'You really won't need them. The refraction,' he added vaguely, 'will be quite different.'

As if this small but unexpected act of violence had brought to the boiling-point her desire for tears, they bubbled over, and because she threw her arms about him in a sort of fond despair, and snuggled close, sobbing vigorously still, he felt the warm drops trickle down his skin, and from his skin she drew into her eyes the saltness of the sea, which made her weep the more. He stroked her hair with a strong but soothing hand, and when she grew calm and lay still in his arms, her emotion spent, he sang quietly to a little enchanting tune a song that began:

> *I am a Man upon the land,*
> *I am a Selkie in the sea,*
> *And when I'm far from every strand*
> *My home it is in Sule Skerry.*

After the first verse or two she freed herself from his embrace, and sitting up listened gravely to the song. Then she asked him, 'Shall I ever understand?'

'It's not a unique occurrence,' he told her. 'It has happened quite often before, as I suppose you know. In Cornwall and Brittany and among the Western Isles of Scotland; that's where people have always been interested in seals, and understood them a little, and where seals from time to time have taken human shape. The one thing that's unique in our case, in my metamorphosis, is that I am the only seal-man who has ever become a Master of Arts of Edinburgh University. Or, I believe, of any university. I am the unique and solitary example of a sophisticated seal-man.'

'I must look a perfect fright,' she said. 'It was silly of me to cry. Are my eyes very red?'

'The lids are a little pink—not unattractively so— but your eyes are as dark and lovely as a mountain pool in October, on a sunny day in October. They're much improved since I threw your spectacles away.'

'I needed them, you know. I feel quite stupid without them. But tell me why you came to the University—and how? How could you do it?'

'My dear girl—what is your name, by the way? I've quite forgotten.'

'Elizabeth!' she said angrily.

'I'm so glad, it's my favourite human name.— But you don't really want to listen to a lecture on psychobiology?'

'I want to know *how*. You must tell me!'

'Well, you remember, don't you, what your book says about the primordial initiatives? But it needs a footnote there to explain that they're not exhausted till quite late in life. The germ-cells, as you know, are always renewing themselves, and they keep their initiatives though they nearly always follow the chosen pattern except in the case of certain illnesses, or under special direction. The direction of the mind, that is. And the glands have got a lot to do in a full metamorphosis, the renal first and then the pituitary, as you would expect. It isn't approved of —making the change, I mean—but every now and then one of us does it, just for a frolic in the general way, but in my case there was a special reason.'

'Tell me,' she said again.

'It's too long a story.'

'I want to know.'

'There's been a good deal of unrest, you see, among my people in the last few years: doubt, and dissatisfaction with our leaders, and scepticism about traditional beliefs—all that sort of thing. We've had a lot of discussion under the surface of the sea about the nature of man, for instance. We had always been taught to believe certain things about him, and recent events didn't seem to bear out what our teachers told us. Some of our younger people got dissatisfied, so I volunteered to go ashore and investigate. I'm still considering the report I shall have to make, and that's why I'm living, at present, a double life. I come ashore to think, and go back to the sea to rest.'

'And what do you think of us?' she asked.

'You're interesting. Very interesting indeed. There are going to be some curious mutations among you before long. Within three or four thousand years, perhaps.'

He stooped and rubbed a little smear of blood from his shin. 'I scratched it on a limpet,' he said. 'The limpets, you know, are the same today as they were four hundred thousand years ago. But human beings aren't nearly so stable.'

'Is that your main impression, that humanity's unstable?'

'That's part of it. But from our point of view there's something much more upsetting. Our people, you see, are quite simple creatures, and because we have relatively few beliefs, we're very much attached to them. Our life is a life of sensation—not entirely, but largely—and we ought to be extremely happy. We were, so long as we were satisfied with sensation and a short undisputed creed. We have some advantages over human beings, you know. Human beings have to carry their own weight about, and they don't know how blissful it is to be unconscious of weight: to be wave-borne, to float on the idle sea, to leap without effort in a curving wave, and look up at the dazzle of the sky through a smother of white water, or dive so easily to the calmness far below and take a haddock from the weed-beds in a sudden rush of appetite.—Talking of haddocks,' he said, 'it's getting late. It's nearly time for fish. And I must give you some instruction before we go. The preliminary phase takes a little while, about five minutes for you, I should think, and then you'll be another creature.'

She gasped, as though already she felt the water's chill, and whispered, 'Not yet! Not yet, please.'

He took her in his arms, and expertly, with a strong caressing hand, stroked her hair, stroked the roundness of her head and the back of her neck and her shoulders, feeling her muscles moving to his touch, and down the hollow of her back to her waist and hips. The head again, neck, shoulders, and spine. Again and again. Strongly and firmly his hand gave her calmness, and presently she whispered, 'You're sending me to sleep.'

'My God!' he exclaimed, 'you mustn't do that! Stand up, stand up, Elizabeth!'

'Yes,' she said, obeying him. 'Yes, Roger. Why did you call yourself Roger? Roger Fairfield?'

'I found the name in a drowned sailor's pay-book. What does that matter now? Look at me, Elizabeth!'

She looked at him, and smiled.

His voice changed, and he said happily. 'You'll be the prettiest seal between Shetland and the Scillies. Now listen. Listen carefully.'

He held her lightly and whispered in her ear. Then kissed her on the lips and cheek, and bending her head back, on the throat. He looked, and saw the colour come deeply into her face.

'Good,' he said. 'That's the first stage. The adrenalin's flowing nicely now. You know about the pituitary, don't you? That makes it easy then. There are two parts in the pituitary gland, the anterior and posterior lobes, and both must act together. It's not difficult, and I'll tell you how.'

Then he whispered again, most urgently, and watched her closely. In a little while he said, 'And now you can take it easy. Let's sit down and wait till you're ready. The actual change won't come till we go down.'

'But it's working,' she said, quietly and happily. 'I can feel it working.'

'Of course it is.'

She laughed triumphantly, and took his hand.

'We've got nearly five minutes to wait,' he said.

'What will it be like? What shall I feel, Roger?'

'The water moving against your side, the sea caressing you and holding you.'

'Shall I be sorry for what I've left behind?'

'No, I don't think so.'

'You didn't like us, then? Tell me what you discovered in the world.'

'Quite simply,' he said, 'that we had been deceived.'

'But I don't know what your belief had been.'

'Haven't I told you?—Well, we in our innocence respected you because you could work, and were willing to work. That seemed to us truly heroic. We don't work at all, you see, and you'll be much happier when you come to us. We who live in the sea don't struggle to keep our heads above water.'

'All my friends worked hard,' she said. 'I never knew anyone who was idle. We had to work, and most of us worked for a good purpose; or so we thought. But you didn't think so?'

'Our teachers had told us,' he said, 'that men endured the burden of human toil to create a surplus of wealth that would give them leisure from the daily task of bread-winning. And in their hard-won leisure, our teachers said, men cultivated wisdom and charity and the fine arts; and became aware of God.—But that's not a true description of the world, is it?'

'No,' she said, 'that's not the truth.'

'No,' he repeated, 'our teachers were wrong, and we've been deceived.'

'Men are always being deceived, but they get accustomed to learning the facts too late. They grow accustomed to deceit itself.'

'You are braver than we, perhaps. My people will not like to be told the truth.'

'I shall be with you,' she said, and took his hand. But still he stared gloomily at the moving sea.

The minutes passed, and presently she stood up and with quick fingers put off her clothes. 'It's time,' she said.

He looked at her, and his gloom vanished like the shadow of a cloud that the wind has hurried on, and exultation followed like sunlight spilling from the burning edge of a cloud. 'I wanted to punish them,' he cried, 'for robbing me of my faith, and now, by God, I'm punishing them hard. I'm robbing their treasury now, the inner vault of all their treasury!— I hadn't guessed you were so beautiful! The waves when you swim will catch a burnish from you, the sand will shine like silver when you lie down to sleep, and if you can teach the red seaware to blush so well, I shan't miss the roses of your world.'

'Hurry,' she said.

He, laughing softly, loosened the leather thong that tied his trousers, stepped out of them, and lifted her in his arms. 'Are you ready?' he asked.

She put her arms round his neck and softly kissed his cheek. Then with a great shout he leapt from the rock, from the little veranda, into the green silk calm of the water far below. . . .

I heard the splash of their descent—I am quite sure I heard the splash—as I came round the corner of the cliff, by the ledge that leads to the little rock veranda, our gazebo, as we called it, but the first thing I noticed, that really attracted my attention, was an enormous blue-black lobster, its huge claws tied with string, that was moving in a rather ludicrous fashion towards the edge. I think it fell over just before I left, but I wouldn't swear to that. Then I saw her book, the *Studies in Biology*, and her clothes.

Her white linen frock with the brown collar and the brown belt, some other garments, and her shoes were all there. And beside them, lying across her shoes, was a pair of sealskin trousers.

I realized immediately, or almost immediately, what had happened. Or so it seems to me now. And if, as I firmly believe, my apprehension was instantaneous, the faculty of intuition is clearly more important than I had previously supposed. I have, of course, as I said before, given the matter a great deal of thought during my recent illness, but the impression remains that I understood what had happened in a flash, to use a common but illuminating phrase. And no one, need I say? has been able to refute my intuition. No one, that is, has found an alternative explanation for the presence, beside Elizabeth's linen frock, of a pair of sealskin trousers.

I remember also my physical distress at the discovery. My breath, for several minutes I think, came into and went out of my lungs like the hot wind of a dust-storm in the desert. It parched my mouth and grated in my throat. It was, I recall, quite a torment to breathe. But I had to, of course.

Nor did I lose control of myself in spite of the agony, both mental and physical, that I was suffering. I didn't lose control till they began to mock me. Yes, they did, I assure you of that. I heard his voice quite clearly, and honesty compels me to admit that it was singularly sweet and the tune was the most haunting I have ever heard. They were about forty yards away, two seals swimming together, and the evening light was so clear and taut that his voice might have been the vibration of an invisible bow across its coloured bands. He was singing the song that Elizabeth and I had discovered in an album of

Scottish music in the little fishing-hotel where we had been living:

> *I am a Man upon the land,*
> *I am a Selkie in the sea,*
> *And when I'm far from any strand*
> *I am at home on Sule Skerry!*

But his purpose, you see, was mockery. They were happy, together in the vast simplicity of the ocean, and I, abandoned to the terror of life alone, life among human beings, was lost and full of panic. It was then I began to scream. I could hear myself screaming, it was quite horrible. But I couldn't stop. I had to go on screaming. . . .

V. S. PRITCHETT

The Voice

A MESSAGE came from the rescue party who
straightened up and leaned on their spades in the
rubble. The policeman said to the crowd: 'Everyone keep quiet for five minutes. No talking, please.
They're trying to hear where he is.'

The silent crowd raised their faces and looked
across the ropes to the church which, now it was
destroyed, broke the line of the street like a decayed
tooth. The bomb had brought down the front wall
and the roof, the balcony had capsized. Freakishly
untouched, the hymnboard still announced the previous Sunday's hymns.

A small wind blew a smell of smouldering cloth
across people's noses from another street where
there was another scene like this. A bus roared by
and heads turned in passive anger until the sound
of the engine had gone. People blinked as a pigeon
flew from a roof and crossed the building like an
omen of release. There was dead quietness again.
Presently a murmuring sound was heard by the rescue party. The man buried under the debris was
singing again.

At first difficult to hear, soon a tune became defi-
nite. Two of the rescuers took up their shovels and
shouted down to encourage the buried man, and the
voice became stronger and louder. Words became
clear. The leader of the rescue party held back the

others and those who were near strained to hear.
Then the words were unmistakable:

> *Oh Thou whose Voice the waters heard,*
> *And hushed their raging at Thy Word.*

The buried man was singing a hymn.

A clergyman was standing with the warden in the
middle of the ruined church.

'That's Mr. Morgan all right,' the warden said.
'He could sing. He got silver medals for it.'

The Rev. Frank Lewis frowned.

'Gold, I shouldn't wonder,' said Mr. Lewis, dryly.
Now he knew Morgan was alive he said: 'What the
devil's he doing in there? How did he get in? I
locked up at eight o'clock last night myself.'

Lewis was a wiry, middle-aged man, but the white
dust on his hair and his eyelashes, and the way he
kept licking the dust off his dry lips, moving his jaws
all the time, gave him the monkeyish, testy and suspicious air of an old man. He had been up all night
on rescue work in the raid and he was tired out. The
last straw was to find the church had gone and that
Morgan, the so-called Rev. Morgan, was buried
under it.

The rescue workers were digging again. There was
a wide hole now and a man was down in it filling a
basket with his hands. The dust rose like smoke from
the hole as he worked.

The voice had not stopped singing. It went on,
rich, virile, masculine, from verse to verse of the
hymn. Shooting up like a stem through the rubbish
the voice seemed to rise and branch out powerfully,
luxuriantly and even theatrically, like a tree, until
everything was in its shade. It was a shade that came
towards one like dark arms.

'All the Welsh can sing,' the warden said. Then he remembered that Lewis was Welsh also. 'Not that I've got anything against the Welsh,' the warden said.

'The scandal of it,' Lewis was thinking. 'Must he sing so loud, must he advertise himself? I locked up myself last night. How the devil did he get in?' And he really meant: 'How did the devil get in?'

To Lewis, Morgan was the nearest human thing to the devil. He could never pass that purple-gowned figure, sauntering like a cardinal in his skull cap on the sunny side of the street, without a shudder of distaste and derision. An unfrocked priest, his predecessor in the church, Morgan ought in strict justice to have been in prison, and would have been but for the indulgence of the bishop. But this did not prevent the old man with the saintly white head and the eyes half-closed by the worldly juices of food and wine, from walking about dressed in his vestments, like an actor walking in the sun of his own vanity, a hook-nosed satyr, a he-goat significant to servant girls, the crony of the public-house, the chaser of bookmakers, the smoker of cigars. It was terrible, but it was just that the bomb had buried him; only the malice of the Evil One would have thought of bringing the punishment of the sinner upon the church as well. And now, from the ruins, the voice of the wicked man rose up in all the elaborate pride of art and evil.

Suddenly there was a moan from the sloping timber, slates began to skate down.

'Get out. It's going,' shouted the warden.

The man who was digging struggled out of the hole as it bulged under the landslide. There was a dull crumble, the crashing and splitting of wood and then the sound of brick and dust tearing down below the water. Thick dust clouded over and choked them all. The rubble rocked like a cakewalk. Everyone rushed back and looked behind at the wreckage as if it were still alive. It remained still. They all stood there, frightened and suspicious. Presently one of the men with the shovel said: 'The bloke's shut up.'

Everyone stared stupidly. It was true. The man had stopped singing. The clergyman was the first to move. Gingerly he went to what was left of the hole and got down on his knees.

'Morgan!' he said, in a low voice.

Then he called out more loudly:

'Morgan!'

Getting no reply, Lewis began to scramble the rubble away with his hands.

'Morgan!' he shouted. 'Can you hear?' He snatched a shovel from one of the men and began digging and shovelling the stuff away. He had stopped chewing and muttering. His expression had entirely changed. 'Morgan!' he called. He dug for two feet and no one stopped him. They looked with bewilderment at the sudden frenzy of the small man grubbing like a monkey, spitting out the dust, filing down his nails. They saw the spade at last shoot through the old hole. He was down the hole widening it at once, letting himself down as he worked. He disappeared under a ledge made by the fallen timber.

The party above could do nothing. 'Morgan,' they heard him call. 'It's Lewis. We're coming. Can you hear?' He shouted for an axe and presently they heard him smashing with it. He was scratching like a dog or a rabbit.

A voice like that to have stopped, to have gone!

Lewis was thinking. How unbearable this silence was. A beautiful proud voice, the voice of a man, a voice like a tree, the soul of a man spreading in the air like the cedars of Lebanon. 'Only one man I have heard with a bass like that. Owen the Bank, at Newtown before the war.' 'Morgan!' he shouted. 'Sing! God will forgive you everything, only sing!'

One of the rescue party following behind the clergyman in the tunnel shouted back to his mates.

'I can't do nothing. This bleeder's blocking the gangway.'

Half an hour Lewis worked in the tunnel. Then an extraordinary thing happened to him. The tunnel grew damp and its floor went as soft as clay to the touch. Suddenly his knees went through. There was a gap with a yard of cloth, the vestry curtain or the carpet at the communion rail was unwound and hanging through it. Lewis found himself looking down into the blackness of the crypt. He lay down and put his head and shoulders through the hole and felt about him until he found something solid again. The beams of the floor were tilted down into the crypt.

'Morgan. Are you there, man?' he called.

He listened to the echo of his voice. He was reminded of the time he had talked into a cistern when he was a boy. Then his heart jumped. A voice answered him out of the darkness from under the fallen floor. It was like the voice of a man lying comfortably and waking up from a snooze, a voice thick and sleepy.

'Who's that?' asked the voice.

'Morgan, man. It's Lewis. Are you hurt?' Tears pricked the dust in Lewis's eyes and his throat ached with anxiety as he spoke. Forgiveness and love were flowing out of him. From below the deep thick voice of Morgan came back.

'You've been a hell of a long time,' it said. 'I've damn near finished my whisky.'

'Hell' was the word which changed Mr. Lewis's mind. Hell was a real thing, a real place for him. He believed in it. When he read out the word 'Hell' in the Scriptures he could see the flames rising as they rise out of the furnaces at Swansea. 'Hell' was a professional and poetic word for Mr. Lewis. A man who had been turned out of the church had no right to use it. Strong language and strong drink, Mr. Lewis hated both of them. The idea of whisky being in his church made his soul rise like an angered stomach. There was Morgan, insolent and comfortable, lying (so he said) under the old altar-table, which was propping up the fallen floor, drinking a bottle of whisky.

'How did you get in?' Lewis said, sharply, from the hole. 'Were you in the church last night when I locked up?'

The old man sounded not as bold as he had been. He even sounded shifty when he replied, 'I've got my key.'

'*Your* key. I have the only key of the church. Where did you get a key?'

'My old key. I always had a key.'

The man in the tunnel behind the clergyman crawled back up the tunnel to the daylight.

'O.K.' the man said. 'He's got him. They're having a ruddy row.'

'Reminds me of ferreting. I used to go ferreting with my old dad,' said the policeman.

'You should have given that key up,' said Mr. Lewis. 'Have you been in here before?'

'Yes, but I shan't come here again,' said the old man.

There was the dribble of powdered rubble, pouring down like sand in an hour-glass, the ticking of the strained timber like the loud ticking of a clock.

Mr. Lewis felt that at last after years he was face to face with the devil and the devil was trapped and caught. The tick-tock of the wood went on.

'Men have been risking their lives, working and digging for hours because of this,' said Lewis. 'I've ruined a suit of . . .'

The tick-tock had grown louder in the middle of the words. There was a sudden lurching and groaning of the floor, followed by a big heaving and splitting sound.

'It's going,' said Morgan with detachment from below. 'The table leg.' The floor crashed down. The hole in the tunnel was torn wide and Lewis grabbed at the darkness until he caught a board. It swung him out and in a second he found himself hanging by both hands over the pit.

'I'm falling. Help me,' shouted Lewis in terror. 'Help me.' There was no answer.

'Oh, God,' shouted Lewis, kicking for a foothold. 'Morgan, are you there? Catch me. I'm going.'

Then a groan like a snore came out of Lewis. He could no longer hold. He fell. He fell exactly two feet.

The sweat ran down his legs and caked on his face. He was as wet as a rat. He was on his hands and knees gasping. When he got his breath again he was afraid to raise his voice.

'Morgan,' he said quietly, panting.

'Only one leg went,' the old man said in a quiet grating voice. 'The other three are all right.'

Lewis lay panting on the floor. There was a long silence. 'Haven't you ever been afraid before, Lewis?' Morgan said. Lewis had no breath to reply. 'Haven't you ever felt rotten with fear,' said the old man, calmly, 'like an old tree, infested and worm-eaten with it, soft as a rotten orange?'

'You were a fool to come down here after me. I wouldn't have done the same for you,' Morgan said.

'You would,' Lewis managed to say.

'I wouldn't,' said the old man. 'I'm afraid. I'm an old man, Lewis, and I can't stand it. I've been down here every night since the raids got bad.'

Lewis listened to the voice. It was low with shame, it had the roughness of the earth, the kicked and trodden choking dust of Adam. The earth of Mr. Lewis listened for the first time to the earth of Morgan. Coarsened and sordid and unlike the singing voice, the voice of Morgan was also gentle and fragmentary.

'When you stop feeling shaky,' Morgan said, 'you'd better sing. I'll do a bar, but I can't do much. The whisky's gone. Sing, Lewis. Even if they don't hear, it does you good. Take the tenor, Lewis.'

Above in the daylight the look of pain went from the mouths of the rescue party, a grin came on the dusty lips of the warden.

'Hear it?' he said. 'A ruddy Welsh choir!'

WILLIAM PLOMER

Ever Such a Nice Boy

You want to know how I first met Freddy? Oh, it's
quite a long story. No, we don't come from the same
place at all. You see, my home's near Gloucester. I
was in service there with Major and Mrs. Trumbull-
Dykes. Mrs. Dykes was ever such a nice lady, she
was just like a mother to me and writes to me every
Christmas, not that I haven't got a real mother, because of course I have, and she's always been good
to me too, I couldn't wish for a better. Well, the
Major used to suffer from rheumatism something
terrible, he was always carrying on and saying the
house was damp, though it was as dry as a biscuit.
He wouldn't rest but they must move to Devonshire,
nagging away all the time.

Well of course Mrs. Dykes wanted me to go with
them, but I didn't like the idea seeing that I hadn't
never been more than a few miles away from home.
It was Mum that persuaded me. 'You've got a good
home with them,' she said, 'you'd better go with
them.' Of course, most of the things was sent off by
train, and we was to follow by car, but there was a
lot of luggage all the same, just like gipsies we were,
all packed in with a kettle and I don't know what
else. Of course, I hadn't never driven so far before
and the Major drove ever so fast and it quite turned
me up, what with the bumps in the road. 'Stop, Gilbert,' said Mrs. Dykes, 'Edith wants to be sick.' 'I
don't *want* to be,' I said. 'I've *got* to be.' Oh, I *was*

ashamed. 'Never mind, Edith,' said Mrs. Dykes, 'you'll feel better now.' 'You'll never make a sailor, Edith,' said the Major. Oh, if I was on the sea I think I'd die.

Of course, it was ever such a nice house that they had, just outside Paignton, everything easy to keep clean and the kitchen all white. The reason I didn't want to go away was I was afraid I would be homesick. It's funny, isn't it, when you get homesick? You see, I was only a kid and me never having been away from home before I just cried and cried. 'Why, Edith,' said Mrs. Dykes, 'whatever's the matter? You're not homesick, are you? Aren't you happy with us?' And, of course, when she spoke to me so gentle that just made me cry all the more. 'If you're so unhappy,' she said, 'maybe it would be better for you to go home at the end of the month.'

Mind you, the Major was always a worry to her, you never knew what he'd be getting up to. I don't believe there was nothing between them and hadn't been for a long time, though I dare say the Major wished there was, so of course they always had separate bedrooms. Well, one afternoon about tea-time, yes, it must have been about tea-time because I was making the toast, the Major must always have his hot buttered toast for tea, there I was making the toast and the Major come into the kitchen. Of course, I didn't take no notice until he come up and caught hold of me. I asked him to let go and stop his games, but he wouldn't, so I hit at his hands with the toasting-fork to make him leave go of me. He had ever such big veins in his hands, they stood right out. 'Oh, you little vixen! You little spitfire!' he said. 'Well, you had no call to lay hands on me,' I said, 'whatever would Mrs. Dykes say?' And as he wouldn't

stop his tricks I said 'Give over, will you!' and hit
him again over the knuckles with the toasting-fork.
'Damn it, damn it,' he said, and then he run out.
Just as I was getting tea ready to take into the drawing-room Mrs. Dykes come in, she'd been out shop-
ping, and 'Oh, Edith,' she said, 'I'll just take the
Major's tea up to him. He's ever so upset,' she said,
'he's hurt his hands something dreadful, he's resting
in his room. He caught them in the mowing machine
and they're all swollen up.' Of course I didn't say
anything, but you should have seen the state his
hands were in. Of course, I didn't mean to hurt him
like that, but it was his own fault in a way, wasn't it?

My homesickness didn't get any better. I seemed
to be always moping, so Mrs. Dykes said I'd better
go home at the end of the month. Well, only a couple
of days before the end of the month I was cleaning
the windows. It was a lovely morning, and when I
was doing the window of the spare room I couldn't
help noticing that there was a boy painting the roof
of a shed in the garden next door, and when I was
looking at him he looked up and saw me and he
grinned and waved his hand. That's ever such a nice
boy, I thought. Of course it was Freddy, though
I didn't know at the time. I was ever so pleased. I
didn't like to be too forward, but I waved back at
him. Then I run downstairs to Mrs. Dykes and I
asked her if I could stay with her instead of going
home at the end of the month. 'Why, Edith, of
course we should be very pleased,' she said, 'but
whatever's made you change your mind so sudden?'
Well, I knew I could tell her everything, so I said
'I've just seen ever such a nice boy painting the roof
of the shed next door, and he waved to me while I
was doing the spare room window.' With that she

run upstairs with me and looked out and when Freddy saw two of us he didn't know what to think. 'Yes, Edith,' said Mrs. Dykes, 'you're quite right, he *is* a nice boy.' So I didn't go away at the end of the month, and I just waited, hoping I'd see him again. I'd forgotten all about being homesick.

Next thing a note came to the house, addressed to 'Miss Edith'. Just like that, 'Miss Edith'. Of course it was from Freddy, asking me if I'd meet him at the corner on my evening out so we could go to the pictures. Oh, I *was* excited. I run and showed it to Mrs. Dykes and 'Of course, Edith,' she said, 'you'll have to go, but I wish we knew something about him. Isn't there anybody we could ask?' Well, next time the butcher's boy come round I said, 'Do you know anything about a fellow round here called Fred Carter?' 'Fred Carter?' he said. 'No, I can't say I do. What sort of work does he do?' 'I believe he's something in the building line,' I said. 'The only Fred I can think of,' he said, 'that's in the building line is Fred Baines, him that was painting that shed next door.' 'And what sort of a fellow is he?' I said. 'Oh, he's all right,' he said, 'but what do *you* want to know for? Has he been round here after you?' 'Don't be so nosey,' I said, but what I couldn't make out was if his name was Baines why did he call himself Carter, but it turned out that his step-father's name was Baines so everybody used to call him Baines's boy though his name was really Carter.

So off I went to meet him, and 'Do be careful, Edith,' said Mrs. Dykes, 'don't let him take no liberties,' she said, 'until you're sure of him.' Oh, and do you know, he was *late*. Oh, I was that worried I could have cried, I thought he was just making game of me. Oh, I *was* upset, I thought I'd have done better to go back home after all. But just then he come up, all smiles, and we went off to the pictures, and we did have a lovely time. Of course after that everything was all right, but Mrs. Dykes said he must come to the house so she could see him for herself, and of course everybody liked him, you know how it is, people always do seem to take to Freddy, and after that he was always coming round, every night he used to come round, Mrs. Dykes was ever so kind, and the Major liked him too.

Then one evening, late it was, Mrs. Dykes come running down to the kitchen, screaming blue murder, 'Edith! Edith! Freddy!! Freddy!! Come quick, there's a man in my room!' Well of course we run upstairs and Freddy grabbed the poker and when we got up to her room there was nobody there but the Major. Do you know he'd got in through the window, thinking to surprise her, she wouldn't let him set foot in her room at all in the ordinary way. 'What on earth's all this?' he said when he see us. 'Why, Gilbert, it's only *you*!' said Mrs. Dykes. 'What do you mean by giving us all such a fright, creeping in at my window like that? Why, I thought it was a *man*!' At that Freddy and me couldn't help giving a laugh. Soon after that I left to get married, and I was sorry to leave in some ways; Mrs. Dykes cried when I went away, ever so good she was. Poor soul, I can't help thinking of her sometimes, with that Major of hers.

EVELYN WAUGH

On Guard

I

MILLICENT BLADE had a notable head of naturally fair hair; she had a docile and affectionate disposition, and an expression of face which changed with lightning rapidity from amiability to laughter and from laughter to respectful interest. But the feature which, more than any other, endeared her to sentimental Anglo-Saxon manhood was her nose.

It was not everybody's nose; many prefer one with greater body; it was not a nose to appeal to painters, for it was far too small and quite without shape, a mere dab of putty without apparent bone structure; a nose which made it impossible for its wearer to be haughty or imposing or astute. It would not have done for a governess or a 'cellist or even a post office clerk, but it suited Miss Blade's book perfectly, for it was a nose that pierced the thin surface crust of the English heart to its warm and pulpy core; a nose to take the thoughts of English manhood back to its schooldays, to the doughy-faced urchins on whom it had squandered its first affection, to memories of changing room and chapel and battered straw boaters. Three Englishmen in five, it is true, grow snobbish about these things in later life and prefer a nose that makes more show in public—but two in five is an average with which any girl of modest fortune may be reasonably content.

Hector kissed her reverently on the tip of this nose.

As he did so, his senses reeled and in momentary delirium he saw the fading light of the November afternoon, the raw mist spreading over the playing fields; overheated youth in the scrum; frigid youth at the touchline, shuffling on the duckboards, chafing their fingers and, when their mouths were emptied of biscuit crumbs, cheering their house team to further exertion.

'You will wait for me, won't you?' he said.

'Yes, darling.'

'And you will write?'

'Yes, darling,' she replied more doubtfully, 'sometimes . . . at least I'll try. Writing is not my best thing, you know.'

'I shall think of you all the time Out There,' said Hector. 'It's going to be terrible—miles of impassable wagon track between me and the nearest white man, blinding sun, lions, mosquitoes, hostile natives, work from dawn until sunset single-handed against the forces of nature, fever, cholera . . . But soon I shall be able to send for you to join me.'

'Yes, darling.'

'It's bound to be a success. I've discussed it all with Beckthorpe—that's the chap who's selling me the farm. You see the crop has failed every year so far—first coffee, then seisal, then tobacco, that's all you can grow there, and the year Beckthorpe grew seisal, everyone else was making a packet in tobacco, but seisal was no good; then he grew tobacco, but by then it was coffee he ought to have grown, and so on. He stuck it nine years. Well if you work it out mathematically, Beckthorpe says, in three years one's bound to strike the right crop. I can't quite explain why but it is like roulette and all that sort of thing, you see.'

'Yes, darling.'

Hector gazed at her little, shapeless, mobile button of a nose and was lost again . . . 'Play up, play up,' and after the match the smell of crumpets being toasted over a gas-ring in his study . . .

II

Later that evening he dined with Beckthorpe, and, as he dined, he grew more despondent.

'Tomorrow this time I shall be at sea,' he said, twiddling his empty port glass.

'Cheer up, old boy,' said Beckthorpe.

Hector filled his glass and gazed with growing distaste round the reeking dining room of Beckthorpe's club. The last awful member had left the room and they were alone with the cold buffet.

'I say, you know, I've been trying to work it out. It *was* in three years you said the crop was bound to be right, wasn't it?'

'That's right, old boy.'

'Well, I've been through the sum and it seems to me that it may be eighty-one years before it comes right.'

'No, no, old boy, three or nine or at the most twenty-seven.'

'Are you sure?'

'Quite.'

'Good . . . you know it's awful leaving Milly behind. Suppose it *is* eighty-one years before the crop succeeds. It's the devil of a time to expect a girl to wait. Some other blighter might turn up, if you see what I mean.'

'In the Middle Ages they used to use girdles of chastity.'

'Yes, I know. I've been thinking of them. But they sound damned uncomfortable. I doubt if Milly would wear one even if I knew where to find it.'

'Tell you what, old boy. You ought to give her something.'

'Hell, I'm always giving her things. She either breaks them or loses them or forgets where she got them.'

'You must give her something she will always have by her, something that will last.'

'Eighty-one years?'

'Well, say, twenty-seven. Something to remind her of you.'

'I could give her a photograph—but I might change a bit in twenty-seven years.'

'No, no, that would be most unsuitable. A photograph wouldn't do at all. I know what I'd give her. I'd give her a dog.'

'Dog?'

'A healthy puppy that was over distemper and looked like living a long time. She might even call it Hector.'

'Would that be a good thing, Beckthorpe?'

'Best possible, old boy.'

So next morning, before catching the boat train, Hector hurried to one of the mammoth stores of London and was shown to the livestock department. 'I want a puppy.'

'Yes, sir, any particular sort?'

'One that will live a long time. Eighty-one years, or twenty-seven at the least.'

The man looked doubtful. 'We have some fine healthy puppies of course,' he admitted, 'but none of them carry a guarantee. Now if it was longevity you wanted, might I recommend a tortoise? They live to an extraordinary age and are very safe in traffic.'

'No, it must be a pup.'

'Or a parrot?'

'No, no, a pup. I would prefer one named Hector.'

They walked together past monkeys and kittens and cockatoos to the dog department which, even at this early hour, had attracted a small congregation of rapt worshippers. There were puppies of all varieties in wire-fronted kennels, ears cocked, tails wagging, noisily soliciting attention. Rather wildly, Hector selected a poodle and, as the salesman disappeared to fetch him his change, he leant down for a moment's intense communion with the beast of his choice. He gazed deep into the sharp little face, avoided a sudden snap and said with profound solemnity, 'You are to look after Milly, Hector. See that she doesn't marry anyone until I get back.'

And the pup Hector waved his plume of tail.

III

Millicent came to see him off, but, negligently, went to the wrong station; it could not have mattered, however, for she was twenty minutes late. Hector and the poodle hung about the barrier looking for her, and not until the train was already moving did he bundle the animal into Beckthorpe's arms with instructions to deliver him at Millicent's address. Luggage labelled for Mombasa, 'Wanted on the voyage,' lay in the rack above him. He felt very much neglected.

That evening as the ship pitched and rolled past the Channel lighthouses, he received a radiogram: *Miserable to miss you went Paddington like idiot*

*thank you thank you for sweet dog I love him father
minds dreadfully longing to hear about farm dont
fall for ship siren all love Milly.*

In the Red Sea he received another. *Beware sirens
puppy bit man called Mike.*

After that Hector heard nothing of Millicent except for a Christmas card which arrived in the last
days of February.

IV

Generally speaking, Millicent's fancy for any particular young man was likely to last four months. It
depended on how far he had got in that time whether
the process of extinction was sudden or protracted.
In the case of Hector, her affection had been due
to diminish at about the time that she became
engaged to him; it had been artificially prolonged
during the succeeding three weeks, during which he
made strenuous, infectiously earnest efforts to find
employment in England; it came to an abrupt end
with his departure for Kenya. Accordingly the duties
of the puppy Hector began with his first days at
home. He was young for the job and wholly inex-
perienced; it is impossible to blame him for his
mistake in the matter of Mike Boswell.

This was a young man who had enjoyed a wholly
unromantic friendship with Millicent since she first
came out. He had seen her fair hair in all kinds of
light, in and out of doors, crowned in hats in succeeding fashions, bound with ribbon, decorated
with combs, jauntily stuck with flowers; he had seen
her nose uplifted in all kinds of weather, had even,
on occasions, playfully tweaked it with his finger
and thumb, and had never for one moment felt
remotely attracted by her.

But the puppy Hector could hardly be expected
to know this. All he knew was that two days after
receiving his commission, he observed a tall and
personable man of marriageable age who treated
his hostess with the sort of familiarity which, among
the kennel maids with whom he had been brought
up, meant only one thing.

The two young people were having tea together.
Hector watched for some time from his place on the
sofa, barely stifling his growls. A climax was reached
when, in the course of some barely intelligible back-
chat, Mike leant forward and patted Millicent on
the knee.

It was not a serious bite, a mere snap, in fact; but
Hector had small teeth as sharp as pins. It was the
sudden, nervous speed with which Mike withdrew
his hand which caused the damage; he swore,
wrapped his hand in a handkerchief, and at Millicent's entreaty revealed three or four minute wounds.
Millicent spoke harshly to Hector and tenderly to
Mike, and hurried to her mother's medicine cupboard for a bottle of iodine.

Now no Englishman, however phlegmatic, can
have his hand dabbed with iodine without, momentarily at any rate, falling in love.

Mike had seen the nose countless times before, but
that afternoon, as it was bowed over his scratched
thumb, and as Millicent said, 'Am I hurting terribly?', as it was raised towards him, and as Millicent said, 'There. Now it will be all right,' Mike
suddenly saw it transfigured as its devotees saw it
and from' that moment, until long after the three
months of attention which she accorded him, he was
Millicent's besotted suitor.

The pup Hector saw all this and realized his mistake. Never again, he decided, would he give Millicent the excuse to run for the iodine bottle.

v

He had on the whole an easy task, for Millicent's naturally capricious nature could, as a rule, be relied upon, unaided, to drive her lovers into extremes of irritation. Moreover she had come to love the dog. She received very regular letters from Hector, written weekly and arriving in batches of three or four according to the mails. She always opened them; often she read them to the end, but their contents made little impression upon her mind and gradually their writer drifted into oblivion so that when people said to her 'How is darling Hector?' it came naturally to her to reply, 'He doesn't like the hot weather much I'm afraid, and his coat is in a very poor state. I'm thinking of having him plucked,' instead of, 'He had a go of malaria and there is black worm in his tobacco crop.'

Playing upon this affection which had grown up for him, Hector achieved a technique for dealing with Millicent's young men. He no longer growled at them or soiled their trousers; that merely resulted in his being turned from the room; instead, he found it increasingly easy to usurp the conversation.

Tea was the most dangerous time of day, for then Millicent was permitted to entertain friends in her sitting-room; accordingly, though he had a constitutional preference for pungent, meaty dishes, Hector heroically simulated a love of lump sugar. Having made this apparent, at whatever cost to his digestion, it was easy to lead Millicent on to an interest in tricks; he would beg and 'trust', lie down as though dead, stand in the corner and raise a fore paw to his ear.

'What does SUGAR spell?' Millicent would ask and Hector would walk round the tea table to the sugar-bowl and lay his nose against it, gazing earnestly and clouding the silver with his moist breath.

'He understands everything,' Millicent would say in triumph.

When tricks failed Hector would demand to be let out of the door. The young man would be obliged to interrupt himself to open it. Once on the other side Hector would scratch and whine for readmission.

In moments of extreme anxiety Hector would affect to be sick—no difficult feat after the unwelcome diet of lump sugar; he would stretch out his neck, retching noisily, till Millicent snatched him up and carried him to the hall, where the floor, paved in marble, was less vulnerable—but by that time a tender atmosphere had been shattered and one wholly prejudicial to romance created to take its place.

This series of devices spaced out through the afternoon and tactfully obtruded whenever the guest showed signs of leading the conversation to a more intimate phase, distracted young man after young man and sent them finally away, baffled and despairing.

Every morning Hector lay on Millicent's bed while she took her breakfast and read the daily paper. This hour from ten to eleven was sacred to the telephone and it was then that the young men with whom she had danced overnight attempted to renew their friendship and make plans for the day. At first Hector sought, not unsuccessfully, to pre-

vent these assignations by entangling himself in the
wire, but soon a subtler and more insulting technique suggested itself. He pretended to telephone
too. Thus, as soon as the bell rang, he would wag
his tail and cock his head on one side in a way that
he had learned was engaging. Millicent would begin her conversation and Hector would wriggle up
under her arm and nuzzle against the receiver.

'Listen,' she would say, '*someone* wants to talk to
you. Isn't he an angel?' Then she would hold the
receiver down to him and the young man at the
other end would be dazed by a shattering series of
yelps. This accomplishment appealed so much to
Millicent that often she would not even bother to
find out the name of the caller but, instead, would
take off the receiver and hold it directly to the black
snout, so that some wretched young man half a mile
away, feeling, perhaps, none too well in the early
morning, found himself barked to silence before he
had spoken a word.

At other times young men badly taken with the
nose, would attempt to waylay Millicent in Hyde
Park when she was taking Hector for exercise. Here,
at first, Hector would get lost, fight other dogs and
bite small children to keep himself constantly in her
attention, but soon he adopted a gentler course. He
insisted upon carrying Millicent's bag for her. He
would trot in front of the couple and whenever he
thought an interruption desirable he would drop
the bag; the young man was obliged to pick it up
and restore it first to Millicent and then, at her re-
quest, to the dog. Few young men were sufficiently
servile to submit to more than one walk in these
degrading conditions.

In this way two years passed. Letters arrived con-

stantly from Kenya, full of devotion, full of minor
disasters—blight in the seisal, locusts in the coffee,
labour troubles, drought, flood, the local govern-
ment, the world market. Occasionally Millicent read
the letters aloud to the dog, usually she left them
unread on her breakfast tray. She and Hector moved
together through the leisurely routine of English
social life. Wherever she carried her nose, two in
five marriageable men fell temporarily in love;
wherever Hector followed their ardour changed to
irritation, shame and disgust. Mothers began to
remark complacently that it was curious how that
fascinating Blade girl never got married.

VI

At last in the third year of this régime a new problem
presented itself in the person of Major Sir Alexander Dreadnought, Bart., M.P., and Hector immediately realized that he was up against something
altogether more formidable than he had hitherto
tackled.

Sir Alexander was not a young man; he was forty-
five and a widower. He was wealthy, popular and
preternaturally patient; he was also mildly distinguished, being joint-master of a Midland pack of
hounds and a junior Minister; he bore a war record
of conspicuous gallantry. Millie's father and mother
were delighted when they saw that her nose was
having its effect on him. Hector took against him
from the first, exerted every art which his two-and-
a-half-years' practice had perfected, and achieved
nothing. Devices that had driven a dozen young
men to frenzies of chagrin seemed only to accen-
tuate Sir Alexander's tender solicitude. When he

came to the house to fetch Millicent for the evening
he was found to have filled the pockets of his evening clothes with lump sugar for Hector; when Hector
was sick Sir Alexander was there first, on his knees
with a page of *The Times*; Hector resorted to his
early, violent manner and bit him frequently and
hard, but Sir Alexander merely remarked, 'I believe
I am making the little fellow jealous. A delightful
trait.'

For the truth was that Sir Alexander had been
persecuted long and bitterly from his earliest days
—his parents, his sisters, his schoolfellows, his com-
pany-sergeant and his colonel, his colleagues in
politics, his wife, his joint-master, huntsman and
hunt secretary, his election agent, his constituents
and even his parliamentary private secretary had one
and all pitched into Sir Alexander, and he accepted
this treatment as a matter of course. For him it was
the most natural thing in the world to have his ear-
drums outraged by barks when he rang up the
young woman of his affections; it was a high privi-
lege to retrieve her handbag when Hector dropped
it in the Park; the small wounds that Hector was
able to inflict on his ankles and wrists were to him
knightly scars. In his more ambitious moments he
referred to Hector in Millicent's hearing as 'my little
rival'. There could be no doubt whatever of his in-
tentions and when he asked Millicent and her mama
to visit him in the country, he added at the foot of
the letter, '*Of course the invitation includes little
Hector.*'

The Saturday to Monday visit to Sir Alexander's
was a nightmare to the poodle. He worked as he had
never worked before; every artifice by which he
could render his presence odious was attempted and

attempted in vain. As far as his host was concerned, that is to say. The rest of the household responded well enough, and he received a vicious kick when, through his own bad management, he found himself alone with the second footman, whom he had succeeded in upsetting with a tray of cups at tea time.

Conduct that had driven Millicent in shame from half the stately homes of England was meekly accepted here. There were other dogs in the house— elderly, sober, well-behaved animals at whom Hector flew; they turned their heads sadly away from his yaps of defiance, he snapped at their ears. They lolloped sombrely out of reach and Sir Alexander had them shut away for the rest of the visit.

There was an exciting Aubusson carpet in the dining-room to which Hector was able to do irreparable damage; Sir Alexander seemed not to notice.

Hector found a carrion in the park and conscientiously rolled in it—although such a thing was obnoxious to his nature—and, returning, fouled every chair in the drawing-room; Sir Alexander himself helped Millicent wash him and brought some bath salts from his own bathroom for the operation.

Hector howled all night; he hid and had half the household searching for him with lanterns; he killed some young pheasants and made a sporting attempt on a peacock. All to no purpose. He staved off an actual proposal, it is true—once in the Dutch garden, once on the way to the stables and once while he was being bathed—but when Monday morning arrived and he heard Sir Alexander say, 'I hope Hector enjoyed his visit a little. I hope I shall see him here *very, very* often,' he knew that he was defeated.

It was now only a matter of waiting. The evenings in London were a time when it was impossible for him to keep Millicent under observation. One of these days he would wake up to hear Millicent telephoning to her girl friends, breaking the good news of her engagement.

Thus it was that after a long conflict of loyalties he came to a desperate resolve. He had grown fond of his young mistress; often and often when her face had been pressed down to his he had felt sympathy with that long line of young men whom it was his duty to persecute. But Hector was no kitchen-haunting mongrel. By the code of all well-born dogs it is money that counts. It is the purchaser, not the mere feeder and fondler, to whom ultimate loyalty is due. The hand which had once fumbled with the fivers in the live-stock department of the mammoth store now tilled the unfertile soil of equatorial Africa, but the sacred words of commission still rang in Hector's memory. All through the Sunday night and the journey of Monday morning, Hector wrestled with his problem; then he came to the decision. *The nose must go.*

VII

It was an easy business; one firm snap as she bent over his basket and the work was accomplished. She went to a plastic surgeon and emerged some weeks later without scar or stitch. But it was a different nose; the surgeon in his way was an artist and, as I have said above, Millicent's nose had no sculptural qualities. Now she has a fine aristocratic beak, worthy of the spinster she is about to become.

Like all spinsters she watches eagerly for the foreign mails and keeps carefully under lock and key a casket full of depressing agricultural intelligence; like all spinsters she is accompanied everywhere by an ageing lapdog.

GRAHAM GREENE

The Basement Room

I

WHEN the front door had shut them out and the
butler Baines had turned back into the dark heavy
hall, Philip began to live. He stood in front of the
nursery door, listening until he heard the engine of
the taxi die out along the street. His parents were
gone for a fortnight's holiday; he was 'between
nurses', one dismissed and the other not arrived; he
was alone in the great Belgravia house with Baines
and Mrs. Baines.

He could go anywhere, even through the green
baize door to the pantry or down the stairs to the
basement living-room. He felt a stranger in his home
because he could go into any room and all the rooms
were empty.

You could only guess who had once occupied
them: the rack of pipes in the smoking-room beside
the elephant tusks, the carved wood tobacco jar; in
the bedroom the pink hangings and pale perfumes
and the three-quarter-finished jars of cream which
Mrs. Baines had not yet cleared away; the high glaze
on the never-opened piano in the drawing-room, the
china clock, the silly little tables and the silver: but
here Mrs. Baines was already busy, pulling down
the curtains, covering the chairs in dust-sheets.

'Be off out of here, Master Philip,' and she looked
at him with her hateful peevish eyes, while she

moved round, getting everything in order, meticulous and loveless and doing her duty.

Philip Lane went downstairs and pushed at the baize door; he looked into the pantry, but Baines was not there, then he set foot for the first time on the stairs to the basement. Again he had the sense: this is life. All his seven nursery years vibrated with the strange, the new experience. His crowded busy brain was like a city which feels the earth tremble at a distant earthquake shock. He was apprehensive, but he was happier than he had ever been. Everything was more important than before.

Baines was reading a newspaper in his shirt-sleeves. He said, 'Come in, Phil, and make yourself at home. Wait a moment and I'll do the honours,' and going to a white cleaned cupboard he brought out a bottle of ginger-beer and half a Dundee cake. 'Half-past eleven in the morning,' Baines said. 'It's opening time, my boy,' and he cut the cake and poured out the ginger-beer. He was more genial than Philip had ever known him, more at his ease, a man in his own home.

'Shall I call Mrs. Baines?' Philip asked, and he was glad when Baines said no. She was busy. She liked to be busy, so why interfere with her pleasure?

'A spot of drink at half-past eleven,' Baines said, pouring himself out a glass of ginger-beer, 'gives an appetite for chop and does no man any harm.'

'A chop?' Philip asked.

'Old Coasters,' Baines said, 'call all food chop.'

'But it's not a chop?'

'Well, it might be, you know, cooked with palm oil. And then some paw-paw to follow.'

Philip looked out of the basement window at the

dry stone yard, the ash-can and the legs going up
and down beyond the railings.

'Was it hot there?'

'Ah, you never felt such heat. Not a nice heat,
mind, like you get in the park on a day like this.
Wet,' Baines said, 'corruption.' He cut himself a
slice of cake. 'Smelling of rot,' Baines said, rolling
his eyes round the small basement room, from clean
cupboard to clean cupboard, the sense of bareness,
of nowhere to hide a man's secrets. With an air of
regret for something lost he took a long draught of
ginger-beer.

'Why did father live out there?'

'It was his job,' Baines said, 'same as this is mine
now. And it was mine then too. It was a man's job.
You wouldn't believe it now, but I've had forty
niggers under me, doing what I told them to.'

'Why did you leave?'

'I married Mrs. Baines.'

Philip took the slice of Dundee cake in his hand
and munched it round the room. He felt very old,
independent and judicial; he was aware that Baines
was talking to him as man to man. He never called
him Master Philip as Mrs. Baines did, who was servile when she was not authoritative.

Baines had seen the world; he had seen beyond
the railings, beyond the tired legs of typists, the
Pimlico parade to and from Victoria. He sat there
over his ginger pop with the resigned dignity of an
exile; Baines didn't complain; he had chosen his
fate; and if his fate was Mrs. Baines he had only
himself to blame.

But today, because the house was almost empty
and Mrs. Baines was upstairs and there was nothing
to do, he allowed himself a little acidity.

'I'd go back tomorrow if I had the chance.'

'Did you ever shoot a nigger?'

'I never had any call to shoot,' Baines said. 'Of course I carried a gun. But you didn't need to treat them bad. That just made them stupid. Why,' Baines said, bowing his thin grey hair with embarrassment over the ginger pop, 'I loved some of those damned niggers. I couldn't help loving them. There they'd be laughing, holding hands; they liked to touch each other; it made them feel fine to know the other fellow was round. It didn't mean anything we could understand; two of them would go about all day without losing hold, grown men; but it wasn't love; it didn't mean anything we could understand.'

'Eating between meals,' Mrs. Baines said. 'What would your mother say, Master Philip?'

She came down the steep stairs to the basement, her hands full of pots of cream and salve, tubes of grease and paste. 'You oughtn't to encourage him, Baines,' she said, sitting down in a wicker armchair and screwing up her small ill-humoured eyes at the Coty lipstick, Pond's cream, the Leichner rouge and Cyclax powder and Elizabeth Arden astringent.

She threw them one by one into the waste-paper basket. She saved only the cold cream. 'Telling the boy stories,' she said. 'Go along to the nursery, Master Philip, while I get lunch.'

Philip climbed the stairs to the baize door. He heard Mrs. Baines's voice like the voice in a nightmare when the small Price light has guttered in the saucer and the curtains move; it was sharp and shrill and full of malice, louder than people ought to speak, exposed.

'Sick to death of your ways, Baines, spoiling the boy. Time you did some work about the house,' but

he couldn't hear what Baines said in reply. He
pushed open the baize door, came up like a small
earth animal in his grey flannel shorts into a wash
of sunlight on a parquet floor, the gleam of mirrors
dusted and polished and beautified by Mrs. Baines.

Something broke downstairs, and Philip sadly
mounted the stairs to the nursery. He pitied Baines;
it occurred to him how happily they could live together in the empty house if Mrs. Baines were called
away. He didn't want to play with his Meccano sets;
he wouldn't take out his train or his soldiers; he sat
at the table with his chin on his hands: this is life;
and suddenly he felt responsible for Baines, as if he
were the master of the house and Baines an ageing
servant who deserved to be cared for. There was not
much one could do; he decided at least to be good.

He was not surprised when Mrs. Baines was agree-
able at lunch; he was used to her changes. Now it
was 'another helping of meat, Master Philip,' or
'Master Philip, a little more of this nice pudding.'
It was a pudding he liked, Queen's pudding with a
perfect meringue, but he wouldn't eat a second helping lest she might count that a victory. She was the
kind of woman who thought that any injustice could
be counterbalanced by something good to eat.

She was sour, but she liked making sweet things;
one never had to complain of a lack of jam or plums;
she ate well herself and added soft sugar to the
meringue and the strawberry jam. The half light
through the basement window set the motes moving
above her pale hair like dust as she sifted the sugar,
and Baines crouched over his plate saying nothing.

Again Philip felt responsibility. Baines had looked
forward to this, and Baines was disappointed: everything was being spoilt. The sensation of disappoint-

ment was one which Philip could share; knowing nothing of love or jealousy or passion he could understand better than anyone this grief, something hoped for not happening, something promised not fulfilled, something exciting turning dull. 'Baines,' he said, 'will you take me for a walk this afternoon?'

'No,' Mrs. Baines said, 'no. That he won't. Not with all the silver to clean.'

'There's a fortnight to do it in,' Baines said.

'Work first, pleasure afterwards,' Mrs. Baines helped herself to some more meringue.

Baines suddenly put down his spoon and fork and pushed his plate away. 'Blast,' he said.

'Temper,' Mrs. Baines said softly, 'temper. Don't you go breaking any more things, Baines, and I won't have you swearing in front of the boy. Master Philip, if you've finished you can get down.' She skinned the rest of the meringue off the pudding.

'I want to go for a walk,' Philip said.

'You'll go and have a rest.'

'I will go for a walk.'

'Master Philip,' Mrs. Baines said. She got up from the table leaving her meringue unfinished, and came towards him, thin, menacing, dusty in the basement room. 'Master Philip, you do as you're told.' She took him by the arm and squeezed it gently; she watched him with a joyless passionate glitter and above her head the feet of the typists trudged back to the Victoria offices after the lunch interval.

'Why shouldn't I go for a walk?' But he weakened; he was scared and ashamed of being scared. This was life; a strange passion he couldn't understand moving in the basement room. He saw a small pile of broken glass swept into a corner by the waste-paper basket. He looked to Baines for help

and only intercepted hate; the sad hopeless hate of
something behind bars.

'Why shouldn't I?' he repeated.

'Master Philip,' Mrs. Baines said, 'you've got to
do as you're told. You mustn't think just because
your father's away there's nobody here to —'

'You wouldn't dare,' Philip cried, and was startled
by Baines's low interjection:

'There's nothing she wouldn't dare.'

'I hate you,' Philip said to Mrs. Baines. He pulled
away from her and ran to the door, but she was
there before him; she was old, but she was quick.

'Master Philip,' she said, 'you'll say you're sorry.'
She stood in front of the door quivering with excitement. 'What would your father do if he heard you
say that?'

She put a hand out to seize him, dry and white
with constant soda, the nails cut to the quick, but he
backed away and put the table between them, and
suddenly to his surprise she smiled; she became again
as servile as she had been arrogant. 'Get along with
you, Master Philip,' she said with glee, 'I see I'm
going to have my hands full till your father and
mother come back.'

She left the door unguarded and when he passed
her she slapped him playfully. 'I've got too much to
do today to trouble about you. I haven't covered
half the chairs,' and suddenly even the upper part
of the house became unbearable to him as he
thought of Mrs. Baines moving round shrouding
the sofas, laying out the dust-sheets.

So he wouldn't go upstairs to get his cap but
walked straight out across the shining hall into the
street, and again, as he looked this way and looked
that way, it was life he was in the middle of.

II

It was the pink sugar cakes in the window on a paper doily, the ham, the slab of mauve sausage, the wasps driving like small torpedoes across the pane that caught Philip's attention. His feet were tired by pavements; he had been afraid to cross the road, had simply walked first in one direction, then in the other. He was nearly home now; the square was at the end of the street; this was a shabby outpost of Pimlico, and he smudged the pane with his nose looking for sweets, and saw between the cakes and ham a different Baines. He hardly recognized the bulbous eyes, the bald forehead. It was a happy, bold and buccaneering Baines, even though it was, when you looked closer, a desperate Baines.

Philip had never seen the girl. He remembered Baines had a niece and he thought that this might be her. She was thin and drawn, and she wore a white mackintosh; she meant nothing to Philip; she belonged to a world about which he knew nothing at all. He couldn't make up stories about her, as he could make them up about withered Sir Hubert Reed, the Permanent Secretary, about Mrs. Wince-Dudley who came up once a year from Penstanley in Suffolk with a green umbrella and an enormous black handbag, as he could make them up about the upper servants in all the houses where he went to tea and games. She just didn't belong; he thought of mermaids and Undine; but she didn't belong there either, nor to the adventures of Emil, nor to the Bastables. She sat there looking at an iced pink cake in the detachment and mystery of the completely disinherited, looking at the half-used pots of powder which Baines had set out on the marble-topped table between them.

Baines was urging, hoping, entreating, commanding, and the girl looked at the tea and the china pots and cried. Baines passed his handkerchief across the table, but she wouldn't wipe her eyes; she screwed it in her palm and let the tears run down, wouldn't do anything, wouldn't speak, would only put up a silent despairing resistance to what she dreaded and wanted and refused to listen to at any price. The two brains battled over the tea-cups loving each other, and there came to Philip outside, beyond the ham and wasps and dusty Pimlico pane, a confused indication of the struggle.

He was inquisitive and he did not understand and he wanted to know. He went and stood in the doorway to see better; he was less sheltered than he had ever been; other people's lives for the first time touched and pressed and moulded. He would never escape that scene. In a week he had forgotten it, but it conditioned his career, the long austerity of his life; when he was dying he said: 'Who is she?'

Baines had won; he was cocky and the girl was happy. She wiped her face, she opened a pot of powder, and their fingers touched across the table. It occurred to Philip that it would be amusing to imitate Mrs. Baines's voice and call 'Baines' to him from the door.

It shrivelled them; you couldn't describe it in any other way; it made them smaller, they weren't happy any more and they weren't bold. Baines was the first to recover and trace the voice, but that didn't make things as they were. The sawdust was spilled out of the afternoon; nothing you did could mend it, and Philip was scared. 'I didn't mean . . .' He wanted to say that he loved Baines, that he had only wanted to laugh at Mrs. Baines. But he had discovered that you couldn't laugh at Mrs. Baines. She wasn't Sir Hubert Reed, who used steel nibs and carried a penwiper in his pocket; she wasn't Mrs. Wince-Dudley; she was darkness when the night-light went out in a draught; she was the frozen blocks of earth he had seen one winter in a graveyard when someone said, 'They need an electric drill'; she was the flowers gone bad and smelling in the little closet room at Penstanley. There was nothing to laugh about. You had to endure her when she was there and forget about her quickly when she was away, suppress the thought of her, ram it down deep.

Baines said: 'It's only Phil,' beckoned him in and gave him the pink iced cake the girl hadn't eaten, but the afternoon was broken, the cake was like dry bread in the throat. The girl left them at once; she even forgot to take the powder; like a small blunt icicle in her white mackintosh she stood in the doorway with her back to them, then melted into the afternoon.

'Who is she?' Philip asked. 'Is she your niece?'

'Oh, yes,' Baines said, 'that's who she is; she's my niece,' and poured the last drops of water on to the coarse black leaves in the teapot.

'May as well have another cup,' Baines said.

'The cup that cheers,' he said hopelessly, watching the bitter black fluid drain out of the spout.

'Have a glass of ginger pop, Phil?'

'I'm sorry. I'm sorry, Baines.'

'It's not your fault, Phil. Why, I could believe it wasn't you at all, but her. She creeps in everywhere.' He fished two leaves out of his cup and laid them on the back of his hand, a thin soft flake, and a hard

stalk. He beat them with his hand: 'Today,' and
the stalk detached itself, 'tomorrow, Wednesday,
Thursday, Friday, Saturday, Sunday,' but the flake
wouldn't come, stayed where it was, drying under
his blows, with a resistance you wouldn't believe it
to possess. 'The tough one wins,' Baines said.

He got up and paid the bill and out they went into
the street. Baines said, 'I don't ask you to say what
isn't true. But you needn't mention to Mrs. Baines
you met us here.'

'Of course not,' Philip said, catching something
of Sir Hubert Reed's manner, 'I understand, Baines.'
But he didn't understand a thing; he was caught up
in other people's darkness.

'It was stupid,' Baines said. 'So near home, but I
hadn't got time to think, you see. I'd got to see her.'

'Of course, Baines.'

'I haven't time to spare,' Baines said. 'I'm not
young. I've got to see that she's all right.'

'Of course you have, Baines.'

'Mrs. Baines will get it out of you if she can.'

'You can trust me, Baines,' Philip said in a dry
important Reed voice; and then 'Look out. She's at
the window watching.' And there indeed she was,
looking up at them, between the lace curtains, from
the basement room, speculating. 'Need we go in,
Baines?' Philip asked, cold lying heavy on his
stomach like too much pudding; he clutched Baines's
arm.

'Careful,' Baines said softly, 'careful.'

'But need we go in, Baines? It's early. Take me
for a walk in the park.'

'Better not.'

'But I'm frightened, Baines.'

'You haven't any cause,' Baines said. 'Nothing's

going to hurt you. You just run along upstairs to the nursery. I'll go down by the area and talk to Mrs. Baines.' But even he stood hesitating at the top of the stone steps pretending not to see her, where she watched between the curtains. 'In at the front door, Phil, and up the stairs.'

Philip didn't linger in the hall; he ran, slithering on the parquet Mrs. Baines had polished, to the stairs. Through the drawing-room doorway on the first floor he saw the draped chairs; even the china clock on the mantel was covered like a canary's cage; as he passed it, it chimed the hour, muffled and secret under the duster. On the nursery table he found his supper laid out: a glass of milk and a piece of bread and butter, a sweet biscuit, and a little cold Queen's pudding without the meringue. He had no appetite; he strained his ears for Mrs. Baines's coming, for the sound of voices, but the basement held its secrets; the green baize door shut off that world. He drank the milk and ate the biscuit, but he didn't touch the rest, and presently he could hear the soft precise footfalls of Mrs. Baines on the stairs; she was a good servant, she walked softly; she was a determined woman, she walked precisely.

But she wasn't angry when she came in; she was ingratiating as she opened the night-nursery door— 'Did you have a good walk, Master Philip?'—pulled down the blinds, laid out his pyjamas, came back to clear his supper. 'I'm glad Baines found you. Your mother wouldn't like you being out alone.' She examined the tray. 'Not much appetite, have you, Master Philip? Why don't you try a little of this nice pudding? I'll bring you up some more jam for it.'

'No, no, thank you, Mrs. Baines,' Philip said.

'You ought to eat more,' Mrs. Baines said. She sniffed round the room like a dog. 'You didn't take any pots out of the waste-paper basket in the kitchen, did you, Master Philip?'

'No,' Philip said.

'Of course you wouldn't. I just wanted to make sure.' She patted his shoulder and her fingers flashed to his lapel; she picked off a tiny crumb of pink sugar. 'Oh, Master Philip,' she said, 'that's why you haven't any appetite. You've been buying sweet cakes. That's not what your pocket money's for.'

'But I didn't,' Philip said. 'I didn't.'

She tasted the sugar with the tip of her tongue.

'Don't tell lies to me, Master Philip. I won't stand for it any more than your father would.'

'I didn't, I didn't,' Philip said. 'They gave it me. I mean Baines,' but she had pounced on the word 'they'. She had got what she wanted; there was no doubt about that, even when you didn't know what it was she wanted. Philip was angry and miserable and disappointed because he hadn't kept Baines's secret. Baines oughtn't to have trusted him; grown-up people should keep their own secrets, and yet here was Mrs. Baines immediately entrusting him with another.

'Let me tickle your palm and see if you can keep a secret.' But he put his hand behind him; he wouldn't be touched. 'It's a secret between us, Master Philip, that I know all about them. I suppose she was having tea with him,' she speculated.

'Why shouldn't she?' he said, the responsibility for Baines weighing on his spirit, the idea that he had got to keep her secret when he hadn't kept Baines's making him miserable with the unfairness of life. 'She was nice.'

'She was nice, was she?' Mrs. Baines said in a bitter voice he wasn't used to.

'And she's his niece.'

'So that's what he said,' Mrs. Baines struck softly back at him like the clock under the duster. She tried to be jocular. 'The old scoundrel. Don't tell him I know, Master Philip.' She stood very still between the table and the door, thinking very hard, planning something. 'Promise you won't tell. I'll give you that Meccano set, Master Philip . . .'

He turned his back on her; he wouldn't promise, but he wouldn't tell. He would have nothing to do with their secrets, the responsibilities they were determined to lay on him. He was only anxious to forget. He had received already a larger dose of life than he had bargained for, and he was scared. 'A 2A Meccano set, Master Philip.' He never opened his Meccano set again, never built anything, never created anything, died, the old dilettante, sixty years later with nothing to show rather than preserve the memory of Mrs. Baines's malicious voice saying good night, her soft determined footfalls on the stairs to the basement, going down, going down.

III

The sun poured in between the curtains and Baines was beating a tattoo on the water-can. 'Glory, glory,' Baines said. He sat down on the end of the bed and said. 'I beg to announce that Mrs. Baines has been called away. Her mother's dying. She won't be back till tomorrow.'

'Why did you wake me up so early?' Philip said. He watched Baines with uneasiness; he wasn't going to be drawn in; he'd learnt his lesson. It wasn't right for a man of Baines's age to be so merry. It made a grown person human in the same way that you were human. For if a grown-up could behave so childishly, you were liable too to find yourself in their world. It was enough that it came at you in dreams: the witch at the corner, the man with a knife. So 'It's very early,' he complained, even though he loved Baines, even though he couldn't help being glad that Baines was happy. He was divided by the fear and the attraction of life.

'I want to make this a long day,' Baines said. 'This is the best time.' He pulled the curtains back. 'It's a bit misty. The cat's been out all night. There she is, sniffing round the area. They haven't taken in any milk at 59. Emma's shaking out the mats at 63.' He said, 'This was what I used to think about on the Coast: somebody shaking mats and the cat coming home. I can see it today,' Baines said, 'just as if I was still in Africa. Most days you don't notice what you've got. It's a good life if you don't weaken.' He put a penny on the washstand. 'When you've dressed, Phil, run and get a *Mail* from the barrow at the corner. I'll be cooking the sausages.'

'Sausages?'

'Sausages,' Baines said. 'We're going to celebrate today. A fair bust.' He celebrated at breakfast, restless, cracking jokes, unaccountably merry and nervous. It was going to be a long long day, he kept on coming back to that: for years he had waited for a long day, he had sweated in the damp Coast heat, changed shirts, gone down with fever, lain between the blankets and sweated, all in the hope of this long day, that cat sniffing round the area, a bit of mist, the mats beaten at 63. He propped the *Mail* in front of the coffee-pot and read pieces aloud. He said,

'Cora Down's been married for the fourth time.' He was amused, but it wasn't his idea of a long day. His long day was the Park, watching the riders in the Row, seeing Sir Arthur Stillwater pass beyond the rails ('He dined with us once in Bo; up from Freetown; he was governor there'), lunch at the Corner House for Philip's sake (he'd have preferred himself a glass of stout and some oysters at the York bar), the Zoo, the long bus ride home in the last summer light; the leaves in the Green Park were beginning to turn and the motors nuzzled out of Berkeley Street with the low sun gently glowing on their windscreens. Baines envied no one, not Cora Down, or Sir Arthur Stillwater, or Lord Sandale, who came out on to the steps of the Army and Navy and then went back again because he hadn't got anything to do and might as well look at another paper. 'I said don't let me see you touch that black again.' Baines had led a man's life; everyone on top of the bus pricked their ears when he told Philip all about it.

'Would you have shot him?' Philip asked, and Baines put his head back and tilted his dark respectable man-servant's hat to a better angle as the bus swerved round the Artillery Memorial.

'I wouldn't have thought twice about it. I'd have shot to kill,' he boasted, and the bowed figure went by, the steel helmet, the heavy cloak, the downturned rifle and the folded hands.

'Have you got the revolver?'

'Of course I've got it,' Baines said. 'Don't I need it with all the burglaries there've been?' This was the Baines whom Philip loved: not Baines singing and carefree, but Baines responsible, Baines behind barriers, living his man's life.

All the buses streamed out from Victoria like a convoy of aeroplanes to bring Baines home with honour. 'Forty blacks under me,' and there waiting near the area steps was the proper conventional reward, love at lighting-up time.

'It's your niece,' Philip said, recognizing the white mackintosh, but not the happy sleepy face. She frightened him like an unlucky number; he nearly told Baines what Mrs. Baines had said; but he didn't want to bother, he wanted to leave things alone.

'Why, so it is,' Baines said. 'I shouldn't wonder if she was going to have a bite of supper with us.' But he said they'd play a game, pretend they didn't know her, slip down the area steps, 'and here,' Baines said, 'we are,' lay the table, put out the cold sausages, a bottle of beer, a bottle of ginger pop, a flagon of harvest burgundy. 'Everyone his own drink,' Baines said. 'Run upstairs, Phil, and see if there's been a post.'

Philip didn't like the empty house at dusk before the lights went on. He hurried. He wanted to be back with Baines. The hall lay there in quiet and shadow prepared to show him something he didn't want to see. Some letters rustled down, and someone knocked. 'Open in the name of the Republic.' The tumbrils rolled, the head bobbed in the bloody basket. Knock, knock, and the postman's footsteps going away. Philip gathered the letters. The slit in the door was like the grating in a jeweller's window. He remembered the policeman he had seen peer through. He had said to his nurse, 'What's he doing?' and when she said, 'He's seeing if everything's all right,' his brain immediately filled with images of all that might be wrong. He ran to the baize door and the stairs. The girl was already there and Baines was kissing her. She leant breathless against the dresser. 'This is Emmy, Phil.'

'There's a letter for you, Baines.'

'Emmy,' Baines said, 'it's from her.' But he wouldn't open it. 'You bet she's coming back.'

'We'll have supper, anyway,' Emmy said. 'She can't harm that.'

'You don't know her,' Baines said. 'Nothing's safe. Damn it,' he said, 'I was a man once,' and he opened the letter.

'Can I start?' Philip asked, but Baines didn't hear; he presented in his stillness and attention an example of the importance grown-up people attached to the written word: you had to write your thanks, not wait and speak them, as if letters couldn't lie. But Philip knew better than that, sprawling his thanks across a page to Aunt Alice who had given him a doll he was too old for. Letters could lie all right, but they made the lie permanent: they lay as evidence against you; they made you meaner than the spoken word.

'She's not coming back till tomorrow night,' Baines said. He opened the bottles, he pulled up the chairs, he kissed Emmy again against the dresser.

'You oughtn't to,' Emmy said, 'with the boy here.'

'He's got to learn,' Baines said, 'like the rest of us,' and he helped Philip to three sausages. He only took one for himself; he said he wasn't hungry; but when Emmy said she wasn't hungry either he stood over her and made her eat. He was timid and rough with her; he made her drink the harvest burgundy because he said she needed building up; he wouldn't take no for an answer, but when he touched her his hands were light and clumsy too, as if he were afraid to damage something delicate and didn't know how to handle anything so light.

'This is better than milk and biscuits, eh?'

'Yes,' Philip said, but he was scared, scared for Baines as much as for himself. He couldn't help wondering at every bite, at every draught of the ginger pop, what Mrs. Baines would say if she ever learnt of this meal; he couldn't imagine it, there was a depth of bitterness and rage in Mrs. Baines you couldn't sound. He said, 'She won't be coming back tonight?' but you could tell by the way they immediately understood him that she wasn't really away at all; she was there in the basement with them, driving them to longer drinks and louder talk, biding her time for the right cutting word. Baines wasn't really happy; he was only watching happiness from close to instead of from far away.

'No,' he said, 'she'll not be back till late tomorrow.' He couldn't keep his eyes off happiness; he'd played around as much as other men, he kept on reverting to the Coast as if to excuse himself for his innocence; he wouldn't have been so innocent if he'd lived his life in London, so innocent when it came to tenderness. 'If it was you, Emmy,' he said, looking at the white dresser, the scrubbed chairs, 'this'd be like a home.' Already the room was not quite so harsh; there was a little dust in corners, the silver needed a final polish, the morning's paper lay untidily on a chair. 'You'd better go to bed, Phil; it's been a long day.'

They didn't leave him to find his own way up through the dark shrouded house; they went with him, turning on lights, touching each other's fingers on the switches; floor after floor they drove the night back; they spoke softly among the covered chairs; they watched him undress, they didn't make him wash or clean his teeth, they saw him into bed and

lit the night-light and left his door ajar. He could
hear their voices on the stairs, friendly like the guests
he heard at dinner-parties when they moved down
to the hall, saying good-night. They belonged;
wherever they were they made a home. He heard
a door open and a clock strike, he heard their voices
for a long while, so that he felt they were not far
away and he was safe. The voices didn't dwindle,
they simply went out, and he could be sure that they
were still somewhere not far from him, silent together in one of the many empty rooms, growing
sleepy together as he grew sleepy after the long
day.

He just had time to sigh faintly with satisfaction,
because this too perhaps had been life, before he
slept and the inevitable terrors of sleep came round
him: a man with a tricolour hat beat at the door on
His Majesty's service, a bleeding head lay on the
kitchen table in a basket, and the Siberian wolves
crept closer. He was bound hand and foot and
couldn't move; they leapt around him breathing
heavily; he opened his eyes and Mrs. Baines was
there, her grey untidy hair in threads over his face,
her black hat askew. A loose hairpin fell on the
pillow and one musty thread brushed his mouth.
'Where are they?' she whispered. 'Where are they?'

IV

Philip watched her in terror. Mrs. Baines was out of
breath as if she had been searching all the empty
rooms, looking under loose covers.

With her untidy grey hair and her black dress
buttoned to her throat, her gloves of black cotton,
she was so like the witches of his dreams that he

didn't dare to speak. There was a stale smell in her breath.

'She's here,' Mrs. Baines said, 'you can't deny she's here.' Her face was simultaneously marked with cruelty and misery; she wanted to 'do things' to people, but she suffered all the time. It would have done her good to scream, but she daren't do that: it would warn them. She came ingratiatingly back to the bed where Philip lay rigid on his back and whispered, 'I haven't forgotten the Meccano set. You shall have it tomorrow, Master Philip. We've got secrets together, haven't we? Just tell me where they are.'

He couldn't speak. Fear held him as firmly as any nightmare. She said, 'Tell Mrs. Baines, Master Philip. You love your Mrs. Baines, don't you?' That was too much; he couldn't speak, but he could move his mouth in terrified denial, wince away from her dusty image.

She whispered, coming closer to him, 'Such deceit. I'll tell your father. I'll settle with you myself when I've found them. You'll smart; I'll see you smart.' Then immediately she was still, listening. A board had creaked on the floor below, and a moment later, while she stood listening above his bed, there came the whispers of two people who were happy and sleepy together after a long day. The night-light stood beside the mirror and Mrs. Baines could see bitterly there her own reflection, misery and cruelty wavering in the glass, age and dust and nothing to hope for. She sobbed without tears, a dry, breathless sound; but her cruelty was a kind of pride which kept her going; it was her best quality, she would have been merely pitiable without it. She went out of the door on tiptoe, feeling her way across the landing, going so softly down the stairs that no one behind a shut door could hear her. Then there was complete silence again; Philip could move; he raised his knees; he sat up in bed; he wanted to die. It wasn't fair, the walls were down again between his world and theirs; but this time it was something worse than merriment that the grown people made him share; a passion moved in the house he recognized but could not understand.

It wasn't fair, but he owed Baines everything: the Zoo, the ginger pop, the bus ride home. Even the supper called on his loyalty. But he was frightened; he was touching something he touched in dreams: the bleeding head, the wolves, the knock, knock, knock. Life fell on him with savagery: you couldn't blame him if he never faced it again in sixty years. He got out of bed, carefully from habit put on his bedroom slippers, and tiptoed to the door: it wasn't quite dark on the landing below because the curtains had been taken down for the cleaners and the light from the street came in through the tall windows. Mrs. Baines had her hand on the glass door-knob; she was carefully turning it; he screamed: 'Baines, Baines.'

Mrs. Baines turned and saw him cowering in his pyjamas by the banisters; he was helpless, more helpless even than Baines, and cruelty grew at the sight of him and drove her up the stairs. The nightmare was on him again and he couldn't move; he hadn't any more courage left for ever; he'd spent it all, had been allowed no time to let it grow, no years of gradual hardening; he couldn't even scream.

But the first cry had brought Baines out of the best spare bedroom and he moved quicker than Mrs. Baines. She hadn't reached the top of the stairs be-

fore he'd caught her round the waist. She drove her
black cotton gloves at his face and he bit her hand.
He hadn't time to think, he fought her savagely like
a stranger, but she fought back with knowledgeable
hate. She was going to teach them all and it didn't
really matter whom she began with; they had all
deceived her; but the old image in the glass was by
her side, telling her she must be dignified, she wasn't
young enough to yield her dignity; she could beat
his face, but she mustn't bite; she could push, but
she mustn't kick.

Age and dust and nothing to hope for were her
handicaps. She went over the banisters in a flurry of
black clothes and fell into the hall; she lay before
the front door like a sack of coals which should have
gone down the area into the basement. Philip saw;
Emmy saw; she sat down suddenly in the doorway
of the best spare bedroom with her eyes open as if
she were too tired to stand any longer. Baines went
slowly down into the hall.

It wasn't hard for Philip to escape; they'd forgotten him completely; he went down the back, the
servants' stairs, because Mrs. Baines was in the hall;
he didn't understand what she was doing lying there;
like the startling pictures in a book no one had read
to him, the things he didn't understand terrified him.
The whole house had been turned over to the grown-
up world; he wasn't safe in the night-nursery; their
passions had flooded it. The only thing he could do
was to get away, by the back stair, and up through
the area, and never come back. You didn't think of
the cold, of the need of food and sleep; for an hour
it would seem quite possible to escape from people
for ever.

He was wearing pyjamas and bedroom slippers

when he came up into the square, but there was no one to see him. It was that hour of the evening in a residential district when everyone is at the theatre or at home. He climbed over the iron railings into the little garden: the plane-trees spread their large pale palms between him and the sky. It might have been an illimitable forest into which he had escaped. He crouched behind a trunk and the wolves retreated; it seemed to him between the little iron seat and the tree-trunk that no one would ever find him again. A kind of embittered happiness and self-pity made him cry; he was lost; there wouldn't be any more secrets to keep; he surrendered responsibility once and for all. Let grown-up people keep to their world and he would keep to his, safe in the small garden between the plane-trees. 'In the lost childhood of Judas Christ was betrayed'; you could almost see the small unformed face hardening into the deep dilettante selfishness of age.

Presently the door of 48 opened and Baines looked this way and that; then he signalled with his hand and Emmy came; it was as if they were only just in time for a train, they hadn't a chance of saying good-bye; she went quickly by like a face at a window swept past the platform, pale and unhappy and not wanting to go. Baines went in again and shut the door; the light was lit in the basement, and a policeman walked round the square, looking into the areas. You could tell how many families were at home by the lights behind the first-floor curtains.

Philip explored the garden: it didn't take long: a twenty-yard square of bushes and plane-trees, two iron seats and a gravel path, a padlocked gate at either end, a scuffle of old leaves. But he couldn't stay: something stirred in the bushes and two illuminated eyes peered out at him like a Siberian wolf, and he thought how terrible it would be if Mrs. Baines found him there. He'd have no time to climb the railings; she'd seize him from behind.

He left the square at the unfashionable end and was immediately among the fish-and-chip shops, the little stationers selling Bagatelle, among the accommodation addresses and the dingy hotels with open doors. There were few people about because the pubs were open, but a blowsy woman carrying a parcel called out to him across the street and the commissionaire outside a cinema would have stopped him if he hadn't crossed the road. He went deeper: you could go farther and lose yourself more completely here than among the plane-trees. On the fringe of the square he was in danger of being stopped and taken back: it was obvious where he belonged: but as he went deeper he lost the marks of his origin. It was a warm night: any child in those free-living parts might be expected to play truant from bed. He found a kind of camaraderie even among grown-up people; he might have been a neighbour's child as he went quickly by, but they weren't going to tell on him, they'd been young once themselves. He picked up a protective coating of dust from the pavements, of smuts from the trains which passed along the backs in a spray of fire. Once he was caught in a knot of children running away from something or somebody, laughing as they ran; he was whirled with them round a turning and abandoned, with a sticky fruit-drop in his hand.

He couldn't have been more lost; but he hadn't the stamina to keep on. At first he feared that someone would stop him; after an hour he hoped that someone would. He couldn't find his way back, and in any case he was afraid of arriving home alone; he was afraid of Mrs. Baines, more afraid than he had ever been. Baines was his friend, but something had happened which gave Mrs. Baines all the power. He began to loiter on purpose to be noticed, but no one noticed him. Families were having a last breather on the doorsteps, the refuse bins had been put out and bits of cabbage stalks soiled his slippers. The air was full of voices, but he was cut off; these people were strangers and would always now be strangers; they were marked by Mrs. Baines and he shied away from them into a deep class-consciousness. He had been afraid of policemen, but now he wanted one to take him home; even Mrs. Baines could do nothing against a policeman. He sidled past a constable who was directing traffic, but he was too busy to pay him any attention. Philip sat down against a wall and cried.

It hadn't occurred to him that that was the easiest way, that all you had to do was to surrender, to show you were beaten and accept kindness . . . It was lavished on him at once by two women and a pawn-broker. Another policeman appeared, a young man with a sharp incredulous face. He looked as if he noted everything he saw in pocket-books and drew conclusions. A woman offered to see Philip home, but he didn't trust her: she wasn't a match for Mrs. Baines immobile in the hall. He wouldn't give his address; he said he was afraid to go home. He had his way; he got his protection. 'I'll take him to the station,' the policeman said, and holding him awkwardly by the hand (he wasn't married; he had his career to make) he led him round the corner, up the stone stairs into the little bare over-heated room where Justice waited.

V

Justice waited behind a wooden counter on a high stool; it wore a heavy moustache; it was kindly and had six children ('three of them nippers like yourself'); it wasn't really interested in Philip, but it pretended to be, it wrote the address down and sent a constable to fetch a glass of milk. But the young constable was interested; he had a nose for things.

'Your home's on the telephone, I suppose,' Justice said. 'We'll ring them up and say you are safe. They'll fetch you very soon. What's your name, sonny?'

'Philip.'

'Your other name.'

'I haven't got another name.' He didn't want to be fetched; he wanted to be taken home by someone who would impress even Mrs. Baines. The constable watched him, watched the way he drank the milk, watched him when he winced away from questions.

'What made you run away? Playing truant, eh?'

'I don't know.'

'You oughtn't to do it, young fellow. Think how anxious your father and mother will be.'

'They are away.'

'Well, your nurse.'

'I haven't got one.'

'Who looks after you, then?' That question went home. Philip saw Mrs. Baines coming up the stairs at him, the heap of black cotton in the hall. He began to cry.

'Now, now, now,' the sergeant said. He didn't know what to do; he wished his wife were with him; even a policewoman might have been useful.

'Don't you think it's funny,' the constable said, 'that there hasn't been an inquiry?'

'They think he's tucked up in bed.'

'You are scared, aren't you?' the constable said. 'What scared you?'

'I don't know.'

'Somebody hurt you?'

'No.'

'He's had bad dreams,' the sergeant said. 'Thought the house was on fire, I expect. I've brought up six of them. Rose is due back. She'll take him home.'

'I want to go home with you,' Philip said; he tried to smile at the constable, but the deceit was immature and unsuccessful.

'I'd better go,' the constable said. 'There may be something wrong.'

'Nonsense,' the sergeant said. 'It's a woman's job. Tact is what you need. Here's Rose. Pull up your stockings, Rose. You're a disgrace to the Force. I've got a job of work for you.' Rose shambled in: black cotton stockings drooping over her boots, a gawky Girl Guide manner, a hoarse hostile voice. 'More tarts, I suppose.'

'No, you've got to see this young man home.' She looked at him owlishly.

'I won't go with her,' Philip said. He began to cry again. 'I don't like her.'

'More of that womanly charm, Rose,' the sergeant said. The telephone rang on his desk. He lifted the receiver. 'What? What's that?' he said. 'Number 48? You've got a doctor?' He put his hand over the telephone mouth. 'No wonder this nipper wasn't reported,' he said. 'They've been too busy. An accident. Woman slipped on the area stairs.'

'Serious?' the constable asked. The sergeant

mouthed at him; you didn't mention the word death
before a child (didn't he know? he had six of them),
you made noises in the throat, you grimaced, a com-
plicated shorthand for a word of only five letters
anyway.

'You'd better go, after all,' he said, 'and make a
report. The doctor's there.'

Rose shambled from the stove; pink apply-dapply
cheeks, loose stockings. She stuck her hands behind
her. Her large morgue-like mouth was full of blackened teeth. 'You told me to take him and now just
because something interesting . . . I don't expect
justice from a man . . .'

'Who's at the house?' the constable asked.

'The butler.'

'You don't think,' the constable said, 'he saw . . .'

'Trust me,' the sergeant said. 'I've brought up six.
I know 'em through and through. You can't teach
me anything about children.'

'He seemed scared about something.'

'Dreams,' the sergeant said.

'What name?'

'Baines.'

'This Mr. Baines,' the constable said to Philip,
'you like him, eh? He's good to you?' They were
trying to get something out of him; he was suspicious of the whole roomful of them; he said
'yes' without conviction because he was afraid
at any moment of more responsibilities, more
secrets.

'And Mrs. Baines?'

'Yes.'

They consulted together by the desk. Rose was
hoarsely aggrieved; she was like a female imper-
sonator, she bore her womanhood with an unnatural

emphasis even while she scorned it in her creased
stockings and her weather-exposed face. The char-
coal shifted in the stove; the room was over-heated
in the mild late summer evening. A notice on the
wall described a body found in the Thames, or
rather the body's clothes: wool vest, wool pants,
wool shirt with blue stripes, size ten boots, blue
serge suit worn at the elbows, fifteen-and-a-half
celluloid collar. They couldn't find anything to say
about the body, except its measurements, it was just
an ordinary body.

'Come along,' the constable said. He was interested, he was glad to be going, but he couldn't
help being embarrassed by his company, a small boy
in pyjamas. His nose smelt something, he didn't
know what, but he smarted at the sight of the amusement they caused: the pubs had closed and the streets
were full again of men making as long a day of it as
they could. He hurried through the less frequented
streets, chose the darker pavements, wouldn't loiter,
and Philip wanted more and more to loiter, pulling
at his hand, dragging with his feet. He dreaded the
sight of Mrs. Baines waiting in the hall: he knew
now that she was dead. The sergeant's mouthings
had conveyed that; but she wasn't buried; she wasn't
out of sight; he was going to see a dead person in
the hall when the door opened.

The light was on in the basement, and to his relief
the constable made for the area steps. Perhaps he
wouldn't have to see Mrs. Baines at all. The constable knocked on the door because it was too dark
to see the bell, and Baines answered. He stood there
in the doorway of the neat bright basement room
and you could see the sad complacent plausible sentence he had prepared wither at the sight of Philip;

he hadn't expected Philip to return like that in the policeman's company. He had to begin thinking all over again; he wasn't a deceptive man; if it hadn't been for Emmy he would have been quite ready to let the truth lead him where it would.

'Mr. Baines?' the constable asked.

He nodded; he hadn't found the right words; he was daunted by the shrewd knowing face, the sudden appearance of Philip there.

'This little boy from here?'

'Yes,' Baines said. Philip could tell that there was a message he was trying to convey, but he shut his mind to it. He loved Baines, but Baines had involved him in secrets, in fears he didn't understand. The glowing morning thought 'This is life' had become under Baines's tuition the repugnant memory, 'That was life': the musty hair across the mouth, the breathless cruel tortured inquiry 'Where are they?', the heap of black cotton tipped into the hall. That was what happened when you loved: you got involved; and Philip extricated himself from life, from love, from Baines with a merciless egotism.

There had been things between them, but he laid them low, as a retreating army cuts the wires, destroys the bridges. In the abandoned country you may leave much that is dear—a morning in the Park, an ice at a Corner House, sausages for supper—but more is concerned in the retreat than temporary losses. There are old people who, as the tractors wheel away, implore to be taken, but you can't risk the rearguard for their sake: a whole prolonged retreat from life, from care, from human relationships is involved.

'The doctor's here,' Baines said. He nodded at the door, moistened his mouth, kept his eyes on Philip,

begging for something like a dog you can't understand. 'There's nothing to be done. She slipped on
these stone basement stairs. I was in here. I heard
her fall.' He wouldn't look at the notebook, at the
constable's tiny spidery writing which got a terrible
lot on one page.

'Did the boy see anything?'

'He can't have done. I thought he was in bed.
Hadn't he better go up? It's a shocking thing. Oh,'
Baines said, losing control, 'it's a shocking thing for
a child.'

'She's through there?' the constable asked.

'I haven't moved her an inch,' Baines said.

'He'd better then—'

'Go up the area and through the hall,' Baines said
and again he begged dumbly like a dog: one more
secret, keep this secret, do this for old Baines, he
won't ask another.

'Come along,' the constable said. 'I'll see you up
to bed. You're a gentleman; you must come in the
proper way through the front door like the master
should. Or will you go along with him, Mr. Baines,
while I see the doctor?'

'Yes,' Baines said, 'I'll go.' He came across the
room to Philip, begging, begging, all the way with
his soft old stupid expression: this is Baines, the old
Coaster; what about a palm-oil chop, eh?; a man's
life; forty niggers; never used a gun; I tell you I
couldn't help loving them: it wasn't what we call
love, nothing we could understand. The messages
flickered out from the last posts at the border, im-
ploring, beseeching, reminding: this is your old
friend Baines; what about an elevens; a glass of
ginger-pop won't do you any harm; sausages; a long
day. But the wires were cut, the messages just faded

out into the enormous vacancy of the neat scrubbed room in which there had never been a place where a man could hide his secrets.

'Come along, Phil, it's bedtime. We'll just go up the steps . . .' Tap, tap, tap, at the telegraph; you may get through, you can't tell, somebody may mend the right wire. 'And in at the front door.'

'No,' Philip said, 'no. I won't go. You can't make me go. I'll fight. I won't see her.'

The constable turned on them quickly. 'What's that? Why won't you go?'

'She's in the hall,' Philip said. 'I know she's in the hall. And she's dead. I won't see her.'

'You moved her then?' the constable said to Baines. 'All the way down here? You've been lying, eh? That means you had to tidy up . . . Were you alone?'

'Emmy,' Philip said, 'Emmy.' He wasn't going to keep any more secrets: he was going to finish once and for all with everything, with Baines and Mrs. Baines and the grown-up life beyond him; it wasn't his business and never, never again, he decided, would he share their confidences and companionship. 'It was all Emmy's fault,' he protested with a quaver which reminded Baines that after all he was only a child; it had been hopeless to expect help there; he was a child; he didn't understand what it all meant; he couldn't read this shorthand of terror; he'd had a long day and he was tired out. You could see him dropping asleep where he stood against the dresser, dropping back into the comfortable nursery peace. You couldn't blame him. When he woke in the morning, he'd hardly remember a thing.

'Out with it,' the constable said, addressing Baines with professional ferocity, 'who is she?' just as the

old man sixty years later startled his secretary, his
only watcher, asking, 'Who is she? Who is she?'
dropping lower and lower into death, passing on the
way perhaps the image of Baines: Baines hopeless,
Baines letting his head drop, Baines 'coming clean'.

H. E. BATES

The Woman Who Had Imagination

I

THE yellow brake climbed slowly uphill out of the town, leaving behind it the last ugly red houses; the two white horses broke into an abrupt trot along the level road, the brasses tinkling softly and winking brilliantly in the noon sunshine, and all the passengers who had leaned forward up the hill to ease the strain on the horses leaned back with relief and then lurched forward again with the sudden onward jerk of the brake, the men's straw boaters knocking against the wide sunshades and the big flowered hats of the giggling women. There were many shouts of mock alarm and laughter: 'Whoops! What ho, she bumps! Whoa! mare! Want to throw us out? Whoa? Get off my lap! Stop the brake, me voice's slipped down me trousers' leg! What's the matter? Horses going to a fire or something? Oh Lord, me bandeau's slipped! Get off my lap I tell you! Whoops! Steady! How d'ye think we're going to sing after this? Stop 'em, me voice's crawling up me other leg! Oh, ain't he a case? Oh dear! Ain't he a caution? What ho! Now we're off! Oh, don't he say some bits? Now we're off! Altogether! Whoops! Dearie! Altogether!'

Gradually the parasols became still and circumspect, the women gave their hatpins little tidying pushes and smoothed their dresses, and the horses fell automatically into a smoother pace, the sound of running wheels and the click-clocking of hoofs becoming an unchanged and sleepy rhythm in the midsummer air.

At the rear of the brake, wedged closely in between a hawking fishmonger who still gave off an odour of red herrings, and a balloon of a woman who was sucking rosebud cachous and wheezing for breath as though she had swallowed a button-whistle, sat a youth of twenty. At the height of the giggling and banting and shouting he sat in unsmiling silence. He looked proud and bored. The brake was filled with the Orpheus Male Voice Glee Singers and their wives and sweethearts. That afternoon and again in the evening they were to sing on the lawns of a big house, in competition with a score of other choirs, ten miles on in the heart of the country. Aloof and sensitive, the youth had made up his mind that he was above such things.

'Like a cachou, 'Enry?' said the stout woman.

'No thanks,' he said.

'Real rose. Make your breath smell beautiful.'

'No thanks.'

He had come on the outing against his will. And now—cachous! He looked about him with a kind of bored disgust in which there was also something unhappy. The whole brake was tittering and chattering with a gaiety that seemed to him puerile and maddening. The strong odours of violet and lavender perfumes and the stout woman's rose-scented cachous mingled with the hot smell of horses and sun-scorched varnish and men's cheap hair-oil. He caught now and then a breath of some dark carnation from a buttonhole, but the clove-sweetness would become mixed with the odour of stale red herrings. At the front of the brake he could see his father, a little man dressed in a straw hat cocked on the back of his head and a dapper grey suit with the jacket thrown wide open in order to show off a pale yellow waistcoat with pearl buttons. Opposite his father sat his mother, plump, double-chinned, with big adoring eyes, dressed in a lavender-grey dress and hat to match his father's suit. Round her neck she wore a thin band of black velvet. The very latest! No other woman in the brake sported a band of black velvet. Yet he thought his mother looked hot and uncomfortable, as though the black velvet were strangling her, and his father sat as though she never existed, bobbing constantly up and down to call to someone in the rear of the brake, talking excitedly to anyone and everyone but her.

It was solely because of his father that Henry Solly had come on the outing. Solly! What a name! His father was conductor of the choir, a sort of musical Napoleon, very small and absurdly vain, who wanted to conquer the world with the sound of his own voice. Stout, excitable, electric, he was like a little Napoleonic Jack-in-the-box, with tiny cock-sure blue eyes, a fair, sharp-waxed moustache, and a kind of clockwork chattering voice that changed as though by a miracle, when he sang, into a bass of magnificent tone, warm, rich and strong. By profession he was a draper, but the shop was gloomily unattractive and poorly patronized, so that Alfred found a good deal of time to sit in the back living-room and practise hymns and oratorio and part-songs on the American organ while Henry attended the shop. It was a boring, passionless, depressing existence. 'When you grow up, Henry,' his father had been fond of saying, 'you'll have to wait in the shop.' He often wondered and sometimes still con-

tinued to wonder what it was he must wait for?
Already he had now been seven years in the shop,
waiting. And he had begun to feel now that he would
go on for another twenty, thirty, perhaps even fifty
years, still waiting and still wondering what he was
waiting for. There he would be, fifty years hence,
still dusting and re-arranging the thick flannel shirts,
pants, waistcoats, corduroy trousers, body-belts,
patent collar fasteners, stiff cuffs and starched white
dickies; still writing the little white cards to pin on
the frowzy articles in the window, *Solly for Style—
Solly for Smartness—Solly for Shirts—Socks—Suits
—Studs and Suspenders—Solly for Everything*; still
dusting and setting out the window every Monday
morning, carrying in the absurd naked dummies,
dressing them and pinning on them, as he did now,
a card saying *The Latest for 1902*, only changing
the style of the dresses and the date as he grew older.
He saw himself as some fatuous patriarchal draper
grown half-idiotic from years behind a counter, his
mind starved and enfeebled by lack of the com-
monest pleasures of the world. And there he would
be, still waiting, with the certainty of achieving
nothing but death. He felt sometimes as if he could
hurl a dummy through the shop window on some
dead and empty Monday morning and then walk
out and never come back again. Or if only one of
those grey, naked ladies' dummies would come to
life!

At the same smooth and now monotonous pace
the brake went on into the heart of the country. All
the time he sat silent and contemplative. He was
fair-haired, with a pale, almost nervously sensitive
face that had something attractive in its very pallor
and in the intensity of the blue eyes and the small

mobile mouth. His body, slight and undeveloped from years of waiting in the ill-ventilated and gloomy shop, had something restless and almost anxious about it even as he sat still and stared from the faces in the brake to the fields and woods, quivering and bright in the noon heat, that travelled smoothly past like some slowly unwound sun-golden panorama. It had about it also something stiff and unsatisfied and unhappy. His straw hat was fastened with a black silk guard to the lapel of his coat; it was his mother's idea: as though on that windless, burning day his straw hat would blow off! And just as his straw hat was tied to him he felt tied to the brake, the absurd giggling passengers and the monotony of his own thoughts. As he sat there, unhappily wishing he had never come, he thought dismally of the afternoon ahead—singing, tea in a noisy marquee, more singing on the lawns in the summer twilight, refreshments, more singing, the ride home, and more singing again. Singing! It would have been different if the word had meant anything to him. But he couldn't sing a single note correctly or in tune. How often had his father offered him half a crown if he could sing, without going sharp or flat, one verse of 'The Day Thou Gavest, Lord, is Ended.' He had never succeeded.

'Can you 'itch up a bit?' said the fishmonger suddenly.

Henry moved along the plush seat a fraction, but without speaking.

'That's better. Ain't it hot? If this weather holds I'm a dunner. Fish won't keep, y'know. I had a case o' fresh whiting in yesterday and the missus fainted. Went clean off. That's the fish-trade. See y' money go bad under your eyes.'

The fishmonger's coarse red skin oozed little yellow streams of sweat, which he kept wiping off with his handkerchief, puffing heavily as he took off his bowler hat and mopped his red bald head. He was renowned for his voice, a light sweet tenor, and for his moving and passionate interpretation of 'Come into the Garden, Maud.'

'Blimey,' he kept saying. 'I'm done like a dinner.'

The road, after climbing up a little, had begun to drop down again towards a wooded valley. The country stretched out infinitely green and yellow under the pure intensity of noon light. In the near distance the road shimmered under the heat like quivering water. Cattle had gathered under the shade of trees, unmoving except for the clockwork flicking of their tails as they stared at the passing brake with its crowd of laughing passengers. By a woodside there was a murmur of doves invisible in the thick-leaved trees, warm, liquid, sleepy, and no other bird-sound except the occasional cry of a jay disturbed by the noise of wheels and voices. The brief cool wood-shade was like a draught of water; the shrill voices and clocking hoofs made cool empty echoes in the deep sun-flickered shadowy silence. Someone in the brake reached up and shook a low-hanging bough that in swishing back again seemed to set all the leaves in the wood rustling with a soft, dry, endless whispering. The scent of honeysuckle was suddenly very strong and exquisite, pouring out from the wood in a sweet invisible mist that seemed to disperse as soon as the brake was out in the sunshine again. After the dark coolness of the overhanging trees the day was blinding and burning. And out in the full glare of the sunlight the world was steeped in other scents, the smell of drying hay, the thick vanilla odour of meadow-sweet, the exotic heavenliness of lime trees.

The road went down to a village. There, at a whitewashed public-house with red geraniums blazing vividly in the window-boxes, the brake pulled up to a concert of cries and laughter.

'Whoa! What's the matter with you, old horses? Whoa there! Are they teetotallers? Whoa!'

Shouting and laughing, the passengers began to alight and vanish into the public-house. Those who did not drink walked about to stretch their legs or stood in the shade of the inn wall. Men reappeared from the public-house doorway with glasses of golden beer, their mouths ringed with beads of foam. From the tap-room a bass voice boomed and pompommed deep impromptu notes of noisy pleasure.

Henry got down from the brake and walked about moodily. His father and mother stood in the shade, each drinking a small lemonade.

'Get yourself a lemon, 'Enry, my boy,' said his father.

'No thanks.'

'Feel dicky?'

'I'm all right.'

'Liven yourself up then. Haven't lost nothing, have you?'

'I'm all right,' said Henry.

He refused to sip of his mother's lemonade and walked away. He felt bored, morose, out of touch with everyone.

With relief he saw the passengers emerge from the public-house and begin to climb back into the brake. He climbed up also and found himself sitting, this time, between a tall scraggy man with a peg-leg who gave off the mustily dry odour of leather, and a girl of his own age who was dressed as if she were going to a baptism, in a white silk dress, white straw hat, long white gloves that reached to her elbows, white cotton stockings, white shoes and a white sunshade which she carried elegantly over her left shoulder.

'Oh! It's going to be marvellous,' she said.

'What is?' he said. 'Don't poke me in the eye with that sunshade.'

'The choir, the house, everything.'

'Glad you think so,' he said.

The brake had begun to move again, the shouting and excited laughter of the passengers half drowning the girl's voice and his own. And above the din of the brake's departure there arose the sound of insistent argument.

'I tell you it's right! Seen it times with my own eyes.'

'You dreamt it.'

'Dreamt it! I *seen* it. Plain as a pikestaff.'

'In a churchyard? Tell your grandmother.'

'Well, if you don't believe me, will you bet on it? You're so cocky.'

'Ah, I'll bet you. Any money. Anything you like.'

'All right. You'll bet as what I've told you ain't on that tombstone in Polwick churchyard? You'll bet on that?'

'Ah! I'll bet you. And I *know* it ain't.'

'Well, go on. How much?'

'Tanner.'

There were shouts of ironical laughter and reckless encouragement. A little black frizzy-haired man was bobbing excitedly up and down on the brake seat urging a large blond man wearing a cream tearose in his buttonhole to increase the bet. 'Go on.

Make it sixpence ha'penny. You're so cocky. How can you lose? You know it ain't there, don't you? Go on.'

'Sixpence,' said the blond man. 'I said sixpence and I mean sixpence.'

'You'll go to ruin fast.'

'I dare say. But I said sixpence and I mean sixpence. And here's me money.'

'All right! Let the driver hold it.'

The blond man handed his money to the fishmonger, who had climbed up to sit by the driver, and then began to urge the little man:

'Give him your money. Go on. And say good-bye to it while you're at it. Go on, say good-bye to it. Ah, it's no use spitting on it. It's the last you'll ever see o' that tanner,'

'You're so cocky. Why didn't you bet a quid?'

'Ah, why didn't I?'

Up on the driving-seat the driver and the fishmonger rolled against each other in sudden storms of laughter. Women giggled and men called out to each other, making dark insinuations, urging the driver to stop at the churchyard.

Opposite Henry and the girl a handsome man with a dark moustache and wearing a straw hat at a devilish angle had rested his hand with a sort of stealthy nonchalance on the knee of a school teacher in pink. She in turn averted her eyes, trying to appear as though she were thinking profound, far-off, earnest thoughts.

'What's the matter?' he said.

'It's so hot,' she murmured.

'So are you,' he whispered.

The school teacher's neck flushed crimson and the blood surged up into her face.

And as if to cover up her own embarrassment the girl at Henry's side began to talk in a rather louder voice to him, but her prim banal voice became lost for him in the giggling and talking of the other passengers, the loud-voiced arguments about the bet, the everlasting sound of wheels and hoofs on the rough, sun-baked road. Down in the valley the sun seemed hotter than ever. The brake passed a group of haymakers resting and sleeping in the noon-heat under the shade of a great elm tree. They waved and called with sleepy greetings. A woman sitting among them suckling a baby looked up with sun-tired eyes. Farther on a group of naked boys bathing in a sloe-fringed pond jumped up and down in the sun-silvered water and about the grass pond-bank, waving their wet arms and flagging their towels. In the brake there was a thin ripple of giggling, the women suddenly ducking their heads together and whispering with suppressed excitement. The blond man and the frizzy-haired dark man argued and taunted each other with unending but friendly vehemence. And under the intense sunshine and the dazzling fierce July light the slowness of the brake was intolerable. Up the hills it crawled as though the horses were sick. Down hill the brakes hissed and checked the wheels into the deathly pace of a funeral. Henry sat drugged by the heat and the wearisome pace of progress. Faintly, through the sun-heavy air, came the strokes of one o'clock from a church tower. Already it was as if the brake had travelled all day. And now, with the strokes of the clock dying away and leaving the air limitlessly silent beyond the little noises of the brake it seemed suddenly as if the journey might last for ever.

Twenty minutes later the brake went down hill

through an avenue of elms towards a square church tower rising like a small sturdy grey fortress out of a village that seemed asleep except for a batch of black hens dust-bathing in the hot road. The sudden coming of the brake sent the fowls squawking and cluttering away in panic-feathered half-flight.

'Ah! Your old horses are too slow for a funeral. Might have had a Sunday dinner for nothing if you'd been sharper. What d'ye feed 'em on? Too slow to run over an old hen. Gee there! Tickle 'em up a bit.' And mingled with these shouts the repeated cry:

'And don't forget to stop at the churchyard.'

The frizzy-haired man began to stand up and wave his arms. He became ironically tender towards the blond man. 'I feel sorry for you. It's like taking money from a kid. Pity your mother ever let you come out.' The blond man kept shaking his head with silent wisdom. The brake crawled slowly by the churchyard wall. 'A bit farther,' cried the dark man with excitement. 'T'other side o' that yew-tree. Gee up a bit.' The passengers were craning their necks, laughing, standing up, bantering remarks. With mock sadness the frizzy-haired man patted the blond man on the back, shaking his head. 'Feel sorry for you,' he said in a wickedly dismal voice. The blond man airily waved his hand with a gesture of pity. 'Not half so sorry as you'll feel for yourself in a minute,' he said.

The frizzy-haired man did not listen. He was beginning to survey the tombstones with great excitement, craning his neck. Suddenly the blond man seized him and held him aloft like a child.

'Now can you see, ducky?' he cried.

'A bit farther! Farther! Steady now. Whoa there! Whoa!'

The brake stopped. The small man wriggled down from the blond man's arms. There arose a pandemonium of laughter and shouts in the brake. The driver stood up and chinked the money in his hand. The small man spoke with twinkling irony.

'Oh! No, it ain't there, is it? It ain't there? It's melted. Well, well, I must be boss-eyed. The sun's so hot it's melted. Would you believe it? Fancy that. Just fancy that. It ain't there.'

The blond man was staring with dumb gloom at a gravestone.

'What are you looking at?' began the small man mercilessly. 'What?—If it ain't a tombstone I'll never. Well, well!'

'I'll be damned,' the blond man was saying slowly. 'I'll be damned.'

'Read it!' yelled the little man in triumph.

'I've read it.'

'Read it aloud.'

'Ah, what d'ye take me for? Three pen'worth o' tripe? You read it.'

'All right. It's worth it.' Solemnly the small man read out the rhyme on the tombstone:

> Let wind go free where'er you be:
> In chapel or in church.
> For wind it was the death of me.

Suddenly the driver clicked at the horses and the brake jerked violently on. The women shrieked, the blond man sat disconsolate, the small man piped in triumph above the bubbling and spluttering of laughter.

Henry sat with a little smile on his lips, faintly aloof, his thoughts lofty and cool. He felt wonder-

fully above and detached from the puerile jokes and
empty laughter of the rest of the brake, his brain
manufacturing little self-conscious philosophies
which seemed very clever, and when the mood
seemed to be dying at last it was suddenly revived
by the spectacle of his father standing up in the
brake, signalling the driver to halt for a moment
and delivering his final words of advice and admoni-
tion to the choir.

'Well, we shall be there in a few more minutes.
And I just want to remind you of a few things. We've
had our little jokes. And now I want to be serious
for ten seconds. This is a serious business. We are
down to start singing at four o'clock. All hear that?
Four o'clock. Four o'clock on the big lawn in front
of the house. We shall start off with 'Calm was the
Sea'; and then after that it will be 'On the Banks of
Allan Water' and then last of all 'My love is Like a
Red, Red Rose'. We shall sing these three in the
afternoon. And then in the evening, at seven o'clock,
we shall sing a test piece chosen from one of these
and three others. It might be one of these three. It
might not. It might be anything. We don't know.
We've got to stand ready to sing anything at a
moment's notice.' He waved his arms up and down
constantly in his excitement. His voice was like that
of a little chattering ventriloquist's doll. 'And one
more thing. Remember the words. When it says
"Calm was the Sea" don't sing it as if it were "The
Wreck of the Hesperus", but sing it as if it were
calm—calm and soft. Imagine it. Lovely day. Boats
hardly moving. Softly, softly, does it, softly. Imagine
it. Imagine you're on Yarmouth pier if you like,
looking at the sea. Water hardly moves. And then
"the wandering breezes". Soft again, very soft. Let

them wander. Let them flow from you. And breezes
—remember it's breezes. Not a thunderstorm. Still
soft—you'll see in the copy is marked *dulce*. Italian
word—means sweet, soft, gentle. Remember dulci-
mer. Close your eyes if you like. Sing it as if you
was dreaming.' He closed his fair-lashed eyes and
put on a rapt, dreamy expression of soft ecstasy.
'Dah—dah-dah—daaah-dah!' he sang in a soft fal-
setto. 'Wand'ring bre-e-e-zes.' He opened his eyes.
'Feeling—that's it—feeling. Expression. That's
everything. Anybody can bellow like a bull. But
that's not singing. That's not interpretation. Not
feeling. And don't be afraid of how you look. The
judges aren't looking to see how pretty you are.
They're *listening*. Well, make them listen, soft,
softly does it, remember, softly.'

His voice trailed off to a fine whisper and he sat
down. Henry smiled and the brake went on, the passengers in a changed mood after his father's words,
the women tidying their hats and smoothing their
stiff puff-sleeves and long dresses, the men fingering
their buttonholes, clearing their throats and sitting
in silence as though suddenly musingly nervous of
the thought of the singing.

The country began to change also. The yellowing
wheat-fields, the dark fields of roots shining and
drooping in the hot sun, the parched hayfields and
woods were replaced by an immense park of old
dark trees under which the grass was still spring
green and sweet. Far off, timid and startled, groups
of young deer, palest brown against the dark tree-
shadows, with an occasional dark antlered, resentful stag, stood and watched the brake go past with
glassy, wondering eyes. Soon, through wider spaces
between the trees, there was the big house itself, a

square, stone tall-windowed place, with a carved
stone balustrade round the lead roof and immense
black cedars encircling the lawns. It looked cold
and sepulchral even against the rich darkness of the
trees in the hot sunlight.

The brake turned into the park through high iron
gates on which the family crest blazed in scarlet and
gold. It was as if it had driven into a churchyard.
The passengers were suddenly transformed, sitting
with a stiff, self-conscious silence upon them. As the
brake drove along under a great avenue of elms ex-
tending like a sombre nave up to the lawns of the
house, the horses fell into a walk. The fishmonger
sat very upright on the driver's seat, preening his
buttonhole, and the fat woman, sucking her last
cachou quickly, wiped her lips clean with her handkerchief. The handsome young man in a rakish
straw hat, taking his hand away from the school
teacher's knee, ceased his seductive whispers. The
carriage-drive emerged in an immense sweep from
under the dark avenue into the sunlight and curved
on between the lawns and the house. The brake
pulled up behind a row of other brakes standing
empty by a tall yew-hedge and the choir began to
alight, the men handing down the ladies from the
awkward back-step and the ladies giving little delicate shrieks and pretending to stumble. Henry's
father dragged out from under the brake seat an
immense portmanteau of music. From over the
lawns gay with parasols and flowing frocks, there
came a scent of new-mown grass and women's
dresses, the swooning breath of lime trees and a hum
of human voices like the sound of bees.

Across the lawn also came a man in an old panama
hat, a yellowish alpaca suit and a faded green bow,

beaming with smiles and gestures of aristocratic
idiocy.

'Oh, pardon, pardon me!' he cried. 'But 'oo are
you? Oh! Orpheus choir! Yes! Orpheus! Marvellous! T'ank you a t'ousand times for coming. Yes!
And if you desire anyt'ing please come to me. Any-
t'ing you like. Anyt'ing. And t'ank you a t'ousand
times for coming! T'ank you a t'ousand times! And
eez it not ze most marvellous day? Most marvellous!'

II

In the full heat of the afternoon, tired from walking
about the crowded lawns in the fierce sunshine and
even more bored than he had been in the brake,
Henry saw people passing in and out of the house
through a side door on the terrace. Following them,
he found himself in a wide lofty entrance hall that
had about it the queer half-scented coolness of a
church and the same hollow silence broken at inter-
vals by the sound of voices and strange receding
and returning echoes. He took off his straw hat and
wiped his sweaty forehead with his handkerchief.
The air felt as cool as a leaf on his hot face. In
answer to his question a negative-faced manservant
standing at ease like a tired soldier at the foot of a
wide stone staircase told him that the house was
open to visitors till five o'clock. He walked quietly
up the stairs, his feet soundless on the heavy carpet,
staring at the magnificence of gilded ceilings, dim
tapestries, old dark portraits, immense sparkling
chandeliers, touching the flower-smoothness of old
chests and chairs with his finger-tips as he passed.
Upstairs he went in and out of innumerable rooms,
staring at vast canopied bedsteads, lacquered cabi-

nets filled with never-opened books and fragile china, dim painted screens and ornate fireplaces of cold blue-veined marble. He wondered all the time who had ever lived and slept there, contrasting it all unconsciously with the room behind the shop at home, with the cheap German silk-fronted piano, the brass gas-brackets, the cane music-rack, the broken revolving piano stool, the flashy green jars containing aspidistras whose leaves his mother counted and sponged religiously every Saturday. The place had an air of unreality. The yellow blinds, drawn to keep out the sun, threw down a strange shadowy apricot light. Here and there rents in the blinds let in streaks of dusty sunlight. When he put his hand on the walls they struck cold and damp. Across the floors he noticed trails of candle-grease dropped perhaps by some servant coming in to lower the blinds at night or let them up again in the morning. How long ago? he wondered. There was a melancholy air of the past, of vague, dead, forgotten things. There was also a curious feeling of poverty about it all in spite of that rich magnificence. The blinds were old and stained, the paint was cracked and dirty, and here and there a ceiling had crumbled away, revealing naked laths draped with black skeins of cobweb.

Going slowly up the second flight of stairs, he stopped now and then to look at the prints on the walls. A clock in the house struck four, the notes very soft and delicate, a silver water-sound. Some visitors passed him, coming down, their voices dying away down the two flights of stairs like a vague chant. Going up, he found himself in a bare corridor.

Walking into a room by one door and out by another he turned along a narrow corridor in order

to return to the stairs, but the passage seemed contained within itself, to lead nowhere. And in a moment he was lost. Trying to go back to the room
through which he had come he tried a door, but it
was locked. He began to try other doors, which
were also locked. It was some minutes before he
found a door which opened.

Relieved, he hurried through the room. But half-
way across the floor, thinking of nothing but escap-
ing by the opposite door, he was startled into a fresh
panic by a voice:

'But unfortunately, in bestowing these embraces,
a pin in her ladyship's head-dress slightly scratching the child's neck, produced from this pattern of
gentleness, such violent screams, as could hardly be
outdone by any creature professedly noisy. The
mother's consternation was excessive; but it would
not surpass the alarm . . .'

At the word alarm he stopped. The voice stopped
too. He felt himself break out into a prickling sweat.
Across the room, with his thin fingers outstretched
to a low wood fire, sat an old man in a torn red
dressing-gown. He was sunk into a kind of sick
trance. By his side there was a woman, a young
woman. Arrested in the act of reading, she sat with
her averted head still and intense, looking across the
room with the blackest eyes he had ever seen, black
not only with their own richness of colour but with
an illimitable darkness of sheer melancholy.

'I'm lost,' Henry said.

'Lost?'

She stood upright as she echoed the word, rubbing the fingers of her left hand up and down the
yellow leather binding of the book. Trying to face
her he was sick with confusion. The old man turned

stiffly and stared at him also. The old eyes were pale and vacuous.

Suddenly the woman smiled.

'It's all right,' she said.

For some reason or other Henry could not answer her. He stood half-foolishly hypnotized by her figure, tall and wonderfully slender, her very long maroon-coloured dress, her unspeakably brilliant eyes. Her voice had in it a kind of mournful sweetness which held him fascinated.

At last he attempted to explain himself. He had no sooner begun than she cut him short:

'I'll show you the way,' she said.

He still could not answer. She turned to the old man:

'Sit still. I'll come back.'

'Where are you going?' he muttered querulously. 'Who's that young man?'

In one swift movement she turned from the old man to Henry and then back to the old man again, smiling at the youth with half-grave, half-vivacious eyes. And there was the same mischievous solemnity in her voice.

'He's the new gardener,' she said.

'Eh?'

'The new gardener. Here, take the book. Read a little till I come back. From the top of the page there. You see?'

'What? I'd like some tea.'

'All right.'

'It's not so frightfully warm in here either,' he said pettishly.

'Keep your dressing-gown buttoned. You're not likely to be warm. See, button it up.'

She fingered the buttons of his dressing-gown,

quickly, impatiently. And then, while he still protested and complained, she walked swiftly across the
room, opened the far door and vanished into the
passage outside. In bewilderment Henry followed
her. She shut the door quickly behind him.

'Well, now I'll see you out,' she said.

She began to walk away along the passage and he
followed her, a step or two behind. She walked
quickly with long, impatient steps, so that he had
difficulty in keeping up.

They walked along in silence except for the sound
of her dress swishing along the carpet until he
recognized a window at which he had stood and
looked down on the choir.

'I'm all right now,' he said. He began to utter dim
thanks and apologies.

'Go and enjoy yourself,' she said. 'Have you seen
the lake?'

'No.'

'Go and see it. Across the park and through the
rhododendron plantation. You'll find it. It's lovely.'

Before he could speak again she had turned away.
There was a brief flash of maroon in the passage,
the sound of her feet running quickly after she had
vanished. He waited a moment. But nothing happened, there was only a curious, almost audible
hush everywhere. Outside the singing had ceased.
He moved towards the stairs in a state of dejected
and tense astonishment.

III

The singing was over for the afternoon. There was
nothing to do but wander about the lawns and
terraces or take tea in the large flagged tea-tent.

Privileged ladies were playing croquet on a small lawn under the main terrace, giggling nervously as they struck the bright-coloured balls. Gentlemen in straw boaters and pin-striped cream flannel trousers with wide silk waist-bands applauded their shots delicately. There was an oppressive feeling of summer languor, a parade of gay hats and parasols and sweeping dresses. Henry went into the tea-tent for a cup of tea to escape the boredom of it all. Coming out again he met the fishmonger.

'Cheer up,' said the fishmonger.

'Oh! I'm all right.' He put on a casual air. 'I was wondering which was the way to the lake.'

'The lake?' said the fishmonger. His eyes began to dance like little bubbling peas as soon as he heard the word. The lake? What did he want with the lake? Becoming quite excited, he took hold of Henry's coat-sleeve confidentially and led him across the lawn. So he wanted to know the way to the lake? Well! Very strange. He wondered what he wanted with the lake? Not for fish by any chance? Oh! no, not for fish. Perhaps he didn't even know there were fish in the lake? Henry protested. He cut him short:

'Ah, you're dark, you're dark.'

Finally, losing a little of his excitement, he began to tell him of the days when, as a young man, he had fished in the lake. Fish! They hadn't breathing room. They were the days. But now there hadn't been fish, not a solitary fish, not a stickleback, pulled out of that lake for twenty years. 'Not since old Antonio came.' It was a shame, wickedness. He began to talk with lugubrious regret. Who was Antonio? Henry asked. The fishmonger echoed the words with tenor astonishment, his voice squeaking.

Antonio? Hadn't he seen him running about all over the place—'T'ank you a t'ousand times! T'ank you a t'ousand times!' So that was Antonio? Yes, Antonio Serelli. It was he who was mad on singing and had the choirs come every summer. It was he who hadn't allowed a line in the lake for twenty years. 'In the old days you could give a keeper a drink and fish all day.' But not now. Antonio wouldn't allow it. The police had instructions to keep their eyes open for anyone carrying anything that looked like a rod. And Antonio would go mad if he heard a fish had been hooked. But then he was mad. They were all mad, the whole family, always had been. The girl and all.

'The girl?' Henry repeated. 'Who is she?'

'Maddalena?' The fishmonger shook his head. He didn't know anything about Maddalena. He'd never seen her. She never came out. He only knew old Antonio.

'And what's their name?'

'Serelli.'

'Which must be Italian.'

'Half and half. Don't do to inquire too much into the ins and outs of the aristocracy.'

Finally he pointed out the path going down through a plantation of rhododendrons to the lake and Henry climbed over the high iron fence of the park.

'Keep your eyes open,' the fishmonger whispered. 'They say he's down there every night. Singing the fish to sleep I shouldn't wonder.'

Henry left him and walked down through the rhododendrons to the lake. It was larger than he had imagined, a wide oval of water, stretching for a quarter of a mile before him and on either hand.

A thick wood came down on the opposite shore to the fringe of reeds and wild iris fronds. The water was still and smooth until a pair of wild duck, frightened by his coming, shot up and flew high and swift over the alders darkening the bank, their feet dripping silver, their long necks craned to the sun, their alarmed quack-quacking splitting the warm silence. The water-rings, undulating gently away, struck islands of water-lilies with a soft flopping sound. Under the sun-shot water countless lily-buds were pushing up like dim magnolias and on the surface wide-open flowers floated like saucers of white and yellow china.

As he walked along the lakeside he could still hear the faint cries that rose from the crowded lawns, and now and then the clock of croquet balls. Hearing them he thought of how he had wandered about the lawns and gardens trying to find courage enough to go into the house again in the hope of seeing for a second time the girl who had been reading to the old man. He could not forget the melancholy intensity of her face. But when finally he had hurried along the terrace the door had been locked.

He walked along by the lake. The grass was spongy and noiseless to walk on, the air very still and warm under the shelter of the rhododendrons, and pigeons made a soft complaint in the silence.

Abruptly he was aware of something moving on the opposite bank. He half stopped and looked. It seemed like a group of yellow irises fluttered by a little deliberate wind. Then he saw that it was someone in a yellow dress. The sleeve was waving. He stopped quite still. The sleeve seemed to be making signals for him to go on.

He began to walk slowly along the bank and the woman on the opposite bank began to walk along in the same direction, hurrying. At the end of the lake, where the water sluiced in, was a wooden bridge. The woman began to run as she approached it. Her dress was very long and hampered her movements and she paused on the bridge to straighten her skirt and then hurried on again to meet him.

'You shouldn't come along here, you know,' she began to say, as she approached him.

She seemed to be very agitated. Henry stopped. He felt that she had not recognized him.

'I am very sorry,' he said.

And then, perhaps because of his voice, she recognized him. Her face broke into a half smile, but the agitation remained:

'But you shouldn't, you shouldn't,' she kept saying.

'But it was you who told me to come.'

'It makes no difference.'

He did not speak. All this time they had stood at a distance from each other, four or five yards between them. Now she came nearer. In the house he had thought of her as very young, a girl. Now, as she came nearer, she seemed much older. He took her now for twenty-seven or eight. And perhaps because of the yellow dress she seemed darker too. Her eyes were utterly black, not merely dark, and brilliant without the faintest mistiness, like black glass. And she seemed taller also and her body finer in shape, again perhaps because of the yellow dress, and her skin had a kind of creamy duskiness, soft, very smooth, a rich duskiness that had covered also her heavy southern lips and her straight black hair.

Staring at her, he was still at a loss for something

to say. She had begun to bite her lower lip, hard, making little white teeth-prints on the dusky flesh, as though in agitation or perplexity. And it occurred to him suddenly why she did not want him there. She had come down not to meet him, but someone else. And she was angry and troubled at finding him there.

'I'm very sorry,' he said again. 'But I'll go at once.'

He put his hand to his straw hat. She startled him by saying instantly:

'I'll walk back with you.' And then added: 'I'm going back the same way.'

It looked as if she didn't trust him. But he said nothing. A path slanted up the slope through the rhododendrons and they began to walk up it. The rhododendrons, old wild misshapen bushes, were full of withered seed-heads. He said something about their having looked wonderful in early summer. She did not answer. He thought she seemed preoccupied. Once, without stopping, she glanced back at the lake as though looking for someone, and as she turned back he remarked:

'It's been a wonderful day.'

'Yes,' she said. She said it unthinkingly, the word meant nothing. And suddenly she added:

'You think so?'

And, as she spoke, she was smiling, an extra-ordinary smile, vivacious, dark, allusive. It had in it something both tender and mocking.

'You don't think so?' she said.

'No, perhaps not.'

She seemed to feel instinctively that he was bored. He felt it. And he felt that she might have triumphed over him for knowing, but she said nothing, and they walked slowly on up the path.

All the time he wondered why she had been so agitated at finding him by the lake. And finally he asked.

'I didn't recognize you,' she said.

That was all. He didn't believe her. And she sensed his unbelief at once. She looked quickly at him and he smiled. She smiled in return, the same vivacious tender smile as before, and in a moment they were intimate. She said then:

'I didn't want you to get into any unpleasantness, that's all.'

'What unpleasantness?'

'Well, the lake is private. The fish are preserved and there are keepers and so on.'

He said nothing, but at heart he was disappointed at leaving the lake.

'You're not disappointed?' she said at once.

'Yes,' he said.

And then she did an extraordinary thing. She suddenly lifted her arms with a gesture of almost mocking abandonment and declared:

'All right. We'll go back.'

He protested. But she turned and began to walk back down the path to the lake, not heeding him. He turned and followed her, a yard or two behind, protesting again. And suddenly she let out a laugh and began to run. For a moment he stood still with astonishment and then he ran after her.

At the bottom of the path she paused and waited for him. She was still laughing.

'What shall we do?' she said recklessly. 'There's a punt. We could go out on the lake.'

'All right.' He was ready for anything.

And then, as suddenly as she had turned and run down the path, she was saying:

'No, I mustn't. You must excuse me. I must go back.'

'Don't go,' he said.

She caught the tone of entreaty in his voice. And it seemed to hurt her. Her eyes filled with pain, then abruptly with swimming wetness, and he stood still, too astounded to speak, while she bent her head and let the tears fall helplessly down her face. She began to cry with the helplessness of utter dejection, like someone worn out, not even lifting her hands to her face to hide it, but letting them hang spiritlessly at her side, not moving. She hardly made a sound, as though her tears were flooding away her strength. And when gradually she ceased crying and at last lifted her head she never uttered a word of apology or excuse or regret. But she gave him one amazing look, her black eyes swimming with many conflicting emotions; anger, helplessness, dejection, bitterness, fear and pain.

A moment later they were walking back up the path again. He could not speak. She dried her eyes with the sleeve of her dress, making a little yellow handkerchief of it. He felt that there was something unforgettably strange and touching about her, about her beauty, her amazing changes of mood, her tears and her silence.

And just as he had given up the idea of her ever speaking again, she made a sort of excuse, half for her tears, half for her behaviour on first seeing him:

'My brother might be very angry if he knew people had been down by the lake. And that might mean the end of the singing contests.'

That was all, it was very lame, very unconvincing, but he said:

'I understand.'

She must have felt that the excuse was poor and that he didn't understand, for a moment later she began to tell him, half apologetically, something about her brother: of how he was passionately fond of music, of singing especially. Twenty years before, her father had brought her mother to live there. Her father had been an English doctor and her mother Italian, an opera singer, a very gay woman, but a little irresponsible. Now that her father and mother were dead the brother and sister lived alone in the place and the brother devoted himself to music.

'He lives for nothing else,' she concluded.

She told him all this quietly, a little disjointedly, offering it as an excuse. But there was a curious bitterness in her voice, sharpest when she said 'He lives for nothing else.' He said nothing at all and by the time she had finished speaking they had reached the crest of the path.

There they paused. Across the park, through the thick summer trees, they could see the tent with its flags, the fluttering panorama of dresses across the lawns, the flowers on the terraces. And as they stood there the evening singing began, the harmony of male voices low and soft but very clear on the still evening air. They listened a moment; the choir was singing 'Calm was the Sea', and the voices, falling, crooned away almost to silence. There was a gate in the iron fence beyond the rhododendrons. The woman put her hand on the latch and he pushed it open and she slipped through and before he could say anything she smiled and was going away in the direction of the trees.

Just before she disappeared she turned as if to wave her hand and then, as though remembering something, she let it fall loosely to her side.

IV

It was nearly midnight, the sky was clear and dark, a pattern of blue and starlight. Down the avenue of elms the line of conveyances gave departing winks of light. The horses hoofs made hollow clock-clocking echoes under the roof of thick leaves. The air was still warm. There was a scent of limes, an odour of horses, an acrid whiff of candles from the carriage lamps. Above the noises of departure a thin emasculate voice kept piping continually:

'T'ank you a t'ousand times! T'ank you a t'ousand times. T'ank you so much.'

It was all over. Henry was in the brake, squeezed between the fishmonger and the school teacher who sat half lost already in a pair of dark entwining arms; the brake was moving away, the lamplight was shining down the avenue, the lawn with its web of fairy-lights, azure and red and emerald and gold, was receding, fading, vanishing at last.

'Well, it's been a grand day. And if you ask me we done well. Yes, it's been grand. I'm satisfied. I shan't be sorry when I'm going up wooden hill, now. I like my rest.' The voices of the women were tired, disjointed, the words broken by yawns. A mutter of dissatisfaction ran among the men. They had won the second prize, there had been some unfairness, they had expected the first, they were sure of it, they had sung beautifully. The judges were too old, they were finicky, they had been prejudiced. The voices of the men, discussing it, were petty, regretful. 'A day wasted, I call it.' Little arguments flamed up in the darkness. 'Ah! not so strong. It's been grand.' Jokes cracked out, someone made the sweet wet sound of a kiss, laughter flickered and died, the petty arguments were renewed. A woman suddenly complained: 'There! and I forgot my honeysuckle,' and a voice quietened her from the darkness: 'Come here and I'll give you something sweeter'n honeysuckle.'

The brake went slowly on into dark vague country. The night was warm and soundless, the houses were little grey haystacks clustered together, the woods were blacker and deeper. It was like a tranquil dream: the lovely glitter of summer starlight, the restfulness of the dark sky after the glare of sunshine.

Henry sat silent, only half-conscious of what the voices about him said. He was thinking of the woman: he could see her in the room with the old man, he could see her crying by the lake and half-waving her hand. He could see her clearly and could hear her voice unmistakably; yet he felt at times that she had never existed.

The fishmonger broke in upon his thoughts, his breath sweetish with wine, his voice a little thick and excited:

'Remember I was tellin' you about old Fiddle-sticks, Antonio? I been havin' a glass o' wine with him.'

Henry only nodded.

'Would make me have it. Dragged me into the house. Drawing-room. Kept shaking hands wimme. Nice fellow, old Antonio. You'd like him. Nice wine an' all—beautiful—like spring water. Made your heart sing, fair made your heart sing.'

His voice trailed off and he sat silent, as though overawed by these memories. Thinking of the woman, Henry said nothing. His mind puzzled over her with tender perplexity. Who was she? Why had she wept? What was she doing now?

The fishmonger broke in again, a little garrulously:

'Did I tell you the old man came in? No? Came in about half-way through the second glass. Dirty old dressing-gown, all gravy and slobber down the front. I tell you, nobody knows how the rich live only those who do know. Had the girl with him. In a yellow dress. Know who I mean? The girl who never comes out, never goes nowhere.'

Henry was listening now. He listened a little incredulously, but gradually there crept into the fishmonger's voice a quality of earnestness, of sober truth:

'I know now why that girl never goes out. Do you know—she didn't drink. That was funny. She just sat looking at the old man. I should like you to have seen her looking at him.'

'How did she look at him?'

'Just as if she hated him. Every time he slopped his wine down his dressing-gown she looked just as if she would shriek. And then another funny thing happened. She went out. Just as if she couldn't bear it no longer.'

'Went out?' His heart was beginning to beat with a curious excitement.

'Yes—and then, perhaps you won't believe me, the old man went mad. Raving mad, all because she'd gone. Jealousy! That's all. Mad with jealousy. In the end he went clean off—sort of fit, and Antonio and me had to rub his hands and get him round. Old Antonio was very upset. Kept apologizing to me. "Excuse," he kept saying. "Excuse. He is so jealous about her. He never wants her out of his sight. And she is so young. And then she is a woman of great imagination." What did he mean by that?—a woman of great imagination?' The fishmonger broke out in answer to himself, in a little burst of disgusted fury:

'Imagination! It needed a bit of imagination to marry that old cock.'

The brake had reached the crest of the hill and had begun to descend on the other side. The dew, falling softly, was turning the air a little cooler. The figures in the brake were silent, the lovers enfolded each other. A clock chimed its quarters over the still fields, the fishmonger took out his watch and verified it and dropped it back into his pocket.

'Half-past one,' he murmured.

Henry was silent and as the brake drove steadily on there was a sense of morning in the air in spite of the stars, the silence and the darkness.

Local Boy Makes Good

SITTING on the fo'c's'le-head, by the last light of the sun sinking behind Lundy, Amos finished her; and knew, in that moment of consummation, that she was his masterpiece. He had put ships into bottles before, and his *Cutty Sark*, which he had sold in the Red Lion for forty shillings, had taken him four years; he'd drunk her price in as many hours. But this *Talavera* had been the preoccupation of his thoughts and hands ever since 1939 when he first saw her picture in the Public Library. He had gone there to keep warm, being unemployed; but he had returned day after day to copy from an old book the rig and dimensions of the vessel in which his father as a boy had sailed round the world. Fifty days from Cardiff to Algoa Bay; twenty-eight from Algoa Bay to Lyttleton; seventy-four from Lyttleton to the Lizard. How many times had his father told him every detail of that voyage! So Amos's clumsy pencil scratched and scrabbled in the silent Reading Room until he had drawn the *Talavera* exactly to scale. That drawing, now almost indecipherable, had voyaged in his pocket for eleven years. It had crossed the Atlantic a dozen times (there being a use now for old broken-down seamen), it had been south to Rio and Buenos Aires, north to Murmansk, through the Mediterranean on Malta convoy, and round the Cape to Colombo and Bombay. It had got wet and smudged once, when a ship was torpedoed; and had tossed for two days in a lifeboat off the Azores. Meanwhile the little wooden model, rough-hewn as yet and without her rigging, had shared the opposite pocket of Amos's duffel-coat with his pipe and a plug of tobacco. These were the whole of his possessions when he climbed out of the lifeboat at Fayal.

The masts and spars were whittled in mid-Pacific in 1945. Thence his tanker steamed to Sydney where a telegram told him that his wife had died, and for a space the half-finished model was neglected and forgotten, rolled up with the drawing in the corner of a mackintosh sheet and stowed in one of those shapeless bundles where dwell the household gods of those who lack a hearth. When Amos returned home, however, he went to live with his sister, and it was she who 'to stop him moping' set him to work once more on his toy. At her small house outside Cardiff he began to fashion the sails.

He also pottered in her garden, and fed the hens, and grew with pride some leeks not much thicker than pencils and some cabbages without hearts; thus discovering for the first time that idleness can be pleasant to a man who has saved fifty pounds. He began to keep his eyes open for a cottage of his own and to dream of keeping a pig. He was thinking about this pig, and meticulously sewing the reef-points into a mains'l, when Cec arrived out of the blue, accompanied by a girl.

Amos couldn't at first remember whether he had seen this girl before, because all Cec's girls were almost exactly alike. They put on a lot of lipstick in a sloppy and haphazard way, they were pale and spiritless and their small breasts seemed to be pressed together by their drooping shoulders; they rarely spoke but chewed gum and disconsolately hummed to themselves tunes out of the films. They were the kind of girls who spent their days playing joyless games in pin-table galleries and their nights, perhaps, making love without passion on desolate bomb-sites.

It turned out that this was a new one; Amos did not, however, have much opportunity of making her acquaintance, for after a few minutes Cec turned to her and said, 'Now you muck off, see. You take a little walk down to the end of the street,' and humming 'I'll do anything for you' she went, with drooping shoulders, disconsolately out of the garden-gate. Cec then said (and Amos had known it was coming):

'Well, Dad, I'm in a bit of a jam again.'

'Yes?' said Amos resignedly.

Hands in pockets, leaning against the window-sill, Cec began to describe his jam. It was something to do with the hire-purchase of a second-hand motor-car—a transaction which Amos, who paid cash for all his little needs, found difficult to understand. Cec had been unable to raise the money for the last three monthly instalments and was being threatened with prosecution. Couldn't he, then, return the car? He could not, because he had 'sort of lent it to a chap,' whatever that might mean. Couldn't he get it back from this chap? No, because it had been involved in a trifling accident and would cost thirty pounds to repair. If, on the other hand, the thirty pounds was forthcoming it could be sold at a handsome profit, the hire-purchase firm could be paid off, and everybody, including Cec, would come honourably and gainfully out of the deal.

Amos listened, only half-comprehending, to the familiar tale. Cec's troubles, like his girls, were always of the same kind. They were never simple or

straightforward troubles. They never *quite* amounted
to theft or forgery, though there was always an uncomfortable hint of police-court proceedings in the
background. Nor were they ever due to the fault or
folly of Cec, except in so far as they were in some
mysterious way to be ascribed to his own cleverness.
Amos himself, after all the wretched years, still
clung to a somewhat tattered faith in the cleverness
of Cec. He had been clever as a kid; and the masters
at the Approved School, after his first bit of trouble,
had said he was a clever lad who ought to make
good. Then there had been that business about a
betting telegram which Amos, who couldn't write
or read, supposed was clever in a way; but again
there had been talk of a prosecution and the book-
maker had to be squared with twenty pounds. 'If it
had come off,' Cec airily observed on that occasion,
'I should have been a wealthy man.' Wealth, and in
a strange way honour too, were always just round
the corner when Cec was in trouble. And now, as
usual, honour could be restored and profit could be
gained for a mere matter of thirty pounds or so.

'*Ectually*,' said Cec, with his hands thrust so deep
into his pockets that the padded shoulders of his
double-breasted jacket were pushed up to make him
look like a hunchback, '—Ectually, Dad, it's thirty-
three quid fifteen.'

Amos did not at first answer. His little toy ship
lay on the table before him, and he went on sewing
the reef-points into the sail. Let him stew, he said to
himself, let him stew for a bit. And he thought about
his fifty pounds, and how it was a nest-egg for a
man's old age, and how one could buy a weaner pig
for a fiver; but in his heart he knew that Cec would
have that fifty pounds in the end.

Cec, however, having described his present trouble said no more about it, but lounged about the room and seemed to take a fleeting interest in the work Amos was doing. At least he picked up the hull of the ship in an inquisitive magpie fashion and remarked that it was a pretty thing.

'You and your ships in bottles,' he grinned indulgently. 'What's she called?'

'*Talavera*. 1796 gross tons. Your grandfather——'

'Oh, I know. You've told me often enough. Sailed round the world.'

'In a hundred and fifty-three days,' said Amos.

'You could fly it now in about three.'

It was clear that Cec could see no virtue in sailing round the world in a hundred and fifty-three days; but to fly round it in three days was wonderful because you 'saved time'. Cec was always full of ideas for 'saving time'. When he put them into practice they sometimes got him the sack from the rather mysterious jobs which he took now and then.

'—Saving,' said Cec, after making a brief calculation, 'twenty-one weeks and six days!'

Amos, in his simplicity, dared to wonder what was the point of saving time when you were then faced with an almost insoluble problem of how to use it up: of 'killing' it, in Cec's customary phrase. 'What have you been doing?' his mother used to ask him when he came in late for dinner. 'Oh, hanging about just to kill time.' Even at the age of sixteen he had found it necessary to kill time. For that reason, and not because he enjoyed the films, he went four times a week to the cinema; for that reason, and not because he liked beer and company, he loafed about in the pubs; for that reason, it seemed, he took up with those queer girls. 'Oh, they help to kill time,' he would say.

And now suddenly the latest of these girls returned from her walk. The front door banged and she came humming into the room, this co-assassin of Cec's hours and minutes. She was an automatic thing. Cec had told her to go for a little walk to the end of the street and she had done so. She said nothing, but stood and drooped and glanced about her without interest. Her jaw moved automatically, chewing gum.

Cec said with a sort of affectation of briskness:

'Well, Dad, what about our bit of business?'

Then Amos knew that there could and would be no further discussion. He couldn't, in any case, argue with Cec in front of the girl; and in a curious way he was glad, because those long disputes with Cec made him so tired. When he was younger he used to reason with the boy, and try to persuade him to learn a trade, or go to sea—'The sea, now, that'd make a man of you.' And then he would lose his temper, and swear at Cec and damn his eyes, and on one horrible occasion he had hit him hard with the flat of his hand across his pale face. But the result was always the same; he paid up in the end, and though he would be ashamed to admit it to himself he knew why he paid. It was simply because, despite everything, he loved this creature. Unreasonably, absurdly, ashamedly; and when Cec went out through the garden-gate and walked away with that girl, Amos·would feel quite alone.

So he put down the sail he was sewing, and got up from the table, and said:

'I'll go and get it.'

When he came back he sensed immediately an

altogether different atmosphere in the room. Even
the girl had brightened, and she spoke once or twice,
though in a very small tired voice, addressing Cec as
'Sizzle'. Cec's manner now had a strange feverish
jocularity. He made nervous jokes and laughed
loudly at them; and he pretended to take a sudden
interest in the model of the *Talavera*, taking it to
the window and holding it up to the light.

'You give yourself too much trouble, Dad, over
these things. There's too much detail in 'em. They'd
look just as good if they wasn't so fiddly. These bits,
now——'

'Davits,' said Amos. 'Her boats'll hang from them.'

'Well, they could be all carved out of the same
piece as the hull-like, boats and davits and all.
They'd *look* just the same, when you'd painted 'em.
Save time!'

Amos knew it would be no good explaining, but
he tried.

'The davits aren't part of the hull. They're part of
her gear. The boats hang from them in the falls. I'll
make little blocks and tackle, see, so's she could
lower her boats away . . .'

'She won't need to lower her boats away, not
when you've got her in a bottle,' laughed Cec. 'Still,
I s'pose it kills time,' he added tolerantly. '"Spect
you find it dull-like, with nothing to do all day.'

He prepared to go. Taking his girl by her thin
arm just above the elbow he propelled her towards
the door; like a sort of animated doll she moved
obediently. They went out and Amos followed them.
At the garden-gate he handed Cec the money in an
envelope and Cec said briefly: 'Thanks, Dad. I'll be
seeing you.' The girl shook Amos's hand; but she
didn't say anything unless a momentary convulsion

of her jaw-muscles as she chewed could be taken as
a farewell. The pair went off down the street, and
Amos watched the girl's weak ankles turning over
at every pace because of her very high heels; he
heard her say, 'Sizzle, let's go to the flicks.' As they
passed out of sight he knew the expected loneliness,
and he leaned on the gate for quite a long time,
thinking. It was rather a relief when at last he made
his decision to go back to sea. He had only seventeen pounds left, and his old-age pension; and because he remembered those days of the dole and the
Means Test he was desperately afraid of being poor.
The cottage and the weaner pig faded out of his
dreams as he stumped back into the house and began
to bundle up his belongings. Right in the middle of
the bundle, for safety's sake, he stowed the hull of
the *Talavera*, wrapped up neatly with her masts and
half-finished sails, with the spools of silk which
would be her running rigging, and the precious
smudged drawing he'd made so long ago in the
Public Library.

And now at last she was finished! Her spread
canvas as white and lovely as gulls' wings in the
setting sun, she rode on an even keel within the clear
glass bottle which would confine her for as long as
she lasted—for years and years, maybe for a century, thought Amos in the full pride and glory of
creation; there were ships in bottles much older than
that. Gazing at her, he knew that he would never
make another model. There would be no point in
doing so, because he could never make one better
than this.

It had taken him the whole of his last voyage to
put the finishing touches to her. The eight-thousand

ton tramp had had boiler-trouble on the outward trip and had tied up at Port of Spain in Trinidad for a month while she was being repaired. By the time she was patched up and had discharged her cargo at Caracas and taken on another at Pernambuco nearly five months had gone by. Aware that there was no hurry, and having unlike Cec no ambition to 'save' the fleeting minutes in order that he might squander them later, Amos spent his leisure fiddling with the sails and rigging of his toy, sandpapering, polishing, making sure that every tiny block ran smoothly; he gave the hull no less than four coats of paint and meticulously varnished and revarnished every mast, spar and yard. At last, within sight of the coast of England—it seemed a fit and proper culmination of the long voyage—he slipped the model through the narrow neck of the bottle, a moment almost as anxious as a real launching, and then went up to the bridge to do his trick at the wheel. When he came off watch the glue had set firmly and there was nothing more to do but to pull tight and make fast the silken threads that raised the masts and sails. This was a matter of minutes only; and it somehow astonished him that the moment of creation should be so brief, the preparation for it so long. 'Thus the heavens and the earth were finished, and all the host of them.'

So now, as Morte Point fell away on the starboard quarter, and the white surf of Woolacombe Bay, he held up the ship against the sunset and the soft yellow light shining through her sails and glinting on her fresh paint made her come wonderfully alive, she was a ship of faerie, magical, unearthly, flying before an imperceptible wind. It occurred to Amos that some watcher on Morte

Point or Hartland might have seen the real *Talavera*
thus as she came winging up the Bristol Channel on
that evening long ago; the sunset glowing behind
her canvas, the strong steady sou'-wester in t'gal-
lants'ls, the crisp white foam dancing beneath her
bow, her wake dying away behind her as it had died
away, hissing and subsiding, right round the great
globe of the world!

And her crew, with Amos's father among them,
crowding the rails, murmurous and excited, seeing
England for the first time in a hundred and fifty
days, cheering the landmarks as one by one they came
into view, there's Baggy Point, there's Ilfracombe,
hurray, from the crow's nest a look-out waves an
arm towards Mumbles Head and old Swansea Bay
on the port bow! How well Amos knew that murmurous animation, that buzzing and reawakening,
that sense of seeing old familiar things for the first
time, which only sailors home from the sea can feel.
How many times in his long life, he wondered, had
he run up on deck and rushed to the rail to catch
that first precious glimpse of England? Three score?
Eighty? It might even be a hundred.

Then suddenly Amos, who had been thinking of
the men on the deck of the *Talavera*, realized that
he was coming home at this moment and that the
landmarks awakened no wonder, no sense of anti-
cipation at all. His mood of exaltation fell away
from him. There was no home. There was only his
sister's house (and for all he knew she might by now
have let his room to a lodger); there was the hostel
in the docks; and there was the Red Lion. There
was also a vague gnawing apprehension lest Cec
might have got into some deeper trouble while he
had been away.

He laid down the ship beside him on the fo'c's'le-
head and was no longer conscious of her loveliness,
was only aware that she had filled his thoughts for
so long, and was now no longer there; she was done,
she had gone, she had sailed out of his mind and had
left a vacuum behind her. He paid now the penalty
which all who create must pay; he felt curiously
empty, deflated, his spirit drained away. And he had
no sense of home-coming when he saw the cranes of
Barry and knew that Cardiff lay beyond the head-
land, only three and a half hours' steaming away.

Amos did not go ashore until next morning; and
Bute Street in the morning wears a blear-eyed and
desolate look, a Chinaman yawns outside his empty
café, coal-trimmers after a night shift trudge home-
wards with the whites of their eyes staring out of
blackened expressionless faces, girls who might look
pretty in the evening come out haggardly from
sombre tenements, fetching milk-bottles, coughing
over first cigarettes; Lascars with the infinite weari-
ness of Lascars slope along on their way to join
their ships, and a few sailors with bundles walk the
opposite way, coming ashore. Only to these few does
Bute Street in the morning appear, miraculously, to
be a delectable place; because it offers the first pavements, the first houses, the first cafés, the first pubs,
a foretaste of hearth and home.

Amos, who had nowhere to go, was nevertheless
aware of the indefinably pleasant sensation which
dry land gives to those whose feet for months have
felt only a moving deck beneath them. Savouring
this pleasure, he walked as far as the end of the
street, where he found a café open and ate a fresh
bread roll; this is generally the first indulgence of
men who come off small ships which lack a bakery.

He sat in the café for a long time, trying to pluck up courage to go and find out if his sister had taken a lodger; but at last, realizing that the pubs were now open, he made his way to the Red Lion.

He knew the old barmaid there and she gave him a welcome, which is another thing sailors hanker after when they come ashore. He leaned with his elbows on the counter (one more queer little pleasure renewed) and bought her a drink. Soon some customers came in, and it was not surprising that three of them should turn out to be old friends of his, for Amos had been using the Red Lion, whenever he was ashore, for nearly forty years. To these, after a few beers, he showed his *Talavera*, unwrapping the whole of his bundle of clothes, towels and oddments to find her where she lay at the secret heart of it. She was duly admired, and the landlord recollected the model of the *Cutty Sark* and how Amos had sold her for forty shillings.

'You'd get twice as much for this one,' he said. 'If you could find a Yank, and he was a bit tight, you'd maybe get a fiver.'

'I wouldn't sell her,' said Amos almost fiercely, 'for anything in the world.' The landlord smiled, thinking no doubt that it would be a different tale one night when Amos had spent all his money and wanted a few more drinks.

And now there came in a man older than Amos, a fireman off a collier just back from Gibraltar, who knew all the tricks by which ships were put into bottles, and who asked an expert's questions, nodding approval over the *Talavera* as she lay on the counter among the pints of beer.

'No longer such beautiful things can they make at all,' said this old sailor. 'A lost art it iss, man, like

thatching iss in the countryside. The patience they
do lack for it.'

'True enough,' said Amos. 'Off and on, she took
me eleven years.'

'Eleven years! But a thing of beauty she iss, man,
and worth the labour. They do not understand today. A godless age. Quick results they do demand.
You know that well.'

It crossed his mind that the man was thinking of
Cec, for most of the Lion's customers knew about
him. Indeed, it had been in this bar, seven years ago,
that a well-meaning fellow had taken Amos aside
and whispered to him, 'Trouble there iss at home.'
That was the trouble which led to the Approved
School. Ever since, Amos had been a little afraid
when he returned to the Lion after a long voyage;
afraid of the sympathetic glance, the kindly hand
on the shoulder, the old friend beckoning him into
a corner. However, the old fireman said no more,
and none of Amos's other acquaintances mentioned
Cec at all. They drifted away one by one, and Amos
himself was preparing to leave when the barmaid
leaned over the counter and whispered:

'That boy of yours. You've been away a long
time——'

'Yes?' said Amos sharply. It was a cry as much as
a question. He thought he knew what was coming.
Some fresh trouble, some confused, complex, incomprehensible misfortune; or perhaps after all Cec
hadn't been able to square up that business of the
hire-purchase car. Perhaps it was worse than ever
this time—a case in the Courts, even prison.

'Tell me,' said Amos, with a dry mouth.

The barmaid's hand, rough and wrinkled from
years of washing up, lay upon his sleeve.

'But he's doing well,' she said gently. 'I thought you'd like to know.'

'Doing *well*?'

'Some little business he has. Quite well-to-do he is getting! I saw the advertisement in last night's *Echo*. Wait a minute: I'll get it for you.'

She bustled away, and Amos discovered that he was sweating, so powerful was the sense of reprieve and release. Cec doing well! Still he could hardly credit it. Yet he'd always believed, hadn't he, that the boy was clever? And hadn't the headmaster of the Approved School written 'ought to do well' on his report? 'If only he will take himself in hand, he ought to do well.'

The barmaid came back with the paper. She had folded it open at the advertisement page.

'There,' she said. '*Situations Vacant*. At the bottom of the column.'

Amos read:

GIRLS WANTED *for clean light work in small factory. Good wages. No Saturdays.*

There followed Cec's name and address.

'His own boss he iss, you notice,' said the barmaid. 'Soon he'll be too grand to know us.'

'I must go and see him,' said Amos, suddenly making the decision.

'Of course. You can get there easily on the tram.' Pleased with herself because she had given him the good news, the old woman grinned mischievously. '"Girls Wanted," I said to myself when I read it. "Now that's just like him, that is!" I said. But they settles down in the end,' she added. 'Even the wildest ones, very often, they settles down and makes good.'

The 'small factory', from the outside, was certainly unimpressive. It consisted of a patched-up building on a bomb-site with a long jerry-built shed at the end of it. The yard was full of rubble and broken bricks. Nevertheless there was a new green gate at the entrance and a notice-board freshly-painted in bold yellow lettering:

TWENTIETH CENTURY NOVELTIES LIMITED

with Cec's name underneath, and then *Managing Director*. Clutching his bundle in one hand and his *Talavera* in the other, Amos stood before this notice. It was in his mind that so splendid and marvellous an event as the vindication of Cec required a splendid gesture on his part to match it. He would therefore make him a present of the *Talavera*. She might not be exactly the sort of gift which would take Cec's fancy; but there was eleven years' loving labour in her and she was in fact the only important property which Amos possessed. Moreover, he reflected, if Cec was really going to settle down, as the barmaid had predicted, he would perhaps one day have a home of his own; he would marry,—a nice steady girl, Amos hoped, instead of one of those sloppy ones. If so, how imposing the *Talavera* would look on the mantelpiece over Cec's hearth; and with what pride would Cec point her out to his guests, business-people perhaps, quite well-to-do and respectable,—

'Pretty thing, ain't she? My Dad made her. *Ectually*, my grand-dad sailed round the world in the *Talavera*, in one hundred and fifty-three days.'

Perhaps Amos would never have indulged in so fantastic a day-dream as this unless he had been slightly tipsy. He had had six pints of beer in the Red Lion—his first drinks for five months. They, and the barmaid's good tidings, and the ride in the rocking bumping tram, had combined to give Amos a feeling of uplift and exhilaration which was, let us say, about half-way between drunkenness and sobriety. In this mood he was capable of such flights of fancy as were necessary to picture Cec as a family man, Cec in the company of 'respectable' people, Cec (who had once pawned his only spare pair of shoes) rejoicing in the ownership of a semi-detached house . . .

Some momentary doubts assailed him when he remembered the pawning of the shoes and also the pawning of an overcoat which, it had turned out, was not exactly Cec's own property but had been 'sort of borrowed from a chap'. He put these unworthy thoughts away. Cec had reformed, Cec had turned over a new leaf. He was the Managing Director of Twentieth Century Novelties Limited, and that sounded to Amos like a very important position indeed.

He went through the green gate into the yard and found a door marked 'Registered Office'. Before he knocked at it he had an afterthought and hid the *Talavera* in his bundle of clothes; for he felt a sudden diffidence at appearing before Cec with the gift in his hand and decided it would be more fitting to produce it casually after he had been shown round the factory.

Nobody answered his knocking, so he went in; and like a wind dying away in the tops'ls of his spirit he felt his exhilaration go. The room was dingy and bare; there was a kitchen table which served as a desk, with a portable typewriter on it; and before this typewriter, on the only chair, sat the sloppy-looking girl, chewing gum.

It was apparent that she did not recognize him. For a few moments she went on tapping at the type-writer with two fingers. Then she looked up and said: 'Yeah?'

'I just called,' Amos said, 'to see my son.'

She remembered him now, for she gave an exclamation which sounded like 'Ow!' and, becoming suddenly ladylike, stood up and extended her hand. Then, as suddenly, she withdrew it, remarking 'Wet nail-vanish. Pardon. I'll fetch Sizzle.' She went out through a side door and Amos noticed once again the high heels and the stockings which wrinkled above the ankles when they turned over at each step.

He lit his pipe and waited nervously. It seemed a very long time before the girl came back, with Cec following her. Cec looked different, somehow, and the difference was nothing to do with his new grey pin-striped suit and his American tie which had a picture of a naked woman on it; the change had happened inside him and Amos, forgetting that in recent years he had only known his son as a suppli-cant and a scrounger, felt almost as if he were meet-ing a stranger. For one thing, Cec slapped him on the shoulder, which he had never done before; and as he did so he exclaimed with a tremendous and rather terrifying jocularity:

'Well, if it ain't old Barnacle Bill back from the sea! How are you making out, Dad?' Amos was glad he had hidden the little ship. He could not, at this moment, have brought himself to give it to Cec; he would have felt a fool. It would have been like giving it to someone he had never seen in his life before.

Meanwhile the girl had returned to her seat

before the typewriter; and Cec, with his hands in his pockets, strode up and down the small room.

'Got those invoices done?' said Cec suddenly in a staccato and curiously artificial tone.

'Yes, Boss.' The girl picked up his manner like a child catching a ball.

'Cashed up?'

'Yeah.'

'Let's see.'

She got up and handed him a Bank paying-in book with a lot of pound notes in it. Amos, as he stood and watched, was aware once again of the sharp sense of estrangement. Cec had become somehow larger than life, unreal, unnatural. Amos didn't go to the pictures, or he would have recognized the amateurish imitation of the behaviour of a tough business man in an American film.

Looking up from the paying-in book, Cec said with a grin:

'Hundred and twenty smackers last week. This week we shall knock it up to a hundred and fifty.'

'I heard in the Red Lion——' Amos began.

'The little old Red Lion,' put in Cec patronizingly.

'How well you were doing. I'm glad, Cec.'

'Yes, we're doing well, ain't we?' said Cec, handing back the paying-in book to the girl and giving her at the same time a friendly and intimate slap on the bottom. 'Doing well. And I owe it all to you, Dad!'

'All to me?' Amos remembered the thirty-three pounds fifteen, and the twenty pounds to square the bookie, and the fiver to get the borrowed overcoat out of pawn; and he was suddenly touched.

'It was nothing,' he said.

'Believe me, it was everything.' Cec put his arm

round Amos's shoulders. 'Come along with me. I'll show you.'

He led the way down a covered passage between the blitzed building and the long shed. There was a door at the other end, and Cec said, 'You'll have to put that pipe out now, Dad. No smoking, because of the paint and the varnish.' Amos obediently knocked out his pipe, and Cec ushered him in.

There was a wooden bench running down the middle of the shed, at which under bright electric lights about a dozen girls were working. Amos did not, at first, understand what they were doing; the whole of his attention was taken up by the girls who seemed to be almost exactly alike. A moment later he realized that this was an illusion; for in fact some were tall and some were short, some dark and some blondes. The illusion, he now realized, was caused by the fact that despite these differences all the girls were of the same type: they were Cec's type. They were the sort of girls he had giggled with at street-corners ever since he was fifteen; and there were twelve of them all brought together under one roof! It was terrifying; it was like a nightmare.

Cec prodded him jocularly in the ribs.

'At your age, Pop! Now then, take your eyes off 'em.'

Some of the girls giggled.

'I'll show you something that ought to be more in your line,' said Cec. 'Take a look at this.'

He went towards the bench; for the first time Amos saw what the girls were doing.

They were putting model ships into bottles.

But these were not ships as Amos knew ships. They were not built, they were manufactured. There lay in the middle of the bench a pile of hulls, haphazardly heaped together, shining and glistening with the sort of paint which is used for the uniforms of lead soldiers. Now and then a girl would pick up one of these hulls and with a few deft strokes of a paintbrush suggest the hatches and the planking-in of the decks; then she would toss it casually on to another pile.

'We mould 'em,' said Cec proudly, following Amos's glance, '—out of papier-mâché.'

Two more girls were cutting sails from what looked like a kind of celluloid material, and glueing them on to the masts; others were tying pieces of white cotton to the mast heads; and at the far end of the bench a girl apparently more skilled than the rest was inserting the finished ships in the bottles. For this purpose she was equipped with an ordinary buttonhook and a long-handled brush. As the bottle lay on the bench before her, with one hand she used the buttonhook to raise the ships' masts, with the other she applied a dab of gum to the base of each.

'Come and see the finished job,' said Cec. As he conducted Amos along the line of girls he patted each in a proprietary way between the shoulders. 'How are you doing, Maisie? Everything O.K., Doreen?' In an aside to Amos, he explained: 'No formality here, Pop. No trade-union rules. We gets on with the job.'

'And now,' he added, as they reached the end of the bench and the last girl of all, who was putting corks in the bottles and sealing them with red sealing-wax, 'Now I'll show the genu*ine* completed article, as sold for two guineas apiece in half the pubs of Cardiff, Swansea, Llanelly and Bristol *and* on the beach at Coney Island where the trippers go. The genu*ine* Bedou*ine* original ship-in-a-bottle which took old Barnacle Bill six months to make with his poor old horny hands!'

He leaned over the girl and picked up one of the finished jobs. As he held it up in front of Amos's bewildered eyes, a further beastliness became apparent. The inside of the bottle had been *tinted*: green for the sea, blue for the sky, white waves in between. Against this gaudy background perched the outrageous model, a painted ship upon a painted ocean. But it was a ship only in name; it bore as much resemblance to a ship as a stuffed bird in a glass-case bears to the winged creature with the throbbing throat. Amos recoiled before it.

Meanwhile Cec was saying:

'*Ectually*, Pop, the gross cost including labour is precisely fifteen and a tanner so that gives us a hundred per cent. clear when the retailer's had his rake-off. Not bad, eh? And you must admit she's a neat job, even though she *is* mass produced and she ain't got the frills that yours have. After all, Pop, you've got to keep pace with the world. Take her in your hands, have a good dekko, and tell me straight if you can see anything *wrong*.'

Amos took it, simply because otherwise it would have fallen to the floor; but he didn't want to touch it any more than he would have liked to touch one of those tarty girls. He was not a very imaginative man, nor was he gifted with overmuch sensibility; what imagination and sensibility he possessed had been spent first on Cec with his terrible twisted cleverness and secondly on those loved children of his hands, the *Cutty Sark* and the *Talavera*. Nevertheless he had enough feeling left to be aware that the prostitution of all he believed in lay within his hands in the painted bottle. All the cheapness and

---

the tawdriness of the street-corners, the whole philosophy of the pin-tables enshrined there!

'—And if you'll accept her, Dad, she's yours,' said Cec with a large and expansive gesture. 'I said I owed it all to you; and that's a fact, cross-me-heart-an'-spit-on-the-floor. Well, I made good in the end, didn't I, and there's a little token to remember it by. Stick her on your mantelpiece, Pop, and when you have your friends in of an evening——'

Amos suddenly realized that he was being gently propelled towards the door. Cec's arm was about his shoulders, and Cec's voice, the voice of a stranger, was loud in his ears. In one hand he still clutched his bundle of belongings; in the other, Cec's gift.

CHRISTOPHER SYKES

The Sacred and the Profane

WHEN I was serving as a staff captain in Cairo during the war, I was very pleased to find Adrian Lally among my GHQ neighbours. I had first met him six years or so before the war. The occasion was a Roman Catholic tea-party in Westminster to which we had both been invited to do honour to a Uniat Bishop (a majestic bearded figure wearing a formalized turban), who had come to London to visit Cardinal Hinsley. There was a great deal of genuflexion, ring-kissing, formal dress, polite laughter, tea and cakes. It was not everyone's idea of fun, but I met Adrian that way and so I was, and remain, glad I went. Before I was introduced to him I was told that he was a recent convert, a fact I believe I might have guessed for myself from his slightly dramatic reverence to the Cardinal when the latter greeted him with outstretched hand.

He became my friend, and our friendship was largely maintained as a going concern by the fact of his being a subject for exploration. I found that for all his continual jesting this fat and sensitive man was serious-minded. I knew he was religious, but I discovered further that he was for ever toying with the idea of entering a monastery, though he feared to take this step because he was pleasure-loving. I found him to be far more contradictory in character than people usually are. When we were together in Cairo I found that he was a prodigiously hard worker, one of the ablest Intelligence officers on the staff, and yet he seemed to spend his whole day in gossip. I found out gradually that he was one of those strange beings whose mind operates most effectively in a crowd, in a babel of discussion, in meetings, committees, lobbyings. To clarify his ideas he liked a debate where he presided. He suffered from what I can but call pathological chairmanship.

This discovery interested me, but it also decided me to give Adrian less of my hours of labour. If he wanted to listen to ignorant opinions to set his mind in motion, well he could get them from somebody else. I had other commitments. But my friend was very angry when one evening he asked me to come to his office in the morning, and in refusing I told him my real reason.

'You are a brilliant delver into the mysteries of human nature, aren't you?' he said, glaring.

'But you know that what I say is true.'

'And suppose everyone behaved like you,' he gobbled, 'suppose all Intelligence officers refused to discuss anything with their colleagues unless they had specialized knowledge—what would happen then?'

'We would win the war.'

'Sometimes,' he said gravely, and without smiling at my stroke of wit, 'I don't say always, or often, but sometimes, on rare occasions, I need your advice. Really, I mean, for its own sake. On one subject above all.'

'What subject is that?'

'The Church . . . Oh, don't misunderstand me. I don't see a great spiritual force in you, my dear hog. I'm far more right than you are about the important part of the Rock, but you inevitably know the un-important part better than I ever can ... I hope you don't think I have spiritual pride.'

'Spiritual pride is in the important part, so I wouldn't know. Why do you want my help?'

'You know how many of our colleagues see the hidden hand of the Axis in all things Roman.'

'Yes I do know.'

'And you know how the resultant rows find their way to my office.'

'Is that why you want me tomorrow?'

'Tomorrow,' said Adrian, 'Father Macdonnel is coming to see me. He has just come back from Mahammadieh where there seems to have been some absolutely appalling ecclesiastical bother. I don't want to ask anyone except you for fear of causing scandal. Now, are you going to come, or are you going to turn up your pompous nose?'

'What happened at Mahammadieh?'

'I don't know. Father Macdonnel has written to me to say he wants my help to lodge a formal pro-test with the authorities at the highest level. It's something frightful, that's all I know. Can I rely on you for eleven o'clock?'

'I can't be with you before a quarter past. I'll come though.'

'You come.'

I kept that appointment.

Father Macdonnel was seated on a chair opposite to Adrian. His eyes flashed fire, his lean neck was red with anger. He had apparently come to the end of a discourse.

'And I'm telling you, Colonel Lally,' he was saying, 'that it is a blasphemous and detestable occurrence to which I have been subjected, and I am demanding the strongest imaginable action by the Commander-in-Chief, both on behalf of myself, and of the chaplains under my command.'

Adrian turned to me. 'Here you are at last,' he said. 'Of course, you know Father Macdonnel.'

I had met him several times before. He was the senior Roman Catholic chaplain in one of the corps of the Eighth Army, a position he disliked as it kept him at Headquarters, and he was a bold, adventurous man. When he first came to Egypt as a battalion chaplain he had the misfortune to become well known on account of certain acts of daring in the course of duty, and this caused the authorities to promote him to his present post, for which he was not happily fitted. Office work, the dull duties of 'welfare' organization, and so on, had a little soured his temper, and the outburst, of which I had heard the concluding phrases, was characteristic of his changing nature. Irish bitterness was taking the place of Irish good-humour.

We shook hands, for we had not met for some months, and I said I was very glad to see him again. Adrian led us to the table and pointed to chairs. He then opened the conference in a formal manner.

'Father Macdonnel has just come from Mahammadieh,' he said, 'which is rear Headquarters of his corps for the time being. Things have been going badly, and the question is whether it would be a good thing to inform the Chief personally. Now, Father Macdonnel, if it is not too much trouble, would you repeat what you have just told me in the fullest possible detail for the benefit of our friend. I also would like to hear the facts again so as to get them straight.'

As he pushed cigarettes in front of us Adrian

caught my eye for a second, and I noted a look of fun. Father Macdonnel began his tale.

In time of war one gets so used to odd things that one's mind becomes like a bin; such quantities of queer trash are flung into it daily, to be emptied out later, that, in the way of bins, a beautiful jewel or other little masterpiece lies confused with the rubbish, and not noticed till later. It was not immediately that I recognized that Father Macdonnel's experiences at Mahammadieh were among very remarkable incidents of sacred history.

In those far-off days the name Mahammadieh was heavily charged with emotion, it was the name of the second most important town in Italian North Africa. It had once been Italian Headquarters. The capture and loss of Mahammadieh under Sir Archibald Wavell, its recapture by Sir Claude Auchinleck, its loss again by us to Rommel in 1942, had all been occasions of extreme excitement, days bright with joy or black with bitterness. At the end of 1942 the place came into the news for the last time. General Montgomery, it will be remembered, attacked at Alamein, and on a great day less than a month later, poor Mahammadieh was liberated for good. There was no battle this time. The Germans and Italians retreated and we rushed in, and among the first on our side to head as fast as possible for this town was Father Macdonnel.

For him the place had special attractions. Among the monuments which the Italians had raised to their colonial rule was a Christian cathedral, a spacious handsome building, not very distinguished architecturally, but well proportioned, and supporting a large very well designed green dome. It was not a stupefaction of the world, as Italian propagandists used to say, but it was a civilized edifice. It conferred genuine dignity on Mahammadieh. To this church Father Macdonnel now sped in his fifteen-hundredweight truck with holy zeal. He wanted to start religious services in it immediately, if possible, so that not one day should elapse in which Mass had not been celebrated within its walls.

He arrived to find expected confusion. All the priesthood, except one, had left in panic. Between the retreat of the Axis army and the arrival of our own there had been an interval of several hours during which there had been some abominable scenes of looting, nowhere worse than in this part of the town; indeed an effort had been made to burn down the whole quarter. After looking round the littered streets Father Macdonnel went into the cathedral. He saw a hideous heap of smashed and upturned church furniture in the centre of the nave, and on this a group of about twenty British soldiers reclining in different attitudes of fatigue. Some of them were dozing. The wakeful ones were smoking. Military kit was strewn all over the floor and rifles piled against the high altar. In a dark corner, gibbering with fear, crouched the one remaining Italian priest, the aged sacristan, who had been left behind. He was simple, in the sense that his mental powers had degenerated into subnormality. Father Macdonnel watched him come out of his corner, and in pitiful fear, like that of an animal exploring some object of fascination and terror, hesitantly creep towards the soldiers, gaze at them with terror-wide eyes, and then appeal to them in broken accents and using pathetic gestures of beseeching. As the soldiers could not understand a word he said they replied facetiously, 'Keep yer 'air on, monkey fice,' said

one. 'Give 'im a burst, Charlie,' said another, and
they used other less restrained expressions. The old
man skipped back into his corner with a little squeal.
The British Tommy's famous capacity to make
friends with foreigners all the world over was momentarily suspended. It was a scene of loathsome
sordidness.

Father Macdonnel swiftly corrected the situation.
He started by ordering the men to remove their hats
and put out their cigarettes, and after an hour or so
he ended by rewarding them for their heavy labours
by assigning them billets in two of the side chapels
of the now thoroughly well-tidied fane. He gave
them this shelter on condition that they behaved
with scrupulous decency and left as soon as other
accommodation was available. There was a look in
his eye and something about his thin set mouth
which made them obey him. Having settled the
men, he began to inspect damage with the poor old
bearded sacristan who was called Father Battino.

There was less than he had feared. True, a great
many window panes were smashed; no lecterns remained; where, Father Battino assured him, there
had been a silver offertory-stand by the high altar,
there was now an ugly rent in the plaster; the golden
door of the tabernacle, the rich sanctuary lamp, and
the candlesticks, had been stolen; and in the sacristy
many cupboards had been wrenched open and all
the copes removed. The 'treasure', the collection of
monstrances and other sacred vessels presented by
the King of Italy after the Lateran Treaty, and by
other people on other occasions, had all gone too.
The Germans had taken a good deal, but most of
the looting had been done by the local people. At
the end of their tour of inspection Father Battino

sat down in the sacristy and wept bitterly; but Father Macdonnel stood fingering his chin and saying to himself: 'Well now, it's not so bad as it might be. Not by any means.'

The Sacrament had not been violated; it had not been removed by the runaways, but it had been well hidden away. The church linen, the chasubles, the stoles and maniples, had, rather inexplicably, escaped the notice of the looters, and, oddest thing of all, the altar wine was standing unhidden and unmolested in a corner. The looters were probably coming back for a final visit when the approaches to the cathedral from the poor quarters were blocked by the advancing army. A merciful chance. Father Macdonnel gave the sacristan a pull at his whisky flask and continued his inspection alone. Perhaps if he had not already found much to surprise him agreeably he would not have been so exasperated at the loss he now discovered. He returned to the sacristy after an intense search and addressed Father Battino. 'Ubi Calix?' he asked in a rich brogue, 'Where is the chalice?' for their conversation was conducted in the decadent Latin of the Roman Rite, in which language Father Macdonnel's Irish intonation was more noticeable than in English.

'Stolen! Stolen!' wailed the old man. 'See, this is where the chalices were kept,' and he tottered pointing to a splintered cabinet, 'and there were other chalices here!' he whirled round and pointed to the battered treasure, 'and they took the copes too, and the Holy Water stoup, and the Offertory-stand, and—'

'Yes, yes, I know,' said Father Macdonnel. 'Repetare non est necessarium. *Who* took the chalices? That's the point.'

'Tedeschi! Germani!' replied the sacristan.

'Oh.' This was serious. 'All of them?'

'All! All! Even the chalice which was used at Mass at the high altar yesterday morning. I myself saw an Arab running away with it.' And with a fresh burst of tears he pointed to a small cupboard over one of the chests of drawers before which the priest is wont to vest himself for Mass.

'An Arab? Not a German?'

'No! No! An Arab!' cried the sacristan, wringing his hands, as though this made it a thousand times more frightful. 'He came in all alone while the rest of his people were in the church, and he tore open the cupboard—like this—like a wild beast—and then he ran away with the chalice. I tell you I saw him! I saw him!'

Father Macdonnel sat down and went over this evidence carefully. He established that while all the other chalices had been taken by the Germans, this chalice, the one used at the high altar that day, had been stolen by a local man. He patted Father Battino on the shoulder and assured him that he would get the chalice back to the cathedral. He meant it, he believed it. Meanwhile, using his own battered mug-like field chalice, he said Mass in the cathedral next morning.

Father Macdonnel had an interpreter, a man called Attar, who accompanied him everywhere. I remembered Attar well, indeed his heavily charged breath, which contrasted so eerily with his name, was unforgettable, and it was through Attar that Adrian, for a little time, as though by a side door, made a minor but personal appearance in the story.

Why Father Macdonnel kept this transparent Syrian scoundrel in his service was an insoluble mystery, unless you remembered the attraction that great sinners have for holy people. Attar had been dismissed from a Greek cotton firm for peculation when he presented himself to Father Macdonnel as a persecuted Lebanese Christian thirsting to work for the glory of God. As with so many people of criminal character, his cunning was inextricably mixed with stupidity, and on this occasion he had not troubled to find out whether Father Macdonnel knew Colonel Lally. He would have done well to investigate this matter as it contained seeds of disaster; a few months previously Attar had presented himself to Adrian as a Moslem grandee who knew every Muhammadan notable from King Ibn Sa'ud downwards. Adrian had dismissed him after a few weeks highly unsatisfactory service, whence he had gone to the Alexandrian cotton business. Father Macdonnel was told all about this, but in vain. Because his nature was what it was, he conceived a sort of mad loyalty to this atrocious being. 'I want an interpreter,' he said, 'not a virtuous man.' Attar was without doubt a very gifted linguist. He could strip all beauty and poetry from at least five idioms. He could make French sound gross and Arabic insipid.

The day after their arrival in Mahammadieh, Father Macdonnel gave Attar his instructions. He was to lurk about the bazaars and find out what had become of the looted church property. He was to get the names of the looters and tell them to bring the stuff to the church. He could promise them rewards and no legal action against them.

'And how much dough am I empowered to promise these people, Sir?' asked Attar.

'You can tell them to come along at eleven on Sunday without fear,' replied Father Macdonnel, 'and I'll give them something out of the collection at Sung Mass.'

'But these people will be at me for one Hell of a lot of cash, Sir.'

'I dare say. I'm not here to subsidize sacrilege.'

With a rather indefinite financial programme, therefore, Attar sneaked off to the poorer quarters.

The bazaars, with their age-long romance of teeming swindle, were to Attar what hot-houses are to flowers of the equator. He did well there. Within three days he had obtained five candlesticks, the door of the tabernacle, a lamp which had been stolen from a private house (as was discovered much later) but which did good service in the sanctuary, and a number of other odds and ends from the great pillage. Attar, mingling promises with threats, got the looters to bring these things to the church. Success, as usual, went to his feather-brained head, and before very long he was promising vast fortunes. The treasure began to flow back again, and several items had to be rejected by Father Macdonnel as being by no conceivable probability part of the furnishings of a Christian place of worship. Father Macdonnel calculated that within a week much more than half the looted property would once more be in the hands of the clergy. On Saturday the silver offertory-stand was returned.

Father Macdonnel was a straight and honourable man. In consequence he made a sorry mess of this business, because, once involved in a shady policy, he lost his way. He was short-sighted in crime. He made an idiotic error in promising this dividend on Sunday: a little thought should have made it clear to him that his interest lay in a firm refusal to pay anything until all the looted property was returned.

But even in the performance of good works he inclined to be impulsive and unreflective. He was lost here.

After Mass on Sunday he went to the sacristy door, as arranged. He found a vociferous and sweltering mob who had assembled on Attar's instructions. Attar himself stood in front of them with a hideous proprietary air, and he greeted the priest with a wave of his hand to this flock. 'Here they are, Sir,' he said.

Father Macdonnel surveyed them from the steps with a scowl.

'What do they want?' he asked.

'Why what the Hell d'ya think they want except to be paid up of course.' Attar could never rid himself of the habit of talking down to his audience. The habit had lost him many friends, but not this one yet.

'These are the looters, are they?' the priest answered with affected surprise. 'I see. Very well, give them twenty-five piastres apiece.'

'Twenty-five piastres!' screamed Attar in horror, but before he could say more the priest, in order to forestall him, shouted in Arabic: 'Twenty-five piastres!'

Immediately a suspicion of the ghastly truth as to how they had been tricked began to spread in the crowd. Many of them turned to Attar to demand what this meant, and Attar, after an unsuccessful attempt to parley with Father Macdonnel, who stood at the top of the sacristy steps looking on with icy contempt, repeated to them that their reward was to be twenty-five piastres each, which in those days was equivalent to five shillings.

'And hurry up and get on with it,' added Father

Macdonnel, dramatically throwing a tied-up roll of notes to him.

There was something so awful in the priest's controlled anger that a hush came for a moment over the crowd. Attar, with a worried expression, had actually begun to perform his task of distributing these paltry wages before he was brushed aside, while there arose a wild loud long wail, followed by another, deep horrible more savage noise—the voice of their loathing of the infidel Christian, the voice of Jahad or Holy War. One or two advanced to the priest with extended palms showing the little crumpled cheap bank notes which they had received in the place of expected millions. But Father Macdonnel raised his hand for silence, and through Attar spoke to them. They listened appalled at what he said.

If they thought they were merchants, he began, they were mistaken. They were looters. Their names had all been taken. It was not customary to reward looters but to punish them. Did they know what the punishment for looting was? It was—death. (He suspected, rightly, that Attar would not like to translate this, so he said it three times, and added some gestures.) Strictly, he went on, they were all under sentence. If there was one more word of complaint their names, all of them, would be given to the Military Police and there would be a mass execution. He had no more to say. The choice was theirs. He had spoken. A minute later dust rose high into the air. Without waiting for their money, with the rapid patter of the feet of fear, they rushed off to their houses and hid in them for the rest of that day and most of the next. Attar was worried.

'Why didn't ya let me speak to these damned natives, Sir?' he asked.

'Because I do it better,' replied the priest angrily.

'You make one Hell of a mess of it, Sir. Who's going to sell me any church gadgets now, eh? You've killed the damned goose who lays the golden calf. You don't understand these bloody people, Sir.'

'I'm not a Moslem, if *that*'s what you mean.'

'No more am I a Moslem. Colonel Adrian Lally is one bloody big liar. He goes round Cairo crying out filthy things concerning me. Who the Hell says I am a Moslem?'

'You do when it suits you.'

But Attar was quite right. Returns of church property dropped to nil immediately, the flow of sacred valuables had been turned off at the main, the spring had been parched by disappointment and fear, and the chalice, the chalice which without doubt was somewhere there in those filthy bazaars, had not been recovered. Father Macdonnel's irritation increased as he thought over this failure. His ultimate realization that, if he had followed Attar's advice, he would almost certainly have succeeded, was bitter in the extreme. Desperately he took to the bazaars himself. He strode about them with a black frown on his face; he glared and peered into every shop where a chalice might be hidden amid piles of junk; he yelled his sixteen words of Arabic into many a merchant's ear; he achieved nothing. At this point an important development began. Attar once more took a hand in the search.

General Montgomery's advance was in full tide. Ten days after Father Macdonnel's arrival in Mahammadieh the rumble of the guns was no longer audible there, and from the poetry and squalor of the front line the town began to turn to the discomforts of restored life. It had been, comparatively speaking, mildly damaged in the campaign, and the army decided to use it as a convalescence and sick leave centre, of course on a modest scale. It had a good hospital, a few large hotels, and excellent sea bathing. It had once hoped to be a tourist-trap.

As Mahammadieh remained the rear Headquarters of Father Macdonnel's corps, he was obliged to stay there until the next big leap forward in the advance, and so he was ordered to help his colleagues to found some sort of a troops' club. The chaplains had a great deal of work to do in devising from slender materials the means for men to enjoy themselves, nor were any of them particularly gifted in this task. Least of all Father Macdonnel. He was not interested in enjoyment. They were all much relieved when a regular 'welfare' officer arrived from Cairo. For Father Macdonnel this meant, above all, that he could give more time to the restoration of the religious life of the cathedral, an undertaking where, in the midst of success, he was never for an instant unmindful of his one great failure: the absence of a certain chalice from the altar.

The welfare officer was an energetic and efficient man. He got a cinema going; he conjured up concerts and theatricals; he saw that the club was well stocked with newspapers, and tinned beer called Rheingold; and he organized a sports meeting . . . At this sports meeting the main event was to be a horse race, and this horse race was to be run for a trophy, and the trophy was to be known as The Mahammadieh Cup. Father Macdonnel was invited to be a steward. The welfare officer was a very able officer indeed.

It was Attar who told Father Macdonnel that the chalice had been discovered. He told him that he had found the man who had bought it from the thief, and—here Attar looked suspiciously mournful—the man had unfortunately sold it to a British officer. Oh yes, he knew who the officer was, yes, he was in Mahammadieh. He was Major Swinstead. Swinstead was the name of the welfare officer . . .

At the time when I heard this story from Father Macdonnel, I was puzzled by Adrian's signal to me with his eyes at the first mention of the horse race, and I would be happy indeed if I could convey to the reader the slow accumulation of enjoyment, the gradual and luxurious sinking into the pleasures of comedy, which I experienced as the truth dawned on me. The Mahammadieh Cup and the chalice were one and the same.

'I took the sacristan round,' said Father Macdonnel as he told the story, 'I took him round and he identified it. Oh yes, he identified it. It was standing in Major Swinstead's office. There was no mistake in it. Attar had told me the truth. It was the cathedral chalice they were intending to run a horse race to win.'

On the morning following this exposure Father Macdonnel sent round an early note to the welfare officer to say that he would call at ten-thirty on a most important matter. He would prefer to see him alone.

Had Attar remained away from the scene, there would have been a slender chance of the misunderstanding between the priest and Swinstead being arranged amicably, but unfortunately, at this moment, Attar, that cunning and foolish man, must needs try his hand at diplomacy.

Before that important ten-thirty he visited the welfare officer. He tried to frighten him. He told

Major Swinstead how Father Macdonnel had summoned the people of the bazaars and threatened them with a massacre if all cathedral property was not returned immediately, and how he had personally ransacked several shops in search of the chalice, and how when he had heard that Major Swinstead had it in his possession he had broken into his office with the sacristan in order to make sure. 'I tell you, Major Swinstead,' he concluded, 'that man is just raving crazy for his chalice. I warn you, Sir, not to make him more crazy. If you do I am damned well blowed if he will not seize the chalice by force and/or violence from you. I know bloody well indeed what I am speaking about.'

Major Swinstead was one of those people who are easily liable to a sense of grievance. After Attar's visit he felt a very considerable sense of grievance. He was not a Catholic. In so far as he thought about religion he did so as a very pure Protestant. Though unacquainted with the term, he disliked ultramontanism, particularly since June 1940.

At half-past ten Father Macdonnel called on Major Swinstead. He was smiling and bent on good manners. He had forced himself to be optimistic about this matter. He was painfully aware of his faults of temper, and he was determined not to be unjust to Major Swinstead, who, after all, was entirely guiltless in what had happened.

'Good morning, Major,' he said, 'I hope I am not discommoding you, but you were good enough to ask me to be a steward at the races ... That is not a thing I believe I should do, strictly in accordance with Canon Law, but I think we may reasonably wave aside these objections in a place like Mahammadieh. Now, Major, I want to talk to you about this very horse race. It is about,' and he shot a glance to the mantelpiece on which the chalice was standing, 'the Cup.'

Major Swinstead was a big fair man whose features in ill-humoured repose took on a look of obstinate surliness. On these occasions his voice sounded low and sullen, like the sound of a bell, the sort of bell, moreover, which might fittingly be hung in a large brick neo-Gothic clock tower in an English market square.

'What about the Cup?' he said.

Father Macdonnel caught the note of hostility.

'I should greatly like to know how you come to be in possession of that cup,' he replied with a quick flash of anger in his eye.

'I bought it,' said the Major, and gazed at him in the manner of some huge short-horn bull, as much as to say: 'If you leave me alone you can quit the field without being gored.'

Father Macdonnel started afresh. For the last time that morning he trod the path of appeasement.

'Well now, that's very understandable and I am sincerely sorry to have to cause you a great deal of disturbance and inconvenience. But the truth is, Major, that cup is church property. It is not a simple golden cup at all. It is a chalice. It is the cathedral chalice. It has been identified by Father Battino the sacristan—you know, the old man who remained behind—and strictly speaking it belongs to me, so long as I am here.'

Major Swinstead's mouth became depressed as in an inverted smile; his face, including the lower of his two chins, became suffused with redness, in the midst of which his fair moustache seemed to sparkle like lightning flashes in sunset clouds. A wonderful sight.

'If you want,' he said with slow and massive irony, 'if you want to put in a claim that it's looted property, all right, well, and good. I'll forward it myself, and at the end of the war, or whenever Claims give you an authorization, the owner of the cup will give it back to you on receipt of compensation from the sub-department concerned. But my God,' went on Major Swinstead, 'coolly walking into my office and just bloody well ordering me to hand over the cup . . . And not only that. Coming along with this bloody Battino or whatever he's called and breaking into my office when I'm not there. Turning my whole office upside down. Bursting into my office as if it was a bloody thieves' kitchen. And then coolly walking into my office and demanding my property. Honestly, padre, I think that's the bloody limit.' Major Swinstead had those extraordinarily morbid feelings of affection and loyalty towards the room where he conducted business which are so common in any form of official life, and particularly in the army.

Father Macdonnel turned on Swinstead in a passion of vehemence.

'You are talking like an uneducated child. Breaking into your office, my goodness! As a steward I have a right to see the cup, and I saw it. The door was open. As a priest I have a duty to identify sacred property and Father Battino has enabled me to identify it. You ought to be ashamed of yourself, Major Swinstead, talking so to me. You say I walk in and demand your property. I have not done so but I will do so now. I tell you that that cup is my chalice and I have a right to demand my chalice. And I do demand it. I demand that you hand over that cup, Major Swinstead. Do you understand that!'

'I bought that cup,' said Major Swinstead, 'and I won't hand it over unless I'm ordered to. That cup,' he went on, 'cost me a bloody lot of money. I can get some of it back, I dare say, but it was a bloody expensive cup. It isn't a lot of fellows who'd pay up more than they can afford with only an outside chance of a rebate, so's the chaps'll have a decent cup to race for. I'm not complaining. I'm simply trying to tell you that I'm not going to give up that cup, church property or no church property, no matter what you, and no matter what Father Bloody Battino, or anybody bloody else says, unless I'm ordered to by the Corps Commander or my senior officer in Cairo.'

Father Macdonnel then posed him a serious question.

'Do you realize, Major Swinstead, that to Roman Catholics that cup is as sacred as any material object can be?'

Major Swinstead replied simply: 'I'm not a Roman Catholic.'

A gulf yawned. Two mighty antagonists faced one another. Major Swinstead was lost in the immense and ghostly company which drew up by his side; the fires of Smithfield roared round him. From him at that moment came the cry of freedom against priestly tyranny, against profitable superstitions, against worldly trafficking in holy things. His voice was the sublime utterance of the English Bible. His strength was the strength which had cast forth the ghost of the Roman Empire sitting crowned on the ruins thereof. And on the other side was unforsaken faith great in rule, and in constancy amid the grief of misfortune as the things of this world are reckoned. The ghosts of More and Campion stood there, and of another company, who had scorned peace and wealth at the price of Irish apostasy. The most superb of all claims fortified Father Macdonnel. 'Upon this rock I will build My Church.'

There was no more to be said. Father Macdonnel rose to his feet.

'I will refer this matter elsewhere,' he said, and stalked in white fury out of the Welfare Office.

Heroic moments beget their contraries: moods of high passion often give way to moods of inventive commonsense. As he walked out of Major Swinstead's office Father Macdonnel was in a state of exalted anger in which he felt he could have passed through the torture of martyrdom with defiant joy, in which the blows of chains would have felt like the blows of feathers. But when he arrived at the cathedral he was in a perfectly calm and practically inclined state of mind. He had said he would refer this matter elsewhere. He would indeed, and not first to the Corps Commander. A terrible smile crept over his thin mouth. He summoned Attar to his little office by the sacristy, and together they were long in conference. When Attar left, Father Macdonnel sent a curt note to Major Swinstead saying that he was not able to act as a steward for the forthcoming races.

'Bloody difficult chap, this R.C. padre,' said Major Swinstead in the mess. 'First he wants to pinch our cup and now he won't act as a steward.'

'Funny,' said his friend, 'I'd have thought he was a sportsman.'

The great day came, and everyone, by which I

mean more than half of the local people, the entire staffs of the various Headquarters, the wounded who could move, and the convalescents, two battalions who were in transit to the front line, and a hundred or so on sick leave, went to the racecourse. There was a greater crowd than had been seen there before in its short history. The sports began at three. The egg and spoon races, the three-legged races, the race for men dressed as women, the hurdles, the camel race, the donkey race, and the auction for a military charity of a case of Chianti wine, went well enough, went, all of them, as the frivolous overture before the performance of the great piece: the Mahammadieh Cup. A cab race had been suggested but it was pointed out that all but a few of the cab horses of the town had been entered for the main event.

The racecourse at Mahammadieh where this sporting festival took place is well designed. It was once madly hoped that horse racing would be one of the main attractions beckoning to tourists across the world, as is the case in Cairo. There is a paddock, an enclosure, a grandstand, and even a totalisator, though unfortunately the latter had recently received a direct hit, having been taken from the clouds for an important military installation, which, for all one knows, it might have been in the insanely practical way of warfare. This mattered little, however. There were bookmakers in the army, and they proclaimed themselves in many parts of the course. Newmarket sprung up like a mushroom in this oasis of Libya. Somebody rang a bell for saddling. When he rang it again five minutes later, a string of horses processed from the stables behind the paddock, each one saddled, and led by a native of the town, except one. This was a nice-looking half-Arab, very much the superior of the others. Arab is a loose term which covers many obscure breeds outside Arabia, but what was noticeably non-Arabian about this particular horse was its size, and a certain easy swing in its gait. It was led by Attar.

Before the bell rang again there was much cheering and jeering as the jockeys entered the sacred ring. Their caps and jackets were surprisingly professional in appearance and cut, but white breeches and mahogany-topped boots were in all cases substituted by khaki trousers fastened at the knee. It was amazing, so I was told by a man who was present, to see how exactly like an English race meeting this farcical competition became. The local people represented the dense noisy crowd, the densest and noisiest of all English crowds, the officers and men on leave became the counterparts of the privileged of the enclosures, and one could see instinctively how this man wore his white top hat at Ascot, or how that one with a bowler tilted forward over his brow, stood in impressive and secret preoccupation on the Knavesmire. The Corps Commander, who had flown over from forward Headquarters, for there was a lull in the advance, made a fitting Lord Lonsdale. Major Swinstead deputized for the clerk of the course.

The riders stood in the ring discussing last-minute instructions with their patrons, as is the custom. Only one stood apart. He appeared on the card as E. Macdonnel. He ground his teeth. He was reflecting that for a priest to dress up in this clownish costume was very nearly sacrilegious in itself. Supposing . . . no, he would not toy with that appalling possibility. He had some faith in Attar's researches into the past racing history of Mahammadieh. He had yet more faith in his own eye for a horse. He had another faith too which exalted him. He wished the 'jockeys up' bell would ring and hasten the end of this blasphemous farce.

The Corps Commander came up to him.

'Well, padre, this is a surprise seeing you here. Very sporting of you. Jolly good.' He laughed.

'Thank you, Sir.' He was tempted to tell him precisely why he *was* there. With blazing eyes he looked at the general, but controlled his feelings.

'Nice horse you've got too. Looks as if he's got some breeding.'

'I selected him with care, Sir. I believe him to be a quarter bred, and if that is true it will be by Gay Crusader by the ugly look of him.' As Father Macdonnel said this he looked at the horse again. There is a kind of equine ugliness which is enjoyable because, as they say in horsy language, it 'fills the eye'.

'I'll back you, padre.' The general chortled with delight.

'You might do worse, though the horse is not young,' replied Father Macdonnel, who was not joining in the general's amusement.

'By Jove, he stands out, doesn't he? How did you find him?'

'My interpreter assisted me. We borrowed him from one of the shaykhs who used to race here. The man has removed what he could from the town as he knew the Germans were leaving. They told him. What other racehorses were here are either killed or as yet untraced, as the thieves are still hiding the live ones. There was much looting and disorder, you may recall, Sir.' The Corps Commander discerned a note of sudden irritation in Father Macdonnel's last words. This puzzled him. Perhaps he imagined it.

'How d'you know the horse's breeding?'

'He was bought by Marshal Balbo from an Egyptian, who specializes in cross-breeding with Arab mares, for what they call country-bred racing.'

The bell rang.

'Ah, you Irish! You can't keep away from a horse, can you?' He held up a finger waggishly. The priest did not smile.

'I have ridden very little since I took orders . . . If you'll excuse me, Sir, I must mount.'

'Good luck, padre.'

There was a parade of horses on the course before the start. One of the first things to be noticed was how one or two horsemen stood out by reason of their professional style, and on the strength of it, number eighteen, E. Macdonnel up, became the favourite. When the beast cantered by the enclosure, wagging his head and lashing with his tongue, the odds on him shortened by yet another point. There were thirty-four in the field.

Starting was difficult because professional starters are rarer than other officials of the turf and there had been no time for experiments or rehearsals on an adequate scale. The starting gate, therefore, was handled in a clumsy manner. The proverb about too many cooks and broth applied well here: the gate was for ever going up and down, and there was a moment when a horse was swept off its hooves which were entangled in the strings. After this the gate was abandoned for the old-fashioned flag. There were six false starts from which several horses never returned. When they did get away number eighteen was last.

With few exceptions the riders flogged their horses into maximum speed from the beginning. Not so E. Macdonnel. It would be inaccurate to say that he rode a waiting race; he rode a professional race. His first object was to keep in the running, holding his horse for a final turn of speed, though beyond a general belief in the power of heredity, he had no means of knowing whether this turn was to be found in the descendant of Gay Crusader. He hoped so and guessed so. The race was ambitious: two miles and a half long. There were many distractions. At the seventh furlong one horse fell down dead. Half a furlong on another crashed into the rails at the bend. E. Macdonnel did not so much fear being shut in as being confused by dizziness from the zigzag path of the horses before him. His chance came at the last corner, a little under a mile from home. Here, while he hugged the rails, the whole field lurched over in a body to the far side, and another sickening splintering crash made him suppose, rightly as it happened, that yet another horse had been thrown off the course through the rails. A sharp competitor, ridden by a steeplechase jockey of former days, was coming up on his right. When he heard that approaching noise he at last liberated the all-necessary turn of speed, on which everything depended. It was there. It was not a great turn of speed, but it was there. He heard the horse on his right blow up with a very audible explosion, whilst his own horse settled into a heavy slogging gallop. It was not a fast horse. It was not a born winner. He heard another coming up behind him. He applied the whip. He spurred with his heels. But no tortures on this earth could accelerate the speed. The other horse grew near him, on his right again, but before it was abreast it also exploded. The descendant of Gay Crusader was a stayer, that was wonderfully clear. E. Macdonnel continued to apply the whip but without avail, only the heavy slogging gallop went on, at a regular speed. But it did go on. It went on and on and on. He was aware of a noise of cheering all about him. He saw the post ahead, and riding as though he was trying to strike out of a dead heat, Father Macdonnel won the Mahammadieh Cup by fourteen lengths. Ad Majorem Dei Gloriam.

When the cup was presented to Father Macdonnel by the Corps Commander, Major Swinstead came forward, beaming with admiration. Though he looked rather like a clock tower, he was a warm-hearted man. But something in Father Macdonnel's expression warned him not to chaff or joke about this matter. The major held out his hand. Father Macdonnel took it in his own. This was not a reconciliation, it was a temporary act of fellowship in honour of the human virtues which show in sportsmanship. The gulf yawned as wide as ever, a bridge had been built sufficient for one passage only. And so the two men shook hands.

'And there,' concluded Father Macdonnel, 'you have the whole story before you. That is the naked fact, told without prejudice, and that is the case I wish your assistance in to lay personally before the Commander-in-Chief, so as to avoid the scandal of a whole lot of people hearing it in the usual channels.'

'Well,' said Adrian, turning to me, 'What do you suggest?'

I said the obvious thing because I believed it to be the right thing.

'If this had happened to me, I would leave it where it is,' I said. 'Father Macdonnel has got the chalice, that's the main thing. To appeal to the military authorities now seems to me to reopen a settled case at an absurdly lower level.'

'Oh?' said the priest, raising his eyebrows high. 'I don't think that I am able to follow you.' He looked at me with a piercing and hostile gaze. 'Unless,' he added, 'you mean miracles.'

'I mean just that.'

He made a sound of contempt. 'I must remind you,' he said, 'that miracles can be tested by the simple rule that an authentic one is an occasion for grace. Can you imagine anything less an occasion for grace than that the clergy should compete as jockeys for sacred vessels? I think that anyone who knew what was going on would have been utterly disgusted and scandalized.'

'But that's just the point,' I replied, 'no one does know. Except Major Swinstead. Is he likely to gossip and make mischief? From your story I do not somehow see him as doing that. Am I right?'

The priest hummed a moment and rubbed his chin. He said: 'Major Swinstead is not an indiscreet man, I think. I had heard no talk about this when I left. He is not a bad man in himself, the Major.'

'I gather that Father Battino need not be taken into account.'

'Father Battino did not attend the races . . .'

'And there is nobody else to know. I think you can forget this question of scandal.'

'But Attar knows . . .'.

This sounded like the Ace of Trumps. I had forgotten the pathological chairman, however. Since he had last spoken Adrian had kept his face covered by his hands as though he was in prayer. He now lowered his hands to the table. His eyes were swimming with tears. Though there was a slight tremolo in his voice from his mastered giggles, he spoke now with assurance.

'Attar,' he said, 'is the solution of your problem. You no longer have a problem. It is solved.'

'In what way?'

'I imagine,' said Adrian, 'that when you go your rounds with that monster Attar he sometimes attends your Mass. Is that right?'

For the first time in our discussion Father Macdonnel smiled, as he thought of his wayward lamb. 'Indeed,' he said, 'he attends quite regularly, the rascal, and I am supposed to be very impressed. Oh dear, oh dear, he's a simpleton, is Attar.'

'Yesterday,' said Adrian, 'I saw Attar at High Mass at St. Joseph's. He was by himself. He had not gone there to impress you or any other mortal. And I will tell you something else about that remarkable publican. I saw him put quite a handsome note into the plate. Not a large part, I dare say, of what he made out of the chalice, but something none the less. At the time I was puzzled, now I am sure I understand. Father Macdonnel, you are wrong to dismiss the idea of miracles. You may win a race by your own exertions, but you don't reclaim Attar that way.'

There was a long silence. Father Macdonnel, I could see, was moved.

He got to his feet. 'Well, Colonel Lally,' he said, 'you know GHQ better than I do, so I will take your advice and not approach the Commander-in-Chief. Thank you for your trouble, both of you. Good morning.' He marched out of the office.

WILLIAM SANSOM

The Vertical Ladder

As he felt the first watery eggs of sweat moistening
the palms of his hands, as with every rung higher his
body seemed to weigh more heavily, this young man
Flegg regretted in sudden desperation, but still in
vain, the irresponsible events that had thrust him
up into his present precarious climb. Here he was,
isolated on a vertical iron ladder flat to the side of
a gasometer and bound now to climb higher and
higher until he should reach the vertiginous skyward
summit.

How could he ever have wished this on himself?
How easy it had been to laugh away his cautionary
fears on the firm ground . . . now he would give the
very hands that clung to the ladder for a safe conduct to solid earth.

It had been a strong Spring day, abruptly as warm
as midsummer. The sun flooded the parks and streets
with sudden heat—Flegg and his friends had felt
stifled in their thick winter clothes. The green glare
of the new leaves everywhere struck the eye too
fiercely, the air seemed almost sticky from the ex-
halations of buds and swelling resins. Cold winter
senses were overcome—the girls had complained of
headaches—and their thoughts had grown confused
and uncomfortable as the wool underneath against
their skins. They had wandered out from the park
by a back gate, into an area of back streets.

The houses there were small and old, some of

them already falling into disrepair; short streets, cobbles, narrow pavements, and the only shops a tobacconist or a desolate corner oil-shop to colour the grey—it was the outcrop of some industrial undertaking beyond. At first these quiet, almost deserted streets had seemed more restful than the park; but soon a dusty air of peeling plaster and powdering brick, the dark windows and the dry stone steps, the very dryness altogether had proved more wearying than before, so that when suddenly the houses ended and the ground opened to reveal the yards of a disused gasworks, Flegg and his friends had welcomed the green of nettles and milk-wort that grew among the scrap-iron and broken brick.

They walked out into the wasteland, the two girls and Flegg and the other two boys, and stood presently before the old gasometer itself. Among the ruined sheds this was the only erection still whole, it still predominated over the yards, towering high above other buildings for hundreds of feet around. So they threw bricks against its rusted sides.

The rust flew off in flakes and the iron rang dully. Flegg, who wished to excel in the eyes of the dark-haired girl, began throwing his bricks higher than the others, at the same time lobbing them, to suggest that he knew something of grenade-throwing, claim-ing for himself vicariously the glamour of a uniform. He felt the girl's eyes follow his shoulders, his shoul-ders broadened. She had black eyes, unshadowed beneath short wide-awake lids, as bright as a boy's eyes; her lips pouted with difficulty over a scramble of irregular teeth, so that it often looked as if she were laughing; she always frowned—and Flegg liked her earnest, purposeful expression. Altogether

she seemed a wide-awake girl who would be the
first to appreciate an active sort of a man. Now she
frowned and shouted: 'Bet you can't climb as high
as you can throw!'

Then there began one of those uneasy jokes, innocent at first, that taken seriously can accumulate an
hysterical accumulation of spite. Everyone recog-
nizes this underlying unpleasantness, it is plainly
felt; but just because of this the joke must at all costs
be pressed forward, one becomes frightened, one
laughs all the louder, pressing to drown the embar-
rassments of danger and guilt. The third boy had
instantly shouted: ''Course he can't, he can't climb
no higher than himself.'

Flegg turned round scoffing, so that the girl had
quickly shouted again, laughing shrilly and pointing upwards. Already all five of them felt uneasy.
Then in quick succession, all in a few seconds, the
third boy had repeated: ''Course he bloody can't.'
Flegg had said: 'Climb to the top of anything.' The
other boy had said: 'Climb to the top of my aunt
Fanny.' The girl had said: 'Climb to the top of the
gasworks then.'

Flegg had said: 'That's nothing.' And the girl,
pressing on then as she had to, suddenly introduced
the inevitable detail that made these suppositions
into fact: 'Go on then, climb it. Here—tie my hanky
on the top. Tie my flag to the top.'

Even then Flegg had a second's chance. It occurred to him instantly that he could laugh it off;
but an hysterical emphasis now possessed the girl's
face—she was dancing up and down and clapping
her hands insistently—and this confused Flegg. He
began stuttering after the right words. But the words
refused to come. At all costs he had to cover his

stuttering. So: 'Off we go then!' he had said. And
he had turned to the gasometer.

It was not, after all, so very high. It was hardly a
full-size gasometer, its trellised iron top-rail would
have stood level with the roof coping of a five or six
storey tenement. Until then Flegg had only seen the
gasometer as a rough mass of iron, but now every
detail sprang into abrupt definition. He studied it
intently, alertly considering its size and every feature of stability, the brown rusted iron sheeting
smeared here and there with red lead, a curious
buckling that sometimes deflated its curved bulk as
though a vacuum were collapsing it from within,
and the ladders scaling the sides flush with the sheeting. The grid of girders, a complexity of struts, the
bolting.

There were two ladders, one Jacob's ladder
clamped fast to the side, another that was more of
a staircase, zigzagging up the belly of the gasometer
in easy gradients and provided with a safety rail.
This must have been erected later as a substitute for
the Jacob's ladder, which demanded an unnecessarily stringent climb and was now in fact in disuse,
for some twenty feet of its lower rungs had been
torn away; however, there was apparently some
painting in progress, for a wooden painter's ladder
had been propped beneath with its head reaching to
the undamaged bottom of the vertical ladder—the
ascent was thus serviceable again. Flegg looked
quickly at the foot of the wooden ladder, was it well
grounded?—and then at the head farther up—was
this secure?—and then up to the top, screwing his
eyes to note any fault in the iron rungs reaching
innumerably and indistinctly, like the dizzying strata
of a zip, to the summit platform.

Flegg, rapidly assessing these structures, never stopped sauntering forward. He was committed, and so while deliberately sauntering to appear thus the more at ease, he knew that he must never hesitate. The two boys and his own girl kept up a chorus of encouraging abuse. 'How I climbed Mount Everest', they shouted. 'He'll come down quicker 'n he went up.' 'Mind you don't bang your head on a harp, Sir Galahad.' But the second girl had remained quiet throughout; she was already frightened, sensing instantly that the guilt for some tragedy was hers alone —although she had never in fact opened her mouth. Now she chewed passionately on gum that kept her jaws firm and circling.

Suddenly the chorus rose shriller. Flegg had veered slightly towards the safer staircase. His eyes had naturally questioned this along with the rest of the gasometer, and almost unconsciously his footsteps had veered in the direction of his eyes; then this instinct had emerged into full consciousness— perhaps he could use the staircase, no one had actually instanced the Jacob's ladder, there might yet be a chance? But the quick eyes behind him had seen, and immediately the chorus rose: 'No you don't!' 'Not up those sissy stairs!' Flegg switched his course by only the fraction that turned him again to the perpendicular ladder. 'Who's talking about stairs?' he shouted back.

Behind him they still kept up a din, still kept him up to pitch, worrying at him viciously. 'Look at him, he doesn't know which way to go—he's like a ruddy duck's uncle without an aunt.'

So that Flegg realized finally that there was no alternative. He had to climb the gasometer by the vertical ladder. And as soon as this was finally settled, the doubt cleared from his mind. He braced his shoulders and suddenly found himself really making light of the job. After all, he thought, it isn't so high? Why should I worry? Hundreds of men climb such ladders each day, no one falls, the ladders are clamped as safe as houses? He began to smile within himself at his earlier perturbations. Added to this, the girl now ran up to him and handed him her handkerchief. As her black eyes frowned a smile at him, he saw that her expression no longer held its vicious laughing scorn, but now instead had grown softer, with a look of real encouragement and even admiration. 'Here's your flag,' she said. And then she even added: 'Tell you what—you don't really have to go! I'll believe you!' But this came too late. Flegg had accepted the climb, it was fact, and already he felt something of an exhilarating glow of glory. He took the handkerchief, blew the girl a dramatic kiss, and started up the lowest rungs of the ladder at a run.

This painter's ladder was placed at a comfortable slant. But nevertheless Flegg had only climbed some ten feet—what might have corresponded to the top of a first-floor window—when he began to slow up, he stopped running and gripped harder at the rungs above and placed his feet more firmly on the unseen bars below. Although he had not yet measured his distance from the ground, somehow he sensed distinctly that he was already unnaturally high, with nothing but air and a precarious skeleton of wooden bars between him and the receding ground. He felt independent of solid support; yet, according to his eyes, which stared straight forward at the iron sheeting beyond, he might have been still standing on the lowest rungs by the ground. The sensation of height infected him strongly, it had become an urgent necessity to maintain a balance, each muscle of his body became unnaturally alert. This was not an unpleasant feeling, he almost enjoyed a new athletic command of every precarious movement. He climbed then methodically until he reached the ladderhead and the first of the perpendicular iron rungs.

Here for a moment Flegg had paused. He had rested his knees up against the last three steps of the safely slanting wooden ladder, he had grasped the two side supports of the rusted iron that led so straightly upwards. His knees then clung to the motherly wood, his hands felt the iron cold and gritty. The rust powdered off and smeared him with its red dust; one large scrap flaked off and fell on to his face as he looked upwards. He wanted to brush this away from his eye, but the impulse was, to his surprise, much less powerful than the vice-like will that clutched his hand to the iron support. His hand remained firmly gripping the iron, he had to shake off the rust-flake with a jerk of his head. Even then this sharp movement nearly unbalanced him, and his stomach gulped coldly with sudden shock. He settled his knees more firmly against the wood, and though he forced himself to laugh at this sudden fear, so that in some measure his poise did really return, nevertheless he did not alter the awkward knock-kneed position of his legs patently clinging for safety. With all this he had scarcely paused. Now he pulled at the stanchions of the iron ladder, they were as firm as if they had been driven into rock.

He looked up, following the dizzying rise of the rungs to the skyline. From this angle flat against the iron sheeting, the gasometer appeared higher than before. The blue sky seemed to descend and almost touch it. The redness of the rust dissolved into a deepening grey shadow, the distant curved summit loomed over black and high. Although it was immensely stable, as seen in rounded perspective from a few yards away, there against the side it appeared top-heavy, so that this huge segment of sheet iron seemed to have lost the support of its invisible complement behind, the support that was now unseen and therefore unfelt, and Flegg imagined despite himself that the entire erection had become unsteady, that quite possibly the gasometer might suddenly blow over like a gigantic top-heavy sail. He lowered his eyes quickly and concentrated on the hands before him. He began to climb.

From beneath there still rose a few cries from the boys. But the girl had stopped shouting—probably she was following Flegg's every step with admiring eyes. He imagined again her frown and her peculiarly pouting mouth, and from this image drew new strength with which he clutched the rungs more eagerly. But now he noticed that the cries had begun to ring with an unpleasant new echo, as though they were already far off. And Flegg could not so easily distinguish their words. Even at this height he seemed to have penetrated into a distinct strata of separate air, for it was certainly cooler, and for the first time that day he felt the light fanning of a wind. He looked down. His friends appeared shockingly small. Their bodies had disappeared and he saw only their upturned faces. He wanted to wave, to demonstrate in some way a carefree attitude; but then instantly he felt frustrated as his hands refused to unlock their grip. He turned to the rungs again with the smile dying on his lips.

He swallowed uneasily and continued to tread

slowly upwards, hand after hand, foot after foot. He
had climbed ten rungs of the iron ladder when his
hands first began to feel moist, when suddenly, as
though a catastrophe had overtaken him not gradually but in one overpowering second, he realized
that he was afraid; incontrovertibly. He could cover
it no longer, he admitted it all over his body. His
hands gripped with pitiable eagerness, they were
now alert to a point of shivering, as though the
nerves inside them had been forced taut for so long
that now they had burst beyond their strained tegu-
ment; his feet no longer trod firmly on the rungs
beneath, but first stepped for their place timorously,
then glued themselves to the iron. In this way his
body lost much of its poise; these nerves and muscles
in his two legs and two arms seemed to work independently, no longer integrated with the rhythm of
his body, but moving with the dangerous unwilled
jerk of crippled limbs.

His body hung slack away from the ladder, with
nothing beneath it but a thirty-foot drop to the
ground; only his hands and feet were fed with the
security of an attachment, most of him lay off the
ladder, hanging in space; his arms revolted at the
strain of their unfamiliar angle, as though they were
flies' feet denying all natural laws. For the first time,
as the fear took hold of him, he felt that what he had
attempted was impossible. He could never achieve
the top. If at this height of only thirty feet, as it were
three storeys of a building, he felt afraid—what
would he feel at sixty feet? Yet . . . he trod heavily
up. He was afraid, but not desperate. He dreaded
each step, yet forced himself to believe that at some
time it would be over, it could not take long.

A memory crossed his mind. It occurred to him

vividly, then flashed away, for his eyes and mind
were continually concentrated on the rusted iron
bars and the white knuckles of his hands. But for
an instant he remembered waking up long ago in
the nursery and seeing that the windows were light,
as if they reflected a coldness of moonlight. Only
they were not so much lit by light as by a sensation
of space. The windows seemed to echo with space.
He had crawled out of bed and climbed on to a chair
that stood beneath the window. It was as he had
thought. Outside there was space, nothing else, a
limitless area of space; yet this was not unnatural,
for soon his logical eyes had supplied for what had
at first appeared an impossible infinity the later
image of a perfectly reasonable flood. A vast plain
of still water continued as far as his eyes could see.
The tennis courts and the houses beyond had disappeared; they were quite submerged, flat motionless water spread out immeasurably to the distant
arced horizon all around. It lapped silently at the
sides of the house, and in the light of an unseen
moon winked and washed darkly, concealing great
beasts of mystery beneath its black calm surface.
This water attracted him, he wished to jump into it
from the window and immerse himself in it and
allow his head to sink slowly under. However he was
perched up too high. He felt, alone at the window,
infinitely high, so that the flood seemed to lie in
miniature at a great distance below, as later in life
when he was ill he had seen the objects of his
bedroom grow small and infinitely remote in the
fevered reflection behind his eyes. Isolated at the
little window he had been frightened by the empti-
ness surrounding him, only the sky and the water
and the marooned stone wall of the house; he

had been terrified yet drawn down by dread and desire.

Then a battleship had sailed by. He had woken up, saved by the appearance of the battleship. And now on the ladder he had a sudden hope that something as large and stable would intervene again to help him.

But ten rungs farther up he began to sweat more violently than ever. His hands streamed with wet rust, the flesh inside his thighs blenched. Another flake of rust fell on his forehead; this time it stuck in the wetness. He felt physically exhausted. Fear was draining his strength and the precarious position of his body demanded an awkward physical effort. From his outstretched arms suspended most of the weight of his body. Each stressed muscle ached. His body weighed more heavily at each step upwards, it sagged beneath his arms like a leaden sack. His legs no longer provided their adequate support; it seemed as though they needed every pull of their muscle to force themselves, as independent limbs, close to the ladder. The wind blew faster. It dragged now at his coat, it blew its space about him, it echoed silently a lonely spaciousness. 'Don't look down', the blood whispered in his temples, 'Don't look down, for God's sake, DON'T LOOK DOWN.'

Three-quarters up the gasometer, and fifty feet from the ground, Flegg grew desperate. Every other consideration suddenly left him. He wanted only to reach the ground as quickly as possible, only that. Nothing else mattered. He stopped climbing and clung to the ladder panting. Very slowly, lowering his eyes carefully so that he could raise them instantly if he saw too much, he looked down a rung, and another past his armpit, past his waist—and focused them on the ground beneath. He looked quickly up again.

He pressed himself to the ladder. Tears started in his eyes. For a moment they reeled red with giddiness. He closed them, shutting out everything. Then instantly opened them, afraid that something might happen. He must watch his hands, watch the bars, watch the rusted iron sheeting itself; no movement should escape him; the struts might come creaking loose, the whole edifice might sway over; although a fading reason told him that the gasometer had remained firm for years and was still as steady as a cliff, his horrified senses suspected that this was the one moment in the building's life when a wind would blow that was too strong for it, some defective strut would snap, the whole edifice would heel over and go crashing to the ground. This image became so clear that he could see the sheets of iron buckling and folding like cloth as the huge weight sank to the earth.

The ground had receded horribly, the drop now appeared terrifying, out of all proportion to this height he had reached. From the ground such a height would have appeared unnoteworthy. But now looking down the distance seemed to have doubled. Each object familiar to his everyday eyes—his friends, the lamp-posts, a brick wall, the kerb, a drain—all these had grown infinitely small. His senses demanded that these objects should be of a certain accustomed size. Alternatively, the world of chimneys and attic windows and roof-coping would grow unpleasantly giant as his pavement-bred eyes approached. Even now the iron sheeting that stretched to either side and above and below seemed to have grown, he was lost among such huge smooth dimensions, grown smaller himself and clinging now like a child lost on some monstrous desert of red rust.

These unfamiliarities shocked his nerves more than the danger of falling. The sense of isolation was overpowering. All things were suddenly alien. Yet exposed on the iron spaces, with the unending winds blowing aerially round him, among such free things—he felt shut in! Trembling and panting so that he stifled himself with the shortness of his own breath, he took the first step downwards . . .

A commotion began below. A confusion of cries came drifting up to him. Above all he could hear the single voice of the girl who had so far kept quiet. She was screaming high, a shrill scream that rose in the air incisively like a gull's shriek. 'Put it back, put it back, put it back!' the scream seemed to say. So that Flegg, thinking that these cries were to warn him of some new danger apparent only from the ground—Flegg gripped himself into the ladder and looked down again. He glanced down only for a fractional second—but in that time saw enough. He saw that the quiet girl was screaming and pointing to the base of the iron ladder. He saw the others crowding round her, gesticulating. He saw that she really had been crying, 'Put it back!' And he realized now what the words meant—someone had removed the painter's ladder.

It lay clearly on the ground, outlined white like a child's drawing of a ladder. The boys must have seen his first step downwards, and then, from fun or from spite they had removed his only means of retreat. He remembered that from the base of the iron ladder to the ground the drop fell twenty feet. He considered quickly descending and appealing from the

bottom of the ladder; but foresaw that for precious
minutes they would jeer and argue, refusing to re-
place the ladder, and he felt then that he could never
risk these minutes, unnerved, with his strength failing. Besides, he had already noticed that the whole
group of them were wandering off. The boys were
driving the quiet girl away, now more concerned
with her than with Flegg. The quiet girl's sense of
guilt had been brought to a head by the removal of
the ladder. Now she was hysterically terrified. She
was yelling to them to put the ladder back. She—
only she, the passive one—sensed the terror that
awaited them all. But her screams defeated their
own purpose. They had altogether distracted the
attention of the others; now it was fun to provoke
more screams, to encourage this new distraction
—and they forgot about Flegg far up and beyond
them. They were wandering away. They were aban-
doning him, casually unconcerned that he was alone
and helpless up in his wide prison of rust. His heart
cried out for them to stay. He forgot their scorn in
new and terrible torments of self-pity. An uneasy
feeling lumped his throat, his eyes smarted with dry
tears.

But they were wandering away. There was no
retreat. They did not even know he was in difficulties. So Flegg had no option but to climb higher.
Desperately he tried to shake off his fear, he actually shook his head. Then he stared hard at the rungs
immediately facing his eyes, and tried to imagine
that he was not high up at all. He lifted himself tentatively by one rung, then by another, and in this
way dragged himself higher and higher . . . until he
must have been some ten rungs from the top, over
the fifth storey of a house, with now perhaps only

one more storey to climb. He imagined that he might then be approaching the summit platform, and to measure this last distance he looked up.

He looked up and heaved. He felt for the first time panicked beyond desperation, wildly violently loose. He almost let go. His senses screamed to let go, yet his hands refused to open. He was stretched on a rack made by these hands that would not unlock their grip and by the panic desire to drop. The nerves left his hands, so that they might have been dried bones of fingers gripped round the rungs, hooks of bone fixed perhaps strongly enough to cling on, or perhaps ready at some moment of pressure to uncurl their vertebrae and straighten to a drop. His insteps pricked with cold cramp. The sweat sickened him. His loins seemed to empty themselves. His trousers ran wet. He shivered, grew giddy, and flung himself froglike on to the ladder.

The sight of the top of the gasometer had proved endemically more frightful than the appearance of the drop beneath. There lay about it a sense not of material danger, not of the risk of falling, but of something removed and unhuman—a sense of appalling isolation. It echoed its elemental iron aloofness, a wind blew round it that had never known the warmth of flesh nor the softness of green fibres. Its blind eyes were raised above the world. It might have been the eyeless iron vizor of an ancient god. It touched against the sky, having risen in awful perpendicular to this isolation, solitary as the grey gannet cliffs that mark the end of the northern world. It was immeasurably old, outside the connotation of time; it was nothing human, only washed by the high weather, echoing with wind, visited never and silently alone.

And in this summit Flegg measured clearly the full distance of his climb. This close skyline emphasized the whirling space beneath him. He clearly saw a man fall through this space, spread-eagling to smash with the sickening force of a locomotive on the stone beneath. The man turned slowly in the air, yet his thoughts raced faster than he fell.

Flegg, clutching his body close to the rust, made small weeping sounds through his mouth. Shivering, shuddering, he began to tread up again, working his knees and elbows outwards like a frog, so that his stomach could feel the firm rungs. Were they firm? His ears filled with a hot roaring, he hurried himself, he began to scramble up, wrenching at his last strength, whispering urgent meaningless words to himself like the swift whispers that close in on a nightmare. A huge weight pulled at him, dragging him to drop. He climbed higher. He reached the top rung—and found his face staring still at a wall of red rust. He looked, wild with terror. It was the top rung! The ladder had ended! Yet—no platform ... the real top rungs were missing ... the platform jutted five impassable feet above ... Flegg stared dumbly, circling his head like a lost animal ... then he jammed his legs in the lower rungs and his arms past the elbows to the armpits in through the top rungs and there he hung shivering and past knowing what more he could ever do ...

FRED URQUHART

Man About the House

WHEN Mrs. Watt opened the gate she saw a fair-haired young man watching her out of the window. Waddling up the path, she was aware of him watching her every step. The road from the bus-stop had been uphill, and the sweat was trickling down her forehead and fat blowsy cheeks. She wiped her face, and as she drew her fingers across her brow, she saw that the young man was still standing at the window, gazing at her. As if he were staring at something in the zoo, she thought. She went to the back door, and as she was raising her hand to knock, the young man opened the door suddenly. She stood with her upraised hand in the air, feeling foolish.

'You'll be the new charwoman?' he said.

She nodded and shuffled past him.

'My mother's not up yet,' he said. 'But you can just begin.'

She put her black oilskin bag on the chair in the scullery and as she unpinned her hat she took stock of him. He was a very pale young man with hollow cheeks pitted with huge pores. He had pale blue, watery eyes that stared persistently at her from between his almost white lashes. She felt vaguely uncomfortable under his stare as she took her apron out of her bag and tied it around her fat stomach.

'What do you want me to do first?' she said.

'You can do the fires,' he said.

He showed her the box with blacklead and

brushes. 'You know how to clean a fire, don't you?' he said. 'You rake out the ashes and you take away the fender and——'

Mrs. Watt laughed. 'Bless me, laddie!' she said. 'I cleaned fireplaces long before ye were born.'

He stood and watched her as she set to work. All the time she was blackleading she was conscious of his watchful pale eyes, and she began to be annoyed at his continued scrutiny. He had to step aside when she took out the ashes to the bin, and she said: 'Ye're just like my first joker, he was aye gettin' in the way. I often used to say to him, "G'wa' oot o' ma road for ony favour and let me get on wi' ma work."'

But the young man did not take the hint. He hovered about the room, moving restlessly from one chair to another. He kept up a persistent breathing through his half-open mouth. It was neither a whistle nor a tune and it began to get on Mrs. Watt's nerves.

'What'll I do next?' she said.

'The dishes.'

He went before her into the scullery and pointed to a pile of dirty dishes on the board by the sink. 'You know how to do them, don't you?' he said. 'You drip them on this tray.'

Mrs. Watt laughed, but she did not say anything. The laddie's surely sort of simple, she said to herself. But she knitted her brows irritably when he lounged against the boiler and watched her. He was behind her, but all the time she was aware of the thin, tuneless whistling. She rattled the dishes noisily, trying to vent her irritation on them. She was relieved when Mrs. Laurie came in. She was a tired-looking little woman with a fretful face and pale eyes like her son.

'Good morning, Mrs. Watt,' she said. 'Has Eric been telling you what to do?'

'Ay,' Mrs. Watt said.

'I don't know what I'd do without him,' Mrs. Laurie said. 'He's such a comfort to me. Far better than many a daughter would have been. He's terribly handy about the house.'

'I can see that,' Mrs. Watt said.

Mrs. Laurie leaned against the sink and began to lament about her troubles. Not that Mrs. Watt could see that she had any cause to complain. Her husband, who had been a well-to-do market gardener, had died several years before, and had left her in very comfortable circumstances.

'Eric was our only child,' she said. 'He's all that I've got left now. Thank goodness, he's never needed to go out and work. I don't know what I'd have done if he'd had to go out every day to business. For all that he would have made, anyway. It wouldn't have been worth it. And I feel that I need somebody to keep me company. It's nice, I always think, to have a man about the house.'

'Well, it depends on the man,' Mrs. Watt said. 'I've had three, and none o' them were the kind o' men that ye like to see sittin' continually by the fireside. No' that that kept them frae doin' that, of course. None o' them were the kind that would break their necks bein' in the front o' ony queue lookin' for work. My first joker especially. Bless me, but he was oftener at hame than he was in a job.'

She sighed as she polished the chairs in the living-room. 'But ye shouldnie speak ill o' the dead. And he's been dead a long time, puir man. Gallopin' consumption he had.'

'I sometimes think that Eric's got consumption,'

Mrs. Laurie said. 'He's been complaining of pains in his chest and head.'

While his mother and Mrs. Watt were speaking, Eric lounged about. He never opened his mouth, but Mrs. Watt was acutely aware of his presence. He seemed to be getting continually in her road. She wished that he would go into another room or go outside, but he remained beside them. He did not appear to be listening to their conversation, but Mrs. Watt felt that nothing escaped him. She felt, too, that Mrs. Laurie would say much more if he were not there. All the time she watched her son, twisting her hands nervously.

Suddenly Eric spoke.

He said: 'Is there any lemonade in the house?'

'No, dear,' his mother said. 'I don't think so, dear.'

Eric said nothing. He stared in front of him, his lips drawn-in in a silent whistle.

'Did you want some lemonade, dear?' Mrs. Laurie said anxiously. 'Take some money and go and get some, dear.'

Eric lifted her bag from the sideboard and took out a two-shilling piece. He tossed it in the air and put it in his pocket. Mrs. Watt felt a sense of relief as he lounged out.

As soon as he had gone, Mrs. Laurie licked her lips nervously and said: 'I really don't know what to do about Eric. He's not feeling well at all.'

'Is it thae pains ye were tellin' me aboot?' said Mrs. Watt.

'Yes, I took him to a specialist and he examined him, but he didn't seem able to find anything wrong with him. I had to pay three guineas for the examination, and do you know what he said? You'll never guess, Mrs. Watt.'

'I dinnie ken,' Mrs Watt said. 'I never was ony guid at guessin'.'

'He said——' Mrs. Laurie gulped. 'He said: "There's damn all wrong with him. You should get him a job."'

Mrs. Watt tittered, but when she saw the look on Mrs. Laurie's face, she changed her titter into a cough and began to fill a pail at the sink.

'I'm terribly worried about him,' Mrs. Laurie said. 'I keep wondering whether I've done the right thing by him. Maybe I shouldn't have kept him at home like this. Maybe I've spoiled him. I don't know. But I felt that I needed company. After his father died, I simply had to have a man about the house.'

'If ye'd been married to ma first joker you wouldnie think that,' Mrs. Watt said, putting her pail on the scullery floor and flopping down beside it. 'He was a lad——' wringing out her cloth and slapping it on the linoleum—'and a half! Never did an honest day's work in his life. He was aye sittin' in ma road. A fair scunner!'

Mrs. Laurie's fingers plucked nervously at the cords of her dressing-gown. 'I wish I knew what to do about Eric,' she said. 'He'll have to register for the army next month.'

'Ach, dinnie worry aboot that,' Mrs. Watt said. 'He doesnie look strong. They'll never take him.'

'It's not that I was thinking about,' Mrs. Laurie said. 'I was wondering what I'd do if they didn't take him.'

The front door banged, and Eric came in with three bottles of lemonade. He stared at his mother and Mrs. Watt, but there was no flicker of expression on his face. Mrs. Laurie stopped talking as soon as the door banged; she went away to her bedroom.

•

Eric switched on the wireless and sat down beside it.
He took three packets of chocolate from his pocket.
Mrs. Watt eyed them, thinking to herself how she
would thank him. But Eric began to eat the chocolate himself, never saying a word. Between bites he
whistled tunelessly. After a while he opened one of
the bottles and drank some of the lemonade. He
nodded his head in time with the music from a jazz
orchestra, his pale eyes staring at the window.

Mrs. Watt did some small jobs in the scullery.
When she returned to the living-room she saw that
Eric had opened another bottle and drunk some of
the lemonade although he had drunk only a little
out of the first bottle. She gave her head a puzzled
shake and went to clean the bathroom.

She was wiping out the bath when Mrs. Laurie
came in to speak to her. 'How many days a week
do you think you'll be able to come, Mrs. Watt?'
she said in a low voice.

'How many days do you want me?' Mrs. Watt
said.

'Well, I'd like you every day, but Eric says it's
nonsense,' Mrs. Laurie swallowed with embarrassment. 'He says we don't really need a charwoman,
and that he's quite capable of doing all the work
himself. But, of course, I can't have him doing that.'
She looked uneasily behind her in the direction of
the living-room. 'Do you think you'd be able to
come three days a week?'

'In the forenoons?' Mrs. Watt said. 'I'd like away
at twelve o'clock if possible.'

'That'll be all right,' Mrs. Laurie said. She lowered
her voice again: 'Don't say anything to Eric about
how often you're going to come. He—er—well, he's
never got on very well with any of the women we've

had. But, of course you're different,' she added quickly. 'He seems to be getting on all right with you.'

'Ay,' Mrs. Watt said.

'Just don't say anything to him,' Mrs. Laurie said. 'Nothing that'll make him angry. He's got an awful quick temper.'

'All right,' Mrs. Watt said.

She finished cleaning the bathroom, then she began to peel potatoes for the dinner. When she finished them, she went to ask Mrs. Laurie what else she would do. The bathroom door was half open, and Eric was busy cleaning the taps that Mrs. Watt had done already. He was whistling tunelessly, his eyes staring through the door at Mrs. Watt, staring straight through her.

'Never heed him,' Mrs. Laurie whispered. 'He's so used to cleaning everything himself that he thinks nobody else can do it. He won't even let me do it. Never mind him. It gives him something to do. We'll just have to humour him until he goes to the army.'

Mrs. Watt was bewildered, but she said nothing; she kept looking anxiously at the clock. She wanted to get into the Cross Keys as soon as it opened; she needed a drink more badly today than she ever needed one. That laddie was just a bit more than she could bear. No wonder his mother looked as though she was being driven potty.

'Do you see that?' Mrs. Laurie cried.

Each of the bottles was open, and some lemonade had been taken out of each. The corks were lying on top of the wireless. Mrs. Laurie shook her head apologetically at Mrs. Watt and corked them. 'Eric's so careless,' she said. 'I don't know how he'll do in the army. I wonder how he'll get on?'

'Oh, he'll get on all right,' Mrs. Watt said.

But she wondered whether he would. She had an idea that the army would not deal with Eric as kindly and as softly as his mother had done. She did not know which of them she felt most sorry for.

Mrs. Laurie came to the door with her and whispered: 'Now, you'll be sure to come back tomorrow?'

'Sure,' Mrs. Watt said.

'That's a promise?' Mrs. Laurie said.

There was something so frightened and pathetic in her tone that Mrs. Watt could not say what she would have liked to say.

'Ay, that's a promise,' she said.

But as she went down the path she wondered whether it was a promise she could keep. And when she turned at the gate and saw Eric staring at her out of the living-room window, she felt panic-stricken. She forced herself to smile, but there was no responding smile from him. He continued to stare straight in front of him. Just like a cat, Mrs. Watt thought, hurrying to reach the Cross Keys. Just like a cat waiting to pounce . . . Or was it like a cat that had already pounced and was licking its lips after eating its prey?

A. L. BARKER

Mr. Minnenick

MR. MINNENICK had spent the morning telling the
Misses Pewsey that being bombed was a more swift
and comforting end than being 'put to sleep'—like
their cat Duffle. The Misses Pewsey lived next door,
they had no man about the house and they were
afraid there was going to be a war; Mr. Minnenick
was more than afraid, he was certain.

But he didn't let the ladies see that. He talked
about empty threats and the power of bluff and the
bad economics of modern war. It sounded reassur-
ing and neither Miss May nor Miss Thea saw anything inconsistent in his passionate defence of being
blown to pieces as a happy ending. It was, he declared—with the warmth of Miss Thea's elder-flower
wine on his tongue—a cleaner death than most
people had. Think of poor Jack Dolley, dying of
cancer for eighteen months, and old Mrs. Lazenby,
ninety-six next week and blown up like a balloon
with dropsy. Whereas, if you were bombed, it was
all over in a second, no pain, no lingering, just
finish——

Mr. Minnenick broke off as he remembered where
he had heard that line of talk before. A man, trying
to sell him a vacuum-cleaner, 'a matter of minutes,'
he had said, 'no dirt, no effort, just performance.'
And here was Mr. Minnenick, trying to sell death to
the Misses Pewsey, trying—if you cared to put it
that way—to sell them a vacuum.

But they didn't notice, they were caught between panic and unbelief. They vacillated. At one moment it would never happen, the next, they should leave everything and fly to the caves of Scotland. Mr. Minnenick, who was quite happy with the elder-flower wine, wondered if there were any caves in Scotland and tried to imagine May and Thea Pewsey without their chintzes and their Coalport china, living in them. They were terrified of moths, there would be moths in caves, and bats as well. Having seen them, countless times, reacting to moths, he thought they might be less upset by a bomber.

Mr. Minnenick drained his glass. Who would have thought those flat prudish elder-flowers would make such delightful wine?

Miss Thea stood holding her trinket-box which the crisis had conjured from its hiding place. Miss May was writing out an enormous grocery list.

'If only we knew how long it will last—I should know whether to include pineapple chunks or concentrate on meat roll.'

'The great thing,' said Mr. Minnenick, 'is not to worry. In my opinion, it will all pass over. And if the worst came to the worst—it couldn't last more than a few months, a very few months.'

'A few months!' Miss Thea sat down so suddenly that all the trinkets jingled in her box. 'We should all be dead—the country would be laid waste!'

'Nonsense!' declared Mr. Minnenick stoutly, though privately he agreed. 'Do you suppose we should sit and wait to be killed, Miss Thea? Attack, you know, is the best form of defence.'

Mr. Minnenick was glad he had been able to sound that manly note because the crisis—or the wine—had aroused a queasiness in his stomach. It was not easy to be stolid with all this talk about bombing. Air-raids were sobering things. There was no funny side—as far as Mr. Minnenick could see —to an air-raid. And they had a peculiarly foreign horror. When they happened in Spain or China they were a dreadful consequence of being Spanish or Chinese. If they happened in England, in the unlikely neighbourhood of Mr. Minnenick and the Misses Pewsey, they would be out of context, they would be monstrously wrong, for here justice was balanced with virtue, there were no dreadful consequences of being English.

He left them in the heights of optimism, having established a mental picture of Hitler as an adventurer with a secret respect for the British Empire. Their gate, he noted as he went out, was wearing its latch smooth. That should be attended to because the gate opened from a bank sheer on to the lane—to the danger of the occasional traffic.

But then, he thought as he opened his own gate, was it worth bothering about such things now? There was the new well-cover, he'd put off making that again and again. Now that there wasn't much point in doing it, he wanted, perversely, to get the planks and set to work.

Mr. Minnenick dawdled out to the back garden and looked at his well. He wondered how many buckets of water he'd drawn up in the past and how many more he would draw in the future. Odd, wasn't it, that what one man did in another country should decide about his well-cover? It was as if Mr. Minnenick and his well were out on the fringe of an enormous ripple which had spread through Europe. No doubt, as the ripple reached them, other people

had wondered about their wells. Now it was Mr.
Minnenick's turn and he didn't like it.

He frowned, digging his little rounded chin into
his chest. The ripple had, so to speak, reached solid
ground. It had reached England and could go no
farther. What happened in Europe was a surface
shudder, there could be no depth nor significance in
unrest where there was never peace.

Mr. Minnenick's old well-cover had some interesting ironwork on it. He could take that off and put it
on the new one. Somewhere about was a half-pot
of green paint, he could have a bright green well-
cover. Sighing, he turned away. It would be foolish
to spend what might be his last days in making
a new well-cover to be blown to smithereens with
him.

This year the apples on his tree were pure amber.
Mr. Minnenick passed under them, passed too the
arctic blue of his Michaelmas daisies, and the huge
flimsy poppies, with a sad affection for the beautiful
but doomed.

He went into his cottage and threw another log on
the fire. He couldn't even fancy a mid-morning cup
of tea, there was such an agitation in his stomach. It
was a bad sign, being upset like this—showed he was
getting old. Too old for such things as wars, anyway.
They were a young man's business.

He hadn't enjoyed the last war, not as some people
had. They put him to guard a dump down in Cornwall and left him there for years. When he was de-
mobbed he had melancholia and had acquired the
habit of talking to himself. Since then, of course, the
pace of warfare had been stepped up beyond belief
by bombs and bombers. That was the best you could
say of it—this next war could not last four months,

let alone four years. They would try to beat us down with wave after wave of bombers, try to flatten us like the summer grass. Mr. Minnenick found that his knees were trembling old man's knees and his thumbs feverishly stroked his lapels.

But they wouldn't succeed. There was the British navy, as well as the British army to contend with, and wave after wave of our bombers too, no doubt. He visualized the sky like a vast loom, with planes shuttling across and across it, weaving something close and dark over the daylight. And in the end, the German towns would lie razed to the earth, Hitler and his grey men would dissolve into dust.

It was so inevitable that Mr. Minnenick didn't see how Hitler could be such a fool as to try it. If he cared at all for his grey men and his Unter den Linden, he surely wouldn't sacrifice them.

The trouble was, of course, that Hitler was mad. He screamed and danced, probably he also foamed at the mouth and his pictures had to be touched up afterwards to hide it. Yes, he was mad, but he was Dictator of Germany. How did Mr. Chamberlain look, facing a madman?

Mr. Minnenick suddenly felt very cold, in spite of his fire. It was this aberration at the heart of things which made it all so unnerving. He found his hat and coat and went out.

He was surprised to see old Grummer Aikens and the lad taking the cart up to their field to cut kale as usual. Somehow, although he knew the cows had to be fed, he expected some show of concern. Grummer was sitting on the shaft where he always sat, with his same disparaging stare, and his pipe smouldering.

'Ah,' he said gloomily as the cart passed. His

gloom could not be taken as a reflection of the times, for he was always gloomy.

Mr. Minnenick watched irritably. These people had lived so long on the earth that they could recognize only those crises which came from or fell upon it. To them there was nothing so bad as drought or late frosts or warble-fly. Well, they would find themselves faced with troubles more shattering than a spoilt crop or a wasting herd.

This was scarcely a village where Mr. Minnenick and the Misses Pewsey lived. There were about fifteen cottages sprinkled in the fold between the hills, two or three farms, and one small shop where you could buy castor oil or striped humbugs or send a wire to the ends of the earth. In spite of the fact that Mr. Minnenick was a foreigner who had only lived here five years, he was jealous for the place, and preferred to forget that most of his life had quite other backgrounds. It suited him so well it was hard to believe it had not been accumulated for him.

But this morning it fretted him that the village should be unchanged. Dance music was bellowing from the open door of the Cadogans' cottage, young Phoebe Cadogan with a bright yellow duster round her hair, shook a mop from the upstairs window and waved to Mr. Minnenick. A white cat yawned on top of a wall and there was the baker's van parked as usual half across the lane. The hills were blue, perhaps a little bluer than last week—but that was because winter, not war, was near. Not one thing had come or gone because of the crisis. Mr. Minnenick could not even see one person talking earnestly to another. The lane was empty.

They were all the same as Grummer Aikens, all involved in their own concerns, hoarding like

squirrels in a tree that is to be felled tomorrow. Mr.
Minnenick would have liked them all gathered in
front of him so that he could ask, in the ringing tones
of revelation, did they know what was going to happen to them? Did they realize that in the space of
moments all their hedging and ditching, their plough-
ing and planting, their dusting, their labour, could
be made to fly apart and disintegrate as if it had
never been? Did they realize, as Mr. Minnenick did,
that there was something tremendous in the offing,
something with martial music, death and glory? Mr.
Minnenick was neither so old nor so frightened that
he could not appreciate that other aspect of war.

It seemed to him, as he came to the bend in the
sunny lane, that he was the only one aware of the
crisis, he and Mr. Chamberlain—and the Misses
Pewsey, of course. They would still be wondering
whether to go or stay.

Someone was walking furiously about in the garden of the last cottage. It was Arthur Colum, and
Mr. Minnenick would have turned back had he not
been seen and hailed. He didn't get on with Colum,
the man was too explosive.

Arthur Colum, tall, ugly, and with a futile violence in every movement, threw the garden trowel
he held into an empty pail and made a great deal of
unnecessary noise. He wrenched open his gate and
stalked out to meet Mr. Minnenick. When they
were almost face to face he turned, strode back, and
was entrenched behind the gate by the time Mr.
Minnenick reached it.

'Good morning, Arthur,' said Mr. Minnenick
mildly. 'Not at work today?'

Arthur Colum glared. 'Work? Ha!' He went
tramping off up his garden path, leaving Mr. Min-

nenick standing in the lane. Suddenly he turned and
came back at a run. 'Work—today? Do you realize
this country's on the brink of war?' He held the gate
and shook it, his red face grew redder. 'On the brink
of war!'

'Yes, I do realize it. I thought I was the only one
who did.' Mr. Minnenick spoke with dignity.

'You realize it, eh?' Arthur Colum gave a short
laugh. 'I wonder!'

Mr. Minnenick bridled. Here had he been wrest-
ling all the morning with the burden of his knowledge, and Colum had the effrontery to doubt his
intelligence.

'I am not a fool,' he said frigidly. 'I think I understand just what it means——'

'Do you?' The gate crashed back on its hinges,
Colum strode into the lane and towered over Mr.
Minnenick. 'Do you understand what it means to
fight thousands of bombers, mechanized columns,
shock troops, parachute armies, crack divisions—
with a few old-fashioned planes, hardly any tanks
and a gang of raw recruits?' Mr. Minnenick opened
his mouth and was at once gripped by the shoulder.
'Do you understand what it means to fight a war
and be defeated?'

'Are you trying to tell me the British Empire could
be defeated?'

'The British Empire!' Arthur Colum roared. 'It
isn't an empire, it's a market. There aren't any guns
or planes or tanks, but there's a lot of wool, a lot of
butter and a lot of cotton pinafores. Can you fight
a war with cotton pinafores?' He thrust his hands
so fiercely into his pockets that his trouser-legs
quivered under the impact.

Mr. Minnenick, trying not to smile at this absurd

rigmarole, was shaken by a sudden sobriety in Colum's voice, a stillness in his face. Looking over Mr. Minnenick's head, he said, 'It isn't the war we have to fear—it's the defeat.'

He turned away, went without another word or a single unnecessary gesture, into his cottage and shut the door.

Next moment the door was snatched open again, Colum filled the narrow entrance. He shouted so loudly that two wood pigeons flapped away in alarm. 'We're not ready! We're not ready for war!'

The door slammed. The man was like a jack-in-the-box, thought Mr. Minnenick, and scurried off before Colum could pop out again.

Of course Arthur Colum was a crank, that was taken for granted, but all the same, he had made Mr. Minnenick profoundly uncomfortable. It was one thing to face up to the prospect of war and even —with commendable courage—to face the prospect of personal destruction. It was another thing altogether to look on the possibility of the annihilation of one's country. Mr. Minnenick wilted at the thought. He stood holding desperately to a field-gate, seeing his world fall apart, the future snap off from the present stem, and all the solid words, the promises and pacts, resolve into gibberish.

If Colum were right, if England were unprepared, lacking armaments, lacking soldiers, lacking time— then England would become a vassal of Germany; the British Empire would melt away; the aberration at the heart of things would reach out to twist this country like a straw.

If Colum were right. Mr. Minnenick came up sturdily from his nightmare. Who would believe Arthur Colum? He was a crank, a panic-monger.

Why should he know better than politicians and Ministers of State? Why indeed?

Mr. Minnenick took out a large handkerchief and wiped round his neck under his collar. Strictly speaking, Arthur Colum ought not to be allowed freedom of speech. There was no knowing how many people he would frighten.

Mr. Minnenick went through into the field. He didn't want to meet anyone else and he felt the need of walking on the grass, on something soft and quiet. From this field he could look down through the trees to the roofs of his cottage and the Misses Pewsey's cottage, each with a fine thread of blue smoke rising from their chimneys. Round his own front garden ran a deep frill of brown daisies. The elms were yellowing, a ring of beeches on the hill burned with copper and brilliant verdigris. Below the village a block of fields had been ploughed, and earth had turned up Indian red.

Mr. Minnenick grunted. A vassal of Germany indeed! One might as well try to parcel up the air. What was more, he decided that he had had his morning for nothing. There wouldn't be a war, there wouldn't even be a shemozzle. It was the land which persuaded him, the land which had the inevitable winter to contend with and no time, no precedent for war.

These were absurd reasons for optimism, but they soothed Mr. Minnenick as he longed to be soothed. They let the daylight in on his nightmare and its dreadfulness was no more than a coat on a hook. He felt suddenly lighthearted enough to hum to himself. Taking off his hat, he let the sun shine on his bald head.

A sound, deepening and amplifying his own

humming, made him stop and look up at the sky. At first he couldn't see anything, and that vexed Mr. Minnenick because he liked to see as well as hear. He stood hat in hand, head bent back, frowning against the sun while the sound grew and acquired a deep insistent pulse. He made it out at last—a plane, larger than usual, painted black and coming low into the hills.

That was nothing unusual. There was an aerodrome near, and the planes seemed to like to come down into the hills and out through the gap. When he couldn't sleep, Mr. Minnenick wrote many imaginary letters to his M.P. about the scandal of low-flying.

He was watching it and grudging every yard of its progress across his sky, every little local sound it drowned, when all at once he felt convinced that it was a German bomber.

Mr. Minnenick knew nothing about planes, he disliked them all indiscriminately, and he had no reason for thinking that this plane was either German or a bomber. But it looked uncouth, it looked malicious, and it was definitely foreign. That was enough. Such words as 'dive-bombing', and 'machine-gunning' had explained themselves in Europe, and they were not meaningless even to Mr. Minnenick. Without stopping to wonder why he, a black smudge in a field, should constitute a target, he began to run.

It was panic, the thing he had condemned in refugees and air-raid victims. He always said that panic caused as many deaths as bombing and he liked to imagine himself in an emergency as caustically, coolly stemming a mad rush by his own example.

But now he ran, head down, stumbling among the

tussocks of grass, breath catching in his throat, thoughts and sensations crowding on each other. It occurred to him that he knew how a rabbit felt while the hawk swooped, and his hearing was shattered again and again by the bomb tearing the air apart like linen, by the rattle of machine-guns and the whine of bullets.

The plane was immediately above him now. Someone had said once, that there was nothing to fear from bombers until they had just passed overhead. He could not hope to reach the shelter of a ditch before it took aim. As the plane hovered, his terror mounted beyond the pitch of effort and endurance. The blood drubbed in his old man's veins, his heart turned in his chest. He fell face downwards in the grass, blind, deaf, half-dead with fear.

When at last he had strength enough to look up again, the plane was slipping casually through the gap in the hills and he could hear the sound of the baker's van labouring up the hill. Mr. Minnenick sat up and watched the plane out of sight. He knew now that it wasn't a German bomber.

He felt sick, sick and old. Shaking, his hands searched about among the grass, finding the odds and ends which had fallen from his pockets. He sorted them over, absently, and stowed them away again. Then he had to sit and wait for the earth and sky to stop running together like a liquid.

He was too ill to feel ridiculous, sitting there in the grass within sight of his own cottage. But when he managed to get to his feet and was walking on, and the dizziness had passed, there was added to the aftermath of violent emotion, a burning shame. His humiliation was the more bitter because it was self-inflicted. He had only one thing to hope and be grateful for—that no one else had seen him panic and run, abject as any poor pill-brained rabbit.

Mr. Minnenick crept into his cottage, shut the door and sat by his fire. He felt cold and shivery, but he hadn't the heart even to go and fetch the old shawl from his bed and put it round his shoulders. He sat holding one hand within the other, miserably watching the white ash mount on the wood. All the shocks he had had this morning seemed to merge with this last shock of finding himself a poor witless coward, as ready to panic and as ready to run as anyone else. Worse, he was ready to run from his own imagination. England, it seemed, was lacking —so, too, was Mr. Minnenick. It would be better then, thought Mr. Minnenick in the depths of bitter nihilism, that such a country should be destroyed, and its cowards with it. He, for one, would raise no finger to save skins like his.

He did not spare himself. At any other time, he would have laughed a little, made a cup of tea and lit a pipe while he got over it. But this morning his own deficiencies lay exactly parallel with a gap so huge that there was no condemnation large enough; for sanity's sake, he must concentrate on himself.

He sat on, too dispirited to bother about lunch, only rousing now and then to drop another log on the fire. The afternoon wore on, the sunlight deepened, and Mr. Minnenick had nodded off into a troubled doze. He woke each time the embers scattered in the hearth, blinked about him, and relapsed into sleep again with a grunt. He dreamed he was the last Englishman left alive, that the Germans were trying to blast him out of his cottage and that he, while the bombs fell and the guns roared, was calmly making his new well-cover. He could hear the sound of his hammer-blows. They were so loud that they woke him up. He blinked, the knocking from his dreams went on. Mr. Minnenick turned and saw Miss Thea Pewsey tapping on his window.

He went reluctantly to the door, feeling vaguely aggrieved that the sun should still be shining. Miss Thea peered in at him. She looked absurdly gay, and there was a bright mauve bow at her neck, but when she saw Mr. Minnenick's sunken jaws and his vague eyes, she was immediately concerned.

'Why, Mr. Minnenick—are you ill?'

He felt a little warmed by her anxiety. 'No, I'm just tired.'

'And you've been asleep?'

'I've been sitting there, dozing and thinking, for the last couple of hours or so,' he said sadly.

'Then you haven't heard the news!'

Miss Thea came closer to Mr. Minnenick, her cheeks pink with excitement.

He looked at her distastefully, 'What news?'

'Why, Mr. Chamberlain had an agreement with Hitler, they've made an arrangement, a—what do you call it—a pact!'

Mr. Minnenick's eyes stopped being vague, his mouth opened soundlessly.

'Isn't it wonderful!' exulted Miss Thea. 'It's all settled. Mr. Chamberlain has arranged everything. There isn't going to be any horrible war after all! When they gave it out on the wireless we didn't know whether to laugh or cry!'

Mr. Minnenick's voice was a mere croak. 'You mean it's all over—it's not going to happen?'

'It's never going to happen,' vowed Miss Thea.

'You were right. You said it was an empty threat, didn't you, Mr. Minnenick? You told us it would never happen.'

Mr. Minnenick was beginning to straighten and stretch himself like a man from whose back an enormous burden has just been lifted. 'I did say so, didn't I?'

'You were positive,' declared Miss Thea. 'Just as if you knew all the time. It was such a very great comfort to us. And now—May and I feel so happy we're going to have a little party tonight. You will come, won't you, Mr. Minnenick? We shall ask just a very few friends—Mr. and Mrs. Canning, Miss Gilpin and old Mr. Essex. We thought—not Mr. Colum because he is so excitable and you and he don't get on very well together, do you?'

'We do not,' said Mr. Minnenick firmly. He looked a changed man. His cheeks filled out and grew ruddy, his eyes were clear and direct, he thrust his hands into his trousers-pockets and briskly jingled his loose change. 'I consider Arthur Colum an unwarranted panic-monger, an empty windbag, and a stranger to the truth!'

'Well, anyway,' said Miss Thea, slightly surprised, 'we shan't ask him. I must go now and issue the other invitations. Shall we see you, then, at a quarter-past seven?'

'At a quarter-past seven—delighted,' agreed Mr. Minnenick, smiling at Miss Thea, at his brown daisies and at the sun which had had the good sense to keep shining.

Miss Thea patted her mauve bow, beamed, and sighed, 'I'm so happy it's all settled so nicely!'

Mr. Minnenick went gallantly to open the gate for her. 'It was the might, the power of the British

Empire which saved us,' he declared, standing very straight.

'It was God's will,' said Miss Thea solemnly, and she went down the lane with a little odd step that was almost a skip.

Mr. Minnenick went into his cottage, leaving the front door wide open. He rubbed his eyes, stretched and added fresh logs to the dying fire. Then he made himself a pot of tea, cut a new white loaf into sturdy slices, packed them with cheese, rummaged for a jar of pickles, and carried it all in on a tray to the fire. It was a long time since he had felt so hungry.

As he ate, he thought of Mr. Chamberlain and Arthur Colum. Two such different men! One, for all his posing and his gestures, was no more than an empty reed, echoing to any wind that blew. The other was a giant by comparison, the father of his time, a maker of treaties, personifying the power of empire, its justice and humanity.

Mr. Minnenick cleared his plate and emptied his teapot. In other circumstances, given opportunity and education, he liked to think he might have been just such a man.

He packed his pipe, lit it and went humming into the back garden. The sky was still blue, slightly more filmy now, a perfect backcloth to his golden apples, his brisk yellow daisies and the bronze mops of the chrysanthemums.

Mr. Minnenick nodded towards the hills and the vivid beeches. They were even more beautiful now, and not so heartless. Yet he had to admit they did well not to be in sympathy with human affairs. Where should we be if there was winter with every crisis?

He did not remember ever having felt so light

and free in himself, although there was, somehow, a kind of familiarity about it. As if he'd been spared something vastly unpleasant—as indeed he had—escaped with honour, and not by trickery, some dreaded event.

He accounted, after a moment, for the familiarity, and was warmed by a pleasant sense of youth. He felt as he did when he was let off a caning at school. One was never so very old, after all.

'We shall be all right now,' said Mr. Minnenick, and went to sort out the planks for his new well-cover.

NIGEL KNEALE

The Putting Away of Uncle Quaggin

As one of his descendants remarked, the twentieth
of June, 1897, was marked by public rejoicings
throughout the Empire: Ezra Quaggin had died in
the night. It was also the day of Queen Victoria's
diamond jubilee.

He had lived alone on his farm, working it with
hired labour, sending out occasional blasts of hate
at the male members of the family. Then one night
when he was concealing money in the chimney he
was choked by a mouthful of soot, fell, fractured
his hip and began a lingering end.

He was visited in hospital by fat Tom-Billy Teare
the joiner, who had married the old man's niece, and
was troubled. But Ezra presently told him he had
forgiven the females, who could not be expected to
know better.

'I've seen to it that your Sallie's all right. Now
listen: me will is in a proper black box on top o' the
kitchen dresser. They all know I've made one; leave
her there till you read her to them. Do the—th'-
arrangements, y'self, Tom-Billy. Keep it in the
family, like. An' then maybe the cost . . . ?' His
niece's husband was an undertaker on occasion.

Teare went away happy, full of his executorship.
He told his wife Sallie, and she was content, and
stayed in town on market day to buy a black dress.

Five days passed. Then the sad news came from
the hospital and she was able to put it on.

After Teare had informed the relatives, carefully pencilling down the expenses, he and his wife shut up their home in the village and moved quickly into the Quaggin farmhouse to look after it.

They found the flimsy black deed-box in its place on the dresser. Having no lock, it invited a look inside.

Under a layer of old receipts, a backless prayer-book, and letters dealing with an unsatisfactory grubber, was the will. A long sky-blue paper. It was in the old man's handwriting, with strange words in places, but clear in their meaning.

Teare hugged his wife delightedly. She had been left the farm itself! A few small bequests disposed of the Quaggins.

'We're made, woman!' he said.

But later he fell into some small dispute with the heiress when she wished to cut down expenses now that there was nobody worth pleasing. He considered a heavy meal would be necessary to keep the family quiet during the will-reading. Particularly this will.

On the day of his funeral, the old man lay clean and tidy in the coffin Teare had made for him, ready for those who came to make sure he was gone.

They arrived earlier and in greater numbers than expected, caused the waiting meat-plates to be recast in more and smaller portions.

Teare received the mourners at the door. Quaggins, most of them, the men short and sandy, sharp-nosed; the women pale-faced and shiftily prim. Black clothes, hastily dyed, showed smothered patterns. And expectation showed through the reverence.

The weather was fine, lighting up the dead man's fields for valuation. People went to the windows under pretence of admiring his industry, and gazed hungrily out.

The mourners' conduct was sober while in the house; sober, too, in the black varnished carriages as they crept in line behind the hearse; sober and musical in the draughty little church, as they listened to a long-winded service. At the graveside they began to cheer up; for the unpleasant part of the day was over.

On the return journey talk in the carriages grew bright. Quaggin the Cruelty, the animals inspector, thrust his red whiskers out of a window to hail a friend. From another vehicle Teare thought he heard something suspiciously like song. He frowned at his wife.

The little procession trotted briskly along the road that ran behind the village, and turned up towards the farm.

A tense proprietary excitement filled each jogging group. Eyes were fixed with modest greed on every field they passed. The dutch barn, the old pigsty, the cows. They rounded the orchard.

Teare's carriage was the first. As it drew in towards the house, he saw a figure moving near the rose-covered porch. As if coming from the side where the dairy was, and the back entrance. Teare had visions of unlocked doors. He scrambled out of the carriage.

'Well, who——?'

'Hallo, there!' called the man. 'I missed the poor ould fella, eh?'

Short and sandy, with a sharp nose. A Quaggin, undoubtedly.

'Don't ye remember me, Tom-Billy?'

'Uh—yes. Of course.' Teare shook hands dubiously. Now he knew; it was some sort of cousin, a man they called Lawyer Quaggin because he had once worked as an advocate's clerk. Then a signwriter or something, and for a time, they said, he had tried to live by raising ferrets. A spry man.

'Hallo, all!' called Lawyer Quaggin. People were descending from the carriages. 'I was just sayin' to Tom-Billy here, business missed a train for me, an' I came too late for to see him under!' The relatives hailed him, crowding round.

Teare hurried in after his wife. He motioned her into the kitchen.

'Sallie, just a minute——'

Outside in the hall they could hear old Mrs. Kneen weeping over 'the beautiful internment' and the bass voices of her three sons.

'Well?' said Sallie.

Teare jerked his head and whispered. 'Did y'see that Lawyer character? Skulkin' round the house just as we come up. Keep an eye on him—he's fit for anythin', that fella!'

The parlour was already seething.

Teare dodged about, fitting people into places for the meal. The three huge Kneen boys were prowling gloweringly about, comparing the size of the plate-fuls. A child cried to be taken home. Then somehow a chicken had got into the room, fluttering among the black legs. Women pulled their skirts out of the way. Men jostled, shooing and hooting.

In desperation Teare grabbed a thin arm that led to a long face. 'Mr. Cain, for pity's sake start a hymn or somethin'!'

The thin man struck a fork on a plate and began to sing 'Abide with Me' in a grating voice that struck piercingly through the uproar. Gradually silence came.

The Quaggins sat, unwillingly, one by one.

'So beautiful,' said old Mrs. Kneen in the hush that followed the solo. She added, to the thin man's confusion and anger, 'I mean the way the table is laid. Look at it, boys.'

Soon Sallie had the tea-urn working, and there were polite murmurs of appreciation. Every one held back patiently while cups joggled perilously round.

Then the food went down with a rush.

Quaggin the Cruelty called for a second cup through steaming whiskers. The Kneen boys tore seriously at their cold beef. Pickle glasses emptied. Faces bulged.

Tom-Billy glanced round. Lawyer Quaggin was at the second table and it was difficult to see him. He seemed very quiet. Teare shifted back uneasily. The meat was tasteless in his mouth.

'My boys say they're enjoying it ever so much, my dear,' called Mrs. Kneen. Her sons chewed on, unnoticing.

Teare whispered to his wife, 'Is anybody out watchin' the kitchen?' She shook her head. His face sagged. 'Come, come, Mr. Teare! Eat up!' said a neighbour. 'Don't let the sad business distress ye too much!'

Plates were collected and fresh courses sent round. Creamy cakes and scones oozing with butter. As appetites grew less, droning reminiscences began. Teare heard everywhere the working-out of remote family connexions.

He suddenly stiffened. His wife had nudged him. She whispered, 'Look—Lawyer!'

He screwed round, trying to make his face seem lightly interested in the company. Lawyer Quaggin's place was empty. He was not in the room.

Tom-Billy half rose. He sat again, heart tapping, and whispered, 'Did ye see him go?'

'No, I just turned round, and—oh, look, look! Here he is again.'

The short sandy man was sliding into his seat, a strange look on his face, it seemed to Tom-Billy. A mixture that might have been self-conscious innocence and satisfaction; uneasy satisfaction. He caught Teare's eye and grinned. A nervous smile that suddenly became too hearty.

Tom-Billy felt his face tighten. He stood up. One or two people looked at him, and his wife's hand touched him warningly.

'Uh—get more bread,' he mumbled, and pushed his way between the chair-backs. Once the door was safely shut behind him, he ran the few steps to the kitchen. He pulled a stool up beside the dresser, climbed on to it, and clutched the tin deed-box down from its place. A bead of sweat fogged his eye as he opened the lid.

The heart folded up inside him, and he grasped a shelf for support.

Ezra's will had gone!

He stumbled down, and scattered across the table all the contents of the box. The loose papers, the prayer-book, the letters. He swayed as the empty black bottom of the tin stared back at him. A moment later an old chair's wicker seat split under his sudden weight.

Like scalding steam, a stream of explosive hissing curses reddened his face. Then the remembered need for silence bottled up his fury, and drove it into his head and muddled his thoughts. They took several minutes to clear.

It was Lawyer all right! He must have found out the will's hiding-place by spying through the kitchen window during the funeral. And now he had stolen it; the guilt was there on his face when he sneaked back into the parlour just now.

Tom-Billy sat trying to control himself and picture the next move.

The other room was full of Quaggins waiting to hear the thing read. If he showed the empty box, they would rend him, the keeper of it. Useless to protest that Sallie had been left everything; each man jack of them would fancy himself cheated out of a huge legacy.

Go in there and denounce the thief? No, that was as bad. Lawyer would be ready, knowing the Quaggins distrusted him nearly as much as they did Tom-Billy. He would have the will hidden somewhere, and brazenly deny everything. And later, in his own crafty time, he would tell the Quaggins in secret what it said.

Either way, the will would never be seen again. The farm would be divided amongst the whole brood.

Tom-Billy groaned with anguish.

Something must be done immediately; he had no idea what. Often he had wondered what a fattened beast felt when it sniffed the smell of slaughter. Now he knew; it prayed for the neighbourhood to be struck with catastrophe, to give it a chance of escape.

An earthquake. At least a whirlwind.

Words were dancing in front of his eyes. 'All your problems solved,' they read. He tried to blink them away like liver-spots, but they persisted. They seemed to be printed on a packet lying by the wall. A little more cold sweat formed on his face.

He rose. He approached the improbable packet.

'Vesuvius Brand Lighters. All your firelighting problems solved!' he read. So he still had his senses. His pulse slackened. He had been tricked by the crumpled label.

A bag of patent things that Sallie must have bought; old Quaggin would have died of cold before spending money on them. 'Vesuvius Brand.' There was a clumsy little picture of people in long nightshirts running about clutching bundles and boxes, and a flaming mountain in the background. He slowly picked up the smelly packet.

A desperate idea was coming. The most desperate he had ever had.

He pulled the split wicker-chair into the middle of the room and stacked the firelighters carefully upon it. Five of them the packet held. Quickly he added crushed newspapers, some greasy cleaning rags he found in a cupboard, and two meal sacks. The old stool and table he arranged close to the chair, in natural positions. A jarful of rendered fat completed the preparations.

He replaced the scattered papers in their tin box, and put it exactly where it belonged, up on top of the dresser.

In fearful haste now, dreading that somebody would come to look for him, Tom-Billy struck a match and put it to the tarry shavings. The flame crept over the problem-solving lighters.

As he closed the kitchen door behind him, he began to count slowly.

One, two, three——

He wiped the sweat from his face. At about a hundred it should be safe to raise the alarm.

Conversation was lively when he re-entered the parlour.

Only the Kneen boys were still eating, urged on by their mother's busy hands. The animals inspector was performing a balancing trick with lumps of sugar. Crammed, a child had fallen asleep.

Foxy Lawyer was sitting without any expression, as if biding his time.

Tom-Billy sank into his place beside his wife. He answered nothing to her questioning eyes.

Twenty-one, twenty-two, twenty-three.

He accepted another cake and ate it slowly, as calmly as he could.

Fifty-seven. Fifty-eight.

He was praying that no one would leave the room yet. Once, to his horror, Quaggin the Cruelty rose and squeezed from his place, but it was only to borrow another basin of sugar. Tom-Billy watched him sit again and go on with his tricks.

Seventy-one. Seventy-two.

The family histories were still proceeding. Near-by, a monotonous voice worked out a line that was proving intricate: '—And this Quine I'm tellin' about was a cousin of Quine the draper, an' he married the widow of a fella that had a brother in the mines; now let me think what his first name would be——'

Eighty-three.

A sandy man leaned across the table and winked. What about the will-readin', Mr. Teare?' he said quietly.

Instantly, it seemed, they were all deathly still; full

of fierce attention. 'Yis, the time is suitable enough now,' said a woman, with a kind of desperate reasonableness.

There were murmurs of, 'The will!'

'He's goin' to read it!'

'Oh, yes, the will! I'd clean forgot about that!'

'Is it you that has charge of it, Tom-Billy?'

Teare was frozen in his chair. Bright eyes were on him from every side. In his head he had counted ninety-one. He nerved himself to pretend that he suddenly heard crackling or smelt smoke.

He was forestalled.

'D'ye smell burnin'?' said a voice. There were sniffs.

'Somethin's on fire!'

There was a moment of silent alarm. Then Quaggin the Cruelty dropped his sugar and scrambled towards the door. He pulled at it. A cloud of thin, foul smoke was swept into the room.

There was uproar. People rushed to the narrow hallway, Tom-Billy Teare fighting to be at the head. Behind, there were frightened, coughing cries; a banging at the jammed window. Somebody was roaring, 'Save the women!'

When they reached the kitchen the smoke became black and choking. Flames could be seen in it. Men hung back unhappily.

'Come on! Quick!' shouted Teare, and dived inside to kick apart the evidence of his fire-raising. His eyes streamed. 'Fling everythin'—out of the—the back door here!' He heaved it open as he shouted, and threw a smouldering cushion into the stone yard. Drew breath, then back into the room.

Men were blundering about the sides of the kitchen, eager to save what might become their own property. Mrs. Kneen's voice was raised somewhere, commanding her sons to keep out of danger.

A chair was tossed outside, then a glowing table leg.

The women crowded in the yard, filling buckets at the pump and passing them from hand to hand.

Watching savagely, Teare was in agony. Through the smoke faces were hard to recognize. He felt a small draught of despair; if Lawyer had run away, the whole plan was wasted.

Suddenly he saw the little clerk on the other side of the kitchen, jostled in from the hall by a bulky helper; he looked nervous.

Teare sprang for the dresser and snatched down the black box. Almost in the same movement he had Lawyer held fast in the hug of a thick arm, and rushed him strongly through the burning room to the yard door. Into clear earshot of everybody; particularly the women. 'Here, take this! An' keep it safe!' he shouted. 'Uncle Ezra's will is inside it!'

For a moment their eyes locked. Seeing the fury in Lawyer's, Teare knew he had been right.

There was a tense pause in the clattering and fuss and sluicing of water. The word 'will' had struck home. Every jealous eye was on the little foxy man clutching the box.

'Watch it close and no monkey business!' Teare yelled after him, with a wink round at the rest. He felt that the wink was a good touch.

Now he had to make sure Lawyer was left alone with it.

'Come on, everybody—one last big slap at it!' With something like cheerfulness, he flung himself at the dying fire. The Quaggins followed suit.

Tom-Billy busied himself in the yard, finding work

for every pair of hands. Except one. Lawyer sat alone in a strawy corner, the box on his knees. But there must be no witness to say he had not meddled with it; Teare kept every one on the move, shouting at them, directing, comforting. His flannel shirt was soaked with sweat as well as water.

Once he caught sight of Mrs. Kneen approaching Lawyer as if to sit and share his guardianship. He ran and caught her arm. 'Oh, Mrs. Kneen, would ye look to the child yonder—I think she's taken with fright!' Lawyer glowered.

A minute or two later, when Teare turned from dousing the last smouldering remains of the table, the corner was empty. He thought he glimpsed Lawyer, slipping round a corner of the cowhouse.

The idea must be working!

'It's all out now!' called one of the Kneen boys from inside. Water dripped from everything in the kitchen and swilled across the stone floor. The ceiling was blackened. Otherwise damage was small, though wives' voices rose when they saw their men's singed suits, and the Cruelty was anxiously feeling the shape of his beard. Dye had run on splashed dresses.

Tom-Billy pulled a sack over his shoulders and looked round. There must be no waiting.

'Where's—who did I give it to? The will box?' He hoped his frown looked honestly puzzled.

They knew.

'Lawyer!' shouted voices. 'Where's Lawyer? I seen him a minute ago!' The unmistakable cry of hungry, suspicious animals. 'Where did he get to? Lawyer! Did you see him go?'

'Lawyer, the fire's out!' shouted Quaggin the Cruelty. 'Where the divil have ye put yeself?'

'Lawyer! Lawyer!'

There was a hush.

The little foxy man was coming from the direction of the cowhouse, the box in his hands. His hair seemed a brighter ginger, or his face was whiter. Suspicious eyes were all on the tin.

Without a word, expressionless, Lawyer handed it to Tom-Billy. This time his eyes told nothing.

'Ah—thanks,' Teare said. 'We wouldn't have had this lost for the world, eh? Thanks for keepin' it safe, Lawyer.'

There was a chorus of excited approval.

'Good oul' Lawyer! Bad job if the will had gone on fire!' 'If they found even a singe——'

'Better make sure it's safe,' said the man who had suggested the reading.

Tom-Billy's hands trembled violently as he put the box down among the trickling water and singed cushion feathers that covered the yard. 'Heat injures the nerves,' murmured Mrs. Kneen, interestedly; nobody noticed her.

The black box squeaked open. Tom-Billy's hand went inside and fumbled quickly. A pause.

He drew out a long, sky-blue paper.

'This aforesaid document,' he read shakily, 'is the only will whatever of me, Ezra John Quaggin, pig, general, dairy and poultry farmer——'

His head sang with relief as he looked round the grimy, eager faces.

'Go on! Go on, Tom-Billy,' they cried.

He found the place, cleared his throat, and read again. Soon, he knew, the real fun would begin.

ELIZABETH BOWEN

Maria

'WE have girls of our own, you see,' Mrs. Dosely
said, smiling warmly.

That seemed to settle it. Maria's aunt Lady Rimlade relaxed at last in Mrs. Dosely's armchair, and,
glancing round once more at the Rectory drawing-
room's fluttery white curtains, alert-looking photographs, and silver cornets spuming out pink sweet-
pea, consigned Maria to these pleasant influences.

'Then that will be delightful,' she said in that
blandly conclusive tone in which she declared open
so many bazaars. 'Thursday *next*, then, Mrs. Dosely,
about tea-time?'

'That will be delightful.'

'It is *most* kind,' Lady Rimlade concluded.

Maria could not agree with them. She sat scowling under her hat-brim, tying her gloves into knots.
Evidently, she thought, I *am* being paid for.

Maria thought a good deal about money; she had
no patience with other people's affectations about
it, for she enjoyed being a rich little girl. She was
only sorry not to know how much they considered
her worth; having been sent out to walk in the garden while her aunt had just a short chat, dear, with
the Rector's wife. The first phase of the chat, about
her own character, she had been able to follow perfectly as she wound her way in and out of some
crescent-shaped lobelia beds under the drawing-
room window. But just as the two voices changed—

one going unconcerned, one very, very diffident—
Mrs. Dosely approached the window and, with an
air of immense unconsciousness, shut it. Maria was
baulked.

Maria was at one of those comfortable schools
where everything is attended to. She was (as she had
just heard her Aunt Ena explaining to Mrs. Dosely)
a motherless girl, sensitive, sometimes difficult,
deeply reserved. At school they took all this, with
her slight tendency to curvature and her dislike of
all puddings, into loving consideration. She was
having her character 'done' for her—later on, when
she came out, would be time for her hair and complexion. In addition to this, she learnt swimming,
dancing, some French, the more innocent aspects of
history, and *noblesse oblige*. It was a really nice
school. All the same, when Maria came home for
the holidays, they could not do enough to console
her for being a motherless girl who had been sent
away.

Then, late last summer term, with inconceivable
selfishness, her Uncle Philip fell ill and, in fact,
nearly died. Aunt Ena had written less often and
very distractedly, and when Maria came home she
was told, with complete disregard for her mother-
lessness, that her uncle and aunt would be starting
at once for a cruise, and that she was 'to be arranged
for'.

This was not so easy. All the relations and all the
family friends (who declared when Sir Philip was ill
they'd do anything in the world), wrote back their
deep disappointment at being unable to have Maria
just now, though there was nothing, had things been
otherwise, that they would have enjoyed more. One
to his farm in fact, said Mr. MacRobert, the Vicar,

when he was consulted, another to his merchandise. Then he suggested his neighbours, a Mr. and Mrs. Dosely, of Malton Peele. He came over to preach in Lent; Lady Rimlade had met him; he seemed such a nice man, frank, cheerful, and earnest. *She* was exceedingly motherly, everyone said, and sometimes took in Indian children to make ends meet. The Doselys would be suitable, Maria's aunt felt at once. When Maria raged, she drew down urbane pink eyelids and said she did wish Maria would not be rude. So she drove Maria and the two little griffons over the next afternoon to call upon Mrs. Dosely. If Mrs. Dosely really seemed sympathetic, she thought she might leave the two little dogs with her too.

'And Mrs. Dosely has girls of her own, she tells me,' said Lady Rimlade on the way home. 'I should not wonder if you made quite friends with them. I should not wonder if it was they who had done the flowers. I thought the flowers were done very nicely; I noticed them. Of course, I do not care myself for small silver vases like that, shaped like cornets, but I thought the effect in the Rectory drawing-room very cheerful and home-like.'

Maria took up the word skilfully. 'I suppose no one,' she said, 'who has not been in my position can be expected to realize what it feels like to have no home.'

'Oh, Maria darling . . .'

'I can't tell you what I think of this place you're sending me to,' said Maria. 'I bounced on the bed in that attic they're giving me and it's like iron. I suppose you realize that rectories are always full of diseases? Of course, I shall make the best of it, Aunt Ena. I shouldn't like you to feel I'd complained. But of course you don't realize a bit, do you, what I may be exposed to? So often carelessness about a girl at my age just ruins her life.'

Aunt Ena said nothing; she settled herself a little further down in the rugs and lowered her eyelids as though a strong wind were blowing.

That evening, on her way down to shut up the chickens, Mrs. Dosely came upon Mr. Hammond, the curate, rolling the cricket-pitch in the Rectory field. He was indefatigable, and, though more High Church than they cared for, had outdoor tastes. He came in to meals with them regularly, 'as an arrangement,' because his present landlady could not cook and a young man needs to be built up, and her girls were still so young that no one could possibly call Mrs. Dosely designing. So she felt she ought to tell him.

'We shall be one more now in the house,' she said, 'till the end of the holidays. Lady Rimlade's little niece, Maria—about fifteen—is coming to us while her uncle and aunt are away.'

'Jolly,' said Mr. Hammond sombrely, hating girls.

'We *shall* be a party, shan't we?'

'The more the merrier, I daresay,' said Mr. Hammond. He was a tall young man with a jaw, rather saturnine; he never said much, but Mrs. Dosely expected family life was good for him. 'Let 'em all come,' said Mr. Hammond, and went on rolling. Mrs. Dosely, with a tin bowl under one arm and a basket hooked on the other, stood at the edge of the pitch and watched him.

'She seemed a dear little thing—not pretty, but such a serious little face, full of character. An only child, you see. I said to her when they were going away that I expected she and Dilly and Doris would

soon be inseparable, and her face quite lit up. She
has no mother; it seems so sad.'

'*I* never had a mother,' said Mr. Hammond, tugging the roller grimly.

'Oh, I do *know*. But for a young girl I do think it
still sadder . . . I thought Lady Rimlade charming;
so unaffected. I said to her that we all lived quite
simply here, and that if Maria came we should treat
her as one of ourselves, and she said that was just
what Maria would love . . . In age, you see, Maria
comes just between Dilly and Doris.'

She broke off; she couldn't help thinking how
three years hence Maria might well be having a
coming-out dance. Then she imagined herself telling her friend Mrs. Brotherhood: 'It's terrible, I
never seem to see anything of my girls nowadays.
They seem always to be over at Lady Rimlade's.'

'We must make the poor child feel at home here,'
she told Mr. Hammond brightly.

The Doselys were accustomed to making the best
of Anglo-Indian children, so they continued to be
optimistic about Maria. 'One must make allowance
for character,' had become the watchword of this
warm-hearted household, through which passed a
constant stream of curates with tendencies, servants
with tempers, unrealized lady visitors, and yellow-
faced children with no morale. Maria was forbear-
ingly swamped by the family; she felt as though she
were trying to box an eiderdown. Doris and Dilly
had indelibly creased cheeks: they kept on smiling
and smiling. Maria couldn't decide how best to be
rude to them; they taxed her resourcefulness. She
could not know Dilly had thought, 'Her face is like
a sick monkey's,' or that Doris, who went to one of
those sensible schools, decided as soon that a girl in

a diamond bracelet was shocking bad form. Dilly
had repented at once of her unkind thought (though
she had not resisted noting it in her diary), and
Doris had simply said: 'What a pretty bangle. Aren't
you afraid of losing it?' Mr. Dosely thought Maria
striking-looking (she had a pale, square-jawed little
face, with a straight fringe cut above scowling
brows), striking but disagreeable—here he gave a
kind of cough in his thoughts and, leaning forward,
asked Maria if she were a Girl Guide.

Maria said she hated the sight of Girl Guides,
and Mr. Dosely laughed heartily and said that this
was a pity, because, if so, she must hate the sight of
Doris and Dilly. The supper-table rocked with merriment. Shivering in her red *crêpe* frock (it was a rainy
August evening, the room was fireless, a window
stood open, and outside the trees streamed coldly),
Maria looked across at the unmoved Mr. Hammond, square-faced, set and concentrated over his
helping of macaroni cheese. He was not amused.
Maria had always thought curates giggled; she despised curates because they giggled, but was furious
with Mr. Hammond for not giggling at all. She
studied him for some time, and, as he did not look
up, at last said: 'Are you a Jesuit?'

Mr. Hammond (who had been thinking about the
cricket-pitch) started violently; his ears went crimson; he sucked in one last streamer of macaroni.
'No,' he said, 'I am not a Jesuit. Why?'

'Oh, nothing,' said Maria. 'I just wondered. As a
matter of fact, I don't know what Jesuits are.'

Nobody felt quite comfortable. It was a most
unfortunate thing, in view of the nature of Mr.
Hammond's tendencies, for poor little Maria, in
innocence, to have said. Mr. Hammond's tendencies

were so marked, and, knowing how marked the Doselys thought his tendencies were, he was touchy. Mrs. Dosely said she expected Maria must be very fond of dogs. Maria replied that she did not care for any dogs but Alsatians. Mrs. Dosely was glad to be able to ask Mr. Hammond if it were not he who had told her that he had a cousin who bred Alsatians. Mr. Hammond said that this was the case. 'But unfortunately,' he added, looking across at Maria, 'I dislike Alsatians intensely.'

Maria now realized with gratification that she had incurred the hatred of Mr. Hammond. This was not bad for one evening. She swished her plateful of macaroni round with her fork, then put the fork down pointedly. Undisguised wholesomeness was, in food as in personalities, repellent to Maria. 'This is the last supper but three—no, but two,' she said to herself, 'that I shall eat at this Rectory.'

It had all seemed so simple, it seemed so simple still, yet five nights afterwards found her going to bed once again in what Mrs. Dosely called the little white nest that we keep for our girl friends. Really, if one came to look at it one way, the Doselys were an experience for Maria, who had never till now found anybody who could stand her when she didn't mean to be stood. French maids, governesses, highly paid, almost bribed into service, had melted away. There was something marvellously, memorably unwinning about Maria. . . . Yet here she still was. She had written twice to her aunt that she couldn't sleep and couldn't eat here, and feared she must be unwell, and Lady Rimlade wrote back advising her to have a little talk about all this with Mrs. Dosely. Mrs. Dosely, Lady Rimlade pointed out, was

motherly. Maria told Mrs. Dosely she was afraid
she was unhappy and couldn't be well. Mrs. Dosely
exclaimed at the pity this was, but at all costs—
Maria would see?—Lady Rimlade must not be worried. She had so expressly asked not to be worried
at all.

'And she's so *kind*,' said Mrs. Dosely, patting
Maria's hand.

Maria simply thought, 'This woman is mad.' She
said with a wan smile that she was sorry, but having
her hand patted gave her pins and needles. But rude-
ness to Mrs. Dosely was like dropping a pat of
butter on to a hot plate—it slid and melted away.

In fact, all this last week Maria's sole consolation
had been Mr. Hammond. Her pleasure in Mr. Hammond was so intense that three days after her coming he told Mrs. Dosely he didn't think he'd come in
for meals any more, thank you, as his landlady had
by now learned to cook. Even so, Maria had managed
to see quite a lot of him. She rode round the village
after him, about ten yards behind, on Doris's bi-
cycle; she was there when he offered a prayer with
the Mothers' Union; she never forgot to come out
when he was at work on the cricket-pitch ('Don't
you seem to get rather hot?' she would ask him feel-
ingly, as he mopped inside his collar. 'Or are you
really not as hot as you seem?'), and, having discovered that at six every evening he tugged a bell,
then read Evensong in the church to two ladies, she
came in alone every evening and sat in the front
pew, looking up at him. She led the responses, waiting courteously for Mr. Hammond when he lost his
place.

But tonight Maria came brisky, mysteriously up
to the little white nest, locking the door for fear Mrs.

Dosely might come in to kiss her good-night. She could now agree that music was inspiring. For they had taken her to the Choral Society's gala, and the effect it had had on Maria's ideas was stupendous. Half way through a rondo called *Off to the Hills* it had occurred to her that when she got clear of the Rectory she would go off to Switzerland, stay in a Palace Hotel, and do a little climbing. She would take, she thought, a hospital nurse, in case she hurt herself climbing, and an Alsatian to bother the visitors in the hotel. She had glowed—but towards the end of *Hey, nonny, nonny* a finer and far more constructive idea came along, eclipsing the other. She clapped her handkerchief to her mouth and, conveying to watchful Dilly that she might easily be sick at any moment, quitted the school-house hurriedly. Safe in her white nest, she put her candlestick down with a bump, got her note-paper out, and, sweeping her hair-brushes off the dressing-table, sat down at it to write thus:

Dearest Aunt Ena,—You must wonder why I have not written for so long. The fact is, all else has been swept from my mind by one great experience. I hardly know how to put it all into words. The fact is I love a Mr. Hammond, who is the curate here, and am loved by him, we are engaged really and hope to be married quite shortly. He is a fascinating man, extremely High Church, he has no money but I am quite content to live with him as a poor man's wife as I shall have to do if you and Uncle Philip are angry, though you may be sorry when I bring my little children to your door to see you. If you do not give your consent we shall elope but I am sure, dear Aunt Ena, that you will sympathize with your little niece in her great happiness. All I beseech is that you will not take me away from the Rectory; I do not think I could live without seeing Wilfred every day —or every night rather, as we meet in the church-yard and sit on a grave with our arms round each other in the moonlight. The Doselys do not know as I felt it was my duty to tell you first, but I expect the village people may have noticed as unfortunately there is a right of way through the churchyard but we cannot think of anywhere else to sit. Is it not curious to think how true it was when I said at the time when you sent me to the Rectory, that you did not realize what you might be exposing me to. But now I am so thankful that you did expose me, as I have found my great happiness here, and am so truly happy in a good man's love. Good-bye, I must stop now as the moon has risen and I am just going out to meet Wilfred.

    Your loving, full-hearted little niece
    Maria.

Maria, pleased on the whole with this letter, copied it out twice, addressed the neater copy with a flourish, and went to bed. The muslin frills of the nest moved gently on the night air; the moon rose beaming over the churchyard and the pale evening-primroses fringing the garden path. No daughter of Mrs. Dosely's could have smiled more tenderly in the dark or fallen asleep more innocently.

Mr. Hammond had no calendar in his rooms: he was sent so many at Christmas that he threw them all away and was left with none, so he ticked off the days mentally. Three weeks and six long days had still to elapse before the end of Maria's visit. He

remained shut up in his rooms for mornings together, to the neglect of the parish, and was supposed to be writing a book on Cardinal Newman.
Postcards of arch white kittens stepping through
rosy wreaths arrived for him daily; once he had
come in to find a cauliflower labelled 'From an admirer' on his sitting-room table. Mrs. Higgins, the
landlady, said the admirer must have come in by
the window, as *she* had admitted no one, so recently
Mr. Hammond lived with his window hasped. This
morning, the Saturday after the Choral Society's
gala, as he sat humped over his table writing his
sermon, a shadow blotted the lower window-panes.
Maria, obscuring what light there was in the room
with her body, could see in only with difficulty; her
nose appeared white and flattened; she rolled her
eyes ferociously round the gloom. Then she began
trying to push the window up.

'*Go away!*' shouted Mr. Hammond, waving his
arms explosively, as at a cat.

'You must let me in, I have something awful to
tell you,' shouted Maria, lips close to the pane. He
didn't, so she went round to the front door and was
admitted by Mrs. Higgins with due ceremony Mrs.
Higgins, beaming, ushered in the little lady from the
Rectory who had come, she said, with an urgent
message from Mrs. Dosely.

Maria came in, her scarlet beret tipped up, with
the jaunty and gallant air of some young lady in-
triguing for Bonny Prince Charlie.

'Are we alone?' she said loudly, then waited for
Mrs. Higgins to shut the door. 'I thought of writing
to you,' she continued, 'but your coldness to me
lately led me to think that was hopeless.' She hooked
her heels on his fender and stood rocking back-

wards and forwards. 'Mr. Hammond, I warn you:
you must leave Malton Peele at once.'

'I wish *you* would,' said Mr. Hammond, who,
seated, looked past her left ear with a calm concentration of loathing.

'I daresay I may,' said Maria, 'but I don't want
you to be involved in my downfall. You have your
future to think of; you may be a bishop; I am only
a woman. You see, the fact is, Mr. Hammond, from
the way we have been going about together, many
people think we must be engaged. I don't want to
embarrass you, Mr. Hammond.'

Mr. Hammond was not embarrassed. 'I always
have thought you a horrid little girl, but I never
knew you were quite so silly,' he said.

'We've been indiscreet. I don't know what my
uncle will say. I only hope you won't be compelled
to marry me.'

'Get off that fender,' said Mr. Hammond; 'you're
ruining it . . . Well then, stay there; I want to look at
you. I must say you're something quite new.'

'Yes, aren't I?' said Maria complacently.

'Yes. Any other ugly, insignificant-looking little
girls I've known did something to redeem themselves
from absolute unattractiveness by being pleasant,
say, or a little helpful, or sometimes they were well
bred, or had good table-manners, or were clever and
amusing to talk to. If it were not for the consideration of the Doselys for your unfortunate aunt—who
is, I understand from Mr. Dosely, so stupid as to be
almost mentally deficient—they would keep you—
since they really have guaranteed to keep you—in
some kind of shed or loose-box at the bottom of the
yard. . . . I don't want to speak in anger,' went on
Mr. Hammond, 'I hope I'm not angry; I'm simply

sorry for you. I always knew the Doselys took in Anglo-Indian children, but if I'd known they dealt in . . . cases . . . of your sort, I doubt if I'd have ever come to Malton Peele— Shut up, you little hell-cat! I'll teach you to pull my hair——'

She was on top of him all at once, tweaking his hair with science.

'You beastly Bolshevik!' exclaimed Maria, tugging. He caught her wrists and held them. 'Oh! Shut up—you hurt me, you beastly bully, you! Oh! how could you hurt a girl!' She kicked at his shin, weeping. 'I—I only came,' she said, 'because I was sorry for you. I needn't have come. And then you go and start beating me up like this—*Ow*!'

'It's your only hope,' said Mr. Hammond with a vehement, grave, but very detached expression, twisting her wrist round further. 'Yes, go on, yell— I'm not hurting you. You may be jolly thankful I *am* a curate. . . . As a matter of fact, I got sacked from my prep school for bullying . . . Odd how these things come back . . .'

They scuffled. Maria yelped sharply and bit his wrist. 'Ha, you would, would you? . . . Oh, yes, I know you're a little girl—and a jolly nasty one. The only reason I've ever seen why one wasn't supposed to knock little girls about is that they're generally supposed to be nicer—pleasanter—prettier—than little boys.' He parried a kick and held her at arms' length by her wrists. They glared at each other, both crimson with indignation.

'And you supposed to be a curate!'

'And you supposed to be a lady, you little parasite! This'll teach you— Oh!' said Mr. Hammond, sighing luxuriously, 'how pleased the Doselys would be if they knew!'

'Big brute! You great hulking brute!'

'If you'd been my little sister,' said Mr. Hammond, regretful, 'this would have happened before. But by this time, of course, you wouldn't be nearly so nasty . . . I should chivvy you round the garden and send you up a tree every day.'

'*Socialist!*'

'Well, get along now.' Mr. Hammond let go of her wrists. 'You can't go out of the door with a face like that; if you don't want a crowd you'd better go through the window . . . Now you run home and snivel to Mrs. Dosely.'

'*This* will undo your career,' Maria said, nursing wrists balefully. 'I shall have it put in the papers: *Baronet's niece tortured by demon curate.* That will undo your career for you, Mr. Hammond.'

'I know, I *know*, but it's worth it!' Mr. Hammond exclaimed exaltedly. He was twenty-four, and intensely meant what he said. He pushed up the window. 'Now get out,' he stormed, 'or I'll certainly kick you through it.'

'You are in a kind of a way like a brother to me, aren't you?' remarked Maria, lingering on the sill.

'I am not. Get out!'

'But oh, Mr. Hammond, I came here to make a confession. I didn't expect violence, as no one's attacked me before. But I forgive you because it was righteous anger. I'm afraid we *are* rather compromised. You must read this. I posted one just the same to Aunt Ena three days ago.'

Maria handed over the copy of her letter.

'I may be depraved and ugly and bad, but you must admit, Mr. Hammond, I'm not stupid.' She watched him read.

Half an hour later Mr. Hammond, like a set of walking fire-irons, with Maria, limp as a rag, approached the Rectory. Maria hiccupped and hiccupped; she'd found Mr. Hammond had no sense of humour at all. She was afraid he was full of vanity. 'You miserable little liar,' he'd said quite distantly, as though to a slug, and here she was being positively bundled along. If there'd been a scruff to her neck he would have grasped it. Maria had really enjoyed being bullied, but she did hate being despised. Now they were both going into the study to have yet another scene with Mr. and Mrs. Dosely. She was billed, it appeared, for yet another confession, and she had been so much shaken about that her technique faltered and she couldn't think where to begin. She wondered in a dim way what was going to happen next, and whether Uncle Philip would be coming to find Mr. Hammond with a horsewhip.

Mr. Hammond was all jaw; he wore a really disagreeable expression. Doris Dosely, up in the drawing-room window, gazed with awe for a moment, then disappeared.

'Doris!' yelled Mr. Hammond. 'Where is your father? Maria has something to tell him.'

'Dunno,' said Doris, and reappeared in the door. 'But here's a telegram for Maria—mother has opened it: something about a letter.'

'It would be,' said Mr. Hammond. 'Give it me here.'

'I can't, I won't,' said Maria, backing away from the telegram. Mr. Hammond, gritting his teeth audibly, received the paper from Doris.

Your letter blown from my hand overboard, he read out, *after had read first sentence wild with*

*anxiety please repeat contents by telegram your
Uncle Philip wishes you join us Marseilles Wednesday am writing Doselys Aunt Ena.*

'How highly strung poor Lady Rimlade must be,'
said Doris kindly.

'She is a better aunt than many people deserve,'
said Mr. Hammond.

'I think I may feel dull on that dreary old cruise
after the sisterly, brotherly family life I've had here,'
said Maria wistfully.

CLEMENCE DANE

The Dearly Beloved of Benjamin Cobb

IT was a shock to see a clerical figure turning, with the air of an owner, into my old home. I rounded on the house-agent's clerk, a friendly enough creature, but new since my day.

'Does he live there? Why doesn't he live in the Rectory?'

'This is the Rectory—oh, you mean the old Rectory. Nobody lives there now—too near the churchyard.'

'Do for me. I only want a place for week-ends.'

'See it if you like, of course!' He turned resignedly up the road. 'Not my place to crab it, but nobody's lived there these twenty years. Old Cobb was the last.'

'Cobb? Little Mr. Cobb?'

'Ah, you lived here once, of course! Know him?'

'A little. I was only a boy. I was never inside the house.'

'Nor anyone else by all accounts. Character, the reverend was, eh?'

I nodded, but half hearing; for we had struck across the churchyard and I was puzzling over the altered look of the place. Yet the square of sky was still set like a turquoise in the belfry, the yew tree still held out propped arms, and the daisied hay of summer was undulating over the graves. But the

oaks? now I had it! The oaks still stood in a row,
but a row without purpose; for the hedge they had
sentinelled was gone and behind them extended a
raw tract of white crosses and dying wreaths.

'Of course!' I decided aloud. 'It's the field!
They've taken in the Rectory field!'

'They'll take in the Rectory soon.' He flung open
the door in the high stone wall like a jailer unlocking
a prison, and laughed, 'Do for you, eh? It's empty.'

'Swept and garnished,' said I and stared.

There it stood, just as it stood in my memory, the
one unfriendly house in that friendly land. With
its sickly stucco, with its two sockets of blackness
where the glass of the upper windows had been
broken or removed, with its pinched and thrust-out
porch like a fretful mouth, it still had its remembered appearance of a wicked human face. A piece
of cloud skimming the blue overhead was reflected
for the instant of its passing in a jag of pane, and it
was as if an eyeball had rolled suspiciously in our
direction. The grimy laurels still hedged its base-
ments, the lean fir tree, always dying, yet never dead,
still scrabbled with spindly fingers on the creeperless
north wall. The stringy rosebush still bunted against
the dining-room window, but its flowers were rotting
under their caps of discoloured outer petals and its
leaves without gloss were so wrinkled and sapless
that you'd think the very blights must starve. The
surrounding garden was a mere rubbish heap. It had
been neat enough once: little Mr. Cobb was his own
gardener, and there had been a bed or two, and
every spring, bean-poles and taut string and a spatter
of hopeful green; but I could see now that, even had
the pence been less pitifully sparse, nothing could
have fruited in such a place. 'Cut down the trees!'

faintly across the years I could hear my mother's indignant voice; but the wife of little Mr. Cobb would
not have even a dead twig broken from its branch.
She had vouchsafed, in the early days of her marriage, with a snap of her fine eyes and a toss of her
handsome head, that 'she liked her privacy, thank
you! *She* wasn't public property whatever her husband might be!' and with that snap and toss had
shut yet another door upon herself for the rest of
her life. The eighties were not tolerant of bad manners in one they considered an inferior, and all the
world knew that little Mr. Cobb had married beneath him. And so the weeded paths grew velvety
with damp and the flowers were choked by the rank
droppings from the all-encircling limes, and the
Rectory remained fenced in from air and sunlight
and the neighbours' eyes till it was as quiet there
and hopeless as hell on Hallow-e'en.

I said—

'It's a marvel they stood it so long. Where are
they living now, d'you know?'

'Living? They're dead,' said the house-agent.
'Dead years ago. Their grave's just over the wall.'
He swished a way for himself through the nettles to
the low rampart that overlooked the churchyard,
saying as he did so, with a nod at the house behind
us, 'They're pulling it down in the spring. Good
thing too. D'you know you couldn't get a man or
woman or child to come through this gate after
dark? Queer couple! They say she beat him.'

'They say—they say!' I cried impatiently.

'Oh, well, some say it was him, of course, that he
kept her locked up. They say if you'd come here, in
the dark you know, that you'd see enough through
those windows——'

'They sleep quiet, I should think,' I said, leaning over to read the plain headstone lying almost under my feet. It ran—

Sacred to the memory of
BENJAMIN COBB,
for 25 years shepherd of this parish.
He entered into rest
on February 27th, 1903.
Also of
EILEEN,
his dearly beloved wife,
who died a week later.

And then in small letters half hidden by the daisies—

Judge not!

'Who had the sense to put that up?' I asked curiously.

'Sense? I don't know about sense. Old Miss Shepperley paid for it.'

'The schoolmistress? Is she alive still?'

'Alive and kicking. Retired, of course. Lets lodgings. Now she might put you up for the time being. There's a place I'd like to show you tomorrow— that is, if you'll go to the hundred.'

'A hundred's my limit. So she put it up, did she?'

'She did. Her own expense too. Would do it. "Penance" was the word she used, they tell me.'

'Penance? She was always good friends with the Rector?'

'Ah, but who wasn't, so far as I make out? They say when the end came——'

But at that I broke in with a promise to look over the house at a hundred the next day, and so got rid of him. I didn't want to hear of little Mr. Cobb's end from that hearsay stranger.

Long forgotten, gallant little Mr. Cobb! All through the flowery walk he danced ahead of me, a black-frocked shadow with arms and legs and coat-tails all at work to hurry him. He was always in a hurry, was little Mr. Cobb, always so eager to get his day's work done, always so joyous in his return to his uncertain welcome; yet always (looking back, that fact stood out very clearly) so determined that not a jot of that work should be ill done, unfitted for it as he must have known himself to be. A successful clergyman must, I suppose, have something of the actor in him and something of the woman, and little Mr. Cobb was pure masculine, stubborn, truthful, precise; yet if he were no Whitefield, at least his parish was properly patrolled and his church as well kept as his surplice. The village vowed that he had but one and that he washed it himself. 'The more credit to him!' said my mother hotly when this reached her; for it was always spotless. When he trotted about the altar in it, zealous and unsmiling, he always reminded me of good dog Toby in a Punch-and-Judy show enduring his ruff and standing soberly on his head. Sometimes indeed we wished that he were a little less thorough: from 'When the wicked man' to 'Remain with you always' he spared us nothing: we progressed every Sunday through prayers, psalms, Litany, Communion and three full-length hymns though characteristically he took them at the briskest of paces and his sermons were short and pithy. Only two or three times a year was the programme varied. When little Mr. Cobb sailed up the nave, his ceremonial bearing not even marred by those pouncing glances that detected

whisperers or empty seats, when the reverend gal-
lopade of the service slowed to a wedding march
tempo and, final proof, the Te Deum gave place to
the interminable Benedicite, we children would nod
at each other and, daring nurse, turn in our seats to
stare; for 'O all ye works of the Lord!' was a certain
sign that the legendary Mrs. Cobb was in the Rectory pew. Why the Benedicite should appeal to him
on such occasions we did not guess: I suppose its
triumphant echoes have little meaning to childish
ears; but to me it is plain enough now. Little Mr.
Cobb was spreading his feathers in the eyes of his
mate, eagerly proving that he could hold his congregation, that he could be master in his own church.
Little Mr. Cobb was showing off to his dearly beloved.

'The dearly beloved!' Ever since I can remember
it was the parish's nickname for the Rector's wife.
Provoked by some ill-considered loyalty of his, born
between a sneer and a smile at some tea-table gathering, it was kept alive, long after the irritation had
been forgotten, by his own habit of never referring
to her without some tender qualification:

'My dear wife is inclined to think——'

'As my beloved wife always feels——' and once,
on that dreadful night when he had come to us with
head held very straight and a painful flush on his
leathery cheek, to beg a sofa to sleep on, it had
been—

'My dear wife, as you know, suffers greatly in
health. At such times, Eileen—my wife, that is—
my dearly beloved wife—is not herself. At such
times——' and so broke off with a twitching lip.
What between the little man's shame and pride, and
chattering teeth, for he was drenched to the skin, it

took my father ten minutes to realize that the woman had locked him out of the house to spend the bitter March night as he could. He had not the keys of the church, he explained, or he would not have troubled them—no, he would not go to bed— if he might sit by the fire till morning—he must be gone early, his wife would be wanting him then. And at that, confidentially, over a glass of port, sipped with judgement—'Nerves, my dear sir! It's her nerves! They exhaust her. They make her wretched.'

He was so obviously distressed at the idea that anyone should sit up with him that my people in the end went off to bed, leaving him with his feet on the hob and an eiderdown tucked round him: and when in the morning my mother stole down before the servants were awake to make him a cup of tea, he looked so surprised and, decorous good man, so shocked, that she did not know whether to laugh or cry at him and was forced to call down my father. And then between them they sent him off with a good breakfast inside him to what he called his home.

Gallant little Mr. Cobb! Turning for a last look at the Rectory, I almost thought I saw him standing once more in the gaping door-hole, and with him my small self of long ago caught in the very act of unlawful entry. I could almost hear his voice, quick and harsh, as if he, not I, were the startled one——

'Shouldn't play here, you know! No place for children. Where's your mother?'

I pointed dumbly to a corner of the bloomy hedge where Mother and my cousins were sitting stringing cowslips, and then and there he marched me off to them, his hand still on my shoulder. My mother must have guessed that something was wrong, for she got up, scattering flowers and children, and came through the long grass to meet us.

'Why, Hughie——' she began quickly, but her eyes were on little Mr. Cobb, and it was then that I first realized that grown-up people have a language of glances.

He gave me a friendly push towards her.

'I've had a visitor. But I'm telling him, Mrs. James, my garden's no place to play in. Too damp, eh?' And then as I jogged off to join the others I heard a hurried undertone—'Mustn't let him come, my dear! Not a place for children! No, no, no! Not a place for children!'

Not a place for children indeed, I thought, as I recalled my one other glimpse of that forbidden ground. I must have been older, for I was sent, I think, to leave a note, and I remember the more sophisticated thrill with which I started out, my curiosity so whetted by the recollection of all the fragments of evil gossip I had heard, that my sister's 'I dare you to go in: I dare you to wait for an answer: I dare you to!' was scarcely needed. Indeed I reached the laurels by the bow window before my courage failed me and, at a movement within, I dived into the bushes to watch and get my breath before attempting the final venture of the doorstep and the knocker.

They were both at home. He was sitting at his desk, writing his sermon I imagine, for it was a Saturday, and she was trimming a hat with the invariable pink roses. I remember that particularly because I thought to myself, What did she want a hat for when she never went out? And when she had finished she put it down and said something. I saw her lips shaping the words that I could not hear.

He turned to her and smiled. He must have said that it was pretty, for she smiled back at him and put it on her head and began twisting the bows about as if she were pleased. At that, with such a brightening eye, he said something again, quickly, jerking his head towards the church. But she frowned and shook her head, and as he went on talking with pleasant urgent gestures, flung off the hat so roughly that it tumbled from the sofa to the floor, and then, as he stooped for it, laughed at him, a hateful loud laugh that I could hear through the shut window. I watched him straighten himself, put down the hat so carefully and look at her with a shutting off of the brightness of his face that touched me. It was like the shutting off of sunlight on a gleamy day of spring. I knew the look so well, and with a stricken conscience, for it was just the way my own mother looked at me when I wouldn't be good. I felt horribly ashamed for her. He spoke a word: it must have been her name; but she merely looked him over insolently and, turning, flounced out of the room. She left the door wide behind her, and I was so busy peering down the passage, so busy storing impressions to tell the others, that I forgot little Mr. Cobb. He must have sat himself down to his writing at once, for he was hard at work when his wife returned, still with that leaden look on her face and in her hands a tray of dinner-things. She swept the tablecloth into a corner and flung on another, carelessly, so that one end dipped to the floor. Even through the closed window I could hear the maddening clatter with which she dumped the tray upon the sideboard and tossed the crockery and utensils into place. She was like an ill-broken mare we had once possessed and sold again after it had nearly

killed my father. I watched her eye glint at her husband after each provocation just as Lady's used to
do, and her mouth take an uglier line because he
would not heed. For he wrote on, drawing aside his
chair to give her passage when she pushed rudely by
him, and catching at his papers without a word when
a swing of her hips in passing would have whirled
them to the floor. His expression did not change: he
still worried patiently and funnily at his pen like a
terrier worrying at a stick; but something in the
stoop of his shoulders made me feel indignant. She
had the meal ready at last, and told him so with one
movement of the lips: and so slouched to her place
and sat down, digging her chin into her fist and letting her other hand and arm sprawl out across the
table so that a glass tipped and the ugly bone spoon
was flicked out of the cellar in a spray of salt.

For a moment the room was perfectly still, with
the two souls in it sitting like statues, she at the table
and he at his shabby desk. Then she flung at him,
over her shoulder, 'Am I to wait all day?'—one read
the words on her pressed lips, her flattened eyelids,
her nostrils twitching like a cat's tail. He rose at that,
rubbing his hands, with a touch of apology in his
cheerful smile, a touch too much of sprightliness in
his step, and sat down at the end of the table with
his back to me. He bowed his head for grace, picked
up the carving knife and fork and set them down
again: then ensued once more one of their odd
pauses, and I saw his hand slip out and close over
hers. But at that she started up like a mad creature,
caught up the heavy cover in front of her and flung
it straight at him. It missed him by an inch and
crashed through the window into the bushes at my
feet. I was too frightened to move. I could hear now

as well as see, and the torrent of words that poured
from her lips dazed me—words that had no meaning, words that stuck in one's mind like one's first
sight of blood, or beastliness, or death.

He let her talk, with no more in the pauses of her
passion than a low 'Eileen! Eileen!' and suddenly it
was over, as a thunderstorm is over, and she dropped
limp and exhausted in her chair. Then to my amaze-
ment he went swiftly to her (I wondered awesomely
what he was going to do to her), and she caught at
him with both her hands as if she were dragging
herself out of a pit and, with a little gasping cry,
down went her head on his shoulder and her eyes
closed. In an instant he had his arms round her and
half lifted, half dragged her to the horsehair sofa.
I thought, I remember, that he looked very funny
dragging that big woman about. I heard her say—

'Don't go! And then—'Benjy, I didn't mean——'

He shook up a pillow and pulled a rug over her,
a bright patchwork thing that distracted my attention for a moment; for our nurse used to make
patchwork quilts, and it was the fashion among us
children to collect scraps of silk for her. When I had
time for those strange actors in my play, little Mr.
Cobb was busy with a sandwich and a plate and
was urging her to eat and drink. But she wouldn't
touch it. She said—I could hear her clearly enough
now—

'Leave me alone! Oh, can't you leave me alone!'
and in the same breath—'Don't go!'

He was murmuring in a distressed voice something about an appointment in the village and—

'You know, my dear, that's why we had lunch so
early.'

She gave him a gleaming look and said again—

'Don't go!'

But he only said with mild finality—

'My dear, you know I must!' and hunted forth his shovel hat from a cupboard in the wall. I can see now, as my childish eyes could not see, how like his little speech was to his little self. I don't suppose that ever in his life it had occurred to him that it was possible to omit a duty even for her sake: maybe that fact was at the root of their misery.

She flounced back on to the sofa with—

'You never do anything to please me!' And at his cheerful—

'Why, it's only to the schools, my dear! I'll be back before you know I'm gone!' she would give him no answering smile. She said—

'I don't care if you never come back!' and as he hesitated in the doorway fumbling with his Prayer-books, looking at her kindly, as if he hoped even then for another sort of speeding, she cried—

'Oh, do *go* if you're going!'

At that he went. I waited till he should have left the garden to make my escape. He came out by the front door and stood a moment on the ill-kept broken steps that betrayed his poverty, and I heard him say to himself very softly, 'My poor girl! My poor girl!' and sigh. Then he jammed the shovel hat firmly down upon his head and jaunted off brisk as ever. I thought to myself that it was queer to call a lady older than mother a girl.

Miss Shepperley still lived opposite her schools, but the road there seemed much shorter than once it had been, and so I arrived as, it amused me to realize, I had always done, punctually at tea-time. Miss Shepperley didn't know me at first; but when she did we were very glad to see each other. In ten minutes I was in the same horsehair armchair that I used to sit in, the same service with the turquoise band round the edges was set out on the table between us, and the same tea-cosy with the hand-painted eschscholtzias that had been my sister's handiwork was covering the same brown teapot with the chipped knob; while from over the road the shrill voices of the afternoon singing class uplifted in 'John Peel' and 'Early one morning' still floated in at the open window as they used to do. Indeed there was only Miss Shepperley's front hair, very grey against the dark brown coils at the back (but it had been all brown when I knew her) to remind me that I was a young man of affairs and not an eight-year-old come to tea with Miss Shepperley for a treat.

We talked: I told her all that I had been doing, and she told me all that she had been doing in the last fifteen years: and I thought how far and fast I had run and how stock-still Miss Shepperley had been sitting. And yet I thought that stagnation suited her, for she had grown out of the masterless fifties into a kind old witch with all the beauty of an old woman and all the energy of a young one. I began to think the world of her again, just as I used to do: and she knew it and twinkled. Within an hour she had heard all about my novel and my editor and my engagement and the rest of my hopes and fears. And then we fell to inquiries after one old friend and another till at last—

'So little Mr. Cobb is dead,' I said. 'I'm sorry.'

'For him?' she said quickly. 'You needn't be!'

'I suppose not. But I liked him. And the woman died also, I hear—*see* rather.'

'Ah, you've been in the churchyard,' she said. And then, flushing, '*I* put that up.'

'So I'm told. Why, Miss Shepperley?'

She smiled at me indulgently—

'What do you want to know for? The editor? Oh, my dear, you can tell the story if you like. Nobody would believe it, so it's quite safe. Besides, there isn't one.'

'There must have been. What was it, Miss Shepperley? Drink? Drugs? What was the matter with her?'

She blinked at me: and suddenly I realized that in Miss Shepperley's eyes I was not much older than the small boy who used to take tea with her, in spite of my editor and my engagement. She said—

'Drink—drugs—we don't run to that sort of thing here. You have your cinemas in London. But in a village, you know, the passions themselves are enough of a stimulant.'

I blurted out, suddenly seeing her with new eyes—

'You didn't live here always?'

She smiled at me.

'No, my dear!'

And that is as much as I ever heard of Miss Shepperley's life story. We sat silent. I didn't know, nor do I yet, whether I had been snubbed or confided in. Presently I said uncertainly—

'The passions?'

'Love, hate, jealousy, grief. And pity, my dear. Pity can be a passion. Yes, you had 'em all in full flower up at the Rectory—passion-flowers—the only flowers that garden ever fruited.'

'What fruit?'

'Dust and ashes. They died, my dear. They point a moral and adorn a tale. D'you want to tell it?'

'Hear it, anyway.'

She said thoughtfully—

'You could call it "The Lovers' Tale", if it weren't used already.'

I looked at her to see if she was joking. But she was quite grave. I said—

'Lovers? Miss Shepperley, she made his life a hell. Even I know that from the scraps I can remember.'

'But she loved him.'

'I've seen them together.'

'She loved him.'

'I'll never believe it.'

'I wouldn't once. And so it's on my conscience that I helped to kill her. And yet not much on my conscience, for you may be sure that wherever she is now, heaven or hell, he'll be looking after her.'

'I'll admit that he loved her, though even that's hardly believable——'

'She was young once, you know!' said Miss Shepperley.

'Well, of course!' I said uncertainly.

'Ah, but I mean *young*. She had the gifts of youth. A fretful mouth even then, and coarse hands, but— she would have charms, I think, for a little man like him. At twenty-five you'd have called her—a fruitful goddess: that is if she hadn't pinched herself so insanely. But she was as vain as a peacock: that began the trouble. She arrived here, you know—they were a honeymoon couple—feathered and bustled, all silk and cheap lace, and he with a hundred and fifty a year! It put people's backs up, knowing what they knew.' And then, answering the lift of my eyebrows —'Oh, she had caught him in his college days—one of the towns-people. He was a catch, you know—

double first and so on. But for his marriage he might
have done anything. All sorts of shining lights used
to come down to see him—at first—till she drove
them away.'

'But why? Why?'

'My dear, she was jealous of the stones he walked
on, of the weeds he pulled out of the garden. D'you
know, I think it pleased him. He had thrown over
all his prospects to marry her, and so that attitude
of hers rewarded him, I suppose, at the start. The
novelty, do you think? He was a learned schoolboy
and she went to his head, I imagine, like bad champagne. He was such a prig, you know, when they
first came here.'

'Little Mr. Cobb?'

'You wouldn't think so, would you? Kind little
man. But he was! Heavens, how intellectual his
sermons were! A real treat if you had the taste—
but what's the use of brilliance in a village? What
with his priggishness and her vulgarity you can
understand that they weren't liked. He weathered
it: he was a quick learner; but she—never! She
offended people right and left—made silly mistakes
and wouldn't let herself be told. Always reminding
one that she was a lady too, poor creature! We'd
have put up with her, of course, if it had been only
that she was underbred, but on the top of it all she
had the temper of a fishwife, and when she lost it
she didn't care what she said or did. In fact I don't
believe she knew. I remember a scene once at a
ladies' meeting, a penny reading committee, when
every woman in the room got up and walked out of
the house except me. I was official in a sense, or I'd
have gone too. But believe me, when they were gone
she turned round to me (remember she'd been im-

possible, simply impossible) and said in a rueful, helpless way that disarmed me, in spite of myself—

'"Aren't they beasts? Oh, aren't they? You can't say a thing to please them!"

'(One didn't say beast in those days, you know! It was a dreadful word.) And then—

'"Oh, and I took such pains with the tea!"'

'So she had, my dear! It was the sort of tea that would have been ostentatious at the Big House, and they with that pittance and what he earned from his learned societies! My eyes ran over the sugared cakes and the satin doilies, and I suppose she saw what I thought, for she came up to me and planted herself in that dreadful attitude of hers, hands on hips like a principal boy—oh, I can see her now, and the way it showed off her figure—and said—

'"Well, what's wrong with *that*?" And then—"You can get out too if you look at me like that."

'But her lip was trembling and I was sorry for her. She was just like an ignorant ill-bred child.'

'I keep my sympathy for him all the same!' said I.

'Why, yes—if it comes to that. D'you know, there was even at one time talk of pressure being brought on him to resign. It came to nothing in the end, I fancy, because the vestry were such cowards. No one, face to face with him, had the heart to give him the reason. But he was learning—oh, he was learning! I tell you he grew into what you knew in the first two years—and after that final flare-up he managed somehow to keep her under control. Indeed it grew easy, what with her declaring that she wouldn't receive so-and-so and the whole neighbourhood avoiding her. For a time she came to the official gatherings, concerts and mission work and so on, and then a child was born and died, and after

that she might have been dead herself for all we saw
of her. But tales still went the rounds. They had a
servant at first, but they never kept one a month.
The girls all said the same thing—a good mistress
till she was crossed, and then—a devil! They stuck
to it that she was kind to them, that they'd like to
stay, but they were afraid for their lives when she
was in one of her fits.'

'And of him? What did they say of him?'

'He chilled them, you know. He never could be
hail-fellow. But they all spoke well of him. But of
her it was always, "Ah, the pore dear! She's a fair
terror, the pore dear!" as if they half admired her.'

'But they didn't stay?'

'No. And between you and me, my dear, that's
what I put his death down to. She took over the
work of the house after a fashion; but she was a
slap-dash useless creature: I've always said he was
undernourished. She fed him on boiled eggs and
cheap sweets, I fancy, and so of course when the
influenza came—no stamina! God forgive me for
saying so, my dear, for he's capable of rising from
his grave to contradict it. *He* never complained.'

'Why on earth he ever married her——' I began.

'You'd never be such a fool, would you?' said
Miss Shepperley. And then— 'Oh, my dear, why do
people marry? Body and soul—but the body has
first say when one's young. Isn't it so? You're a
young man and I'm a woman and an old one—but
isn't it so?' And then, as I made her no answer—
'No, no! It's what she saw in him that occupies me.'

'It's pretty obvious, isn't it? You said yourself—'

'Yes, I said she was out to catch her man, and he
was not the first by all accounts——'

'Oh, that sort!'

'I've never been sure. His friends were very loyal. There was never a hint, never the flicker of an eyelid. Too loyal—that was what made one suspicious. But if she were—what we've thought her sometimes and whispered and said and shouted from the thatch (you know what a village is), does it say she didn't love him? Body and soul—but the soul might have had first say perhaps with her, for a change. Suppose now that he hadn't married her? He saved her from something: d'you think she didn't know it? But *I* say didn't she save him too? Better to break your heart than shrivel it, my dear! I'm old-fashioned: I believe marriages are made in Heaven, even this one. At least he died with her hand in his. Dr. Davis told me that. What do you think his last words were?'

I said—

'It should have been, "Dearly beloved!"'

'"Doctor, make her rest!" Davis said that finished him, and he's accustomed to queer scenes. They had been on their feet for pretty well a fortnight, you know, with half the village paralysed by the influenza scare, and they'd no sooner got it under than the Rector dropped where he stood. They sent for her—the first time she'd been in a neighbour's house for years—but she shocked everyone. She didn't seem to consider how ill he was: to move him—to get him back to the Rectory—that was her whole concern. He was her husband and it was her place to decide, and there was a conspiracy against her, and so on—oh, dreadful! Davis was pretty rough with her at last, they tell me, but he couldn't forbid her the room because the Rector was asking for her. And so she sat there all through the night while he sank, quarrelling with Davis under her breath.

But at dawn little Mr. Cobb began to pull at her hand, Davis said, and craned from his pillow till his lips touched it, and then, as I tell you, while Davis straightened him, "Doctor," he says, "make her rest!" and with that drowses and, after a while, dies. He was only fifty.'

'Well?' I said at last softly.

'Well?' she returned. And then I saw that her mouth was unsteady and wished I had held my tongue. But she had herself well in hand, all but her mouth.

'It's not much to you, my dear,' she said steadily, 'but we—we were fond of him.'

I said—

'So was I, I think, or he wouldn't have stuck in my mind so all these years. But that's only half the tombstone, Miss Shepperley?'

'Ah, poor soul, yes!' she said. 'I'd forgotten her. We all forgot her. Such a funeral! All the village came. We *were* fond of him. And everyone saying it in whispers, you know, in a wondering way, as if it were a surprise to us. It was only afterwards that we thought of Mrs. Cobb. She hadn't come—that wasn't anything: women didn't till lately—but it got around that she'd been quite unpardonable to Dr. Davis and the Squire. She as good as told Dr. Davis that his treatment was responsible for the Rector's death, and then began to bargain with the Squire about moving and the fittings of the house—yes, before her husband was so much as buried—and there was a row royal with the undertaker's people. They said that the only thing she seemed to care about was her mourning. Lady Sarah, who had called with the Squire, offered to lend her clothes, knowing, of course, that there was no money: and I'm sure she

offered it nicely; but no! She was all for ordering
crapes and alpacas from the draper's till old Brown
went up to see her himself and told her bluntly that
he would help her, and so would the rest of the
vestry, for the Rector's sake, but that he wouldn't
give credit for fallals. He came back quite shaken,
d'you know, and said that she'd screamed him out
of the house. And after that nobody went near her
for two or three days, and I can't say that I blame
them. But on Saturday, a week from the day he died,
I was in at Brown's, at the grocery counter, and
while he was serving me he told me something that
made me uncomfortable. He said that he'd had no
orders from the Rectory since the day he went up,
and that his boy had told him that morning that the
milk-jugs hadn't been touched for two days. The
boy had left them at the gate, and when Brown told
him to go up to the front door, he said he was afraid
to, because the garden was all over scarecrows.
Brown said, quite rightly, that something ought to
be done, but that he himself wouldn't go near her
for a sovereign nor let his wife. He said, and I'm
sure he believed, that she was possessed of a devil.
It is a devil too, a temper like hers.'

'So you went!' I told her.

She flushed.

'How did you know?'

'Old times,' said I, smiling at her; but she only
answered with her familiar, anxious frown—

'Oh, I know I meddle.'

'Is that what you call it?' said I.

She put out her hand and touched mine.

'Nice boy!' said Miss Shepperley. And then—'But
this bit of meddling wasn't so easy. It was years
since I'd spoken to her. She'd taken a dislike to me

because of the concerts. Mr. Cobb used to depend on me, you know, to run them, and she was unpleasant about it. I don't mind telling you. I'm too old to mind. But going up to the Rectory I thought to myself that it was rather good of me to trouble. But there, it was for his sake I was meddling, not for hers. The boy was quite right: there were two jugs of milk by the steps and thickened, with dust on the cream, and when I opened the door in the wall you never saw such a sight! The whole garden was strewn with black garments, spread on bushes, hung from twigs, flapping and bellying in the wind till the place looked like a picture I once saw of vultures on a battlefield. I thought she must have run mad, till I noticed the pools and trails of black water on the gravel and up the steps. Then I understood. It was her mourning, my dear. She had been dyeing all her ·clothes. Queer, isn't it, how trouble takes people! I could see her as I came up the path, sitting at the table in the dining-room, driving her machine till I thought she'd break it; but though the dining-room window was two yards from the porch and though I know she saw me, there was no answer when I knocked. But I wasn't going to be stopped when I'd got so far—dear knows I truly hoped to help her! —so I went straight in, down the passage and into the room—and found myself face to face with her as she sat between the table and the wall. I said—

'"Forgive me—may I come in?"

'She didn't get up. She barely lifted her head, and I began to think that she wasn't going to speak at all and to wonder what I should do next. But after a minute she said—

'"What do you want here—now?"

'I said—

'"I thought I might be of some use to you, Mrs. Cobb."

'She went on turning the handle and guiding the stuff past the needle as she said, without a look at me—

'"A pity you didn't come sooner!"

'I said, holding on to my temper——

'"One is diffident about intruding."

'"Yes," she said, "you've been diffident about intruding for twenty years, the lot of you! But you think you can come and go as you please, I suppose, now my husband has left me in the lurch." Yes, she said that. Imagine it! I was so shocked that I could only get out a—

'"Mrs. Cobb!"

'"Well!" she said, stooping her face to the cloth and biting off a thread, "hasn't he left me in the lurch?" And then—"What call had he to go grubbing round in those muck-heaps they call cottages?"

'I said, trying to be gentle, trying my hardest, my dear—

'"Mrs. Cobb, don't you realize——?"

'She flung up her head.

'"I realize that he thought more of his tin-pot parish than of his wife. D'you think he'd listen to me when I begged him to stay at home—begged him and prayed him? Not he! It's as if he'd died to spite me."

'Well, at that, my dear, I lost my temper completely, utterly, as I've never in my life done before or since. I said—

'"To please you, I should think!"

'At that she dropped her work and got to her feet with a—

'"What the hell d'you mean?" speaking in a rau-

cous street voice, the way drunken women speak:
her face was flaming. But I didn't care. I said—

'"You know the hell I mean—" and with that I
launched out. I told her what we thought of her and
him. I told her how we'd watched them all these
years and how we'd grown to like and pity him, and
in the end been glad to hear that he was dead and
free of his bitter troubles. I told her in so many
words that if ever a woman had ruined a man's life
then she had ruined his, with her selfishness and her
cruelty and her crazy rages. And that if the epidemic
had been his way of release, before God and in the
sight of the congregation he was none the less a
murdered man and that she had killed him.

'Then I stopped; and for a minute we stared at
each other without a word. I was panting, and so
was she, and her face had gone a queer mottled
colour, patches of red on dead white, and her mouth
was half open. She said at last quite quietly, like a
lady, not like a fishwife (it was a side of her I'd
never dreamed of)—

'"You must be mad!"

'I said—

'"Must I, Mrs. Cobb? Then we're all mad in this
village, for I'm saying what we all think."

'She looked down at her work thoughtfully, as if
it were something that she'd never seen before, and
then back again at me with just the same look, and
then she said, stammering a little—

'"But—but I loved him!"

'I laughed: not maliciously, but because I couldn't
help it. I suppose I was rather near hysteria. It had
shaken me to say what I'd said. But she went on
quite gently—

'"Why do you laugh? I loved him." And then,

with a sort of hastening of her speech in the quiet
room, like a storm blowing up on a leaden day, "I
loved him. It's not true what you say. I tell you
I loved him—I loved him." And then—"Benjy, you
know! Benjy, tell her! Benjy!" She waited, as if for
an answer, moving her hands to and fro as though
she were feeling for a support: and when no answer
came—I had no words, my dear—she suddenly fell
back into her chair, bowed her head in her hands
and began to cry. No, and it wasn't hysterics either:
it was grief finding outlet—grief: such grief as I had
never dreamed of, and yet I've had my share, I dare
say. It wasn't like a woman crying: it was like the
crying of a lost soul on judgement day—after sentence. I didn't seem to see her, if you understand: it
was like watching a storm of nature. I thought—
don't laugh at me—I kept on thinking of the Flood
when the rain came down, pulping and battering
and beating the world flat, drowning it. It went
through my head over and over again, in his voice,
you know, little Mr. Cobb's dry Sunday voice, reading the lesson in church, "The fountains of the great
deep were broken up and the windows of heaven
were opened." I tell you it was the most terrifying
and inhuman thing I've ever dreamed of, that bitter,
wicked creature sitting there, crying, crying, crying,
like a drowning world.

'I suppose I sat there an hour watching her, not
daring to speak.

'She'd cry herself quiet, you know, after a time,
and sit there twisting her hands. Then she'd lift her
head at last with a listening air and her poor drowned
eyes would wander weakly round the room and fix
their gaze on something, the leather chair by the fire
it was once, and another time the dyed breadths of

stuff in front of her, and then her lip would begin
to quiver and her eyes fill and the muscles of her
throat strain, and you'd see her fighting and struggling with herself, her face all twisted up like a
comic mask, and then—down would go her head
again, and the rain, the rain renew. I tell you, you
could see it and hear it, with the forests snapping
like matchwood, the cities swept away, the ridges of
the world crumbling into mud beneath that downpour: and still the storms sweeping on in gusts of
wind and lightning and water, wiping away all
things human, blotting out the face of the world.

'Only it was not the world: it was a woman crying.

'And then she began to beat her head against the
wall.

'You can imagine that I talked to her, put my arm
round her, tried to bring her to some sort of reason.
Oh, *my* anger was gone, gone in the first five minutes,
overwhelmed, swept away. I tell you it seemed a
pretty trivial thing, my anger. I was not even sorry:
how can you be sorry for a grief like that? But I
wanted her to restrain herself. Such grief wasn't
decent, it wasn't liveable with, it had got to be
covered up. I said what I could that was comforting,
but it was like trying to uphold a ruined cliff that
is sliding into the sea. I didn't know what to do or
what to say. And when she began to beat her forehead against the wall, yes, and when I went to her,
threw me off as if I were a fly to be brushed away
—she was a big strong woman—then I went for
help. I thought she'd kill herself.'

'Was she trying to, d'you suppose?'

'I don't think so. I think she was just easing her
pain. She was always a violent creature, and so
when she suffered, it was violently. But you can

imagine that I couldn't let it go on. I had to have help. I went out, late as it was, running all the way, to find the district nurse, but she was away looking after a patient, and when I went on to the sexton's wife, she was out too. It must have been an hour before I found anyone, and when we did get back to the Rectory, Mrs. Cobb was gone. She was not in the room, not in the house.

'That was a night, I tell you. We went first to the doctor, and he knocked up Wills, the constable—you remember Wills? By that time half the village was up and out with lights and lanterns. Somebody, I don't know who, put the word about and in a moment they were all whispering and then shouting, "The ponds! Try the ponds!" You know the two ponds at the side of the road, opposite Oulson's down at Drake's Bottom?'

'I know,' I said. 'They're deep.'

'And used, my dear, and used these hundred years! I could tell you tales! Well, we all set off helter-skelter the mile and a half down Drake's Hill, and a time we had when we got there! We knocked up Oulson's to get a drag, but he had nothing: and at last men got out the netting he used for his cherry trees and made shift with that. It all took time, and what with the darkness and the wet—oh, we were a set of fools, and after an hour we knew it! Kettles and pots and pans we found, but we didn't find Mrs. Cobb. It was grey daylight when we got to the top of Drake's Hill again and back to the Rectory. It was just as we left it, and we were beginning to break up—for what were we to do?—we were soaked and tired out!—when one of a parcel of boys going off home across the churchyard let out a whoop and yell, and then they all came running back, crying

out that they'd found her. Fools that we were—
we'd never thought of the churchyard! As I said to
Mary Wills, "Call ourselves women! We might have
known!"

'She was lying on her face on his grave, with the
earth scattered all round her as if she'd been digging. Her poor hands were torn and her arms clayed
up to the elbow, and she was dead—dead and peace-
ful.'

'Poor thing!' said I. And after a moment, 'What
was it—heart?'

'Exposure. Exhaustion too, I daresay, after all
that crying; but they brought it in "exposure". She
must have lain there all the time we were searching.
There was frost on her dress and hair. Oh, you
know, that cut me to the heart, to think how he must
have grieved to hear her above him in the darkness,
calling to him and getting no answer, getting no
help, when he'd cherished her so. I suppose that was
his punishment. "Little children, keep yourselves
from idols!" I heard him preach on that once—one
of his sound sermons, all Greek derivations and the
Athanasian Creed.'

'Poor things!' I said again. And then—'At least,
poor him! I can't get up much sympathy for her,
can you?'

But Miss Shepperley did not answer, and lifting
my eyes I saw that she was listening, not to me, but
to the voices of the children, very loud and nasal all
of a sudden in the hot little silent room:

> *Ye gentlemen of England,*
> *That live at home at ease,*
> *How little do you think upon*
> *The dangers of the seas!*
> *Give ear unto the mariners—*

She turned with a gesture sharp as a cry. I never knew before that old eyes could hold such passion—

'"The dangers of the seas," my dear! That's it! "The dangers of the seas!" Have we ever sailed to the gates of hell and heaven, and seen the face of Love? Oh, it may come to you still. You're young. But I? What right have I to judge? Have I been where they've been? Grant that they wrecked themselves; but—think of the stars they steered by! To bury the bodies when they come ashore and commend the souls to the wind of God that drove 'em —that's our business. But not to judge them, my dear, never to judge them; for we've not been on their journey, and we don't understand.'

ROSAMOND LEHMANN

A Dream of Winter

In the middle of the great frost she was in bed with influenza, and that was the time the bee man came from the next village to take the swarm that had been for years buried in the wall of her country house; deep under the leads roofing the flat platform of the balcony outside her bedroom window.

She lay staring out upon a mineral landscape: iron, ice and stone. Powdered with a wraith of spectral blue, the chalky frost-fog stood, thickened in the upper air; and behind it a glassy disc stared back, livid, drained of heat, like a gas lamp turned down, forgotten, staring down uselessly, aghast, upon the impersonal shrouded objects and dark relics in an abandoned house. The silence was so absolute that it reversed itself and became in her ears continuous reverberation. Or was it the bees, still driving their soft throbbing dynamo, as mostly they did, day in, day out, all the year round?—all winter a subdued companionship of sound, a buried murmur; fiercer, louder, daily more insistent with the coming of the warm days; materializing then into that snarling, struggling, multiple-headed organism pinned as if by centripetal force upon the outside of the wall, and seeming to strive in vain to explode away from its centre and disperse itself.

No. The bees were silent. As for the children, not one cry. They were in the garden somewhere: frost-struck perhaps like all the rest.

All at once, part of a ladder oscillated across the window space, became stationary. A pause; then a battered hat appeared, then a man's head and shoulders. Spying her among the pillows, his face creased in a wide grin. He called cheerfully: 'Good-morning!'

She had lost her voice, and waved and smiled, pointing to her throat.

'Feeling a bit rough? Ah, that's a shame. There's a lot of nasty colds and that about. Bed's the best place this weather, if you ask me.'

He stepped up on to the little balcony, and stood framed full-length in the long window—a short, broad figure in roll-collared khaki pull-over, with a twinkling blue small peasant's eye in a thin lined face of elliptical structure, a comedian's face, blurred in its angles and hollows by a day's growth of beard.

'Come to take that there swarm. Wrong weather to take a swarm. I don't like the job on a day like this. Bad for 'em. Needs a mild spell. Still, it don't look like breaking and I hadn't nothink else on and you wanted the job done.'

His speech had a curious humming drawl, not altogether following the pattern of the local dialect: brisker, more positive. She saw that, separated by the frosty pane, they were to be day-long companions. The lady of the house, on her bed of sickness, presented him with no problems in etiquette. He experienced a simple pleasure in her society: someone to chat to on a long job.

'I'll fetch my mate up.'

He disappeared, and below in the garden he called: 'George!' Then an unintelligible burr of conversation, and up he came again, followed by

a young workman with a bag of tools. George felt
the embarrassment of the situation, and after one
constricted glance through the window, addressed
himself to his task and never looked towards her
again. He was very young, and had one of those
nobly modelled faces of working men: jaw, brows
profoundly carved out, lips shutting clearly, salient
cheek-bone, sunk cheek, and in the deep cavities of
the eye-sockets, eyes of extreme sadness. The sorrow
is fixed, impersonal, expressing nothing but itself,
like the eyes of animals or of portraits. This face
was abstract, belonging equally to youth or age,
turning up here and there, with an engine-driver's
cap on, or a soldier's; topping mechanics' overalls,
lifting from the roadmender's gang to gaze at her
passing car. Each time she saw it, so uncorrupted,
she thought vaguely, romantically, it was enough to
believe in. She had had a lot of leisure in her life to
look at faces. She had friends with revolutionary
ideas, and belonged to the Left Book Club.

'Be a long job this,' called the bee man. 'Looks
like they've got down very deep.'

A sense of horror overcame her, as if some terrible
exploratory physical operation of doubtful issue, and
which she would be forced to witness, was about to
take place. This growth was deep down in the body
of the house. The waves of fever started to beat up
again.

The men disappeared. She waited for the children
to appear upon the ladder; and soon, there they
were. John had taken the precaution of tucking his
sister's kilt into her bloomers. In his usual manner
of rather disgusted patience, he indicated her foot-
ing for her. They pranced on the balcony, tapped
on the pane, peered in with faces of lunatic

triumph, presenting themselves as the shock of her life.

'A man's come to do the bees!'

'It's perfectly safe,' yelled John, in scorn, fore-stalling her. But voiceless, she could only nod, beam, roll her eyes.

'Shall we get Jock up?'

Frantically she shook her head.

'But he's whining to come up,' objected Jane, dismayed.

The hysterical clamour of a Cairn terrier phenomenally separated from his own rose up from below.

'We'd better go down to him,' said John wearily, acknowledging one more victory for silliness. 'Here come the workmen anyway. We'd only be in their way. Here—put your foot *here*, ass.'

They vanished. Insane noises of reunion uprose; then silence. She knew that Jane had made off, her purely subjective frivolous interest exhausted; but that John had taken up his post for the day, a scientific observer with ears of deepening carmine, waiting, under the influence of an inexpressible desire for co-operation, for a chance to steady the ladder, hand up a tool, or otherwise insinuate himself within the framework of the ritual.

Up came the bee man and his mate. They set to work to lift the leads. They communicated with each other in a low drone, bee-like, rising and sinking in a minor key, punctuated by an occasional deep-throated 'Ah!' Knocking, hammering, wrenching developed. Somebody should tell them she could not stand it. Nobody would. She rang for the curtains to be drawn, and when they were, she lay down flat and turned her face to the wall and sank into burning sleep.

She woke to the sound of John shouting through her door.

'They've gone to have their lunch. He's coming back this afternoon to take the swarm. Most of the roof's off. I've seen the bees. If only you'd drawn back your curtains you could have too. I called to you but you didn't seem to hear. The cat's brought in two more birds, a pigeon and a tit, but we saved them and we're thawing them behind the boiler.'

Down the passage he went, stumping and whistling.

Three o'clock. The petrified day had hardened from hour to hour. But as light began to fail, there came a moment when the blue spirit drew closer, explored the tree-tops, bloomed against the ghostly pane; like a blue tide returning, invading the white caves, the unfructifying salt stones of the sea.

The ladder shook. He was there again, carrying a kind of lamp with a funnel from which poured black smoke.

'Take a look,' he called cheerfully. 'It's worth it. Don't suppose you ever see nothink o' the kind before.'

She rose from her bed, put on dressing-gown and shawl and stumbled to the window. With a showman's flourish he flung off the black sacking—and what a sight was revealed! Atolls of pale honeycomb ridging the length and breadth of beam and lath, thrusting down in serrated blocks into the cavity; the vast amorphous murmuring black swarm suddenly exposed, stirring resentful, helpless, transfixed in the icy air. A few of the more vigorous insects crawled out from the conglomeration, spun up into the air, fell back stupefied.

'They're more lively than you'd think for,' said the bee man, thoughtful. She pointed to his face, upon which three or four bees were languidly creeping. He brushed them off with a chuckle. 'They don't hurt me. Been stung too often. Inoculated like.'

He broke off a piece of honeycomb and held it up. She wished so much to hold it in her hand that she forced herself to push down the window, receiving the air's shock like a blow on the face; and took it from him. Frail, blond, brittle, delicate as coral in construction, weightless as a piece of dried sponge or seaweed.

'Dry, see?' said the bee man. 'You won't get much honey out of here. It's all that wet last summer. If I'd 'a' taken this swarm a year ago, you'd a' got a bagful. You won't get anythink to speak of out of here now.'

She saw now: the papery transparent aspect of these ethereal growths meant a world extinct. She shivered violently, her spirit overwhelmed by symbols of frustration. Her dream had been rich: of honey pouring bountifully out from beneath her roof tree, to be stored up in family jars, in pots and bowls, to spread on the bread and sweeten the puddings, and save herself a little longer from having to tell the children: No more sugar.

Too late! The sweet cheat gone.

'It's no weather to take a swarm,' repeated the bee man. Dejectedly he waved the lamp over the bubbling glistening clumps, giving them a casual smoke-over. 'Still, you wanted the job done.'

She wished to justify herself, to explain the necessity of dispossessing the bees, to say that she had been waiting for him since September; but she was dumb. She pushed up the window, put the honeycomb on her dressing-table, and tumbled heavily into bed again.

Her Enemy, so attentive since the outbreak of the war, whispered in her ear:

'Just as I thought. Another sentimental illusion. Schemes to produce food by magic strokes of fortune. Life doesn't arrange stories with happy endings any more, see? *Never again*. This source of energy whose living voice comforted you at dawn, at dusk, saying: We work for you. Our surplus is yours, there for the taking—vanished! You left it to accumulate, thinking: There's time; thinking: when I will. You left it too late. What you took for the hum of growth and plenty is nothing, you see, but the buzz of an outworn machine running down. The workers have eaten up their fruits, there's nothing left for you. You've had it this time, my girl! Supplies are getting scarce for people like you. An end, soon, of getting more than their fair share for dwellers in country houses. Ripe gifts unearned out of traditional walls, no more. All the while your roof was being sealed up patiently, cunningly, with spreading plasters and waxy shrouds.'

Through half-closed eyes she watched him bending, peering here and there. Suddenly he whipped out his knife, plunging his arm forward out of sight. A pause; then up came knife, hand again, lifting a clot of thick yellow sticky stuff. Honey.

'Honey!'

There it was, the richness, the substance. The knife carried a packed edge of crusted sugar, and as he held it up, the syrup began to drip down slow, gummy, amber-dark. Isled in the full attack of total winter there it hung, inviolable, a microcosm of summer, melting in sweet oils.

'Honey!' yelled John from below.

'*Now* we're all right,' called back the bee man in a happy voice, as if released all at once from his own weight of disappointment. 'Plenty here—right in the corner. Did you ever see anythink so artful? Near shave me not spotting it. Oh, we'll get you some! Run and beg us a dish off Cook, Sonny, and I'll dish you out a nice little lot for your tea.'

She heard the urgency of the start of her son's boots. It was as if he ran away with her, ran through her, bursting all obstacles to be back with the dish before he had gone, to offer it where it was required: his part in the serious task. This pure goodwill and disinterestedness of children, this concentration of spirit so entire that they seemed to fuse with and become the object, lifted her on a cool wave above her sickness, threw her up in a moment of absolute peace, as after love or childbirth, upon a white and abstract shore.

'That's a nice boy you've got,' said the bee man, cutting, scraping busily. 'Sensible. I'm ever so glad to see this honey. There's one thing I do hate to see, and that's a swarm starved.'

The words shocked her. Crawling death by infinitesimal stages. Not a question of no surplus, but of the bare necessities of life. Not making enough to live on. A whole community entombed, like miners trapped.

A scuffle below. John's fluting voice came up:

'This do?'

'Fine. Bring it up, Sonny.'

The largest meat platter from the kitchen dresser hove in sight.

'Thanks, mate. Now we'll get you a bit o' somethink to sweeten you. Need it? What does your Mammy think, eh?' He shouted with laughter.

Unable to cope with repartee of so personal a character, John cast her a wry self-conscious grin, and rapidly vanished.

Light was rapidly failing, but the rising moon arrested the descent of darkness. In the opaque bleached twilight his silhouette persisted on the pane, bending, straightening. He hummed and whistled. Now and then he spoke softly to the bees. 'Run off, my girl, run off.' Once he held up his hands to show her the insects clustering upon them.

'They don't worry me, the jokers. Just a sore sort of a tingle, like as if I'd rapped myself over the fingers with a hammer.'

He brushed them off and they fell down like a string of beads breaking. They smiled at one another. She closed her eyes.

Roused by a rap on the pane, she lay in confused alarm. The lower window ran up with a swift screech, and, heaving towards her over the sill in the semi-darkness, she saw a phantasmagoric figure climb in and straighten itself. A headless figure. Where the face should have been, nothing but swaying darkness. It's the fever. Wait, and it will go away.

She found courage to switch on the lamp and saw the bee man. He was wearing a round hat with a long circular veil of thick gauze that hung to his shoulders.

Fishing up a fragment of voice she croaked:

'Is that your hat for taking swarms?'

'Oh, him,' he said laughing, removing it. 'Forgot I had him on. Did I give you a scare?'

'Stylish,' she said.

'Thought you'd like to know the job's done. I've got 'em down below there. Got you a nice bit of honey, too. I'm glad of that. I hate to see a swarm starved.'

He drew her curtains together. 'Better dror 'em or you'll get into trouble with the black-out, bother it.' Then he moved over to the fireplace. 'Your fire's gone right down. That's why I come in. Thought I'd make it up for you.' He knelt down, riddled the ashes, and with his bruised, swollen, wax-stuck fingers piled on more coal. 'That'll be more cheerful soon. Ain't you got nobody to see to you then?'

'Oh, yes,' she whispered. 'There'll be somebody coming soon. I forgot to ring.' She felt self-pity, and wanted to weep.

'You do seem poorly. You need giving your chest a good rub with camphorated. I believe in that.'

In another few moments he would be rubbing her chest.

But he remained by the fire, looking thoughtfully round the room. 'This is a nice old place. I knew it when I was a young lad, of course. The old Squire used to have us up for evening classes. Improve our minds. He was a great one for that.' He chuckled. 'Must be ten years since he died. I'm out o' touch. Went out to Canada when I was seventeen. Twenty years ago that was. Never got a wife, nor a fortune, nor nothink.' He chuckled again. 'I'm glad I got back before this war. Back where I started—that's where I am. Living with my married sister.'

She said:

'Won't you have a cup of tea?'

'No, I'll be off home, thanks all the same. I'd best get that swarm in. They're in a bad way.'

'Will they recover?'

'Ah, I couldn't say. It wasn't no weather to take a swarm. And then it demoralizes 'em like when you steals their honey. They sings a mournful song— ever so mournful.' He strode to the window. 'Still, we'll hope for the best. George'll be up in the morning to put them leads right. Well, I'll wish you goodnight. Hope you'll be more yourself tomorrow.' At the window he paused. 'Well, there's no call to go out that way, is there?' he remarked. 'Might as well go out like a Christian.'

He marched briskly across the room, opened her bedroom door, closed it quietly after him. She heard his light feet on the oak staircase, dying away.

She took her temperature and found it was lower: barely a hundred. He had done her good. Then she lay listening to the silence she had created. One performs acts of will, and in doing so one commits acts of negation and destruction. A portion of life is suppressed for ever. The image of the ruined balcony weighed upon her: torn out, exposed, violated, obscene as the photograph of a bombed house.

What an extraordinary day, what an odd meeting and parting. It seemed to her that her passive, dreaming, leisured life was nothing, in the last analysis, but a fluid element for receiving and preserving faint paradoxical images and symbols. They were all she ultimately remembered.

Somewhere in the garden a big branch snapped off and fell crackling down.

The children burst in, carrying plates of honey. 'Want some?'

'Not now, thanks. I can't really swallow anything, not even delicious honey.'

'It isn't delicious. It's beastly. It looks like seccotine and it tastes *much* too sweet. Ugh!'

It was certainly an unappetizing colour—almost brown; the texture gluey. It had been there too long. She croaked:

'You oughtn't to be in this room. Where's Mary? Don't come near me.'

'Oh, we shan't catch your old 'flu,' said John, throwing himself negligently backwards over the arm of the sofa and writhing on the floor. 'Look here, Mum, what on earth did you want to get rid of the poor blighters for? They never did any harm.'

'Think what a maddening noise they made.'

'We liked the noise. If you can't stand the hum of a wretched little bee, what'll you do in an airraid?'

'You had a lovely day watching the bee man.'

'I dare say.'

But now all was loss, satiety, disappointment.

'Think how everybody got stung last summer. Poor Robert. And Mr. Fanshawe.'

'Oh, your old visitors.'

What an entertainment the bees had been, a topic, a focusing point at week-ends. But from now on, of course, there would be no more week-end parties. It was time for the bees to go.

'Remember Jane's eye, all bandaged up for days.'

'I remember that.' Jane flushed, went solemn. 'It didn't 'alf 'urt.'

'Your *English*!' cried John, revolted.

'I got not 'alf off Pippy Didcock,' said Jane, complacent. 'They all says that. It's Oxfordshire accident.'

She started to run up and down the room, kilt flying, hair bouncing, then stood still, her hand on her chest.

'What's the most important thing about a person?' she said.

'Dopey,' said her brother. 'What's biting you?'

'Don't you know?' said Jane. 'Your heart. If it stops, you die. I can hear mine after that running.'

'It won't stop,' said her mother.

'It will some day,' said John. 'It might stop to-night. Reminds me—' He fished in his pocket and drew out a dark object. 'I brought up this tit to give it a last chance by your fire. It was at the back of the boiler, but the cats would keep prowling about. They got the pigeon. It must have been stiff eating.' He examined the tit. 'It's alive!'

He rushed with it to the fire and crouched down, holding it in his palms before the now leaping flames. 'Its eyes opened. It's fluttering.'

Jane came and knelt beside him.

'Isn't it a *sweet* little tiny bird?'

Suddenly it flew straight up out of his hands, dashed against the mantelpiece, fell down again upon the hearth-rug. They were all perfectly silent.

After a moment his hand went out to pick it up again. Then it flew straight into the fire, and started to roast, to whirr and cheep over the coals.

In a split second she was there, plunged in her hand, out again. Smell of burnt feathers, charred fragments flaking down. It was on the hearth-stone. Everybody stared.

Suddenly it revived, it began to stagger about. The tenacity of life in its minute frame appalled her. Over the carpet it bounced, one wing burnt off, one leg shrivelled up under its breast, no tail; up and down, vigorously, round and about.

'Is it going to be alive?' said Jane.

'Yes,' said John coldly, heavily. 'We can't do anything about it now.'

OXFORD

MORE OXFORD PAPERBACKS

This book is just one of nearly 1000 Oxford Paperbacks currently in print. If you would like details of other Oxford Paperbacks, including titles in the World's Classics, Oxford Reference, Oxford Books, OPUS, Past Masters, Oxford Authors, and Oxford Shakespeare series, please write to:

UK and Europe: Oxford Paperbacks Publicity Manager, Arts and Reference Publicity Department, Oxford University Press, Walton Street, Oxford OX2 6DP.

Customers in UK and Europe will find Oxford Paperbacks available in all good bookshops. But in case of difficulty please send orders to the Cash-with-Order Department, Oxford University Press Distribution Services, Saxon Way West, Corby, Northants NN18 9ES. Tel: 0536 741519; Fax: 0536 746337. Please send a cheque for the total cost of the books, plus £1.75 postage and packing for orders under £20; £2.75 for orders over £20. Customers outside the UK should add 10% of the cost of the books for postage and packing.

USA: Oxford Paperbacks Marketing Manager, Oxford University Press, Inc., 200 Madison Avenue, New York, N.Y. 10016.

Canada: Trade Department, Oxford University Press, 70 Wynford Drive, Don Mills, Ontario M3C 1J9.

Australia: Trade Marketing Manager, Oxford University Press, G.P.O. Box 2784Y, Melbourne 3001, Victoria.

South Africa: Oxford University Press, P.O. Box 1141, Cape Town 8000.

THE WORLD'S CLASSICS

The World's Classics series makes available annotated editions of the major works of such important women writers as Jane Austen, the Brontë sisters, Fanny Burney, Maria Edgeworth, George Eliot, and Elizabeth Gaskell.

VIRGINIA WOOLF

Edited with notes and introductions by leading scholars, Virginia Woolf's most popular works are now available in ten World's Classics.

Between the Acts   Edited by Frank Kermode
Jacob's Room   Edited by Kate Flint
Mrs Dalloway   Edited by Claire Tomalin
Night and Day   Edited by Suzanne Raitt
Orlando   Edited by Rachel Bowlby
A Room of One's Own, and Three Guineas   Edited by Morag Shiach
To the Lighthouse   Edited by Margaret Drabble
The Voyage Out   Edited by Lorna Sage
The Waves   Edited by Gillian Beer
The Years   Edited by Hermione Lee, with Notes by Sue Asbee

Also available:

Virginia Woolf: A Writer's Life   Lyndall Gordon

OXFORD BOOKS

Oxford Books began in 1900 with Sir Arthur Quiller-Couch ('Q')'s *Oxford Book of English Verse*. Since then over 60 superb anthologies of poetry, prose, and songs have appeared in a series that has a very special place in British publishing.

THE OXFORD BOOK OF ENGLISH
GHOST STORIES
Chosen by Michael Cox and R. A. Gilbert

This anthology includes some of the best and most frightening ghost stories ever written, including M. R. James's 'Oh Whistle, and I'll Come to You, My Lad', 'The Monkey's Paw' by W. W. Jacobs, and H. G. Wells's 'The Red Room'. The important contribution of women writers to the genre is represented by stories such as Amelia Edwards's 'The Phantom Coach', Edith Wharton's 'Mr Jones', and Elizabeth Bowen's 'Hand in Glove'.

As the editors stress in their informative introduction, a good ghost story, though it may raise many profound questions about life and death, entertains as much as it unsettles us, and the best writers are careful to satisfy what Virginia Woolf called 'the strange human craving for the pleasure of feeling afraid'. This anthology, the first to present the full range of classic English ghost fiction, similarly combines a serious literary purpose with the plain intention of arousing pleasing fear at the doings of the dead.

'an excellent cross-section of familiar and unfamiliar stories and guaranteed to delight' *New Statesman*

Also in Oxford Paperbacks:

The Oxford Book of Short Stories   edited by V. S. Pritchett
The Oxford Book of Political Anecdotes
edited by Paul Johnson
The Oxford Book of Ages
edited by Anthony and Sally Sampson
The Oxford Book of Dreams   edited by Stephen Brock

POETRY FROM OXFORD PAPERBACKS

Oxford's outstanding range of English poetry offers, in a single volume of convenient size, the complete poetical works of some of the most important figures in English Literature.

WORDSWORTH

Poetical Works

This edition of Wordsworth's poetry contains every piece of verse known to have been published by the poet himself, or of which he authorized the posthumous publication. The text, which Thomas Hutchinson based largely upon the 1849–50 standard edition, the last issued during the poet's lifetime, was revised for the Oxford Standard Authors series by Ernest de Selincourt.

The volume preserves the poet's famous subjective arrangement of the Minor Poems under such headings as 'Poems Referring to the Period of Childhood', 'Poems Dedicated to National Independence and Liberty', and 'Sonnets Upon the Punishment of Death'. *The Prelude* is given in the text of 1850, published shortly after Wordsworth's death, and *The Excursion* as it appears in the 1849–50 edition. Two poems of 1793 are included, 'An Evening Walk' and 'Descriptive Sketches', and a group of other pieces not appearing in the standard edition. The text reproduces Wordsworth's characteristic use of capital letters and in most cases his punctuation, though spelling has been regularized. The poet's own Notes to the 1849–50 edition, as well as to some earlier editions, are reprinted, along with his Prefaces.

The edition also contains a chronological table of Wordsworth's life, explanatory notes on the text, and chronological data for the individual poems.

Also in Oxford Paperbacks:

The Prelude   William Wordsworth
Poetical Works   John Keats
The Golden Treasury   Francis Turner Palgrave

OXFORD POETS

Oxford Paperbacks has one of the finest lists of contemporary poetry. It includes well-established and highly regarded names, as well as exciting newcomers from Britain, America, Europe, and the Commonwealth.

Winner of the 1989 Whitbread Prize for Poetry

SHIBBOLETH

Michael Donaghy

This is Michael Donaghy's first full-length collection. His work has a wit and grace reminiscent of the metaphysical poets, and his subjects range widely, responding in unexpected ways to his curiosity and inventiveness. Among the varied pieces collected here are a number of love poems remarkable for their blend of tenderness and irony; a terse 'news item'; playful 'translations' of a mythical Welsh poet; and an 'interview' with Marcel Duchamp.

As the American critic Alfred Corn says:
'Michael Donaghy's poems have the fine-tuned precision of a ten-speed bike, the wit of a streetwise don, a polyphonic inventiveness . . . Poems so original, wry, and philosophical as these are hard to come by. Don't think of passing them up.'

Also in Oxford Poets:

Blood and Family   Thomas Kinsella
Selected Poems   Fleur Adcock
Adventures with My Horse   Penelope Shuttle

PAST MASTERS

General Editor: Keith Thomas

Past Masters is a series of concise and authoritative introductions to the life and works of men and women whose ideas still influence the way we think today.

'Put end to end, this series will constitute a noble encyclopaedia of the history of ideas.' Mary Warnock

SHAKESPEARE

Germaine Greer

'At the core of a coherent social structure as he viewed it lay marriage, which for Shakespeare is no mere comic convention but a crucial and complex ideal. He rejected the stereotype of the passive, sexless, unresponsive female and its inevitable concommitant, the misogynist conviction that all women were whores at heart. Instead he created a series of female characters who were both passionate and pure, who gave their hearts spontaneously into the keeping of the men they loved and remained true to the bargain in the face of tremendous odds.'

Germaine Greer's short book on Shakespeare brings a completely new eye to a subject about whom more has been written than on any other English figure. She is especially concerned with discovering why Shakespeare 'was and is a popular artist', who remains a central figure in English cultural life four centuries after his death.

'eminently trenchant and sensible . . . a genuine exploration in its own right' John Bayley, *Listener*

'the clearest and simplest explanation of Shakespeare's thought I have yet read' Auberon Waugh, *Daily Mail*

Also available in Past Masters:

Paine   Mark Philp
Dante   George Holmes
The Buddha   Michael Carrithers
Confucius   Raymond Dawson

LITERARY BIOGRAPHY AND
CRITICISM IN OXFORD PAPERBACKS

Oxford Paperbacks's impressive list of literary biography and criticism includes works ranging from specialist studies of the prominent figures of the world literature to D. J. Enright on television soap opera.

BRITISH WRITERS OF THE THIRTIES
Valentine Cunningham

'He has steeped himself in the period . . . *British Writers of the Thirties* is by far the best history of its kind published in recent years . . . and it will become required reading for those who wish to look back at a society and a culture in which writers, for all their faults, were taken seriously.' Peter Ackroyd, *The Times*

'a serious and often brilliant book, provoking one to argument, forcing one back to known texts and forward to unread ones . . . it is simply so packed with information that it will speak as much to readers with an interest in social history as to the students of literature for whom it was first intended.' Claire Tomalin, *Independent*

'this should henceforth be the standard treatment . . . a minor classic of literary history' Frank Kermode, *Guardian*

'brilliant survey and analysis . . . Mr Cunningham's narrative is cleverly constructed, wonderfully detailed, and he deploys his findings to great effect.' Charles Causley, *Times Educational Supplement*

Also in Oxford Paperbacks:

Fields of Vision   D. J. Enright
Modern English Literature   W. W. Robson
The Oxford Illustrated History of English Literature
edited by Pat Rogers
The Pursuit of Happiness   Peter Quennell

ILLUSTRATED HISTORIES IN
OXFORD PAPERBACKS

Lavishly illustrated with over 200 full colour and black and white photographs, and written by leading academics, Oxford Paperbacks' illuminating histories provide superb introductions to a wide range of political, cultural, and social topics.

THE OXFORD ILLUSTRATED HISTORY
OF ENGLISH LITERATURE

Edited by Pat Rogers

Britain possesses a literary heritage which is almost unrivalled in the Western world. In this volume, the richness, diversity, and continuity of that tradition are explored by a group of Britain's foremost literary scholars.

Chapter by chapter the authors trace the history of English literature, from its first stirrings in Anglo-Saxon poetry to the present day. At its heart towers the figure of Shakespeare, who is accorded a special chapter to himself. Other major figures such as Chaucer, Milton, Donne, Wordsworth, Dickens, Eliot, and Auden are treated in depth, and the story is brought up to date with discussion of living authors such as Seamus Heaney and Edward Bond.

'[a] lovely volume . . . put in your thumb and pull out plums' Michael Foot

'scholarly and enthusiastic people have written inspiring essays that induce an eagerness in their readers to return to the writers they admire' *Economist*

Other illustrated histories in Oxford Paperbacks:

The Oxford Illustrated History of Britain
The Oxford Illustrated History of Medieval Europe